*'history with
a mystery'*

CELTIC KNOT

In this twist of history,
Ann Shortell's protagonist,
Irish immigrant housemaid
Clara Swift, is a spirited
narrator who uses wit
and intuition to shed light
on a mystery for the ages.
This elfin girl with an old
soul must step beyond
the horror of her hero
D'Arcy McGee's slaughter —
and four other deaths linked
to the assassination — before
she truly understands the
cost of crossing a new
country's threshold.

www.annshortell.com

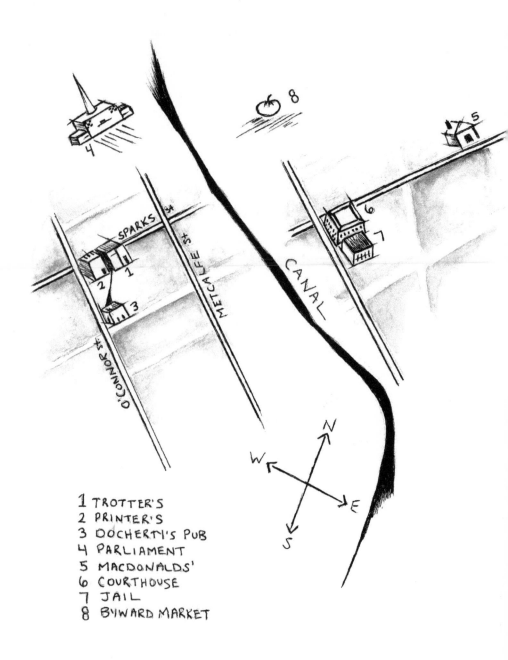

1 TROTTER'S
2 PRINTER'S
3 DOCHERTY'S PUB
4 PARLIAMENT
5 MACDONALDS'
6 COURTHOUSE
7 JAIL
8 BYWARD MARKET

A sketch of the interior of Trotter's Boarding House can be found at www.annshortell.com

CELTIC KNOT

ANN SHORTELL

Celtic Knot is a work of historical fiction, using well-known historical and public figures. All incidents and dialogue are products of the author's imagination and are not to be construed as real. Where real-life historical or public figures appear, the situations, incidents and dialogues concerning those persons are entirely fictional and are not intended to change the entirely fictional nature of the work. In all other respects, any resemblance to persons living or dead is entirely coincidental.

 FriesenPress

Suite 300 - 990 Fort St
Victoria, BC, V8V 3K2
Canada

www.friesenpress.com

Copyright © 2018 by Ann Shortell
First Edition — 2018

A SYDENHAM PUBLICATION

ISBN
978-1-5255-2090-7 (Hardcover)
978-1-5255-2091-4 (Paperback)
978-1-5255-2092-1 (eBook)

1. FICTION, MYSTERY & DETECTIVE, HISTORICAL

Distributed to the trade by The Ingram Book Company

For Herb

and for Susan,
who knows the territory

A NOTE ON HISTORY

Celtic Knot is inspired by a series of historical events which occurred in Canada in 1868 and 1869.

Some of what appears in these pages is vintage fact; some of this is pure fiction, cut and fashioned out of whole cloth. Much is a weave of those two strands.

Some of the strangest material presented here is true.

Certain scenes are designed to be true to events. Certain crucial scenes, dates and characters deviate from historical details for purposes of story. Links to historical resources, and information about historical personages who may bear similar names to the novel's characters, are detailed at www.annshortell.com

A NOTE ON LANGUAGE

The Gaelic used in these pages conforms, when possible, to mid-nineteenth-century spelling. However, those words which require dotted accents, rather than Roman letters, are written in a more modern form. Some words are used with North American spelling and pronunciation.

Clarity was the author's primary motivation for these choices. She also took into account the backgrounds, and personal story arcs, of various characters.

All the Gaelic, Latin, and French is meant to be comprehended by the context in which it appears. For a list of words and their meanings, please consult the website above.

DRAMATIS PERSONAE

Mr. Bernard .... Secretary of the Cabinet, M'Lady's brother
Bonnie .... maid at McGees' house
Paddy Buckley .... spy
The butcher .... inquest jury member
John Hillyard Cameron, Q.C .... Jimmy's defence attorney, Orangeman
Father Clement .... parish priest
Monsieur Desbarats .... Trotter's landlord, printer
Barney Devlin .... Mr McGee's political opponent
Eamonn Docherty .... owner of Docherty's Tavern
Hannah Docherty (Walsh)................... Eamonn's niece, barmaid
Major Pierce Doyle .... Prime Minister's aide, investigator
Dr. Gillivray M.D. .... inquest witness, local medic
Hortense................................ baby nurse
Miss Keough .... housekeeper at the McGees' house
Mr. Lacey .... Editor of the *Ottawa Times*
Jean-Baptiste Lacroix .... witness at murder trial
Suzanne Lacroix .... glove-maker, artisan
Mr. (Sir) John A. Macdonald .... Prime Minister of Canada
Miss Margaret Mary Theodora
Macdonald (the baboo) .... baby girl
M'Lady (Susan) Agnes Macdonald .... Prime Minister's wife
Miss Frasa McGee .... elder McGee daughter
Mrs. Mary McGee .... widow of Mr. McGee
Miss Peggy McGee........................ younger McGee daughter
Mr. (Thomas) D'Arcy McGee M.P. .... orator, author, politician
Mrs. Polly O'Neill .... police officer's wife
Sergeant Tommy O'Neill .... Ottawa Police detective
Mr. James O'Reilly, Q.C. .... Crown Attorney
Judge Richards .... Trial Judge and Appeal Court Justice
Monsieur Theodore Robitaille M.P. .... boarder at Trotter's
Sow .... Clara Swift's pet piglet
Miss Stewart .... housekeeper at the Macdonalds' house
Clara Swift .... housemaid, Mr. McGee's amanuensis
Mrs. Nancy (Mary Ann) Trotter .... proprietor of Trotter's Boarding House
Willy Trotter .... Parliamentary pageboy, journalist
Dr. Van Courtlandt, M.D. .... Coroner
Mike Walsh .... Hannah Docherty's sweetheart, trial witness
Bridie Whelan .... wife of suspected Fenian rebel
Jimmy (Patrick James) Whelan
(alias Sullivan) .... suspected Fenian, alleged murderer

CONTENTS

"I have been weighed in the balance, and not found wanting."

—*Secret Fenian password, revealed by Thomas D'Arcy McGee*
in The Montreal Gazette, August 19th, 1867

I'm wasting my new beeswax candles, staring at the pages of the past.

I should be keeping watch over Miss Macdonald. Sweet little baboo, she's finally asleep, thanks be.

Mr. Macdonald did have this desk placed by the nursery window, for my personal use. My *escritoire*, M'Lady calls it. She's gifted me the oak box for my tapers, and a pewter candelabra.

M'Lady says beeswax gives twice the light of tallow. Which is for the best, as I wish never to touch tallow again.

I do need the light.

The moon is the merest bowline in the night sky. There's no snow left to reflect the stars above, not since the Easter melt. Suzanne Lacroix told me at the market yesterday that the promise of snow is in the air, and will wrap round us again soon. She says the *Métis* have their own ways of forecasting weather.

Me, I've learned it's best not to twig what spring may bring in this country.

This is the anniversary of Mr. McGee's murder. The last night Mr. McGee will laugh with the faeries. At a year and a day, his soul will be free to move on. It's right that I do too.

I only pray this annal sets me on the road to redemption.

I run a finger along the loops and spikes of my opening sentence. The ink is stiff, the words are weighted in place. 'Tis the Prime Minister himself who's tasked me to write down all of what I know, and even what I think.

Now I've crossed out, corrected, and blotted the last of my pages. I've seen this job through. Come morning, I'm to hand over my words—and my pledge that this is the only copy—and leave final judgement to the higher-ups.

Yet I'm missing something in my telling.

How I came to be at the centre of this saga. How I know what matters, and as much as anyone alive will ever know of the truth.

I'd best set my thoughts straight, before I drip ink onto another piece of good linen rag paper. A quire of fresh paper rests next to my copying hand. Whiter than I can make a bed sheet with three lye bleaches. With a watermark that shows the fool under his cap. The same paper as Mr. McGee used—'twas one of his little jokes, how every man needs to remember he's more fool than king.

There's barely any India blue left, though. Mr. McGee called an empty inkpot a message that enough words had been used on a matter.

"A story's well told when you give away a bit of your heart, Clara." That's what Mr. McGee used to tell me. He always started with himself. And he was the finest storyteller I'm ever likely to hear.

So I'll dip my pen one more time, and lay out my own past, simple.

I'm Clara Swift. Irish girl, British subject and a Canadian all twenty-one months we've had a country. Housemaid, nursemaid, politician's scribe and now an author myself. And me only fifteen. I wonder if Mr. McGee had written this many words by the time he was my age, for all that he wrote after.

I'm lucky enough that Mr. Thomas D'Arcy McGee, a saint of a man, was born in Carlingford, County Louth, Ireland. Two years ago he wrote to our priest for a girl to help around his house in Montreal, Quebec.

The priest knew my father had bid Gram to school me, and I'd worked hard at my hedge-school lessons—and at my English, to please my father. Da, he'd finally shown up in Carlingford when Gram was failing, only to say he wouldn't be taking me to Kilkenny to join his new family. I could see my face in the lines of his, but Da didn't see my place in his life.

So after Gram died, I left Ireland.

The priest had arranged a half-fare ticket as I could easily share a cot. I'd signed a pledge—after the priest never heard a yea or nay from Da—to help sponsor the passage of another girl, five years hence.

"Sure, you're fourteen your next birthday, I'm told . . . you may be married by then, with a home of your own to welcome an Irish girl into," the priest had told me.

Then he'd hoisted my trunk onto a cart.

4

As I'd climbed in beside it, he'd added a warning. *"That's if you leave off with the Shakespeare and those foreign writers—no man wants a girl with so much learning as to seem uncanny."*

I knew that look. I'd seen it often enough from the other villagers when I pulled a book from my pocket. He meant he didn't think an elf like me could ever grow into a proper woman.

My trunk and I made it safely to Dublin, then off to Cork, onto a packet ship, and through a journey in the steerage hold where I hardly ate or slept for weeks on end, and still fared better than most of those crowded all around me.

Mr. McGee met me at the dock in Montreal. As he rode with me to his home in a one-horse hackney carriage, he told me his first story.

How he'd been chased from Ireland as a rebel back in '48. He'd donned a priest's own robes to escape. He'd settled first in America, where he'd found they weren't running their country right either.

In Montreal, he was gobsmacked to find a British colony where Catholics had equal rights.

So in 1857, he moved his family north. There, Mr. McGee joined the big men to help lead the province. It was his idea to link all the Canadian settlements, and create a country. One that would look after us Irish—and also show England, by way of Canada's fine self-governance, that *Éireann* could safely be granted the same freedoms.

By then, he'd seen Fenian rebels for the dangerous sinners they are.

The Fenians had invaded Canada from south of the border, in a failed bid to draw British troops to these shores—so their brethren in Ireland would have fewer redcoats to fight when next they rose up.

Mr. McGee had rediscovered his religion, and he had all the conviction of a convert to the cause of reason and responsible government.

The Fenian devils cursed him as the worst kind of traitor.

It didn't work out well for me with the McGees in Montreal. None's my fault, though I shouldn't talk against Mrs. McGee. Anyway, I've offered it up to Mary Mother of God.

Mr. McGee, bless his soul and good nature, brought me here to Ottawa after he'd been elected to the new Canadian Parliament. To work at Mrs. Trotter's boarding house—and to keep on copying Mr. McGee's writing.

I had caught on to his shorthand codes right away, which pleased him as much as the way I made my letters: a slight slant, proper capital letters, and words big enough for sore eyes. He praised me up for having such a fine hand.

The boarding house wasn't a proper home. Still, it housed quality gentlemen while they were at Parliament. And Mrs. Trotter had sympathy for me doing my own studies—my lollygagging, so Mrs. McGee would call it.

"Clara is thinking," Mr. McGee would say, in his grand-for-the-public voice. *"Which makes her closer to the Lord Jesus and all great men."*

I like to think that it made me closer to him.

It's hard to think Mr. McGee's been dead these twelve months. Since that night, all the talk has been of the new word, assassination, which means murder and politics mixed together in a devil's brew. With all Irish as suspects.

I've been twisting this way and that myself, looking for whom to trust.

John A. Macdonald is our Prime Minister and so boss of us all, as well as me in particular. He was Mr. McGee's close friend. I must believe he knows best.

The Prime Minister's right to think that Mr. McGee would want me to parse out the truth. Mr. McGee believed in laying out the hard facts of the matter, with no weight given to what it may cost a body.

There's no question but I was there from start to finish, for sure, and I beg forgiveness nightly for any hand I had in the course of events.

I suspect Mr. Macdonald may tuck away this testament, leaving for posterity's judgement the strict moral of the choices made. There's plenty to answer for, with a man shot dead and a man hanged for it. That's the simplest accounting, though I must tot up three others, whose deaths are in some way linked to the McGee assassination—and two more whose hearts' *cuislean* may yet flow beyond the sea.

And little hope now that Mr. McGee's own *Apologia* will be published, to help set his family's affairs to rights.

As for the rest of the country—it's a heavy weight on me that so many folk believe a lie. Even as I do see it's safest, while lives are still at stake.

Mr. Macdonald isn't a dreamer like Mr. McGee. His tools are people; he knows how they can best be set to use. He looks at me, he sees a maid of all work. When he found me crying the other day because my words aren't high-minded poetry like Mr. McGee's, he said I should write my account of this past year the way I'd do dishes. So that the facts shine, once I've cleaned all the muck off them.

And that I've done. I haven't dropped the gravy boat in first, so the water wasn't fit for fancy china. My water's been clean enough to come back and rinse the brandy glasses. If I've had to stay up late to scrub the worst of the stew pots, that's the job done right, and I can take pride in it.

No matter the mess the gentlemen have made.

So here's the clearest reason why I'm the one to set down this tale. I was on the other side of the door when Mr. McGee was shot.

ASSASSINATION

Tuesday April 7th, 1868

Mrs. Trotter didn't allow me in the parlour when it was open for service as a public house. After she closed at ten, we'd mop up, rinse the spittoons, and use the parlour bar as our own sitting room while we awaited the menfolk.

This particular night, just before midnight, Mrs. Trotter saw in three of her boarders. She swept their entryway after they'd gone up to their rooms. Then she lay down and dozed on the men's settee.

I propped a candelabra on the table nearest the window, so as to catch the moonlight, and set to copying Mr. McGee's new speech. He was going on about all the secret Fenians in Montreal's Griffintown, and even here in Ottawa. He believed the rebels might stage another border raid soon.

The tower bell on Parliament Hill rang one o'clock in the morning, startling Mrs. Trotter.

"Clara, you won't be able to do your day's work," she started in with me.

"The gentlemen won't want an early breakfast," I said, "after sitting late at Parliament."

"I don't like my Willy working these hours, and him a year younger even than you," she said. Her son Willy Trotter was a Parliamentary pageboy. "I don't know what to do with the pair of you."

A key scraped in the lock of the boarders' door.

"Have a look out, Clara," Mrs. Trotter said. "See which of our trio of truants that is."

I breathed against the windowpane, and wiped off the frost with my apron. With the close moon, I could see the sharp outline of a grown man. His beaver hat was flush with the lintel, his boots tamping off snow on the stoop.

"It's Monsieur Robitaille," I said.

Monsieur Robitaille was a foot taller than Mr. McGee and Willy both. Though Willy claimed he'd be as big a man, when he came into his full height. More of Willy's nonsense talk, that was.

A knock followed. Three sharp raps.

"You'll have to let him in, Clara," Mrs. Trotter said. "I double-locked that door, an hour ago."

"Why would you ever?"

"There've been some shiftless lads in the bar this week," she said. "Asking after Mr. McGee—when he's around, what he's up to. They've right spooked me."

"Mr. McGee says—in this new speech—that for all their threats, the Fenian rebels are only succeeding at uniting us Canadians." I waved the paper in my hand, as I walked past. "We good Irish, the Frenchies, and even the Protestants."

"Mr. McGee would be better to stop railing against the Fenians," she said. "Even if it's Mr. McGee they're het up at, any of us could be hurt. And I want no shenanigans in my boarding house. And no backtalk, Clara."

'Twas true that we were blind to whoever was entering the boarders' door. The landlord, Monsieur Desbarats, had knocked together two buildings that had long stood cheek-by-jowl on the same lot, to make Trotter's Boarding House at 71 Sparks Street.

The public rooms were in this, the newer of the two buildings, and to reach the boarders' entryway Mrs. Trotter and I had to step through a connecting archway. She'd even had the landlord cut out a new door at the front, just for the boarders. The idea was that the boarders would let themselves in with their own keys. Then they had only to scrape their boots, and they could head up their own staircase. In fact, only Mr. McGee and Monsieur Robitaille were careful to clean the street off their feet. I had to mop up after the rest.

Meantime, their entry hall was so narrow that whenever I had call to open the men's door, I had to step back into the archway to let the blasted door swing wide. Then I couldn't see who was traipsing inside, until they stepped up onto the bottom stair. Of course, a wide-open door attracted snow in winter, dust and wind in all seasons. Mrs. Trotter complained daily that the boarders' door let the City of Ottawa into her home, without her say-so.

Tonight I stood in place to greet Monsieur Robitaille, who had to crouch to fit on the first step, so as not to hit his head on the ceiling. "Good evening, Monsieur," I said. "Did you see Mr. McGee speak?"

"Shut that up tight after him, Clara," Mrs. Trotter called out. She was comfy under a pink woollen blanket, so she didn't bother rising. "Did you speak yourself, Monsieur?" she asked.

"I did say a few words, Madame Trotter."

Monsieur Robitaille had an orator's voice like Mr. McGee's, so he didn't have to raise it for her to hear his reply. Out of courtesy, though, he followed me into the parlour.

"And, Mademoiselle Clara," he sketched a bow at me, "D'Arcy had me read his speech and make a few notes while an Opposition Member was on his feet. My friend McGee knows I can't absorb all his ideas this late—or should I say this early. He's due to be speaking now."

"It might just as well be day, anyhow," Mrs. Trotter said, "with the moon hung so full and low."

"It's the snow," I said. "There's moon-glow all over the snow banks tonight."

"It isn't good for a body, when night turns into day like this," Mrs. Trotter said.

"The faeries will be out for sure," I said.

"Call them the Good People, Clara," she said. "You know 'tis safer."

We both crossed ourselves, Father, Son, Holy Ghost.

Mrs. Trotter didn't mean to put a portent to the moon being this big and bright. She was a God-fearing biddy, and wouldn't want anyone to think otherwise.

"Do make the Sign of the Cross, Monsieur," I said. "To forestall any ill will."

He smiled, then made the blessing.

"Anyway, the sheen's helping me make out Mr. McGee's words," I said. "I need the aid, the way this tallow smokes so."

"I'm frightened you'll catch fire from the flame yourself, Clara, with the amount of lamb's fat you slather on your hands each evening," Mrs. Trotter said.

"I need to keep them supple—" I said.

"*La lune* lit my way here," Monsieur Robitaille said. "And she'll light McGee's. *Bonsoir, Mesdames.*" He had heard this argument, over my coddling my fingers to protect my penmanship, more than once before. Ever polite, he bobbed a bow in Mrs. Trotter's direction, smiled at me, and headed upstairs.

"You've double-locked that door, Clara?" Mrs. Trotter gave me a sharp look.

I retraced my steps, turned the key, and pulled the latch bar.

She drifted off to sleep again as I read over my work.

Mr. McGee wrote that the Fenians had caused havoc, but so far had gained no ground against our militia—and no reaction from London, either. He'd scribbled a note to himself about the Prime Minister— *"Macdonald confides no troops will be sent to aid us, under any circumstances."* Mr. McGee had crossed out that bit, so I hadn't copied it. He'd also written another note, which was mixed in with the speech pages—his elder daughter, Miss Frasa, was in need of a good visit at home, after Easter.

I tucked that scrap away, to hand him directly on his return. Then I rubbed my eyes, and went over to rest on the little chaise. Glad Mrs. Trotter hadn't caught me tiring, after my bold talk.

The bell rang two o'clock.

About half an hour later, I awoke to Mrs. Trotter's snoring, and a scratching like a cat's claws—a key running across the door. There were only Mr. McGee and Willy not yet home. One of them was trying to garner our attention without waking the household.

Willy wasn't so polite.

I rolled off the chaise. I'd best be careful, though. If it were Willy, he might hit me with a snowball.

I stepped through the passage and once again lifted the bar on the latch. When the door was half-open, there was a noise—like a firecracker had been set off.

No one came across the threshold.

"Did somebody shoot a gun?" Mrs. Trotter yelled from the settee.

"I can't see—" I said.

"Gunfire," she yelled. "Shut that door, Clara."

She was behind me, suddenly, shoving me right against the door. Ice-cold wood pressed against my forehead, and I pushed with all my strength.

The door slammed shut. I pressed my ear to it hard, but heard nothing.

Monsieur Robitaille came running downstairs double-quick in his dressing gown, holding his boots in one hand and a kerosene lamp in the other. There was clomping on the floor above; the other boarders stirring.

"Monsieur Robitaille, there've been no more shots," Mrs. Trotter said, as he crouched on the first step. "D'you think we're safe to check?"

He nodded.

"Clara," Mrs. Trotter said. "Turn the knob, and ease open the door enough that Monsieur Robitaille can reach that handle —there, now scoot back here."

She and I crowded close in the archway, as Monsieur Robitaille reached forward from his perch.

He stared out. *"Tabarnac,"* he said. *"Arrêtez-vous—votre châtelaine—la clé du verrou de la cuisine."*

He slammed the door shut once more.

Mrs. Trotter handed me the candelabra she'd carried over, and untied her key ring from her apron. She pointed the kitchen door key at the floor, near the entrance. "Of all the—" she said.

In the light cast by candles and lamp, I saw that on the hardwood lay a set of teeth. The kind you order from a catalogue.

"Don't go any closer, Mesdames."

Monsieur Robitaille grabbed the key, and ran.

I squeezed around Mrs. Trotter.

"Be sure to bar that again, Clara," Mrs. Trotter said.

But I stepped up onto the Monsieur's place on the stair, and pulled the door full open—so I could see outside.

A heap of clothing was piled like laundry on the stoop. It was not Mr. McGee lying face down there, not looking like that. The best part of a man's body was there, sure, in clothes uncommonly like his. And next to it a walking stick. That was Mr. McGee's, yes. And his white top hat.

Where the back of his head should be, there wasn't anything to see but bloodied flesh and bone. Blood staining the door, blood muddying the hoarfrost that lay over the stoop.

I swallowed and looked beyond, to try and stop gagging. There was blood in the snow bank too, blood in the moon-glow. And down the road, the ghost-grey outline of a buggy, turning onto O'Connor Street.

The wail of my keening filled the night. Mrs. Trotter pulled me back, and held me to her as I wept.

II

Monsieur Robitaille had eased Mr. McGee over, so the wound didn't show. Then he had gone for the police. Mrs. Trotter, the three other boarders and I had posted ourselves between Mr. McGee and the street.

By now, the blood was frozen stiff all around Mr. McGee's mouth. He had the voice of an angel. Everyone said so. Nobody else was looking down at him anymore.

I hiccupped, and choked back another sob.

"Clara, you can't stay here, standing over Mr. McGee and howling like that," Mrs. Trotter said. "Go round again and in the back way, girl. The gentlemen and I will set up lamps out here, to make sure Mr. McGee's remains are safe."

Safe. Mrs. Trotter was daft, for sure. She'd double-locked the door so she could be safe. So Mr. McGee couldn't open it with his key, in time to save himself. Now Mr. McGee would never be safe again, no matter how many lanterns or people were crowded round him.

"Inside, Clara."

I took a long breath of the frozen air, then another. "I'll hand out the lamps through the window," I said.

I scuffed my boots along down the alley's caked snow. Now I wanted nothing so much as to be with other people again.

In the dining room, I picked up the tray of kerosene lamps I'd just filled for the boarders' use, and ran into the parlour. As I pushed up the window, I noted my candle had guttered out.

The bell rang three o'clock. At that moment, Willy yelled from across the street. "Ma, Ma, is that Mr. McGee?"

"Willy, where in the name of Our Lord Saviour have you been?" Mrs. Trotter said.

"Christ on a crutch," Willy said when he reached his mother. "I saw somebody slumped against our door, so I ran into the *Times* office."

Mr. Lacey, the newspaper's editor, came across after Willy. "It is D'Arcy, by God." Mr. Lacey said. "I'll go for a doctor."

A look passed between Mr. Lacey and Willy. I'd heard them before, talking about 'stories', and how to be first to the telegram office.

"I don't see as—oh, the man's gone already," Mrs. Trotter said. "Willy, take that load from Clara."

Willy grabbed at the tray I'd set on the windowsill, knocking me off-kilter. My tummy gave a great heave, and I spewed dinner's remains. Some landed right on Willy's mitts.

"Clara," Mrs. Trotter called out. "Lay down until you're needed."

"Jesus, Clara, what—" Willy said.

I shook my head and shut the window. Then I pulled aside my cape, to wipe my mouth with my apron. But I didn't head off through the kitchen to my back-alley room. Instead, I relit the candle, and retraced my earlier steps. Mr. McGee's denture was still lying on the floor . . . I'd been told not to touch.

If I'd only pretended to double-lock the door . . . if I'd done as I felt was right, and not as I was told . . . Mr. McGee may have made it inside to safety.

I made my way upstairs, plucking Mr. McGee's room key from my own *châtelaine* and rubbing the blade-edge along the underside of my right arm—where I'd burned it on the washing mangle.

The pain helped a bit.

Mr. McGee's pipe tobacco was all around the room. I'd left the curtains open wide, the way he liked, so he could see without a nightlight.

"Don't think a full moon uncanny, Clara. Shedding light on any matter can only make it better. Remember that."

That's what Mr. McGee had told me when he came home after dinner, to fetch his speech for the special evening Parliamentary session.

I picked up his favourite cream-coloured sweater from his reading chair, folded it. *"That's Aran wool, Clara, 'twas my own father's,"* he'd told me. *"And what's better, knitted by my blessed mother."*

I understood the comfort in that. I had Gram's cape on, didn't I. I hadn't shed it at the door as I usually did.

Still, I shivered as I crossed the room. The window seat was always piled high with his books and papers. The police might want to look through these. I could straighten them up for Mr. McGee.

As I leaned over the pile, I couldn't help checking on Mrs. Trotter's little ring of light, set between Mr. McGee and the street.

Neighbours were now helping Willy, Mrs. Trotter, and her other boarders. They were piling up logs, on the far side of the wooden walkway. A few were even rolling stones, to make the barrier a stronghold.

I noticed that the three respected Parliamentarians, whom I served daily, struggled with any heavy lifting. *"Lightweights all three,"* Mr. McGee had scrawled on scrap paper after a particularly difficult dinner conversation.

These other boarders had expressed amazement, and a measure of disgust, that Mr. McGee wanted to give the vote to *"the feckless Indians"*.

When Mr. McGee had caught me reading that note, he'd admonished me to erase it all from my mind.

From that moment—though I always cleaned all three of their rooms to a spit-shine, and I daren't meet their eyes when serving their sausages—I'd never been able to address any of them as anything more than 'Mister,' or 'sir'.

Lest I slip up.

It didn't matter that they were, in reality, Messrs. Wodehouse, Henderson and Buttle. I could think of them only by the nicknames he'd penned in frustration. *Woodmouse, Hedgehog, and Bat,"* he'd called them—all foolhardy and venal creatures from old Irish tales.

Still, I was glad to have even the likes of those jokers out there, between Mr. McGee and the rest of the world. For on the far side of the street, more and more people were gathering with each passing moment. They were sharing flasks and bottles as they ogled Mr. McGee's body.

Monsieur Desbarats must have arrived from his fancy home in Sandy Hill while I was on the stairs. He was waving people away from this property he owned, and from his printing shop as well. No-one was paying him the least attention.

A man jumped from a carriage, swinging a leather physician's kitbag. How was it the doctor had arrived before the police?

I settled myself among the books on the floor, and inched up Mr. McGee's window. The voices cut through the winter night.

"Dr. Gillivray." Mrs. Trotter let him step inside the circle.

I tilted forward to see. Knocked a pile of snow from the sill, and held my breath. Nobody looked up at the sudden dusting.

Dr. Gillivray turned Mr. McGee's body over again, so that he lay exposed.

Jesus, Mary, and Joseph.

I pulled my cape tighter against the chill.

Dr. Gillivray raised Mr. McGee's cane in the air, then pointed it toward the door.

He stepped right over Mr. McGee, shouting, "Bring my bag, will you?" Then, "Got it. From the head wound, I figured the bullet would be in the door—the cane helped with the trajectory."

"This is Mr. D'Arcy McGee on the ground." I was gladdened by the anger in Mrs. Trotter's voice. "I'd ask you not be talking of wounds and—tragedy."

"A tragedy indeed, Mrs. Trotter," the doctor said, like he was gentling her.

At which point, saints be praised, Monsieur Robitaille emerged out of the back alley with Sergeant O'Neill, a line of coppers trailing after them.

Mrs. Trotter held out a hand in greeting. "Tommy . . .."

He took her hand in both of his. "Nancy, I'm sorry for the trouble life's brought to your door tonight."

The doctor stepped forward. "I have the bullet, O'Neill," he said.

"You have, Gillivray?" Sergeant O'Neill's voice hardened. "And who roused you for this?"

The sergeant ordered the other coppers to herd Willy, Mrs. Trotter and the boarders— save Monsieur Robitaille—down the alley and inside.

Another carriage hightailed it up the street, this one a four-in-hand Clarence. The driver jumped down. He wore a banged-up cowboy hat, and he never wore a red coat, but I knew from Mr. McGee that Pierce Doyle held the rank of Major. First in the British Regulars, now as one of the first officers in the Canadian government's new Dominion Constabulary, which was about to be tasked with protecting Parliament.

So when Major Doyle opened the carriage door, I wasn't surprised to see Prime Minister Macdonald step down.

"Clara?" Mrs. Trotter rapped on the door. She'd checked my room first thing, no doubt. "Are you in there?"

She pushed the door open but hung back, like she didn't want to be too close to Mr. McGee's belongings.

I motioned her over. "The Prime Minister's down below."

Mr. Macdonald passed by the sergeant's outstretched hand. He knelt by Mr. McGee.

"D'Arcy," he said, touching Mr. McGee's near arm. "The Goddamned evil buggers." He looked up at his man Doyle, then at the sergeant. "I want them all rooted out," he said. "D'you hear me? These Goddamned rebels must all be caught."

Mrs. Trotter stepped across the room, her meaty fingers snatching at me. "Out of here, Clara. Lest Tommy O'Neill catches you mucking about with Mr. McGee's papers."

"Look, Willy's snuck back out," I told Mrs. Trotter. "He's watching from the alley."

Mr. Macdonald stared up at the moon a moment, then all around the lot. "Robitaille," Mr. Macdonald said. "We need to carry D'Arcy inside. Pierce—"

Mr. Macdonald's aide came up to his side.

"I'll deal with the skull," said Dr. Gillivray.

"No," Mr. Macdonald said. "I'll hold D'Arcy where he's bleeding."

Mr. Macdonald pushed himself up on one foot, pulled his scarf from his neck and draped it over his gloves. Then he placed Mr. McGee's head ever so gently on his cradled hands.

Monsieur Robitaille, Dr. Gillivray, Mrs. Trotter's friend and Ottawa Police Sergeant O'Neill, and Major Doyle, all squatted in position on either side of Mr. McGee.

"Rise," the Prime Minister called out.

Slowly, steadily, the five men lifted Mr. McGee up, and carried him out of my sight.

At the last, Willy crept out of the alley. He picked up Mr. McGee's white hat and walking stick, and followed the parade of living and dead.

III

There was no peace to be had in my room. As I changed my apron, shouts of orders being issued to troops travelled through the pane of my alley window, mixing with the more-distant clamour of citizens gathering on Sparks Street. And, with my being so close to the kitchen, I could hear Mrs. Trotter having a cozy chat with Sergeant O'Neill.

I emerged to find them seated by the hearth, her refilling his ale jar. A couple of coppers also nursed jars, as they milled around the back door.

A red-coated foot soldier entered and held the door for a militiaman to follow behind him, letting in the chill wind. The Regulars and a volunteer unit both must have been summoned to the scene, to supplement the Sergeant's Ottawa Police Service.

"Clara, could you stoke the fires in the front rooms?" Mrs. Trotter said.

"Yes'm."

The parlour, I found, was quiet enough.

Willy had placed Mr. McGee's top hat and stick atop the new speech. Mr. McGee's body had been laid out on the bar.

If his shade were still hovering, it didn't shine through him. It was as if he'd shrunk away from us, in the time he lay on the doorstep.

Not that he was ever a big man; he just seemed a giant when he spoke. Mr. McGee was always a soulful man; his ideas had been the biggest part of him. He was always talking, singing, speechifying, or dreaming up ways to better all our lives.

Whereas his bone and muscles only filled a boy's pants. Even I could almost look him in the eye. Those as didn't like him called him 'all hat and swagger.' He laughed and made a joke of it on them, wearing the beaver or the white hat as if to say 'what of it?' to all naysayers.

21

Until someone's bullet knocked it off his head.

I'd seen the dead before, of course. Back home in Carlingford, there was always a funeral, a wedding, or a baptism in the offing. There was a comfort in the pattern—the church ceremony, the house visit. I'd sat with the departed along-side Gram, too, when the family needed to catch some rest. We all did such for one another. It was as the Lord wanted, that a man be with his own kind until he was laid in his grave.

I'd even seen my own Gram's shade, as sometimes happens right on a loved one's passing. She'd been stretched out, silent, on her deathbed, and rising above it, too. As if to comfort me, though she'd rarely done so in life.

"You were there?" The voice was quick and sure.

Major Doyle was standing where Mr. McGee's boots hit the lace antimacassar. His glanced fell on the archway. "You were there—when D'Arcy was shot?"

For all the times Mr. Macdonald had sent Major Doyle with messages for Mr. McGee, this was the most I'd ever heard come out of him.

"I live in, here," I said.

"Clara Swift, I know you've been working for McGee. Didn't I see you at his own house in Montreal?" he said. "And now you're here at his boarding house in Ottawa. Some folks may be wondering at that."

Major Doyle liked to let on he was one of the lads, in a boiled-wool shirt and ill-fitting trousers. A glorified errand boy. I knew better.

"*Driver, indeed,*" Mr. McGee had said, when this man had accompanied Mr. Macdonald 'round town. "*Doyle's to be a big part of Macdonald's new special federal police, Clara. The man's driving John A.'s private forces faster than he is the Prime Minister's horses. Watch out, there's a coming lad.*"

"Mr. McGee was kind enough to find me employment here," I said. "When the missus—they didn't need so many staff at their house."

Major Doyle nodded. "Look, it won't be me saying it, that he wanted to keep you close— where're you going, girl?"

"Over to the settee." I picked up Mrs. Trotter's blanket, then eased behind a few barstools. Toward Mr. McGee's head.

"No." Major Doyle snatched at the blanket before I could lay it down.

I didn't let go. His fingers were twice my size and chafed from rough use, though his nails were clipped straight. He pressed, and my own fingers lost their feeling. My teeth clenched, but I didn't whimper as he peeled away my hands.

"There's to be an inquiry, held right here, come daylight," Major Doyle said. "The Right Honourable Coroner and his jurors must view McGee. With no blanket messing him up or causing questions later."

"How is a blanket any different from the Prime Minister's scarf?" I said.

"You'd best clean yourself, Little Miss. You can't come near the body again like—that." The major flicked a thumb at one of my braids.

I realised my cape hadn't half done its job. There was vomit on my dress, right above the waistband of my clean apron. I'd unpinned my hair after supper, ready for the bedtime that hadn't come. Now the rags I'd knotted round the ends of my plaits were stiff with my spit.

"The girl's primping can wait, Pierce—I've need of you."

The Prime Minister had opened the door connecting the parlour to the dining room. His gaze took in Major Doyle, me, Mr. McGee.

"D'you think I should have let D'Arcy's blood pool in my hands, girl?" he said. "And you, Pierce—picking on such a wee, poor thing?"

I'd first seen Mr. Macdonald before he was Prime Minister. When he'd spoken from the platform, that sunny day the previous summer, I'd thought he looked like nothing so much as a bird. With his pumpkin-coloured waistcoat and green velvet walking coat for plumage, his short hop of a walk, and his head tilting to one side, he'd nipped and pecked at his opponents' arguments.

He always had the last word, so Mr. McGee said—and he was quick with it.

"*You can't help but admire John's way of viewing the whole field at all times,*" Mr. McGee told me. "*And picking his spots, so you never see him coming at you. John bests his opponents in such a way that, as irked as they are when he wins, they like him despite it and respect him for it.*"

Tonight, I understood what it was to feel the sharp edge of that tongue.

"I didn't mean to say . . . .." I bobbed my head. "Sir—"

"Pierce," he said. "Needs must, man. The Mayor's agreed; you're in charge of O'Neill and his lot of locals. The telegrams—"

"Shoo now, Clara," Doyle said.

"Miss," Mr. Macdonald said. "Come in here a minute and clear us a space, if you would."

The dining table had already been set for the morning meal.

"One of our men has gone to rouse the operator," Major Doyle said, as I stacked dishes onto the sideboard. "The alert should've gone out to all militia units across Ontario, Quebec and both maritime provinces."

"It better have," Mr. Macdonald said. "Now the Premiers all need details. Disraeli, the Queen . . . Tupper—he's top of the list. He'll let Howe know loud and clear, that popinjay must cease all rabble-rousing against us with the Lords in London. Mary McGee . . . ." Mr. Macdonald's voice faded. "This news had best come from her priest. Come to think, we'll telegraph the Vatican. D'Arcy would want to be in the Pope's prayers."

"Bring me that writing kit, Clara," Major Doyle said, waving toward the parlour.

I ran for my pen, inkbottle and paper, set them all in front of Mr. Macdonald, and swept up cutlery, willy-nilly.

"We'll need another—" Major Doyle said.

"There's Mr. McGee's kit," I said.

"I've suggested O'Neill set a police guard on McGee's room," Major Doyle told the Prime Minister.

"Clara, is it?" Mr. Macdonald said. "Could you fetch the police sergeant?"

There was no need of that. I opened the door to see Sergeant O'Neill right out in the hall, being calmed down by Monsieur Robitaille.

"Theodore," Mr. Macdonald said to Monsieur Robitaille, when the pair had entered. "Excellent—you're best to write to the government in Quebec City, and the Montreal mayor."

Monsieur Robitaille hurried off to fetch his own portable mahogany *secretaire*.

"Now, Sergeant," Mr. Macdonald said.

O'Neill nodded, as slightly as possible without it being seen as a sign of disrespect. He and the major looked at each other, with no friendly eye between them.

"This is a Fenian raid. New Brunswick, Niagara, Quebec--and now tonight they've struck in Ottawa," Mr. Macdonald said. "It's not merely some local shooting."

Monsieur Robitaille returned, set his kit and himself down next to Mr. Macdonald, and began composing correspondence. He passed on a page to the Prime Minister for approval.

"With all respect, Sir John," Sergeant O'Neill said. "About you setting up a war room here. I'll need this space for the inquest. 'Tis, after all, a murder I'm looking into right here—Sir."

"Just the right tone, Robitaille, thank you," Mr. Macdonald said, scanning the page he'd been handed. "You're right, of course, Sergeant," he added, without looking up. "I can better deal with affairs of state from my office. Doyle, is there another driver about?"

"I've plenty of militia patrolling out front now," Major Doyle said, "but none of my own men are about . . . ."

Monsieur Robitaille motioned me from the room. But I couldn't go without asking him. "Monsieur? Shouldn't we be preparing Mr. McGee . . .?"

"Do not go near that body," Major Doyle said.

Mr. Macdonald cast a look at me. "Some sustenance, perhaps, to carry us through . . ." he said. "Have I—?"

"She's D'Arcy's own servant from Montreal," Major Doyle told Mr. Macdonald. "I suppose—she might not know what she *does* know. A girl like her can be in a room, and no one notices," he said. "D'you know, that could be handy . . .."

"She's a *jeune fille*, gentlemen," Monsieur Robitaille said.

"I'll fetch a tray, Sir," I told Mr. Macdonald. "Toast with cheese?"

"Wrap it, if you could, miss," Mr. Macdonald said. "A few boiled eggs as well, if you've any about . . . and a cut of meat?"

From the heat that flushed the sergeant's face, I thought he still may be looking to argue about Pierce Doyle being boss. But he was smarter than that.

"You're needing a driver, Sir?" Sergeant O'Neill said. "Nancy Trotter's son works for you already."

It was a big step up for Willy to drive the Prime Minister's fancy four-horse carriage. He'd been angling to meet Mr. Macdonald, snagging rides on the rearboard whenever the Prime Minister offered Mr. McGee a ride home of an evening. Preening as the carriage pulled up, laughing at how I wheezed whenever I was around horses.

It made me fierce with grief to watch Willy and Mr. Macdonald bundle up, and think of those times Mr. Macdonald had ensured Mr. McGee arrived home safe. If only he and Doyle had done the same after the speeches . . .. I supposed Mr. Macdonald had been anxious to hurry home to his new wife.

Once they'd left, Mrs. Trotter and I jammed open the connecting doors and pushed the bar tables against the parlour windows, while three coppers shifted the dining table to the far wall. The coppers collected every stray seat—including Mr. McGee's—and we ranged them behind the settee, sticking in kitchen and bar stools, all so tight together that their eventual occupants needed to tuck up their feet—and still the tables pushed against their backsides.

Meantime, Sergeant O'Neill dragged twelve men from their beds to hear from those of us who've had to live through this night.

By dawn, all of us were watching Mr. McGee's blood clotting on the bar, the sight growing clearer as the morning light peeked through the curtains.

If I had any tears to waste, I'd have almost felt sorry for this bunch of so-called jurors. I was becoming used to the sight, and they were only now having their first look at Mr. McGee.

The butcher from down the lane ran right off to retch. I didn't tell him I'd done the same—Major Doyle had warned me not to fraternize.

The rest of these gormless gents I didn't know, excepting an old whitebeard I'd sat near in at church of an odd Sunday.

A few of these lads may even be dancing a jig as if on Mr. McGee's grave at Docherty's Tavern tonight.

"Any of them could be Fenian rebels," Mr. McGee once said as we all walked into Mass. *"Some believe they're true Catholics, killing in the Lord's own name. As for the rest—this is the best place for them to hide, among the holy."*

Mr. McGee knew this to be true as only a former rebel and sinner could. Thanks be he had made his peace with the Infinite.

So far there'd been no praying or toasting inside the house at all, to carry Mr. McGee along his way. Outside, though, the racket was growing louder, as the town awoke to the news.

While the jurors shifted in their front-row seats, Father Clement appeared from the kitchen. I was that glad, to see he'd managed to make his way through the fray.

He pulled a narrow purple silk prayer stole out of his pocket.

"The Extreme Unction," I said, going to meet him. I crossed myself, in anticipation of the Blessed Sacrament. "You know, Father, I can sit with Mr. McGee—turnaround with Mrs. Trotter—as long as is needed." I took his coat from him, and shuffled some others, so his could fit without the coat stand tipping.

"Bless you, child," Father Clement said. "Of course the parish—"

"Just to be clear, Father Clement." Sergeant O'Neill caught the priest on his way over to Mr. McGee. "I'll arrange who's to sit anywhere near the body. There's to be no wake here at all, no viewing of the body until McGee's back in Montreal. And Father—no oil can go on that body until there's been an autopsy."

It was an order, not a petition. I'd never heard a priest spoken to so.

"Father, what's an 'autopsy'?" I asked.

"Never you mind." Sergeant O'Neill waved me off.

Father Clement smiled, squeezed in front of the jurors, and said the Latin as he anointed the air, then kneeled and prayed over the stains on the floor under Mr. McGee's remains.

When he rose, he placed a hand on the sergeant's arm. "I'll be sure to have a chat with your good wife on Sunday, Tommy," Father Clement said. "She often asks me to send up a prayer on your behalf."

Sergeant O'Neill looked like he'd rather have to answer to Our Maker than the missus. He stuck two fingers in his mouth, and blew a piercing whistle. "This inquest is set to start," he said. "Everyone—" He looked at Father Clement. "Move away from the bar."

Mrs. Trotter motioned me to join her in the back row.

"Clara, Tommy O'Neill's only doing his job, after all, and it's made worse for him by having that Pierce Doyle set over him," she said. "You have to feel for the man."

"For Sergeant O'Neill?" I said.

"You and I will have our chance to mourn Mr. McGee. Once they all leave us be. There'll be time enough and more, then," she said.

I nodded. She was right. I'd be doing my own mourning for some time to come.

The man they were calling Coroner this morning was old Dr. Van Cortlandt. He'd been here last week to check on Mr. McGee's gout. I was glad 'twas him in charge. And that he chose to question that prize rooster Dr. Gillivray first.

Gillivray was all long gobbledygook words again. "The pistol ball impacted above the keyhole . . . ."

Why didn't he just say the bullet was in the doorframe? So chuffed with himself. I could tell from the press of Mrs. Trotter's hand against my arm, she was reliving that shot too.

Suddenly, Dr. Gillivray was talking about Mr. McGee's teeth. "When the bullet escaped the upper jaw," he said, "it carried with it four artificial incisors."

What was he going on about, a bullet carrying teeth?

"As soon as we entered, the Sergeant and I found these teeth lying on the floor next to the threshold—with their fitting of *gutta-percha*."

We'd all seen the teeth, hadn't we?

"They were lying about eighteen inches inside the front door sill." He stopped. "So the door must have been open when the shot went through McGee's skull."

No. It couldn't be that I—how could Gillivray suggest such a thing?

I'd thought it was a firecracker. Mrs. Trotter yelled to close the door and bar it, quick. She rushed upstairs . . . .. Monsieur Robitaille re-opened the door to Mr. McGee.

To Mr. McGee.

"Nobody thinks you're to blame, Clara." Mrs. Trotter pulled my nails from my arm. "Quiet now, there's a lamb."

"It's luck that you weren't shot, too, girl." The butcher had turned around. The sergeant tapped on the man's shoulder with his billy stick to bring his attention back to Dr. Gillivray.

Did they all know it had been me?

The room turned toward me, as Dr. Gillivray went on telling how smart he was, to figure out how I'd swung the door shut right as the shot was in the air. Maybe the second before the bullet hit the jamb and lodged itself in the wood. And, the doctor told the inquest, a mere second after it tore through Mr. McGee.

IV

Monsieur Robitaille and Mrs. Trotter both testified to finding Mr. McGee.

Monsieur Robitaille was thanked and excused, to go and provide aid and advice to the Prime Minister. Woodmouse, Hedgehog and Bat followed behind, without thought as to whether they were needed at Parliament, or could better help out at the house. The trio all eyeballed me before they left, then looked at Mrs. Trotter as if to say I already should have been fired, and perhaps arrested to boot.

"Major, am I to speak next?" I had made my way up to the Coroner's table, where the witnesses and officials were still gathered, while Coroner Van Cortlandt stepped away to stretch his legs in the outhouse.

Sergeant O'Neill said he didn't think the jurors needed me to go over the facts a third time.

"Neither Monsieur Robitaille nor Mrs. Trotter mentioned the buggy," I said.

"What buggy, Clara," Major Doyle said.

"When I looked out—" I started.

"She was that sick, poor thing," Mrs. Trotter said.

Major Doyle stroked his moustache, like he could still smell it on me. I'd boiled water and washed my face and body twice—then scrubbed the ends of my braids and rubbed in oil infused with attar of roses, before pinning them up and donning a kerchief.

"That was after," I said to Mrs. Trotter. "You didn't see the street right after the shooting like I did, you were behind me, in the archway."

"You saw a buggy?" Major Doyle asked again.

"It was just that wisp of a carriage, I spied it as it disappeared round the bend . . . onto O'Connor."

"A wisp?" Sergeant O'Neill said. "That's all you have for us?"

"'Twas there but a moment—then gone," I said.

"One or two horses?" Major Doyle asked. "Open buggy, or closed coach? How many men were there?"

"I don't—I didn't see . . . it was a buggy . . .."

"I hardly think we need tell the inquest about a carriage you can't describe, and no men sighted, let alone identified," Sergeant O'Neill said. "The point here today is to rule on a cause of death. We'll have enough time for a girl's tales of ghostly visions, once we've crossed all our legal Ts. Maybe once we're able to investigate, we'll even find someone who saw a corporal being who we can pull in and question."

The major nodded. My being silenced was the first matter on which the police sergeant and the Prime Minister's special constable had agreed.

When the coroner returned, the jurors importuned him to have a break of their own. They all huddled in the kitchen, while Mrs. Trotter and I boiled tea and served them ham sawed off the bone. Sure it was providence, the butcher-juror said, that only the day before Mrs. Trotter had ordered the hock from him.

As they were all eating the blessed pork, Major Doyle pulled out a black leather cigar tube. He gave a bare nod to the coroner and the sergeant. All three stepped outside, and shut the kitchen door tight behind them.

Mrs. Trotter was hauling out a soup pot for the ham bones, though there was barely elbow room to set it on the stove. She motioned to the jurors, like she wanted to take a broom to them. "You men will have to scoot, now you've been fed."

The jurors didn't budge.

Mrs. Trotter appealed to one of the young coppers. "Make them go sit in the rooms we set up for them, so I've my own kitchen to work in." Then she called out, "Clara, go out to the root cellar for onions and potatoes. It seems I'm to feed people all day, so I'd best start a broth."

I grabbed my boots, stuffed the untied lacing inside to make haste, and eased open the door to scoot around to the back garden.

The major, smoking on the stoop, blocked my way. "Not a chance you're coming out here," he said.

Further down the alley, Coroner Van Cortlandt and Sergeant O'Neill were in a snit.

"We should be there," the coroner was saying, his plummy accent ringing strong and clear, for an old gent. "The jurors and I should hear what the Prime Minister has to say."

The jurors turned toward the raised voices, to a man.

"We all know how McGee died," we heard Sergeant O'Neill's reply, just as strongly. "Give us a verdict—so we can get on with catching and hanging the Fenian bastards."

The butcher muttered that he would find out what in blazes was going on. He pulled the door from my grip, and swung it all the way open.

"It's my ruling. We're going." Coroner Van Cortlandt motioned the major aside, and addressed us all from the stoop. "The Prime Minister is about to tell Parliament what he knows about Mr. McGee's death. There should not be an inquest ruling, on cause of death, until we hear Mr. Macdonald on this matter."

"Even if *they* go and hear the politicians' orate," Sergeant O'Neill said, coming right up, a hair's breadth behind the coroner, "you, Van Cortlandt, need to perform that autopsy. Right quick."

Coroner Van Cortlandt made to protest—until Major Doyle coughed.

"But we're to go?" the butcher said.

"'Tis Himself's decision," the sergeant replied.

With that, the jurors couldn't move quickly enough. They grabbed their coats from where they were piled up on the washing mangle in the laundry room, rushed out the back door and up the alley. Gone. Major Doyle loping up the rear, like their sheepdog.

I fetched the vegetables, climbing down and under the house into the cellar, ruminating over what I'd heard, my laces hanging loose, and sodden, by the time I emerged with a full peck. The sergeant had the right of it, to be put out about this cut-and-run. Yes, Mr. Macdonald had helped carry Mr. McGee inside last night. Yet I didn't see how fine words in Parliament could contribute to men's ruling on the cause of the murder.

Yet it would be something to tell their grandchildren, that they heard the Prime Minister's speech on the day of Mr. McGee's murder. And while I'd never been inside Parliament, it had to be a better place to think on the matter than Mrs. Trotter's parlour, where Mr. McGee's corpse was seeping into the very air around us. Even here in the kitchen, the ham hock and tea had carried the aroma of death.

Mrs. Trotter moved for her cloak. "They've no more right to hear the eulogies than we have—less, as they don't care a whit about the man," she said.

I set down the onions and picked up a brush to rub the dirt off the potatoes. "Is anything about this right?"

Sergeant O'Neill leaned against the threshold. "Only the jury goes, Nancy. Those of us who are working today have business here still—Paddy, Brian," he called out for his coppers. "I need you to carry McGee."

Mrs. Trotter rehung her cloak. "You'll be taking him up to his room, then, Tommy?"

"I'm sorry, Nancy." Sergeant O'Neill did look abashed, all of a sudden. "We haven't yet looked at his things . . . we need a different room . . . ."

"I'll not have a boarder left before you're done with me, Tommy. Nor a night of sleep in my own house. Dr. Van Courtlandt is to cut into poor blessed Mr. McGee, here?"

Autopsy. Now I wished I didn't have to know the meaning.

It took some back-and-forthing, and more sympathy for Mrs. Trotter from the sergeant—and a suggestion from a copper that they use my room, it being downstairs—before Mrs. Trotter offered up the attic.

The coppers spread the pink blanket under Mr. McGee's body like an army stretcher, his head lolling off it.

'Twas clear Mr. McGee was bound to face more desecration before he would rest in any sort of peace. No, peace was a ways off yet.

Praise be, then, that as Mrs. Trotter and I swabbed down the bar I realised that—for the moment—I'd moved past my heart's pain and my stomach's sickness. To the numbness that sets into a body with a long Lenten vigil.

Coroner Van Cortlandt cut into Mr. McGee's head wound, so he could rule that Mr. McGee had been shot once, clear and simple. Then he sewed up the back of Mr. McGee's head, quick as a wink.

As he set out, the coroner gave me permission to clean the attic floor.

I climbed two flights with the mop and pail, but cleaning the unbleached floorboards wasn't my true purpose. I hadn't been given permission to prepare Mr. McGee for burial—but I washed his face and hands anyway.

I handled him with the care I'd given Gram when she was fevered. Even so, it felt wrong to be doing such. Like touching the wounds of Jesus—though I knew that to be blasphemy. Mr. McGee was human enough, touched by age and care. His hands were like a gentleman's—except for the scarred, inky callus on his pen finger. That I'd noticed before, of course. He had a lump on his left temple, hidden by the waves of his hair. I'd never known that.

For the remainder of the afternoon, Mrs. Trotter and I prepared food for the jurors' return. But when Sergeant O'Neill arrived at six o'clock in the evening, he was accompanied only by a lady. The biddy holding his arm so tightly was about Mrs. Trotter's age and height, though lacking her heft. She was a long piece of string, as they would say back in Carlingford.

"Nancy, you're to pack up the food and join the exodus to Parliament," the sergeant said. "By order of Major Doyle."

There just wasn't room now for the inquest to be held at Mrs. Trotter's, he told us, as all manner of politicians had chosen to sit in on the hearing.

"Polly says she'll sit upstairs," the sergeant said, "—my wife. This is Nancy Trotter."

He didn't bother to introduce me.

"She thinks McGee needs a proper mourner," he told Mrs. Trotter. "I'll leave one of my men as guard on the landing, mind."

So Father Clement had the right of it. Mrs. O'Neill could change her husband's mind on religious matters.

"I've brought my own dinner," Mrs. O'Neill said. "Didn't you say the inquest might go on into the night, Tommy?"

"I was about to mention that, Polly." Sergeant O'Neill looked at Mrs. Trotter like she was to give him sympathy for having an interfering wife.

Mrs. Trotter thanked Mrs. O'Neill kindly, declaring she'd have an easier mind once she was in the same room with Willy again. "Come on, Clara." She looked around. "Best to clear our heads with some cold air, in any case."

I tied my boots tight this time, before I threw on my cape.

"Doyle's meeting you in the alley," the sergeant said. "You don't want to go out front with the crowd that's now gathered."

I didn't want to open the boarders' door, for certain. Not because of the crowds out there now, but because of the one man who wouldn't be out there ever again.

The new Dominion Constables must've been seconded from the Regulars, since they were wearing British redcoats. We certainly needed their protection, and that of the Ottawa coppers beside them, as we carried the victuals out and down the alley. It seemed there were as many people outside now, as there had been in the streets of Griffintown on Election Day. Only now, the mood was like Mr. McGee had lost, and the voters didn't know how they'd go on without him.

We reached Sparks Street, to witness men carving out bits of the bloody sidewalk boards for souvenirs.

Militiamen wearing the uniform of the Carleton Blazers—the battalion of local volunteers who helped the redcoats safeguard Parliament—had been posted outside the house. They moved in, shooing the scavengers. Then they themselves began removing the walkway boards entirely.

"Those have to go to the station. Sorry, Nancy," Sergeant O'Neill said. "I'll be sure they're replaced."

The soft look Sergeant O'Neill gave Mrs. Trotter made me wonder if he remembered his good wife was right inside.

I fell back, to walk beside Major Doyle. "Major, what you said to the Prime Minister about me—"

"Don't start with me now," he said. "I've no time for a colleen's blather."

"No. I don't mind how you picture me, even to the Prime Minister," I said. "You thought I might be of some use. And as I was the one . . . . I couldn't help Mr. McGee. So Major, if I can be of use in any way . . . in ferreting out Mr. McGee's murderers, why that would save my soul alive."

We weren't carrying our fare in the Prime Minister's private carriage, of course. Major Doyle was now driving a four-wheeled battlefield cart, with two dray horses who couldn't measure an inch under nineteen hands. Sergeant O'Neill helped Mrs. Trotter onto the back seat of the open cab upfront, and climbed in alongside her.

"Climb up, Clara." The major nodded that I was to hop up, in the back with the provisions. "And quit calling me Major. Or even Doyle. Make it Pierce. I don't like to alert every passer-by to my position."

"You can call him anything you want, Clara." The voice came from behind a pile of boxes labelled *Docherty's Pub*. "Just so you don't call on him with the collection plate."

I knew that voice. I looked through the slats of the cart to see Hannah Docherty, of all people.

"Clara," Hannah said, throwing aside a fur rug. "I'm sorry for the night you've had." She gave me a hand up, and a hug I wasn't prepared for.

I was glad enough to see her. If anyone could sashay through this mess, it would be Hannah. I'd met Hannah three months earlier, when Mrs. Trotter first sent me to the butcher. I walked in to find the man looking at a beauty, like all his problems would be solved if she just stood there and let him keep looking. Since then, Hannah had become the young lady I studied, to figure out what being a pretty colleen was about.

I was introduced to Hannah soon after, at Trotter's, as she lived at the pub down the lane, and was close to Willy and his mother. She first paid attention to me, though, when Mrs. Trotter told her I'd been raised by my grannie, just like her.

Mrs. Trotter told me that Hannah had been in need of a bosom friend, ever since Mrs. Trotter's daughter, Maisie, passed away the year before.

I was ever so chuffed when Hannah began to single me out. Sometimes she came over to borrow a bottle when her uncle needed extra for his pub. Sometimes I saw her on the way to Mass, and she invited me to sit in her uncle's pew.

I was shy and proud when she did, and Mrs. Trotter was pleased, and Willy looked so jealous that it was me who'd been chosen. Any man in the vicinity always acted the same around her as the butcher had, even a boy like Willy.

My schooling by Hannah wasn't a practical apprenticeship. I would get older, but even when I reached eighteen like Hannah, I wouldn't have gained her looks or her sparkle or her eyes that changed from honey to tawny brown with the light. I looked on her glamour more like the way I studied Mr. McGee to figure out how a great mind works.

So, as soldiers packed in Mrs. Trotter's victuals, I settled under the rug and let Hannah cuddle me.

"You poor dear, what you must be suffering." Hannah took my hands in hers as Doyle hied the horses and we set out on the four-block ride. Her coat sleeves, edged in rabbit fur, slipped under my cape. "I'm glad I can be here—thanks be Pierce is my cousin."

That I hadn't known. They had the same Dubliner's Viking colouring, true. But in Hannah I saw the fire, in Doyle, the ice.

"Just call him Pierce, Clara," she said. "You'll find he's more human that way. Look, he's even letting me come along."

"Letting you?" I asked. "Surely the favour's yours."

"There's been all sorts of military men, sweeping through the pub all day long." Hannah nodded at the soldiers. "British troops, these new Canadian Constables of Pierce's, the Ottawa coppers, even the militia. All hauling off Irish lads. Lord knows where they're taking them, but I heard Parliament . . . .. You see, I need to check my Mike's safe."

"Mike—the dark-haired fellow I saw you walking with last month?"

"No, not that lad. Mike's moved here from Montreal. Mike Walsh—if you hear anyone say his name, come find me? We've been courting on and off for a while bytimes, but it took this scare for me to know. He's the one, Clara."

I was surprised to hear that.

"And I'm so scared he's been scooped up, along with all the others. Once I find him, Pierce'll get him out."

"Will he now?" Sergeant O'Neill called out from the cab.

"I never said that, Hannah." Major Doyle—Pierce, I must remember—sounded ticked. "I said I need help with chores at the inquest—and I'd like to see what's what, with this new favourite beau of yours."

V

"A cathedral in which we worship democracy, Clara."

That's how Mr. McGee liked to describe the new Parliament Building.

It was even bigger than Notre-Dame in Montreal, which Mr. McGee told me is the largest church in the New World.

I'd walked by Parliament often in these past few months. Mainly going to and from the ByWard Market, to fetch provisions. Yet I was shy of it still. In all its loftiness and grandeur, it did make me want to sink to my knees.

I'd learned to admire from afar how the solid, pearly sandstone was set off by the rough grace of the slate roof. Mr. McGee had told me to look for glints of fire amid the window dressings, from a stone he said had been imported from New York State.

"Some of the best of the building made its way from the States to this new home, even as I did," he said—that last bit with a wink.

Last week, swinging an empty basket on my way to market, I'd worked up the nerve to come close.

Mr. McGee had been het up that morning about a Maritimer, a Mr. Joseph Howe, sailing to London to tell the Queen there shouldn't be a Canada after all. It only took one trickster, he reminded me, to undo years of honest men's toil.

So I'd darted up to the cornerstone of the main building and touched it, quick—thinking if I sent up my wish for the betterment of the entire country, it wouldn't matter 'twas just a maid doing the bargaining.

The luck seemed to rub my way, though. That night, Mr. McGee promised to show me inside. Well, it wasn't a promise as such, more one of his grand statements.

"The girl who can write out these words for me, and understand them too, deserves a tour of our Parliament building," he said.

I'd arisen extra early the next morning to iron out a dress handed down from Mr. McGee's daughter, Miss Frasa; a blue silk, almost new as she didn't need it at the convent, and already cut to size. I suppose I was dawdling, to make it perfect, because Mrs. Trotter called out to me to set on the kettle—and by the time I'd dashed to the kitchen and back again, I smelled singed cloth. I'd set the iron on the table like a booby, and though I'd pushed the dress well to the side, I'd burned a tiny hole in the back of the skirt.

I cried so hard, and felt so stupid about it, that I burrowed into the closet where Mrs. Trotter stored out-of-season garments and her late husband's old things, so no-one would hear me.

After I finally straightened myself out, I spent my free daylight hour sewing a new tuck in the dress. The patch almost didn't show. I made sure to finish that very day, so as to be ready whenever Mr. McGee should choose to conduct the tour.

Now I was here without him, or the dress—in my last clean apron and my worst dress, in point of fact. One of Mrs. Trotter's that, even cut down, was all bunched-up funny at the chest. Not that it mattered, as Mr. McGee wouldn't be the one touring me. Still, I didn't like to appear a slattern in his cherished halls.

As I stood staring at all the fancy carvings— were those rude *sheela na gigs* above the staff entrance?—Pierce Doyle hurried Sergeant O'Neill up the steps. Hannah walked right in, no man saying her nay.

Mrs. Trotter and I were barred entrance.

"You with the jury?" the redcoat asked.

"Witnesses," Mrs. Trotter said. "And my own son works here—running around for Mr. Macdonald." She sounded so proud. "Willy Trotter."

"Trotter—where McGee was shot." The soldier looked at her like that made the shooting her fault, somehow. "I've heard you're related to that Buckley who's been arrested?"

"Who are you, talking such nonsense?" Mrs. Trotter grew fierce. "I'm Nancy Trotter—here by order of the Coroner, my son works here, and I know no such Buckley."

Willy ducked out the door, around the guard like a pickpocket on the docks. "Ma—Pierce sent me to see what's keeping you —" he called.

"The major?" Willy nodded, and the soldier waved us in. "Why didn't you say as much?"

The hallway was full of men who didn't look at us as they rushed past. *"Big Men,"* Mr. McGee had called them, his tongue in his cheek. *"Like my fellow boarders—barring Robitaille, of course, he's earned his stature."*

"The coroner's just told all the details about Mr. McGee's injury—" Willy said.

"Well, he should have done his job at his own surgery," Mrs. Trotter said.

"Ma, our boarding house will be famous," Willy said. "Not that I'm wishing ill off Mr. McGee—but don't look at it as a curse on our house, Ma. We were the boarding house of D'Arcy McGee, and we can be proud of that. Besides, Monsieur Robitaille told me he and the others are staying put—they won't have a bunch of assassins running them off."

"Have you given your testament as well, Willy?" said Mrs. Trotter.

"I told the jury I didn't see anyone on the street—and no buggy, neither," Willy said, with an eye-roll in my direction.

I should never have told Willy a thing, when he'd quizzed me on what happened while I was packing the Prime Minister's early-morning snack. And I should have known from Willy's reaction—he'd grabbed the package and took off for the carriage, muttering that girls were full of vapours— that the investigators wouldn't believe me either.

"I don't see what you could share," I said. "You only came near after the shooting."

"I heard the noise," he said.

"And when you did see 'something' on the stoop—which is all you could make out from across the street—you ran inside that newspaper and hid," I replied.

"I spoke right after I delivered John A. here," Willy addressed his mother. "Then I made a special run to the telegraph office."

"Call him Sir John A. Macdonald, son," Mrs. Trotter said.

Willy steered us around a sharp corner, into yet another corridor lined with gilt-framed portraits. I had to think such fancy people were all members of the monarchy.

Mrs. Trotter looked upon one fat, bald, mustachioed gentleman's painted image with particular distaste. "The colour of that man's cheeks, 'tis like the bloom of an eggshell," she said. "That's just the way Sir John looked when he arrived last night."

"He doesn't like to be 'Sir' around here, Ma," Willy said. "It reminds the others he's the only one to have been so honoured by the Crown. Anyway, John

A.'s been operating without sleep—or liquor. You'll hear by the croak in his throat that he can't hold out much longer."

"Mr. Lacey didn't get to the telegraph office first?" I asked Willy.

"He and the other journos arrived a bit ahead of time," Willy said, "but they had to wait for Mr. Macdonald's messages about the 'assination' to go through, before they could send off any news."

"Assignation, Willy?" I said. "That's a secret meeting."

He flashed a page, quickly so I couldn't see. "The word's *ass-assi-nation*, Miss Clara Bluestocking Swift. It means murder of a big-shot politician, Mr. Lacey says."

"Don't be a goose, Willy, let Clara see what the Prime Minister wrote," Mrs. Trotter said.

Willy shifted the pages more slowly, to show off the important messages with which he'd been entrusted. I saw only snatches.

> *. . . guards will be posted at the house . . .*
> *. . . no solace to offer but our protection . . .*
> *. . . pray for us all.*

That last was from the note that Monsieur Robitaille had written to the McGee family priest, Monsignor Ryan. One sentence stopped me.

> *A black night for our country.*

The night hadn't been black, though. The moon had been unusually close.

"The railway lines are all on watch —all the villages around have been alerted, and the lock stations too," Willy said.

"They think the killers have left town?" Mrs. Trotter said.

"There's all kinds of stories. That there'll be more killings, that they're trying to get to John A." Willy said. "That maybe none of us should even be here now, lest they've rigged this building to blow when the Parliamentarians are inside lamenting for poor D'Arcy."

"Mr. McGee, Willy—may the saints bless his soul and keep him," said Mrs. Trotter.

Surely, she could give over on trying to teach Willy what's proper, tonight of all nights.

"What's that other message, Willy?" I said.

He shrugged. "He asked Mr. Tupper to look out for Mr. McGee's book."

"His book," said Mrs. Trotter. "At such a time as this?"

How excited Mr. McGee had been to finish his *Apologia*.

"If I succeed," he'd said, *"this book will change this country—and the one to the south of us, Clara. It has that much fire, and brimstone too."* And he'd looked for a moment like a devilkin himself.

"You should've been here for the speeches, Ma," Willy said. "Mr. Macdonald broke down. The Prime Minister, crying in Parliament."

"How much more must I walk, Willy?" Mrs. Trotter said.

"Through those double doors ahead, Ma," Willy said. "Promise. I walk these halls ten times daily."

"Mr. Macdonald would have spoken well of his friend," I said.

"Not so any of us could hear. You know how low John A. talks, bytimes. Now Monsieur Cartier, he gave the finest speech of all," Willy said.

"Monsieur Cartier didn't even like Mr. McGee," I said. That man had lobby-talked Mr. McGee out of the government's Cabinet. Too many Irish, he'd said.

"He's the second-most important man here," Willy said. "And he's not about to speak ill of the dead, Clara. None of them are. Though we all know it was the Fenians as did in Mr. McGee, even Parliamentarians need to have clean noses today."

Fenians. I didn't doubt there were more than one of the rebel buggers in on the plot. I'd have to say penance for using the word, even in my thoughts, but it kept repeating inside me. *Buggers.*

That's what Mr. Macdonald had called them. Mr. McGee's shooting must've been planned, all those Fenian leaders in on it. Mr. McGee had raised a ruckus when he'd published, in the *Montreal Gazette,* that the schemers had some success in seizing upon our Irish community groups. That they'd been using good men as pawns, so they could raise funds and support for insurrection.

Yes, a conspiracy, among all their leaders. No one man could have done something so—soulless. Such a big evil. Mr. McGee had poked at the Irish rebels until they were flaming angry. And they had threatened him more than once, the Fenian so-called Brotherhood.

Willy was right. When we finally arrived at the new site for the inquest, I was staggered to enter such an immense chamber—a hall as large as Trotter's entire downstairs—and find its every square foot already occupied.

I spotted Monsieur Robitaille seated among a phalanx of men, who had the look of Members of the House of Commons, or Senators. Woodmouse, Hedgehog and Bat were in the back row, but Monsieur Cartier was right up front; he'd become Mr. McGee's friend in death.

Mrs. Trotter groaned when she saw that not even Hannah had been able to snag a seat among the interested parties.

We manoeuvred to stand near her, amidst the crush by the wall.

Wild stories were running around the room, shared among the seated great and we crowded commoners, as everyone waited with equal impatience for the inquest to start up again. New tales, fear and panic travelled in and out every time the doors were opened and closed. Told by people who had nothing to do with it . . . or maybe some of them did?

I was suddenly full of questions.

Willy was as full of answers, working at Parliament and all. And he liked knowing his way around even more, when it was Hannah asking.

"John A.'s the Attorney General as well as Prime Minister, you know?" Willy said to Hannah. "He'll have this inquest wrapped up double-quick and a real trial well in hand. You'll see."

"They need some Fenians to put up for trial," I said.

"Oh, they've locked up a bunch of lads already. With the notices they've sent out across the country, there'll be scores arrested," said Willy. "They're scooping up any lad who's even been seen talking to a Fenian."

Hannah stroked her neck, Willy's eyes following her downward movement. "Who?" she said. "Have you heard any names, Willy?"

"I hear Patrick Buckley's in jail, for certain," he offered. "Though that could be for a number of reasons, Mr. Lacey says."

"Do you know this Buckley, Son?" Mrs. Trotter grabbed Willy's arm.

"Oh, he's the younger brother of another of Macdonald's so-called 'drivers', only John Buckley's not as important as Pierce. Both Buckleys understand the Gaelic—I wish you'd taught me, Ma, it would be useful now."

"You're saying this man Patrick Buckley's in there to spy," Mrs. Trotter said. "Have you been chumming around with these Buckleys, Willy?"

"I'm saying Paddy Buckley'll be released right quick and he'll be telling stories," Willy said, shaking off his mother's arm. "Ma—leave off, will you? Not here—"

"They're being held in the jail?" Hannah said. "I'd heard lads are being questioned right here in the building."

"I don't rightly know—yeah, they may be bringing over some lads to testify," Willy said. He pulled at the inside of his collar like it was too tight.

"Would you mind touring me around, Willy?" Hannah had only to smile.

For a moment, I thought I'd twit Willy that his *mavourneen* Hannah was looking for another lad altogether.

Then Hannah caught my eye.

I rubbed at the puffed-up skin under my right sleeve. These people telling the jury over and over about Mr. McGee's murder made me jumpy, like I couldn't breathe and I wanted to scream at them, all at the same moment. After a solid hour of this, I needed to be moving around. Doing something useful.

I edged to the door. Sergeant O'Neill waved a finger at the guard—I wasn't going anywhere. I was close enough by, though, when the major strode back in— Pierce, as I was to remember to call him now. Willy followed—without Hannah. Both of them began scanning the crowd.

"Willy." I caught his arm. "Surely we should serve the jury something liquid."

"They should follow Mr. Macdonald's approach to the matter, and carry their own fuel," Willy said, shrugging me off.

"Willy—mind your betters." Mrs. Trotter came over to smooth her son's hair. She pulled his ear, hard, while she was at it.

"Hannah was supposed to bring tea in to another committee room for me," Pierce said. "But the damn girl's disappeared. Come with me, Clara."

Me walking out past Sergeant O'Neill, with Pierce waving me through, was a small enough victory. But while they wouldn't hear me say my piece about what I'd seen, at least the major was letting me help—in accordance with what these men saw as my capabilities.

Mr. Macdonald's face had gone all pasty, and he was sweating cold.

"Get me Desbarats," he said.

There were four well-suited men around the table, besides the Prime Minister. They leaned forward as one.

I understood why. I was right behind him with my tray, after all, and I could hardly hear his voice.

"That printer on Sparks St.," one of them said.

"Desbarats is renting to that Trotter woman, and his print shop is next door." Mr. Macdonald said. He was peering at a scrap of paper. "Now his former night watchman has done himself in?"

"The night watchman killed himself at his own home," another man said.

"Mighty convenient timing," said a third.

"Roust out Desbarats," Mr. Macdonald repeated, tilting his head up for a moment, and taking in all their faces.

"Is it true Nancy Trotter's somehow related to your man Buckley?" said the first man.

"What about this other fellow?" said Mr. Macdonald. "Whelan."

The Prime Minister accepted the teacup. "Thank you, Miss Clara——?" he said, with the cup poised in the air. He looked right at me, remembering, probing— dismissing. "No cream—can you credit it was poor D'Arcy who stopped us selling liquor here in Parliament?"

He was still looking at me, but the remark was meant for the table.

"Well, he closed the public bar, at least," the third man replied.

Mr. Macdonald turned his focus to lifting out a flask from his pocket.

"I'm with you John," that man continued. "And none of your black-leaved brew for me, girl."

The men all laughed, without taking any pleasure in it.

Mr. Macdonald poured a nip into the cup. "That's more like mother's milk. Now—how many have been rounded up?"

"Twenty here in Ottawa," Pierce said, from where he'd pressed himself against the wall. "I hear as many again already, in Montreal. We're waiting on reports from Toronto and points between."

"What about this?" Mr. Macdonald held up a page. "Is this true? Sweeney's up and died, and over the border in Buffalo?"

Sweeney—*The Times* said he was one of the biggest rebels of all.

Pierce nodded. "God must be listening, once in an odd while."

"The Fenian bastard," said the first man. He accepted a cup from me, then pointed to the sugar bowl, two fingers raised.

"There's some justice left in this world," said the second. That gentleman waved me on by.

"And the Fenians are talking of giving the damned rebel a right royal funeral, in Toronto," Mr. Macdonald read out. "Same day as McGee's to be buried in Montreal."

"That's about perfect, isn't it?" Pierce said.

"We won't let that happen," said Mr. Macdonald. "Now about Whelan——"

Pierce tilted his head toward the tea tray, then the door. 'Twas a look and a hook for me.

Pierce gave me directions like I was a simpleton, before slipping back into the meeting. But still, there were so many corridors, and as it was full dark, the window glass reflected the hall's marble and stone in strange ways. So I made a wrong turn.

A very wrong turn. To an open door, with six men tied up inside. Four redcoats were beating on each lad. They were shackled, eyes swollen eyes, lips cut and bleeding. The air smelled of urine, and worse. Two of the men in chains looked more like boys. One was a carrot top, who gleamed grey with sweat as he watched a Black Irishman take a drubbing with a sally rod. One of the older men was running his tongue around the inside of his mouth like he'd lost a tooth.

A soldier hauled back and pounded the stomach of the Black Irishman.

I flinched, and stepped back without looking.

A hand grabbed my elbow, and hustled me a few steps further away from the scene.

"How'd you get through that corridor?" The soldier who asked was English, the kind whose *r*s sound like *w*s. He was twice my size, and he'd pulled my back in against him so I couldn't see his face. His hand slid around my waist, and he pulled tighter. His belt pressed into my back.

"I was serving . . . Mr. Macdonald," I said, my voice falling with each word. "I couldn't find my way back to——"

"Serving Cabinet? I haven't seen you before."

"Pierce—Major Doyle—brought me ——"

I felt him stiffen. "You his cousin?"

I said nothing.

His other hand came around me, groping my chest, digging through all the extra folds of Mrs. Trotter's cloth while I made myself as small as possible, until his knuckles squeezed the knob of my right breast.

I shuddered, and he lost his grip a minute, then squeezed tighter.

I was stiff as a scarecrow after a frost, my hands clenched—I wanted to have at him, but I was terrified to move an inch.

"I've more tit than you do, girl," he said. "Pierce must have more than one cousin. Should've known you weren't the one--I hear you can see that beauty get a wiggle on across a dark street."

"Pierce is right behind me," I said, willing him to let me go.

"Turn back where you came from, you." He wiped his knuckles on my shawl as he released me. "Then take a left. Don't think of looking back. And I'll be around to hear, so don't think of telling any story about this, either."

I ran the moment he let me go.

Back the way I'd come and then up the first side corridor. Were there voices ahead? Had I taken the wrong path again—what would I find this time?

Then I couldn't run, suddenly. I slid down to the floor, and curled into myself. No man had ever touched me like that. Not even on the ship, though I'd learned then that careful meant lucky, when I was stuck too close to certain people. And I'd seen others touching, being touched . . . heard women fighting off men at night.

I was fine though. I took off my shawl and reversed it, in case his knuckles had left a stain.

Nobody could tell now.

A couple of men passed a lamp on the wall further down the hall. These were older men. Wearing suits, not uniforms. I pushed against my hands to stand, then hurried toward them.

How could men act like that?

I tamped down my feelings, the press of his hand . . .. I'd been in luck, indeed. I knew what could happen to women who had the misfortune to be caught near a battle. You only had to read the Holy Bible to know that truth, never mind the Greek and Roman classics I'd studied at the hedge school.

Mr. McGee had told me we had to be prepared for another fierce fight. That this was a war. Canadians of all kinds against Irish Fenians. He'd said that some of the battle wouldn't be fought on a field, either. That 'twas better to have the government hunt down the enemy, rather than drag innocents into a pitched battle. *We'll find them, to a man,* he said. *We'll show ourselves to be a proud warrior nation.*

I didn't think he'd meant someone like me might be hurt in any way, though.

Well, I had been, and him not here to protect me.

I'd seen it now myself, how this type of war was fought.

Those soldiers might have already faced the Fenians in the Battle of Ridgeway, or at Fort Erie. They might have seen the men beside them lose their lives during one of the Fenian raids. What I saw was men acting under officers' orders . . . and I'd just had a taste of soldiers' rules.

It didn't matter that the lads being beaten were all Irish Catholics, without doubt. It didn't matter how that Saxon redcoat had touched my person.

Maybe I was punished . . . to make me realise . . . well, maybe it had been my fault, for even being there.

"Canadians against Fenians," Mr. McGee had repeated, time and again. *"Your own future depends on our winning, Clara."*

At least those young Irishmen back there could see their attackers' faces.

Still . . . as I forced myself to walk forward, I hoped, hard, that Hannah had found her fellow.

Was this the correct corridor? Yes— I saw Willy, ahead of me, leading Hannah to a lineup outside the inquest room. I ran to reach them.

"Where've you been, Clara?" Hannah said. "You're all out of breath."

"I'm done in," I said.

"Of course you are." Hannah patted my shoulder. "Any news?"

"What's up with this crush?" Willy called, as two guards stepped up to block the door.

"Everyone has to wait for the men in custody to go in," one of the guards replied. "Hey, Willy, are you for jail next?"

"What d'you mean by that?" Willy said.

"There's talk about your mother. That she's tied in somehow."

Four prisoners were marched through the crowd. They weren't the ones I'd just seen. They were just as badly beaten, though.

"Sweet Jesus." Hannah's voice fell.

I wiped the back of my hand across my mouth.

Others around us began to speak up, and to curse.

The inquest doors opened. Pierce stuck out his head. "Move aside," he told all of us agitated onlookers. "Let them bring in the boys."

So they were led into the inquest, and we followed, falling into single-file as if we'd just received Communion. The prisoners' arrival imposed order inside the room as well. The people who'd been speculating earlier were silent, craning to see.

It turned out that one of the men—the one with only a few scratches on him, but the beginning of a shiner—was the famous young Patrick Buckley. He was questioned first by Coroner Van Courtlandt, and the others all repeated Buckley's refrain.

And they all only named one name. And named him again and again. A man who had been watching Mr. McGee speak from the gallery the previous night. A man who'd been het up—agitated, so Buckley told the inquest. A man who'd been seen examining a gun in his waistcoat pocket. A man with a brother already jailed back home in Ireland as a Fenian rebel. A man who went by the name of Whelan. Patrick James Whelan. Not Patrick, this Paddy Buckley was quick to tell the coroner. This man was known by his middle name, people should be asking for a lad named Jimmy.

Jimmy Whelan.

I'd never heard of the man, and by that night's end I hated him already.

VI

The twelve men left us sitting there, hour after hour, while they were set up else-where. Finishing off Mrs. Trotter's fine food, no doubt, while making a decision. In my present dark mood, I imagined they'd then settled in comfortably in the Parliamentary library, with wing chairs and brandy. It mattered not where they'd been sequestered, though, or when they would finally take it upon themselves to return to the inquest. Nobody doubted what the ruling would be. Murder, though they couldn't say yet who fired the gun. And a manhunt for one Jimmy Whelan.

Coroner Van Cortlandt had fallen asleep in his chair. By nine o'clock in the evening, we couldn't hold out any longer, either. Sergeant O'Neill said that as his wife had been sitting alone all these hours, he'd let us leave.

No, she'd not been alone, I wanted to tell him. She'd been with Mr. McGee. I suddenly needed to be the one sitting beside him.

Pierce and the Sergeant led we witnesses from Trotter's, and Hannah, through the unruly pack of politicians, soldiers, and other reprobates still milling about.

"Keep close, Clara," Pierce said. "You don't want to be lost in this crowd."

Did he know? About that Saxon soldier? I'd heard lads talked . . . but grown men?

I craned my neck to keep sight of the lantern Pierce held up as a beacon. There was a break in the grey and brown woollens all around me. And a familiar face.

He was a right smart-looking young man. Sandy curls, wearing a finely cut double-breasted tweed coat. He'd turned himself right around, looking for someone, when he saw me noticing him. It had been a few months, but I was sure he recognised me.

He ducked, then elbowed his way forward. Out of my sight.

I pushed up on my toes. Was the lad from Montreal rushing away from me? Or from someone else?

The crowd surged forward, and I tripped. "Clara?" Pierce said. "What the—"

"It's just that—fellow. There." I spied him again as I righted myself—his curly hair brushing the collar of the heather tweed. "The laddie who's knocked that other man aside, trying to cut ahead."

"With the burnt-orange whiskers?" Pierce said. "And?"

"His name's Sullivan," I said. "He's one of Mr. Barney Devlin's men."

"So he worked on behalf of McGee's Fenian-loving opponent, during last summer's election," Pierce said.

I thought of the Irish lads who'd traipsed through the inquest, and the beatings they'd taken first. "Pierce—that doesn't mean—I'm not saying there's anything particularly off about him, mind."

"What *are* you saying, Clara?"

"Sullivan came to the McGee house on New Year's Eve."

"That's the lad who spooked the McGees with a bomb scare?" Pierce said.

"He seemed sure Mr. McGee was in danger."

"It's worth asking the man just where he conjured up the notion that you were all about to be blown to Kingdom Come."

Pierce signalled a group of volunteer militiamen to fall in, around those of us returning to Trotter's. And a second group, of redcoats, to follow him. "Good eye, Clara," Pierce said. "Tell O'Neill he has my permission to drive the government cart, Clara—let me go by, man."

"There was nothing found that night at the McGees', Pierce," I called out. "'Twas no more to it than all the talk among people here tonight—suggesting Parliament's about to be bombed."

But I was speaking to Pierce's receding back.

Was Sullivan now to be knocked about, on my say-so? Sure, anyone with any news of a threat to Mr. McGee should be questioned, I knew that was right . . ..

I stepped into the midst of our group, as we moved outside our country's seat of power. Seeking safety from both the crowd, and the militia escort.

A gargoyle stared down at me. 'Twas a devilkin, sticking out his tongue, an icicle hanging from his spout. A patch of snow was pockmarked with the shards that the demon had recently spit out.

"So what do you think of Parliament, Clara?" said Willy. He'd pushed his way out first, and now was awaiting the rest of us with some impatience.

"It makes me feel small and in the wrong of it, somehow," I said.

"It makes me feel bigger. And everything right," said Willy. "But then, this is not a place for girls."

Mrs. Trotter came out next, nattering on to Sergeant O'Neill as he offered her his arm down the stairs—about the talk of her and the Buckleys.

"I told you, Ma, it's all smoke," Willy said.

"So they're dirtying my skirts, to hide a government agent amidst traitors?" Mrs. Trotter said. "I don't care why—I don't want my name smeared to further their ends, Willy."

Mrs. Trotter turned to Sergeant O'Neill. "Tommy, is there nothing you can do for me?"

"I'll get you a story in the newspaper, Ma," said Willy. "You're part of the biggest news since Confederation, and Mr. Lacey likes me, he'll help me write up your complaint for the *Times*. I'll do your 'eye-witness account', as the newsies say. That's the answer to this."

"I wouldn't trust Lacey to handle it," said Sergeant O'Neill. "An ad in the paper, Nancy, that's what you need. Say it plain and simple. 'I, Nancy Trotter, am not related to, nor do I know, either of these Buckley characters'."

They slowed down to talk. Her voice carried, though. "That Mr. Lacey is filling his head with promises," Mrs. Trotter said. "Using my Willy—to gain information from Parliament."

"A mother never likes to see her son grow away from her," Sergeant O'Neill said.

"You'll help me with the wording," she said to the sergeant, "so it'll sound legal-like."

"I'll bring the advertisement over, ready for placement, when we come for McGee."

Mrs. Trotter began to weep. Sergeant O'Neill took the opportunity to pull her in, and patted her back.

Willy ran ahead to the buggy, bumping them as he passed.

I didn't wonder. The sergeant held her too close. He and Mrs. Trotter had been friendly enough the odd time the sergeant had dropped by these past few months. The first time he had come for police business, to inquire about someone who Mrs. Trotter may have served in the parlour bar. She had said, as he left, how sorry she was she couldn't help—but it was always nice to have the visit.

I hadn't heard any of the other conversations; they'd closed the door.

I'd never thought anything of it. Though now that I did think, maybe it had been one of those chats with the sergeant that had spooked her into double-locking the door.

Finally, Hannah stepped onto the path. "The man's in Montreal," she said, skidding into me. "He never made it back."

"You mean that Jimmy Whelan?" I said.

"My Mike." Hannah looked at me as if I'd truly lost my senses. "He's been picked up, along with half of Irish Montreal. It's not good to be Irish anywhere in this country tonight, Clara. And won't be—until they've found a man to hang the shooting on."

Mr. McGee had taught me justice wasn't ever so simple, especially for we Irish. Yet, after these hours in our halls of government, I didn't see my way to telling Hannah she didn't quite have the right of it.

"A tot of brandy will set you up," Hannah said, carrying a bottle and alighting on my bed. "For the night you've had, and the one in front of you."

"That's Mr. McGee's special brandy," I said. Hannah must have rooted around in the bar until she'd found the best.

"'Tis only right that we use it then." She poured for me first, and laughed something fierce when I choked over my drink. "So you've never snuck a swallow before?" she said.

"It's not my first," I said. "I took part in the toast when Gram died. And our priest gave me two bottles of whiskey in case I needed to steady my stomach on ship."

"For medicinal use," Hannah said. "Wise priest."

"I had one tot before they were stolen from me," I said.

Mrs. Trotter walked into my room.

"What are you two up to in here?" she said. "Have you got Clara drinking now, Hannah?"

"She's an old hand at it," Hannah said.

"Mrs. Trotter, I swear, I don't take a drink at all but—"

"Settle down, Clara. Hannah may have the right of it. It'll help you have a few hours' sleep," Mrs. Trotter said. "I'll ask the copper Tommy's posted here to knock on your door, Clara. He'll rouse you at about four o'clock in the morning. Now up and out with you, Hannah. You've need of sleep too."

"I'll be asleep before I'm halfway down the lane to home," Hannah said, and hugged me goodbye.

"You can relieve Clara, tomorrow," Mrs. Trotter told Hannah as she saw her out. "If you could be back here, come dawn?"

I did lay me down, and kept my sore eyes closed—until I heard the tread of feet near my door, and a man's strong knock.

I couldn't say I was any more rested, though, when I climbed the attic stairs. I found Mrs. Trotter knitting in the dark. There were no windows up here to let in the moonlight, and she had a great fear of a candle, or worse still, a kerosene lamp, being knocked over and setting off a fire in the house's rafters.

"You're up for this, Clara?" she asked. "I can last out the night myself."

"I want to do this," I said. "Please. For Mr. McGee."

I knew, though, my sitting with Mr. McGee was purely selfish. I was hoping Mr. McGee could provide me with at least cold comfort.

And so I told Mr. McGee about the men I'd seen being knocked about, how I'd pointed out a likely lad to Pierce, and now I feared the worst would happen to him, and on my account. I couldn't tell him about—the other—but I thought of it, and hoped that amounted to the same thing—him being no more able to hear me, than he was to read my mind.

I told him how I wanted to make up for not helping him over the threshold. "The soldiers—was that their revenging your blood split, Mr. McGee? Or did it arise from the soldiers' fears of what could happen to them and theirs?"

I was stupidly surprised, somehow, when The Holy Spirit did not descend upon me, and I had no epiphany. And left scrambling, because from here on forward, I'd never be able to turn to Mr. McGee for direction again.

I'd have to make do, by thinking on what he'd already told me.

"When you're about to take a course of action, Clara," he once said, *"ask yourself the cost. And know you'll have to pay it."*

I edged forward. Mr. McGee's body was beginning to ripen and turn in earnest. I'd pulled one of his pocket squares from the dirty linens pile in the laundry, before climbing the stairs, for just this reason. I burrowed my nose into it, and breathed in his sweat and liniment.

Mrs. McGee had been good all last fall and winter about slathering on that liniment, for her husband's bad leg . . ..

She'd just sent me to her room for more of the special salve. Murmuring an apology of sorts, even. For keeping me up through the night on New Year's Eve, when the other maid, Bonnie, had family to go home to.

There had been an insistent knocking, as I rushed down the front-hall stairs. I'd answered the door, jar of liniment in hand, to see before me one of Barney Devlin's roustabouts. A flashy dresser, for some reason he'd let his raccoon-fur coat fall open. His silk vest made me think he'd been to a party already, and his boots reflected a high shine.

I recognised him from six months earlier, when Devlin had fought dirty at the election speeches. This particular lad had yelled lots of questions at Mr. McGee from the back of the hall.

One time, Mr. McGee stopped mid-speech, to say the young gentleman shouldn't let himself get so het up. "Why, sir," he said, "you're sweating enough to ruin your lovely white linen shirt."

The lad couldn't run together a sensible sentence in reply.

Devlin had run down Mr. McGee's reputation most effectively, though, all over Griffintown. That man had almost succeeded in keeping Mr. McGee out of Parliament. And Mr. McGee had called Devlin a Fenian on numerous occasions during speeches, and had even come close to that charge in writing.

Four months later, the bells of Notre-Dame Cathedral were ringing in 1868, Mr. McGee lay suffering from the gout, and this stylish lout who'd voted for the Fenian candidate was stomping his feet on the Member of Parliament's front porch.

"I must speak to McGee, Miss," he said, blowing on his hands, so I backed up a little and let him take one step inside. "It's his life in the balance." His hat was crushed under an armpit. There was sweat on his forehead, like when he'd questioned Mr. McGee, and now I could smell the liquor on his breath. But there was something—his eyes were uncanny.

"You stay right here—?"

"Sullivan, Miss."

I knew not to let one of Devlin's men into the house. Not with the death threats Mr. McGee had been finding in his mail for months. Yet I'd left the door ajar when I'd run for Miss Keough, the McGee's housekeeper.

She'd stood up to Sullivan. Mr. McGee was ill, Miss Keough told the man. Mr. McGee was receiving no visitors. Sullivan could state his business or go.

"You need to get old D'Arcy out—all of you, get out of the house before the bombing."

By this time, Mrs. McGee had come to see the fuss. "Bombing? Jesus Mary and Joseph, what are you saying, man?" Mrs. McGee'd grabbed Sullivan by the arm.

"Pardon, Ma'am, I didn't think you—"

"Tell me. At once."

Sullivan responded to that maternal command, and the story soon all poured out. The house was to be blown up, he claimed, when we were all in our beds.

"By three in the morning, you'll all be with Christ in heaven if you stay here," the man at the door—Sullivan—had said.

Sullivan had promised he'd go to alert the coppers. "Make sure you get your girls out," he'd told Mrs. McGee—though Miss Frasa had stayed at the convent, so Mrs. McGee had only Miss Peggy to worry over.

"Beid lá eile ag an bPaorac," I'd heard him mutter as he left. "But not tonight."

'Twas the Fenian cry.

"Mrs. McGee Ma'am," I called out. "That man just said, 'the poor will have another day'."

So Mrs. McGee had roused Miss Peggy herself, while Miss Keough went to the pub down the alleyway, and fetched four strong men. Those lads who didn't help came up the lane from the local anyway, and stood in the street drinking jars, while Mr. McGee was carried in his invalid chair up the front stairs to the neighbours. Acting as if 'twere all staged, for their New Year's entertainment.

There Mr. McGee stayed until morning, waiting for the coppers to show.

Mrs. McGee had led all the females around to the parochial house, where we knelt on the floor and prayed with the priest. All night, even Miss Peggy.

I offered it up, asking Mother Mary that the Lord take this scare into account, and save Mr. McGee from worse.

Finally come dawn, Mrs. McGee shepherded us all home. To find Mr. McGee had already insisted on returning to his writing, New Year's revellers again transporting him.

Miss Keough went around right then, and raised heck at the police station. The coppers said no one had arrived with any such alarm, what was she talking about?

Mr. McGee told his wife and housekeeper to calm down, everyone was fine despite the feathers and fuss.

He did say, though, that it was like one of his dreams, where he'd been saved by an angel from the devils. And he sent out word around Griffintown that he wanted to see this lad Sullivan.

But Sullivan wasn't to be seen. Devlin, when visited by the police, swore he hadn't come across the man in some time.

"Done's done," Mr. McGee had told his wife and housekeeper, when weeks passed with no sign of any such man. "I believe the visit was providential. Now we'll leave the man be."

"Clara?"

Mrs. Trotter shook me. "I don't suppose we should have expected a girl your age to keep vigil. Anyway, now you need to meet another morning."

I brushed the knob of Mr. McGee's wrist, as I jerked upright. It had been stiff when I'd washed him, but now it had gone limp.

I set his cold hand back in place, ashamed and horrified.

"Yes'm." My throat was raspy. I ran my tongue around my gums. It was all the fault of that liquor. Mr. McGee had warned me that it had taken hold of him young, and I should guard myself against the same fate.

I made a face at Hannah.

She was hunched behind Mrs. Trotter, under the slanted rooftop. She paid me no attention. Her own nose was wrinkled, and her eyes were set on Mr. McGee. She didn't look any too thrilled to be taking a shift.

"Did you know Mr. McGee, Hannah?" I said.

"He'd been in the pub—sorry, Clara, but he wasn't always a saint." Hannah waved me aside and took the chair. "We never had a real conversation as such. He looks like he's resting peaceful."

Hannah had a point. With clean hands and face, and his eyelids shut, he could've been dreaming—as long as you didn't get close to his sunken-in mouth or the mess that was the back of his head.

"Come on now, Clara," Mrs. Trotter said. "Hannah will be sitting with Mr. McGee until the funeral procession arrives. He's to go home to Montreal in a few hours. Willy says he's to have our country's first State Funeral. One like President Lincoln's."

"Mr. McGee wouldn't want to be buried like an American," I said.

"Whatever it's to be, he'll be buried in style." Mrs. Trotter started downstairs. "And we're needed to pack up his things."

"Couldn't we send them on later?" I said.

"The things are to go to the jailhouse, not to Montreal," Hannah said as she settled herself in and took some fine lacework from her bag. "So Pierce told me."

"The boys have already set up his trunk in the parlour, Clara." Mrs. Trotter called up. "Nothing for it, but we've to do the job now. And I'm afraid you won't rest even then; you're to go along with the body. Doyle is taking Hannah along too."

"I'm—we're off to Montreal?"

Hannah shrugged and nodded that I'd best hie downstairs if I wanted answers. I followed Mrs. Trotter.

"I've put your best things in your kitbag, not to worry," Mrs. Trotter called back at me. "Mrs. McGee will have to make arrangements for your trunk . . .."

Neither my kitbag nor my little trunk was my worry. Mrs. McGee wouldn't be happy to see me at her door at the best of times. To arrive this way . . .. I missed my footing. "I'm to stay there?"

"Have a care, Clara." Mrs. Trotter steadied me.

Once I was safely on the second floor, she motioned me to take the next flight before her.

I heard Sergeant O'Neill's whistle before I was all the way downstairs.

The sergeant was already making himself comfortable in the parlour. He patted his pocket, and the place next to him on the settee.

"I'll place this later today, Nancy," he said as she followed me in. "It could be in the paper tomorrow, and it'll run the week complete."

Mrs. Trotter and I worked quickly, but carefully, with no wasted motion. I pretended for a few moments that we were sending Mr. McGee on a voyage by sea to the Old Country. He'd been so uplifted, when he spoke of his last visit to Louth. I took special heed of the china cat Miss Peggy had given her father last Christmas. I thought a moment, then wrapped it in Mr. McGee's own da's sweater.

While his clothing, books and few mementoes were all tucked in, the young coppers toted down Mr. McGee's writing, and dumped papers onto the bar stools.

Mrs. Trotter rubbed her back. "Clara, if you could pack up the papers, there's a girl." She patted my hand before she took the seat next to the sergeant. "It's best done and over with."

Sergeant O'Neill smiled. "And doesn't the girl work for you, Nancy?"

"Truth to tell, she worked for Mr. McGee as well, Tommy," she said. "Half of those papers are in her handwriting."

The sergeant shaded his eyes against the mid-morning light. "Give me some of those, Pat," he said. A smooth-shaven lad with jug-ears handed him a stack of speeches. "This is your writing, girl?"

I nodded. *"Your script is as even as that of the scribe who copied the very Book of Kells, Clara,"* he'd told me.

The sergeant shifted Mr. McGee's notes. "A right terrible scrawl he himself had."

"Mr. McGee had his own style of note-taking," I said. "Sometimes he used just a letter to make do for a word. He had other tricks too—to catch his thoughts before they ran away on him. And he used, Latin, Gaelic and English, sometimes all mixed together, when he jotted down ideas. 'It's like making a sketch before a painting'—so he said."

"And did he teach you his tricks, then?" Sergeant O'Neill crumpled the papers slightly, and handed them back to Pat. "Well, those are lessons best forgotten, girl. Poor McGee's thoughts ran away on him too often; his tongue too. And now his wife's a widow for it."

I kept my head down. Sergeant O'Neill was right about that much. Mrs. McGee hadn't been happy about Mr. McGee writing that new book, while so ill all last fall. Writing through the pain, he'd told me; that was the secret. Though the pain was clearly with him as he punched his pen into the paper.

Come to think—there were far too few pages here.

"Where is Mr. McGee's book?" I asked, turning to the copper named Pat.

"You just packed that trunk full of them, girl," Sergeant O'Neill spoke for his copper.

"Not the books he owned, Sergeant. The book he'd only finished writing. His *Apologia*, he called it. The manuscript's as has just gone to Mr. Tupper in London."

I'd sewn a grey flannel sack for it, from an old pair of Mr. McGee's boiled-wool pants. The book manuscript had been much smaller than I'd expected it would be . . .. I'd had to wind the twine 'round twice, to secure the bag.

"Yes, Willy toted it up to Parliament, to be added to the High Commission's pouch," Mrs. Trotter said.

I'd offered to copy the book, but Mr. McGee had been having none of that.

"Oh, I trust you, Clara girl. But it's best that there aren't too many eyes on this book yet."

"Is it about the Fenians, then, Mr. McGee?" I had asked, only a few weeks back.

"And a lot more. The Yankees will feel the flame from this roasting. They call themselves a fine republic, and treat Irish immigrants like their new slaves."

Sergeant O'Neill stood. "What about those books?' He pointed at a high bookshelf, where the books were encased in glass.

"That's my own collection of first-edition, T. D'Arcy McGee books," Mrs. Trotter said. "I had him sign them all on first meeting, then put them in that display case, to properly preserve them."

I wasn't even allowed to dust those books. In truth, it would have been a danger for me to attempt it. Even Mr. McGee had joked with me that he was afraid to grab a stool, climb up, and borrow one, *"lest I stumble with it, and catch the dickens from my good landlady for daring to damage a book for which she'd laid out good money. Anyway, Clara, you and I have both had a chance to read my words for free."*

I understood he'd meant that tale as a warning—this wasn't Montreal, where I could peruse any book in his library, so long as Mrs. McGee didn't notice.

As much as I wanted to reread them all, so far I'd followed the house rules.

"Well, that makes good sense, Nancy," Sergeant O'Neill said. "But there's still one missing?"

"A manuscript," I said. "It's not a printed book yet, Sergeant."

He turned to his coppers. "You picked the room clean?"

"Yes, Sergeant," Pat said.

"A book's like a brew that's best kept in the bottle, Clara, until it's ready for public consumption." Mr. McGee had been so chuffed with himself, that morning he'd sent the new book off to his friend Mr. Tupper. *"I'll say this, mine will burn its way down the throats of America."*

"Surely Mr. McGee didn't let the book travel 'cross an ocean," I said, "without making himself a copy. . . he had twice as many pages piled on his desk, as he sent in that package."

"Maybe Mr. McGee left his copy in Montreal," Mrs. Trotter said. "He did go home for his little girl's tenth birthday."

And I'd packed his trunk . . . he'd taken his diary, I knew. He often wrote his thoughts in that first, then transferred the best of them to the *Apologia* . . .. He made sure I knew, in the nicest possible way, that the diary was off-limits as well.

"D'Arcy McGee was a social enough man," Mrs. Trotter said. "If anyone has heard of an extra copy of that manuscript, they'll surely speak up—or send it to his wife."

Sergeant O'Neill waved over the young coppers. "Off to the station with this lot, boys," he said. "Who knows, the man clearly did other rash things in his lifetime."

VIGIL

Wednesday April 8th, 1868

VII

Mr. McGee's coffin was not fine rosewood, nor even poor man's pine, but a silvery, leaded-metal box. I'd never seen the like of it. Who would think to lay a man down so?

The coppers carried Mr. McGee downstairs and laid him onto the coffin's pillowed casing, and an undertaker locked down its hatches. Perhaps the government feared the Fenians would be able to do more harm to Mr. McGee, were his shrouded body encased in ash or oak—as 'twould surely have been at home in Ireland. Perhaps they wanted to seal him up tight in a tin case, so no more trouble could rise from his wounds.

The casket was placed onto a wooden bier, whose wheels wobbled, as if to buckle from all that weight. The bier was pulled up, in turn, onto a cart, to which there were saddled four dray horses uncommonly like those Pierce had driven to Parliament. I couldn't say they were the same drays, though they had the same glossy sheen to their roan coats. I always keep myself a safe distance from such large, powerful creatures.

Prime Minister Macdonald had soon shown up outside again, this time with all his cabinet ministers, our bishop, the mayor, and a host of other dignitaries. They all made a show of walking alongside the cart, and it seemed the whole of Ottawa fell in behind the men. Along Sparks Street we went, north on Metcalfe, east on Wellington, then along Sussex to Ottawa's Catholic cathedral.

All the way, shops were shut up tight, and there were no hawkers or tinkers, no drunks, no biddies sweeping or doing their marketing. Just strangers and neighbours falling in line behind us—Mrs. Trotter and Willy; Hannah and me; everyone grouped in twos, like the animals heading for the ark, Frenchies and Indians from Lowertown joining the ragged march. All of us keeping our heads down, as if in fear of a deluge ahead.

The mourners were all whispering—then shushing one another, as we entered the church. Then, when the silence broke during the Mass marking Mr. McGee's farewell to Ottawa, it was with a wail of words, everyone at once crying of *poor D'Arcy* and *his poor family* and *a dark day for Ireland*. People who barely knew Mr. McGee were lamenting his death like they were his very own brothers.

I had no will to do aught but step forward to my pew and sink down, thankful to kneel and nod off, while the bishop, and all the priests from miles around, blessed and censered and prayed over Mr. McGee's stitched-up, sealed-off corpse.

Too soon, we were ordered up on our feet and down the aisle again. Mrs. Trotter tucked a note in my cape pocket, and squeezed my hand. I saw her lay a rosary into Hannah's.

Then Hannah and I were placed ahead of the crowd, following close to the casket so we could climb up the ramp and into the funeral cart. We were to be the women who performed the traditional wailing over the corpse, though I planned to intersperse my Gaelic keening with the Latin decades of the rosary.

People may have wondered at the choice of two young maids rather than older, more experienced keeners from the Irish community. It did make some sense, though. Pierce needed female family members to cry in public over the deceased. Hannah was Pierce's family, and he thought of me as belonging to the McGees. I was glad for that mistake. It mattered not, in that moment, that I did not know what would happen to me, once I'd completed this final task as Mr. McGee's servant.

Pierce followed us up into the cart. The bier was secured with ropes, and Hannah and I held tight to one another as the drays pulled off with their heavy load. Pierce braced himself upright, one leather-gloved hand pressed against Mr. McGee's casket, and the other resting on the butt end of a rifle.

I still didn't twig, at first, to why Pierce chose to make that trip across Ottawa standing, alongside we handmaidens, in the open cart, in the freezing air, with the crowd surging all around.

I looked him up and down. There was the outline of a gun handle, beneath his left pant leg, jutting out from a boot holster.

And then I realized, our public position was exactly why he was with us—this vantage gave him the best view of the throng.

Pierce must have guards stationed, I figured, to catch his signals, lest he see the Prime Minister in any danger.

With that knowledge, his constant squint into the bright sun became painful to contemplate. And I noticed that he kept biting lips that were already chapped raw.

So worry ate away at him as well.

Mrs. Trotter waved from the street. Willy had pushed his mother and himself to the front of the crowd, by once again hanging on the coat-tails of *Times* editor Mr. Lacey. Willy was not so sad to see me go, but miserable to stay behind while Hannah and all our boarders, being Members of Parliament, were travelling on the special train.

I stroked one of the metal hinges that held Mr. McGee in place. Then I pulled out the rosary Mr. McGee had given me.

"Hannah," I said. "Do you want to lead the first mourner's keen? Or should we begin together?"

"I don't know those old Irish songs," she said. "I've my bits of Gaelic from grannie, but as for those ancient chants, I don't twig how even you've managed to master them."

"But you can wail, surely."

"Aye, I'll join you in wailing," she said. "But you won't find me mouthing the Latin for the midnight rosary, either. Mr. McGee will have to be content with me saying my prayers in English." She fingered Mrs. Trotter's beads, which hung from her hand in full display.

"Then why—"

"Pierce trusts me, Clara—and I've vouched for you. Now you keen, and I'll do my best to mouth something that at least looks like it matches the Gaelic."

And so I began with a part of the lament *Úna Bhán*, which it struck me fit this tragedy.

> *Tá an sneachta ar lár agus barr air,*
> *Chomh dearg le fuil . . .*

Hannah had no way of knowing the words meant *'the snow is on the ground, and the top part of it, as red as blood'*. But my choice prompted Pierce to flick his gaze my way.

After repeating the entire Úna-Bhán, I raised my voice, in the open-throated scratch that creates the uncanny, chilling wail that is an Irish keen.

There, Hannah was a match for me.

Barn-sized doors swung wide, and the coffin was hoisted between facing green-leather benches screwed onto the floor of a compartment half the size of Mrs. Trotter's parlour. Four of Pierce's men wrapped ropes around the bench legs, strapped down the coffin tight to its form of transport, then lifted up chunks of river ice wrapped in burlap, and placed them on the lid. I had my question answered. The coffin had to be metal, as that amount of ice might warp or even crack wood. The government was taking almighty care, so that Mr. McGee's body would be in shape for the Montreal wake.

Once those army men jumped down, Pierce walked up with a stepstool. "Sit over there, Clara," Pierce pointed up at the bench on the left. "So as to move along with the train." He and Hannah exchanged a sly glance.

I hated that he knew I'd tossed my stomach. I hated that he was right about me now. My only other train trip had been coming up from Montreal with Mr. McGee, in January. I was fine with the train's motion then, even sitting backward, what with my excitement about going there to help him. Now my stomach didn't feel at all settled . . .. Of course, instead of Mr. McGee's voice spinning tales from the seat across from me, these three months later, I had Mr. McGee's body under ice in front of me.

Once I climbed in, Hannah followed, using Pierce's arm as a rail. With her seated on the rearward bench, there was just enough room for each of us to tuck in our boots on either side of Mr. McGee. The baggage man handed up hot bricks. "Be careful where you place those," Pierce said from the platform. "You need them to last until Prescott."

"I don't see how bricks will warm us," Hannah said. "With this ice laid here, we might as well be sitting in the middle of the Ottawa River."

The baggage man handed up a stack of blankets next. "Wrap up," Pierce said. "Pretend you're ice-fishing, Hannah."

"Do you have rags we can use to mop up melting water?" I said.

The baggage man dug around the bottom of his wagon, and came up with the rest of the burlap roll. Pierce tossed it in my lap. "Do what you can with that," he said. Then he slammed and latched the door.

Hannah and I set to work with the length of burlap. We were soon soaked by the runoff, and pulling at the wisps of cordage that stuck through our gloves and pricked our fingers.

"All the pomp and to-do, and the entire government didn't think to bring along any serviceable cloth," Hannah said. "That's men for you. Clara, what would our grannies think about this show?"

I shook my head. I was already too woozy to carry on a conversation. So I shut my eyes, and let Hannah ponder the mysteries of mourning in this new world.

The wheels ground against the rail. My bit of sleep had left me bone weary, but unable to drift off along with the train's motion. So I schooled myself to sit still, for what seemed like hours, no matter how I wanted to fidget, until Hannah was finally dozing.

I listened a while longer to her steady breathing . . . .. When it seemed safe, I dug into the pocket of my cape. Now I could finally read Mrs. Trotter's note. I'd been worrying it, there was even a trace of soggy burlap cord stuck to the inside of the envelope.

Mrs. Trotter hadn't time for much, of course. There wasn't even a date, but it was on her Trotter's Boarding House stationary.

> *Clara,*
> *You're a good girl, and I'd have you back in a trice.*
>
> *Nancy Trotter.*
>
> *Show this to Mrs. McGee, or the housekeeper, if you like.*

Until I saw the words written, I hadn't let myself look at how much I was counting on that offer. Although neither reminded me of any particular person from back home in Carlingford, both Hannah and Mrs. Trotter had become a little bit of home for me.

Mr. McGee had seen that Mrs. Trotter and I would fit. She'd only just lost her own girl Maisie to typhoid . . . and he must've figured out how I'd been hollow with loneliness, since Gram passed.

As for Hannah, even though she had been born here in Canada, she talked and thought like a daughter of *Éireann*. Folks say that's what it's like. Those as have never stepped on the sod become more Irish than the Irish.

For sure, I was closer to both of them, than to any female I'd found in my months in Montreal. Oh, Miss Keough and Bonnie, who worked for the McGees, were nice enough. But they'd both caught right away that I wasn't to be any favourite of Mrs. McGee. It was her mood that ruled the McGee house.

Of course the McGee daughters were well above me. I was even a bit closer in age to the elder of the Miss McGees, seventeen-year-old Miss Frasa, than I was to Hannah; but the distinctions had been observed.

Was I now to lose my two friends? Or could I send a note back with Hannah, thanking Mrs. Trotter kindly and . . .. That thought pressed in upon me, so that I could hardly breathe. So I did what I'd had to do more than once, this past twelve months. I made myself stop looking at the world I was leaving behind, for just this moment, and force my eyes to see the one I was moving toward.

Until, slowly, my heart settled.

The road running north alongside the train track was all dried ruts, under snow and ice. On either side, fields flashed by as patches of melted water and dry stubs from last year's harvest. The season to come was still shrouded in snow, even though tomorrow was Holy Thursday. Still, I could tell these were corn fields. In Ireland, corn is for the pigs. Here we ate it, and it wasn't half-bad.

We hit the smell of bog sulphur, and the train hooted a warning whistle. Hannah stirred. We were pulling into Prescott station. Two rail lines met here, and we'd be switching from the Ottawa route, to follow the St. Lawrence River east to Montreal.

The station's stubby limestone walls had been prepared for our passage with a wrapping of black crepe, even a black bow in the window.

We stopped short of the station. I thanked Our Lady for that, as there was another delegation waiting. We had stopped three times already, so Mr. Macdonald could speak to those who had gathered along the way to witness our passing. Each time, his speech held his own sorrow, and his need to push past it already.

Our martyred McGee belonged to all of us, I'd heard him say. His funeral would be *our first national event,* and *a moment to knit our new country together . . ..*

The feeling in Mr. Macdonald's voice was real each time, but it bothered me the way he tailored the same words, slightly differently, for each audience.

I didn't much like Mrs. McGee, truth to tell. But when I heard the Prime Minister say that that her husband's death had a saving grace to it, I felt angry for her. Of course, Mrs. McGee would take Mr. Macdonald to rights, if he said as much to her. His widow would never accept, either, that Mr. McGee had belonged to anyone but her and her girls. She'd be as mad as a wet hen that Mr. Macdonald was letting strangers horn in on their grief.

For myself, I knew I couldn't listen to Mr. Macdonald giving Mr. McGee over to the country one more time. And this time with a brass band playing *The Londonderry Air* while the people waited on his comfort. I pounded on the window when Pierce strolled past.

Pierce pulled out his pocket watch, and checked it as the town officials conducted the Prime Minister to his public. Then he opened our door. "Two o'clock," he said. "Not bad time, considering—" Pierce nodded at the citizenry. "And now the Ottawa-Prescott railway is to shuffle these cars across on the side rail, and link us with the Montreal line's engine. Prime Minister's privilege. You two want to hear the man do his best by D'Arcy once more?"

"I need air," I said, "and a privy."

Pierce ushered us to an unpainted side shed.

After that necessary stop, I headed toward the St. Lawrence. Snow was mixed with hard mud at the edge of the riverbank. Stiff weeds caught at my cape. It was too cold for a melt, yet, as ever, water leaked into my boots. You couldn't go any further south from here and still be in Canada, Mr. McGee had told me when we'd switched trains here.

Then, it had been frozen solid. Now, cracked patches of ice looked set to break, mid-river, and slivers floated in the wash.

"You can almost see the Yankees from the riverbank, Clara," Mr. McGee had said. *"But you don't want to go any closer."*

There was a crackle of boots, breaking a new path through the snow.

"Pierce just told me that when the Fenians next attack," Hannah said, "they may come across here. Or just west, where the river's flow is cut by islands."

"Exactly how are you related to Pierce, Hannah?" I said.

"A cousin once removed, as they say. On the Docherty side of my family. He and Uncle Eamonn are really the first cousins." She glanced over her shoulder. "Not that family matters overmuch to Pierce. Hard to say what matters."

"He brought you along," I said.

"To report rebel talk at the wake," Hannah said. "He needs a female around the women of the McGee house, and all the visitors they'll be having. I'm kin— he trusts me to do that much. And I have helped him out, from time to time. You wouldn't believe what men say, when I've served them a few."

Hannah and I stared out together.

"I wish Mike were safe over that border, for now at least," she said.

"You're not courting with a Fenian sympathiser?"

"My Mike's a right fool bytimes, like men can't help but be. But he's no Fenian," Hannah said. "Pierce knows that well enough, else he wouldn't be helping me at all. Oh, Mike's all for the St. Patrick's Society, sure, and he nods along at the lads' talk of soldiering for Ireland," she said. "But shooting a man from behind? No, Mike's no assassin."

"With all the men you could have?"

"You sound as old as Mrs. Trotter, Clara. I'm telling you my worries, aren't I? I'm scared," she said. "Mr. Macdonald, he's after blood for blood here. And you're as close a friend as I've got, since Maisie." Hannah crossed herself. "Though I'd tell a stranger in the street, Clara, if that would help Mike."

"Not a wise thought, Hannah." Pierce had snuck up—how had his boots not crunched the snow? "What was I just telling you, about the thousand islands? There are fifty miles of stepping stones, from Brockville, stretching all the way to Mr. Macdonald's home in Kingston. A thousand, think of it. That's also the number of Fenians we know by name, girls," Pierce said.

That was way, way more rebels, in Irish Canada, than even Mr. McGee had speculated there may be.

"We also know that, for every name we have, there are three or four more men."

"Among our neighbours?" I asked.

"These are men whose homes lie on both sides of the border," Pierce said. "They can creep across, here, say, nice and quiet; they can walk across for much of the winter. It's not like my men and I are watching out for a band of Iroquois or Algonquin. Fenians, they look just like you and me. Sound like us too. Some of them may be our sweethearts."

"Pierce, Mike's not—" Hannah protested.

"Now, don't be looking like that, Hannah m'dear. I'm sure Mike will be sprung soon. He's a fine lad, isn't he?"

Pierce led us back to the train, now set to roll down the Montreal track. Hannah sat beside me this time.

She was not happy when Pierce accepted a basket from one of the linesmen, jumped in, and took the opposite seat.

Metal slammed against metal right outside the wall, as we were coupled to the rest of the machinery. We jerked forward; I grabbed for Hannah, my head tilted, and there was Pierce, watching me. His lips smiled, his brown eyes stayed vacant as a dairy cow's. He pulled at his moustache. "I know we have a bloody murder here," he said, "and with the looks on your faces, you both could take your places on stage alongside the original three weird hags."

Hannah's face flashed anger. I didn't expect she'd ever been called an ugly name before. I wanted to tell her I believed Pierce was merely thinking about the witches from *Macbeth*—then thought better of showing off my learning again.

Hannah glanced at the window, pushed off her hood, and tossed her hair. She seemed reassured enough by her reflection.

"Have a cup of tea, ladies." Pierce reached into the hamper for a stoppered bottle, and cups. "Here we are, then," he said. "All Dogans together."

He delivered this Proddie slur against our people as if 'twere a benediction.

"And good Canadians too," I said.

"And of course, with Mrs. Trotter's *Times* ad," Pierce smiled over the tea things, "all of Ottawa will know the right of it, that she's no connection to any rebels. Maybe you should write out an ad too, Hannah."

The right of it. We sat with that in the air.

Then Hannah waved off Pierce's suggestion for the malarkey it was. "You know how I take mine, Pierce—two dollops of cream."

He handed hers over. "Best you drink it black, Clara," he said.

I took a sip of the cup he handed over. The tea was barely warm, but still a comfort. There was a sudden scent of coal ash, another long, loud whistle, and the rails began to hum again.

I gulped the tea.

Mr. McGee had laughed, sharing tea like this, when I'd told him I couldn't imagine how any such contraption could work to hold us fast, while pulling us along so quickly. Yet sitting here without him, I thought I was in the right of it. The wheels swayed on metal tracks that looked solid, but were merely mounted, after all, on piles of sod next to that grand stream of water. How much this car alone must weigh. I'd seen the bulk of the engine that was pulling us now as we moved slowly, then, with a jerk or two, more quickly out of the station.

I half-shut my eyes, and the scene blurred into one band of silver ice. Yes, 'twas a miracle the earth beneath did not give way altogether.

"Pierce," Hannah said, all sweetness now. "You will help me find Mike? I don't know where to look, in Montreal."

"You're better off not looking, Hannah," Pierce said. "It's no time to be running after some joker. Here, Clara. Read us something, to take our minds off our trouble."

This time, when Pierce reached into the hamper, it was to pull out a thumbed-over copy of Shakespeare's plays. I'd completely forgotten it, next to my writing things, in Mrs. Trotter's parlour.

He handed it over, with a bookmark tucked into the opening scene of *Macbeth*.

VIII

That Wednesday night, the whole of Griffintown—which meant all of Irish Montreal— was blackened. I couldn't think where they'd found so much cloth to drape across all the buildings. Why, Prescott had been nothing compared to it.

Mr. Macdonald spoke outside Bonaventure Station, of course, and then again at Gallery Square, so all the English and French—and especially the Irish who filled McCord Street and Basin Street— could feel that they were part of the death of D'Arcy McGee, Father of Confederation. The Prime Minister was still having trouble with his voice. Yet though they could barely hear him, the people all nodded, like they treasured every word. As we snaked our way past the shuttered doors of Drummond Street, the Prime Minister's words were repeated around us, mouth to mouth to mouth. Hannah and I kept up our howling, but we were nothing now, compared to the roil of grief that built from behind us like a storm tide, until the hollow, senseless screech of thousands of Gaelic voices keening carried us round the corner of St. Catherine Street, to Number 2 Montmorency Terrace.

There, Mr. Macdonald and his contingent halted. Pierce and his military guard cleared bystanders away, so the procession could enter the front door of the McGee house.

Hannah and I were no longer needed, as the real mourners were about to receive their dead. We were escorted off the bier by the draymen, who made sure the beauty and her friend were safely deposited back at the staff entrance.

"Clara Swift, I didn't expect to see you back," Miss Keough said, when she finally answered the door. Then she motioned me inside, shut the door in the draymen's faces, and stepped forward to hug me.

"A sad day, for us all," she said, speaking to me but now looking beyond me, at Hannah.

When I introduced Hannah, I could tell that Miss Keough wasn't so sure about her, with Hannah being so beautiful.

"How is Mrs. McGee?" I asked.

"As well as could be expected," Miss Keough said.

"Whatever gets her through," said Hannah.

A wailing started up in the front hall, then another. The latter sounded like sweet Miss Peggy.

"Bonnie's with the wee one," Miss Keough said.

Some minutes passed, with Hannah doing all the talking about the events in Ottawa, while clearly wondering why Miss Keough and I were avoiding the subject of my return—and all of us pretending not to hear the fuss out front— before Bonnie swung into the kitchen.

"She's undone, she is," Bonnie said, in a big-eyed whisper. "Mrs. McGee's taken the girls up to sleep with her tonight —Clara?" She stopped, struck by my presence. "I guess the whole world is coming, then."

"Clara, and her friend here," that said by Miss Keough with a slight nod to Hannah, "helped return Mr. McGee to us."

"You were keeners? Thank you kindly for that," Bonnie said.

"Bonnie, you must keep in mind the family's not to be bothered," Miss Keough said. "No one else need worry about going upstairs this week."

"Mrs. McGee doesn't like strangers," I told Hannah, in a low tone. "Especially in her own house."

Hannah looked at me, then at Miss Keough. "Clara's not a stranger."

"I'd appreciate anyone's help to set up," Miss Keough said. "Lord knows how we'll keep the onslaught of mourners fed."

"Where are we two to stay?" Hannah said.

There was a pause, then Miss Keough took pity on me.

"There's a cot in Mrs. McGee's sewing room, back beside the boot closet— what used to be your room, Clara," Miss Keough said. "You'll have to sleep in shifts, I'm afraid."

"The way I'm feeling right now, give me a blanket and I'll sleep on the floor," Hannah said. She looked at me. "Clara's small enough, she can sleep almost anywhere."

"I'll stay wherever Mr. McGee's to be," I said.

Pierce walked in at that. "D'Arcy's all set in the alcove, by the front door." His boots were shedding slush, which Miss Keough took note of.

"Pierce, this is Miss Keough—and Bonnie? Clara's talked about you both," Hannah said, though I hadn't. I didn't blame her for trying to charm them, though.

"Don't worry, cuz. I've visited with the McGees before," Pierce said. "Miss Keough, you'd best keep all the curtains shut tight."

"All of Montreal must be outside this home, I swear," Miss Keough said.

"And it will continue that way, all through the waking," Pierce said. "McGee's funeral is now set to surpass Lincoln's. There's talk of eighty thousand on the street for the funeral march Monday. Now, I'm off to check on lodgings for my men."

He left behind two tiny puddles, and a soggy trail all the way out the back door.

"If this is the way they do things in the States," I said to Hannah, "I'm never going there."

Miss Keough looked Hannah up and down again. "All right, Clara," she said, "you may as well sleep on the settee. I've already had it shifted, so mourners can sit next to the casket."

Then Miss Keough put a restraining hand on Hannah's arm, stopping her beeline for the sewing-room bed. "Easy enough for your—cousin?—Major Doyle to talk about the political import of the public outside our door, Miss Hannah," the housekeeper said. "He doesn't have to feed the gathering of tribes, all of whom will be tracking through this house."

The McGee house had been a gift to the family from Mr. McGee's supporters. It was built with red brick, and the lintel stones were marvels in themselves, carved as a line of shamrocks. Each plant had been given its own stem, and the very shadows between each shamrock were formed in the image of the Sacred Trinity. 'Twas an entranceway most fitting for a son of Ireland. When I'd arrived there with him, I'd thought it blessed magic, the chance to live in such a house.

Miss Keough kept the cherry-wood banister that led to the family quarters gleaming, and the oak floors too. They were fitted out with large silk-wool carpets woven in countries I'd read about in Scripture. The neighbourhood had paid for most of the furnishings as well, and it was a house built for entertaining. My experience, though, had been that when he was well, Mr. McGee mostly went out—and Mrs. McGee stayed upstairs.

Mr. McGee's coffin had been placed on the long mahogany refectory table, in the square front reception room. Both had little use when I lived there, but the large space right inside the front door was strangely suited for Mr. McGee to 'lie in state', as had been deemed fitting.

Nigh unto dawn of Holy Thursday, the undertaker unhinged the metal casket.

Pierce reached into his pocket and passed me a bit of cloth, wound 'round something hard. He stepped around Miss Keough and followed the coffin lid, to ensure the undertaker's men set it in the McGee bier, safe until needed on Monday.

Miss Keough watched Pierce manoeuvre out through the chancers and the gawkers of Griffintown.

"McGee's mouth's sagging," the undertaker said. "I'll need to do some work here."

At that moment, it felt powerful good to press against the wall for support; no wonder Pierce always did so. I unrolled the parcel Pierce had left me, and there lay Mr. McGee's shattered denture.

"Can you believe this, Miss Keough?" I said. "For the love of all things holy, he's to have his teeth back. Sir, you'll need these."

The mortuary man pinched Mr. McGee's mouth open, and tucked the teeth inside. "Young lady, that's done the trick." He pulled a threaded needle from his pocket. "Now a few stitches . . . like this . . . and our dear departed Parliamentarian's ready for his public."

"Miss Keough—I'm worried," I blurted. "When Mrs. McGee finds out 'twas me who slammed the door . . . .

"Clara," Miss Keough said, grabbing my hand, but still staring outside, "she's beyond caring. To think it's Good Friday tomorrow. I've asked Major Doyle to corral some militia to shift more furniture. What do you make of Major Doyle?"

"At first—well, he's a hard man, isn't he?" I said. "But now—as I know his cousin—"

"Ah, the fair Hannah."

"Pierce thinks maybe he'll let me help in some small way . . . ."

"Pierce, is it? And is that so?" she said. "You can be sure that if he wants your services, it's to his benefit. Clara, don't be pulled into someone else's trouble. You're too much like—" She nodded at the casket. "Look what good that did."

"Mr. McGee's murder *is* my trouble, Miss Keough."

"Then right now," she said, "you can trouble yourself to help me."

We set to, right then. Bonnie, and then Hannah joined us, as they awakened. Miss Keough directed Pierce's seconded soldiers as needed, too, when the work was too heavy for us.

First, we rolled out dun-brown carpet runners from the undertakers. We ran them along a path past the corpse, through the parlour, then round the dining room. We laid four tablecloths on top of the dining table for protection, before setting out buns with cheese and butter tarts. We did the same for the sideboard, where we set out the undertaker's mugs and tea things.

"People will be squeezed, passing out of here through the garden to the alley, but there's no helping that," said Miss Keough. "We can't let them out through the kitchen, or they'll never leave. We'll have to trust the militia to keep the crowd moving."

We only kept a few dining room chairs downstairs, in case someone felt faint, or was crippled. This was Pierce's idea. "We want there to be no encouragement for anyone to set themselves down," he said.

"What about Mrs. McGee's personal friends?" I said.

"She'll invite them up to the family rooms, if she really wants them," Miss Keough said.

Miss Keough had been turning people away when they arrived with roast pork, cabbage champ and cottage pie. She asked them to bring only more buns and butter tarts. To feed the multitudes, we were in need of manna. "If you can bring us bread you've already sliced," she asked, "or better yet, ham sandwiches, there'll be a blessing for you."

When a soldier swung open the front door, the line was already there, and eager. One of the first to crowd through called out, "Look at D'Arcy; even in death he's enjoying the party."

The man behind, and the one behind him, passed on the thought until all agreed that McGee liked nothing better than a crowd of admirers.

I hated that they had a point. As violent as his end had been, that's how peaceful his body looked now, here in his front hall chamber. The ice may have done some good. Mr. McGee even looked to be smiling. Though I'd witnessed the undertaker run the needle through and pull those lips tight, I took strange comfort in that smile.

Mrs. McGee and her girls breakfasted in their rooms. Then two priests, one from St. Patrick's and one from Notre-Dame, said a private Mass.

About an hour after the wake began, she finally appeared, all on her own. Mrs. McGee set herself, not in a chair beside Mr. McGee, but at the back of the parlour. Away from the door, and from the people visiting at the dining table.

Mrs. McGee stayed too calm, head bent as people genuflected past her. Only a few favourite faces were permitted to step off the pathway, bend and pat her hand. Even those she turned away from.

What was going through her head? She seemed to be the only one *not* lamenting. She and Mr. McGee hadn't gotten on well at all, when I'd lived with them. She didn't like the speeches and the trips to Ottawa and even less his sojourn the year before to Ireland and on to London and Rome. She was still complaining about that desertion, and she'd been mourning her mother last year too. I'd heard she was much closer to that lady than to her husband. She'd even been heard to say she was happiest when he was at the legislature. Yet after his leg ulcer laid him low and close to home, that was the only time I saw her happy.

Now, Mrs. McGee barely allowed the girls downstairs. When she did let Miss Frasa sit with her, midway through that afternoon, the pair of them didn't speak. They looked down at their hands and prayed, as if in a place of worship. Miss Frasa hadn't yet committed to taking the veil, but she seemed relieved when a group of grey-robed nuns arrived from the Woodlands Convent. She retreated with them, upstairs into Mrs. McGee's sitting room.

Hannah and I carried a tea set and buns upstairs to the nuns, despite Miss Keough's warning. I was hesitant to walk in while the beads clicked and their circle thought on the mysteries and mouthed the Glory Be. I could certainly see it was from Our Mother Mary on High that Miss Frasa sought comfort, not her mother Mary McGee.

Hannah stepped forward, to set down her tray on a table next to the Mother Superior. Miss Frasa shook her head at us, without actually looking up. I felt like we were wanting to spread out a picnic on the church altar.

Then Miss Frasa's eyes lit on the blue silk of my dress—her old dress—and stuck there for a moment. She looked up further, and as good as shuddered when she saw the cut of Hannah's rose muslin.

Hannah set down the tray anyway, with a toss of her head.

I left mine on the floor just inside the room. "Don't let it bother you, Hannah," I said as we retreated below stairs. "Miss Frasa never wants anyone to interrupt her prayers."

"She won't see me trying again," Hannah said. "I've never twigged to why nuns think they're so much better than those of us who are living out this life, rather than yearning to jump ahead into the next one."

I crossed myself as soon as I had the chance.

Miss Peggy, who took after her father in size, came downstairs a short while later. She was holding Bonnie's hand all the way to her mother. Then she sat on the floor, and held on tight to her rag doll with one hand, and to Mrs. McGee's shawl with the other. As soon as Miss Peggy became restless, her mother glanced at Bonnie, who whispered for Miss Peggy to stand. I knew Mrs. McGee doted on Miss Peggy, but today she took no comfort from her youngest.

I paused a moment on my way to the food tables, thinking how Mr. McGee used to roll on that floor with Miss Peggy in play.

At that moment Miss Peggy spotted me, and my platter of warm oatmeal biscuits. "Clara?" she called, as anxious as any child would be to have a treat— particularly as I often used to slip her something sweet.

Mrs. McGee's head rose at my name. She shook her head, as if nothing made sense, and my being back in her house was the least of her worries.

Bonnie pulled at Miss Peggy's arm. "Mrs. McGee wants you to rest, Miss," she said. "This isn't the time for Clara."

Miss Keough, following with another platter, frowned and motioned me to go ahead. "She's buried three children, Clara, and now this," Miss Keough said as we set down our loads. "Leave Mrs. McGee be. She'll sort you out soon enough."

Pierce instructed me to find him, should I recognise someone who had baited Mr. McGee during a speech. Then he decided that I should let him know, if anyone showed up who had so much as looked at Mr. McGee askance during the election. I wasn't to approach Pierce, I was simply to walk up close to him, then go on by. He'd said he'd follow me to where the fellow was hanging about. I wasn't even to so much as nod at that point. "I'll be able to read which rotter he is," he said, "from the raging within you."

The first such man I knew by name, he was Mr. Francis McNamee. He'd been involved in a scuffle at one of the election gatherings. A few hours later, there was another lad I'd noticed acting in a dubious manner at those meetings. And shortly thereafter, a third lad walked in, who I'd seen throw a stone at Mr. McGee after a speech.

Each time, Pierce was near enough by, usually leaning against a wall, reading a book. Each time, he left the room shortly afterward.

I looked out the window as each man left, and sure enough, one of Pierce's men from the train, not wearing any uniform, followed after the miscreant.

I saw Hannah nodding to Pierce a few times throughout the day as well, though she couldn't have known any of the lads. She must have sweet-talked each of them into an admission of some kind. I couldn't tell which lads she had pointed out, though, she was that discreet.

The mourners were all certainly well enough lubricated for their mouths to run loose. After the first few hours, Mrs. McGee couldn't have her own way even on keeping the house dry, in honour of Mr. McGee's long struggle with the pledge.

At noon, the pub down the street sent up a box of its best whiskey and a keg of beer.

The way Pierce marched the bar men through, I figured he'd been expecting the delivery.

"Bring us along that tray of glasses, Clara," he said.

Miss Keough stopped us both at the library door.

"Mrs. McGee insists there'll be no spirits." She looked leery to say as much to Pierce, but determined. "Her husband took the pledge time and again, from when he was Clara's age." She lowered her voice. "It made their marriage easier these past months, that he made good on it at last."

"You're not saying we can't have a drink on a day like today, Ma'am." Mr. Macdonald spoke from a chair near the fire.

Miss Keough bowed her head to address the Prime Minister. Taking advantage of the moment, Mr. Macdonald flagged Pierce to steer ahead. "This must be an Irish wake, even for the Scotsmen. Miss——?"

"Miss Keough," said Pierce.

"Miss Keough. Grand to see you again, despite these circumstances." Mr. Macdonald had a way of charming. He could make you feel special, even while reminding you of his place in the world.

"D'Arcy was dry these past months, but he understood when a man needed a drink, none better," Mr. Macdonald said. "Put the beer keg out there with the buns, Pierce, but for God's sake bring the whiskey in here."

Miss Keough didn't thaw much, though, at the idea that the Prime Minister might remember her face, if not her name. "'Tis his widow's wish," she said. "Sir Macdonald."

She did look like she could hardly believe she was standing up to the Prime Minister.

Mr. Macdonald smiled and nodded, like he was agreeing. "Oh, no 'Sir'ing me, please, I'm a Canadian just like you. And Mary's not to worry on it, Ma'am," he said. "We'll keep it civilised. Any hijinks, and Doyle's men will escort the carousers out."

Pierce moved past Miss Keough. I followed, trying not to catch Miss Keough's glare.

I was so unfortunate as to catch Mr. Macdonald's instead.

"What's the girl doing here, Pierce?" Mr. Macdonald was swallowing his words again, but I could still make them out. "I spied your pretty cousin downstairs too. Did you bring a harem?"

"Hannah swears the girl's sound," Pierce said. "And you'll recall McGee himself favoured her?"

"Your cousin's a bonny lass, Pierce, but how does that make her a true judge of who's a traitor?" Mr. Macdonald asked.

"Hannah's more light than bright, I know," Pierce said. "Still, she has a barmaid's native cunning."

As the bells of Notre-Dame tolled Our Lord's death, the crowd kept pouring into the house—instead of hieing to three o'clock Mass like proper Christians on Good Friday.

Maybe they were feeling like Mr. McGee could grant them their absolution. They began to press too close on their way past his coffin. First one man reached out to touch him, then the next, then they were all rubbing him as if he were a lucky charm. It was his head they were touching, again and again and again. I worried they'd be pulling out his very hairs next, for a blessing. Would someone soon be sticking a hand in his wound?

I ran up to the library and pounded on the half-open door. "Please, Pierce— Major Doyle."

"What's this caterwauling, Clara?" he said, coming out to me.

"Downstairs—you have to stop them." I pulled hard on his arm.

"The hellcat—"

Mr. Macdonald appeared, his nose to the wind. "I should go down and circulate in any case . . ." he said.

I fairly ran back, and they weren't far behind, "Christ on a crutch," Pierce said. "They're picking at D'Arcy's carcass like scavengers."

"Doyle, go lift out a couple of windows next door," Mr. Macdonald said. "Get your crew to board them up quick, tell the neighbours we'll have the glass back in a trice. We'll lay that over D'Arcy, until we can have a glazier fit a piece that's plumb."

So Pierce's men shoved two windows between Mr. McGee and his brethren, and within a few hours Mr. McGee was glassed in proper. In some way, this sealed display made it seem that Mr. McGee's death was all for show. Even Christ's body hadn't been left hanging so long as a lesson to his people before he'd been decently interred.

IX

"Clara—quick."

Hannah pulled me out the kitchen door. She had piled her coat and my cape on the veranda, next to the neighbours' dirty dishes.

"Grab yours, you goose," she said. She didn't put her coat on, though it was cold as the dickens, just draped it over her arm.

"Is Pierce sending us off?" I said.

"Pierce needn't know about this." She began moving across the yard. "There's an alley on the other side of this fencing, I've been told."

"There's work to do inside, Hannah."

"We've worked since the dawn of this Holy Week, Clara. You know the neighbourhood," she said. She tied up her skirt and swung her body to the top of the wooden paling. "A few of these Griffintown lads told me they'll be at the local tonight. The Rebel House, they call it?"

"Yes," I said. "For all of the troubles here in Quebec thirty years back. You've a new lad already?"

Hannah landed outside the paling. She gave me a dirty look as she shook snow from her dress and shawl. "Toss me my coat, Clara. I've found out nothing about Mike—but a lad said someone there tonight may know whether he's in *Pied-du-Courant* Prison. Now throw me your cape."

"I'm too young to be in such a place."

"You'll never know if you don't try. C'mon Clara, I can't walk in alone. The lads will get entirely the wrong idea."

"Hannah—"

"I'll bet your Mr. McGee was a regular there, once upon a time. It can't be so bad, do it for me."

It was harder for me to boost myself over, of course. I grabbed an empty wooden case from the pickup pile and stood on it, to gain purchase. I landed hard, and winded. Thank goodness for the snow. It broke my fall, even if it left me rubbing my eyes, and smelling the horse's leavings that had sullied the flakes on landing.

Hannah picked me up, dusted me, and held my cape open. When I shrugged into it, she wrapped me into a spoon hug. "There, I knew you were true, Clara. We'll be but a moment."

That wasn't the way it worked out, of course.

Hannah was everyone's friend within minutes. She amused the room by showing the barmaids how she could pour two ales at a time, both with perfect heads of foam and not a drop spilled.

Then she sat and let the lads wait on her in turn, with whiskey chasing the ale.

I was glad they were all lamenting the loss of Mr. McGee, and none of them speaking treason. The consensus among those who knew him was that Whelan was a fool, who'd wed a smart lady with a comfortable nest, though she was getting on in years. Then couldn't man up to making an old biddy smile and sigh on a daily basis. My ears burned as they teased about the way an older woman wants a young husband to make her happy.

The lads looked at me askance, though, saying, "Why'd you bring your pet, Miss Docherty?" and "Come back when you're full grown, *bogcailín*."

"Clara's brain is big enough to best ye, no worries," Hannah told them. "Tell them about that buggy you saw the night of the murder, Clara." She turned to them and started the story. "Outside McGee's house. . ."

The buggy wavered, in my mind's eye. "It was . . . a form, yet not solid. The lines of it were . . . disappearing away from me, d'you understand? Yet it was there, I know . . . 'twas a one-horse rig, open to the elements, not a fancy, glassed-in carriage . . . moving through the night, gliding around the corner without a jingle . . . "

"Now you're talking of ghosts and the land of the *Síde*, sure," one of the men scoffed.

I couldn't describe it properly, or convince any of them. But every time I thought of the buggy, it was more real to me.

"This one's more a little owl than a girl. I'll call her *ulchabhán beag*," said another lad. "Does your pet need a drink?"

84

That lad went to pull me to him.

After the last time, I was ready for a man's attack. I grabbed on, and hung from this arm. Swinging like a bell, until I pulled him down with me, while his friends cheered me on.

Once he stumbled, I leapt clean away from him.

"I warned you lads," Hannah said, when she could talk for laughing. "She's little, but she can think her way right around you."

"Hannah, it's time we leave," I said.

"Don't worry, Clara, that one's bacon's fried—his eyes dropped when I mentioned Fenians," she said, smiling all the while at the lad who'd tried to manhandle me. "A few are good lads, they know Mike well, the rest . . .. This pub may have the right name, I'd say."

I downed a brandy and hardly choked at all this time.

When I looked up, they'd forgotten all about me. Hannah, surrounded by her new Griffintown admirers, was asking the boyos who knew Mike to tell her all their best stories. She paid no more notice than they did, when I skipped off into the alley.

Even the strangest of days fall into a rhythm when there are people to look after and chores to be done. At sunrise on Saturday, we carried the carpets that had been brought over by the undertakers out back to beat them. They were so stained with filth, we considered not putting them down again. But we needed the pathway. Instead, we came to accept that we couldn't keep the place clean or the tables stocked with buns and tea; we could only do our best and offer the rest up to the Lord's mercy.

The line outside grew all Saturday, and there was hardly any room to manoeuvre in the house.

Midday, Mrs. McGee retreated, and a guard was posted to stop people from even trying to head upstairs to see any family. The neighbourhood listened to Miss Keough, and she had a long list of who had brought cheese buns and who the sandwiches, which pattern of dishes belonged to which house. Another guard had to watch over the stacked empty, unwashed plates, piled ready for pickup just inside the garden door.

The vigil ended on Saturday night just before midnight, with the Prime Minister the last out of the library.

Hannah and I dragged ourselves to the kitchen. Bonnie was still inside the laundry, scrubbing. Miss Keough came out with a bucket of water, and set it back to boil on the hearth. Someone, it transpired, had knocked a pot of tea all over Mrs. McGee's best linen tablecloth.

We could hear Bonnie humming as she pushed the cloth against the washboard. 'Twas the *Lament of the Three Marys*.

"Here—I've saved this for us all as a bedtime snack," Miss Keough said. She carried over an apple cake and a jug of hot milk, frothed and laced with chocolate.

We settled around the table. I was too tired to eat, but I made myself take a bite and a sip, for sustenance. Hannah closed her eyes and licked froth from her lips.

"Bonnie, leave be with the cloth for now and join us," Miss Keough called. Bonnie walked in, wiping her hands on her apron.

She began singing, low,

> *Come to me, you two Marys, and mourne with me,*
> *Óchón agus óchón ó . . ."*

"You've said it there, dear," said Miss Keough. "*Alas and woe is me*, indeed. Give us the song then—all you girls."

"You're not wanting us to croon him out now," said Hannah, her eyes still closed. "Not with the day we've had, and the ones before it, surely. Clara, tell her you're too tired for a mourning dance. Do."

And so I was, surely. Long beyond tired. Yet this was our chance to mourn Mr. McGee as Irishwomen should. As Mr. McGee deserved.

I pushed myself up from the table and placed my hands behind my back.

> *Who is that fine man upon the Passion Tree?*
> *Alas and woe is me,*

I sang along with Bonnie, kicking softly behind me, tapping out a mourning jig. She crossed the room to step beside me, our voices soft and high, our steps full of the feeling we'd been tamping down.

"Up with you, Hannah, you're too young to cry off," Miss Keough said.

Hannah shook her head. "Am I to sing the part of the Mother, or the Magdalene?" Instead of standing to sing the third Mary role in the sacred song, she lay her head upon the table, and curled her arms around her ears, so as to muffle our voices.

And is that the hammer that drove the nails through You?

Miss Keough rose to join us. We lifted one another's voices, our backs straight and shoes clicking in time on the wood floor.

When we finished, I felt a bit more . . . settled. It was time for Mr. McGee to join his own blessed mother. I placed a hand on Hannah's shoulder. She raised her head, finally, and let me lead her to the cot in the sewing room.

For Easter Sunday, those of us working in and outside the house were invited to join the McGee family for morning Mass in the library, being as it was the holiest day of the year. We didn't actually go in, just gathered in the hall so we could hear the priests' chants, and their reciting the Scripture for the miracle of the morning. From the way their lips weren't moving, I saw I was the only one of the workers who understood the Latin, but 'twas meant more to soothe than to enlighten.

Afterward, the McGees' doors were supposed to stay closed to mark the Holy Day of Resurrection. We'd have no joy or celebration, certainly no rebirth, but at least we'd be let well enough alone and maybe able to rest before the funeral, while those not in a house of mourning went to Mass and then had a big feed with their families.

At least that was how Mr. Macdonald and Pierce planned it.

It turned out the Easter miracle didn't stem the delivery of food to the kitchen door. Nor did it prevent close friends and politicians from pounding on the locked front entrance, each one believing himself the exception, the person the McGees needed, the person who should be seen to be of comfort.

By noon Pierce had unlocked the front door and instructed the guard to let only the community leaders come on through.

The militia made one big mistake.

Barney Devlin, failed candidate for office in Mr. McGee's Griffintown, and a man Mr. McGee had as good as named as a Fenian in the *Gazette*, had the nerve to show his face in the front parlour. If ever a man needed to be at Mass praying, Devlin did, begging for forgiveness both from the Lord and Mr. McGee. Why, only a month earlier, Devlin had marshalled the votes to have Mr. McGee kicked out of the Fenian-ridden St. Patrick's Society. I'd have thought the coppers would have him locked up.

Now here he was, large as life, saying how d'ya do.

Mr. Macdonald was murmuring to the bishop as Devlin swanned into the room.

"And to think he was about to finally spend time with his family," the bishop said. "Mary would have moved to Ottawa if need be, once you gave D'Arcy such a good job."

Macdonald shushed the bishop, his head suddenly tilted to the doorway.

"Mary McGee is resting, Devlin." Mr. Macdonald was polite. He couldn't help but be a diplomat. But he wasn't friendly. "The house isn't open. She's had three full days of waking D'Arcy."

"I understand, John—Sir John, that is, and congratulations on the Queen's honour." Devlin stepped closer, smiling. "With all D'Arcy's wild talk during the election, I want the Missus to know we're all Irishmen in the end. D'Arcy said some hard things, made terrible claims—but that stops at the grave for me."

Mr. Macdonald put his hand, soft, on Devlin's arm. "I'm assuming the local authorities have been round. To ask what you knew, Barney, and when."

"I would never—Look, I knew D'Arcy was done in Irish Montreal. The people of our community had lost their faith in him, even as he did barely win re-election. I'd been hearing the rumour you were going to set him up with a fancy job title." He nodded to the bishop, to show he'd heard the earlier conversation. "The man wasn't well and he wasn't prospering. I didn't need him dead."

"Just be sure you aren't seen dancing on his grave." Pierce had stepped forward in turn. "You and the rest of the St. Patrick's Society."

Devlin raised his voice in turn. "I'm telling you, Sir John, there were many times we were just Irishmen together. Looking at D'Arcy there"—he nodded to the casket— "why, I remember a time with him dead drunk, and me and one of the boys dropping him down nice and gentle on the floor here. With just such a sweet look on his face. Oh, the young miss—"

Indeed, Miss Frasa stood in the doorway.

"Sorry, m'dear," Devlin said. "But 'twas so."

Miss Frasa looked through Devlin rather than at him. "My father had kept his pledge to temperance, Mr. Devlin. Despite the demons he had threatening him during the election."

Then Miss Frasa flicked her gaze at me.

There was one particular memory that she and I shared.

Mr. McGee had stayed off the bottle. Excepting a single night, last summer. It was after a run-in with some of Devlin's boys. I'd gone to the hall to hear Mr. McGee speak. Those lads were throwing words at him, though, and outside, they were throwing rocks. Mr. McGee walked away from their ranting, with all of us who'd been cheering him now surrounding him for safety.

He didn't join the men who asked him to step into the pub with them.

When we arrived at the house, he didn't invite anyone in, and he walked into the library and shut the door without thanking me for coming out, or wishing me a good night.

Mrs. McGee had taken Miss Peggy to a friend's country home, and she'd given Miss Keough and Bonnie the week to visit family.

But while we were at the meeting, Miss Frasa had come home from the convent to the McGee house, for a surprise weekend visit with her family.

Her father wasn't any happier to see her than he had been to have me hanging around him.

About an hour after Mr. McGee and I had returned, I was reading at the kitchen table.

I heard a thump, from the direction of the library.

I ran there from the kitchen, lickety-split.

Miss Frasa had heard the noise too--she ran downstairs and reached the library door at the same moment I did.

She was still fully dressed, though it was well past bedtime. "I've been praying," she said, though she certainly didn't have to answer to me.

I curtseyed in reply, and she opened the door.

Mr. McGee was passed out, stone drunk, on this very carpet.

Miss Frasa put a finger to her lips, and reached for the throw on the settee. She'd bent to cover him, then motioned to me to follow her from the room.

"You're to leave him be, Clara. You won't take a peek back here tonight," she said. "My father is fine as he is. And we won't speak of this tomorrow."

Devlin had no comeback for Miss Frasa.

She pulled out her rosary beads. With a glance that landed next on Mr. Macdonald, and Pierce beside the Prime Minister, she left the room behind.

She'd be saying her decades of *Pater Nosters* and *Ave Marias* on those beads all night, to make up for that one falsehood.

Mr. Macdonald cleared his throat. "You'll be able to pay your respects by attending the funeral, Mr. Devlin."

Then Pierce guided the giant fool out the door.

Around five o'clock in the afternoon, on Easter Sunday, Hannah tapped my shoulder. "Clara, you're to go to the library and then grab a bite."

"Every floor in the house will need a good sanding next week," I said. I handed her my broom.

"I hate to leave you to this mess, Clara," she said.

I glanced back before I knocked at the library door, to see Hannah leaning the broom against the wall.

Mrs. McGee was seated behind Mr. McGee's writing desk, staring at the piles of paper and murmuring, with Miss Frasa perched off to one side. A few of Mrs. McGee's friends sat a ways back, in their Sunday best.

I walked in front of the desk, bowing my head in what Miss Keough had told me was the 'appropriate manner'.

"What was your father thinking, writing out all these lists?" Mrs. McGee was saying to Miss Frasa. "A book to Clara Swift, a coat to some fellow I've never met . . .. The gout brought him low, but I never thought he was already planning how to persuade people to pray for him in heaven."

Miss Frasa cleared her throat. "Clara," she said. "You're to choose your book, when you've a moment."

"Her choice?" Mrs. McGee looked up then. "He didn't say a thing about that here. If he wanted to give her a goodbye present," Mrs. McGee said, "why did he not do it then?"

Miss Frasa kicked her mother's chair leg.

"Clara?" Mrs. McGee said.

"Yes'm," I said.

Mrs. McGee seemed to lose track of the fact that she'd addressed me.

"All the fine talk in Parliament of a widow's pension to come won't feed my own girls at the moment," she said in a louder tone.

Her lady friends sat up.

She turned to Miss Frasa again. "Your father had to borrow from Sir Macdonald himself to pay last month's bills. We've no money to pay him back. That's why D'Arcy was to take that postal appointment, and finally make his family a living. As it is, I may have to let Bonnie go."

"Mother, we can talk of this later," Miss Frasa said.

"As for you Clara." Mrs. McGee shook her head. "Well, you know you're not built for service. 'Tis partly D'Arcy's fault." Her voice thickened with a phlegm of sorrow and frustration. "Him putting ideas in your head, about how he rose so far above the village of Carlingford, through wild ideas and charm—and by writing everything down so quickly it was like he was doing conjuring tricks, in three languages. Never you imagine a slip of a girl could do the same, Clara."

"He was still paying me to help him, Ma'am," I said.

"He had two daughters," Mrs. McGee said. "And another three of our children to pray for. Oh, I know what D'Arcy was, bless him." She looked at the bookshelf. "How the man loved to hear himself talk. How he loved those who saw him as a prophet, how he loved to see himself in their eyes."

I wanted to say that Mr. McGee didn't love his own girls less, for all that. But I didn't dare.

"It's my own I've to think of now," Mrs. McGee said. "Unlike my blessed husband, I can't look after every stray."

"How will you find work?" Miss Frasa asked me.

I handed her Mrs. Trotter's letter—I didn't trust myself to read it aloud.

"Well that's fine then . . ." Miss Frasa said. "Clara still has a job in Ottawa, Mother."

"Mrs. McGee, I'm sorry for your loss," I said, in a rush of words.

"Thank you." Mrs. McGee averted her eyes. "You're a useful enough girl, Clara, I suppose. It's more than I can stand, all this." Her voice had steadied. "There's no money in my hand, nor likely to be for some time. Take the book, though. Being as D'Arcy gave you your start. Just be sure you don't take any that he authored. Those are for my girls."

I near as ran to the kitchen. Bonnie was all in tears as well, even as she stood frying up boxty pancakes on the griddle pan, her apron spattered with grated potatoes and flour.

Miss Keough joined us from the larder. "At least we can all rest after tomorrow," she said. "Once Mr. McGee's laid in the ground."

Bonnie flipped the boxty, and sniffled.

"Buried on his birthday," I reminded them both.

Miss Keough nodded. "And it the thirteenth. 'Tis bad luck doubled, isn't it?"

I didn't see where luck came into any of this.

X

I sat down at the library desk at six the next morning, bold as could be, using Mr. McGee's favorite pen and his own foolscap, and wrote out everything I knew, had heard, and suspected about Barney Devlin. So it was ready to hand to Pierce, when he next showed his face. I did hope my thoughts could be of service— though I was hoping even more that by showing cooperation, I may gain myself passage on the train returning to Ottawa. No matter what I had to work at there, it couldn't be worse than what I was facing here.

When that was done, I picked out my book.

Mr. McGee had a special Swift collection. All the Dean's writings, bound with leather and gold edging. He used to tease me about the Dean, how I may be related to the biggest English Protestant that Ireland ever laid claim to.

Until the day I told him about my own father.

It was after the election, late fall. When Mr. McGee's gout was setting in, but before it laid him low. I'd thrown on my bonnet that morning and headed to the rock back by the paling where the sun first hits the garden. It was my reading hour, before the others were up. For Sundays, the Holy Bible. I'd been making my way through it since Mr. McGee said it would lead me to better understand the priest's lessons. Gram always said to listen to the priest and be quiet about it.

I was careful not to finger the pages of the McGee Bible, or dirty the fine leather binding. It was enough that Mr. McGee had said I could look at it this way, anytime, and Mrs. McGee hadn't stopped me.

We didn't have paling like the McGees' back in Louth, all painted fine and even. Fencing, they said in Canada.

I was keen to finish the tale of Esther. A girl no better than me, who married a king. And saved her kin from slaughter.

"Clara's swift, she is—in deed as in name, out and about so early." Mr. McGee had called out as he came across the garden. "What book of our Lord's Word are you reading this day, girl?"

He was walking slowly, side to side like a sailor. His leg had swollen overnight.

"About Queen Esther."

"Oh, and it's a beauty she was. Yet there's a frown on your little face, Clara girl. What could be bothering you about our Holy Bible?"

"It's that—Mr. McGee, it says here that she married outside the faith. And it was a good thing too." I bit my tongue that I had said such a thing.

His left eyebrow quirked up, but his voice was still kind. "You're not saying that an intermarriage can be good in the eyes of the Lord, girl?"

"Why, she was the Lamb of God—the way we are now—and she married the king—"

"Ah yes, King Aha-su-erus." Mr. McGee sounded it out for me, as he had a wont of doing when it was a lesson.

"Yes, him. And he wasn't a Jew, was he? He was against the Jews. It's like he was British, and a Proddie. She married him and 'twas a good thing. Elsewise she couldn't have asked the king to save the other Jews."

He puckered his mouth but no whistle came out, just a long sigh.

"You've got me there, Clara. I'll have to think on it. How did you come to this, girl?"

"The Jews used to be the Lamb of God, in the Old Testament. And now we are. I learned that much from Gram and the hedge school teacher before she sent me to the Proddie National School."

"'Tis so, yes. I won't be nay-saying your Gram on that. Mind you, the Jews still believe that of themselves, though we know best, never fear. As for the Proddies, let's call them Protestants outside the house, now we're building this new country with them, Clara. 'Tis only polite." He smiled, to soften the words. "Even I'm getting along with them, the good ones at least." He was trying to get a measure of me now. "But the intermarriage, you'll not be tying that knot so easily, girl." And softer, "You're not thinking about it for anyone in particular?"

I was hot under my freckles again, even my nose would be red. "My own mother, Mr. McGee."

"Ah, so that's where we're headed." He nodded. "There are Swifts on both sides of the Irish divide, my girl. And some of them pretending to be Proddies and they're

94

Catholics in their hearts, the poor souls." He was still speaking soft, as if to tame me. "He was a Kilkenny man, wasn't your old da?"

"He is."

"I should have thought of it, Clara. Dean Jonathan Swift himself was one of the Old English whose relatives settled in Kilkenny. You may be somehow related to a great writer, and a great champion of the Irish."

An English Proddie our champion?

"Have you read him, girl? Why, Clara, there's no shame in claiming that tie, surely."

"My da's a Superintendent, Mr. McGee. For the trade schools the English think we Irish should learn at, instead of studying our classics in the hedge."

"Well, I may have to hold that sin against him—och, Clara, no smile for me today?" he said. "Still, your da should've been proud to marry a daughter of Ireland, and a Louth girl to top it. And your mother a Gavan, one of the finest Catholic names."

"Gram said Ma was wicked, or she never would have looked at a Proddie. And him gone shortly after the churching was done. She died for her sin. So Gram said."

"Did she now?" He shook his head, with another silent whistle. "Oh, and the girl has to be Irish, to belabour the past this way."

His chin rose, and his voice with it. "I had a grand plan, Clara, back in Boston. I was to take as many good Irish folk as possible away from the Know-Nothings and the Orangemen, from their slums and their pride, and bring them to Canada, Lower Canada as it was then called here.

So they could live proud Catholic lives and learn in good Catholic schools. Bring them to the freedoms here that the Yankee republicans would never give us. Nor the British in Ireland, and I weep for that daily."

"But here in Canada, the British saw their way to letting settlers keep their Catholic ways. I saw what this could mean for us Irish. And I planned how we should all come here, together, with me leading the way like Moses through the desert."

"And I failed, Clara. A failure as grand as the vision in my Black Irish heart. I couldn't find the money or beg the land or band together our people to follow me. I couldn't be the proud Moses I imagined myself."

"Finally I arrived here with just Mrs. McGee and the children Our Lord chose to leave with us. As well as we've prospered here, these many years, I couldn't help but keep thinking about my brothers and sisters in America—my own kin, even. And how I had failed them, though I tried not to speak of it. For shame, that was."

"'Twas weighing on me still, when our small family needed a bit of help in this house last fall. So I wrote home to the Blessed Isle to say, 'Find me an Irish girl, in need of work. An Irish girl who can pull herself up in a new country.' The same as I did in America at just your age, Clara. I wrote, 'Send me a girl who has the heart strength of a Ceridwen, and a soul seeking our St. Brigid.'"

"Here you arrived, Clara Swift. Bright as could be and a Louth girl by God's good fortune. So it's up to you to prove my aim true. If I can see you grow into a strong Canadian, then I will have made my mark on this blessed community of Catholics, and the Protestants and Jews too, may we save their souls yet. Don't lose this chance by dwelling on your old Gram's judgements, Clara. You've left that house and wiped the dust on the mat on your way out."

I knew then, that I wouldn't have my answer from Mr. McGee. He couldn't forgive my mother, though he wouldn't say it. He was doing his best by me, in his way, turning it to himself and the good he had done for me. He was talking grand to work loose the knot he felt in me. 'Twas a fair story too, for one he'd spun on the spot. I could tell he liked it himself. I thought I might hear bits of it, when next I went to hear him address a crowd. I'd hear my own road from Louth, to Boston and Montreal, all speechified into a fine tale for a night's talk.

That was his offer of comfort then. That he had given me a hand, so I could raise myself up. When he wrote the letter, it was any Irish girl he wanted to help. Now it was me he'd be speaking of, when he wove this story in the meeting hall. I would be the only one who knew it was Clara Swift he was caring about.

Well I knew my luck to be in that position. Mr. McGee was the first one to take any interest, since Gram passed—and he was telling me to forget about Gram's penchant for holding a grudge.

Mrs. McGee's voice came from the house then. "Miss Keough, where's that Clara gotten to? And D'Arcy too?" she said. "The girls and I are ready to walk to Mass."

Mrs. McGee knew where we both were, though. She was looking out the window as she spoke.

She didn't like my helping copy Mr. McGee's speeches, or that I was the only one who could make out his special shorthand, or that I was from Louth, same as him.

I was what was wrong in her house. I was his public, horning into his private family time.

Thus, I wasn't surprised when Mr. McGee took me aside, after he recovered from the gout, and told me he'd found a place for me elsewhere. I was surprised, though, to

*hear I was moving to Ottawa. And that I'd still be helping him, as well as his landlady.
But, he told me, we didn't need to be worrying about all of that until I was settled with
Mrs. Trotter.*

*I knew he meant for me not to talk about it in front of Mrs. McGee. Or she might
put an end to the whole idea.*

So it was that, although I looked longingly at the set of Dean Swift's works, I
reached for the McGees' Holy Bible. Such a grand, heavy book, with those wonderful woodcut drawings. And it held that special memory.

I had a time pulling it from the shelf. When I did winch it out, I saw why.
A pile of Mr. McGee's notebooks had been shoved behind it. I pulled them out
as well.

Mr. McGee had sat in here all fall, had lain in here when the gout was worst.
Scribbling notes, to transfer to his manuscript. He'd fit each new notebook into
his special leather cover. When he'd filled a notebook, he'd replace it, and add the
old one to a pile on his desk. When I left in January, the desk looked like a rat's
nest.

The desk had been empty, though, since I'd arrived. I'd thought 'twas cleaned
up for the wake.

Who would shove these notebooks behind a bible, of all places?

I lay the bible open and turned to the Queen Esther chapter. Then I tore out
a page of notes. One page, one small piece of Mr. McGee. And I placed that page
in the bible. Then another page, and another. I turned the pages of the Holy Bible
carefully, layering in Mr. McGee's notes. Page by blessed page, until I had taken
them all.

The wooden box that had held the liquor was now sitting, empty, in the corner.
I carried it over and lowered the family bible inside. I didn't want the bible to be
knocked about and scuffed, so I stuffed the box with newspapers from a pile by
the fireplace. I'd have to tell Pierce about my having been left a gift, in order to
take the box onto the train. If he checked, Miss Frasa would back me up on that,
if need be.

She wouldn't know that Clara Swift was a thief. That I was sneaking around
with bits of her father's daily journal—maybe parts of his new book.

I couldn't make what I'd done right in my mind, and I didn't want to undo
it either.

This was what Mr. McGee and I shared—my taking so quickly to his codes, my copying out his notes in a fine hand. I knew my worth to Mr. McGee, and it was all in pages like these.

Still, I knew tonight I had poked well into Mr. McGee's most private life.

"Clara?"

I was tying down the box with twine when Miss Peggy walked in on her way to breakfast. "What're you doing?"

She meant, 'What are you doing in my da's library?' So Miss Peggy was learning well from her mother, though she still had her father's sweetness.

"Miss? Your ma's calling for you." Hannah walked in. "Morning, Clara. What does the paper say, then?"

I had pulled the papers apart to stuff the box. I hadn't paid any mind to the stories.

"Pierce came in the kitchen earlier with Mrs. Trotter's ad—that's in the *Times*. And Bonnie's abuzz about a photograph in there, of Jimmy Whelan. She says the papers are all repeating what the boys said at the inquest, that he's the one as pulled the trigger. Pierce won't tell me yea or nay about that, the bugger."

Miss Peggy took it all in. "Is that the man who killed my da?"

"Your ma won't want you to be worrying about that, Miss McGee." Hannah uncurled Miss Peggy's fingers from the newspaper and shooed her to the door, keeping hold of the paper herself.

"Pray to Mother Mary my Mike's not in this story." She scanned it, then opened the pages to check inside.

"Pass me the first page," I said. The stories were by Willy's hero, Mr. Lacey. The biggest letters read STARTLING AND DIABOLICAL MURDER.

Here were all the details about how the bullet moved through Mr. McGee's head. These papers shouldn't have been left around for Miss Peggy to try and make out.

Mr. Lacey had even quoted our Willy—*"pageboy William Trotter"*—on how he saw Whelan pacing the Parliamentary gallery as Mr. McGee delivered his address.

"Willy knows my Mike's likely locked up, and shouldn't be, and others like him are too," Hannah said. "Why didn't he have Mr. Lacey put that in his story?"

Of all the arrests, Whelan's had been all the talk at the wake. People said as he was a young tailor who'd moved from Montreal to Ottawa with the sole purpose of bringing harm to Mr. McGee. He'd been arrested at his Ottawa lodgings while we were on the train coming here. Yet, the coppers and Mr. Macdonald's own men were still pulling in Irish rogues in Ottawa, up the Ottawa Valley and here in Montreal too. And keeping them in lockup.

Including Hannah's Mike. She hadn't yet wheedled permission from Pierce to go to the jail here.

I was guessing she wouldn't leave town until she did.

Behind Hannah, Miss Peggy peeked around the door frame.

"Isn't Miss Peggy to go in to breakfast, Hannah?" I folded the paper, and signalled to Hannah as the child sat down on the hall carpet. "I can smell the sausages, can't you?"

Hannah shooed Miss Peggy into the kitchen once more, though not without her protest. "Doesn't Clara know I'm ten now?" Miss Peggy said. "I've been reading for five years—"

She was right. Even I had discounted her, because of her small stature.

With the *leanbh* safely in the other room, I reopened the paper. They'd printed a stiff portrait, the kind a man would pose for, to give to his sweetheart. Whelan had been married last year. The talk in this house said she was older, and well-to-do. His wife hadn't gone with him to Ottawa, she lived right in this neighbourhood.

The photo didn't show that his hair was sandy and that he stared through you rather than at you. I knew that for myself.

Hannah hurried in again. "What'd you think of Whelan, Clara?" she asked.

I didn't look up from the picture. "I know this man. But his name's not Whelan."

"You don't mean it?" Hannah said.

"This is Sullivan," I said. "I met him here, on New Year's Eve."

And I'd identified him as such to Pierce, in that corridor of Parliament. I was the reason this man had been arrested.

Now this newspaper said he'd been charged with murder. A political assassination. As the evil Fenian devil who shot Mr. McGee.

Miss Peggy peeked her head around the door again. "I remember that night, Clara."

"Hannah—" I said. How careless could she be?

"Ma woke me up, special," Miss Peggy said. "At the priest's house we all watched the sky, 'member? But there were no sparks."

"No, 'twas all a false alarm, Miss," I said. "Hannah, where's Pierce?"

"He's out checking the route—all right, Miss McGee," Hannah said, "this time I'll deliver you straight to your mother."

I watched until Pierce came back, recalling bits of the conversation that had been swirling all around during the wake, and on occasion seeping in.

I'd heard people describing Whelan. He was five foot eight at least, and some men made him sound like a looming giant.

"Do you think it was this Whelan for sure," one man asked as he walked by Mr. McGee.

"It could be any Fenian, of course," another said. "This Whelan's the one the investigators have plumped on, and they're painting a dark picture of him."

"Whoever it was, don't you think they had to have help? Or direction?" That man had looked around, fear plain on his face.

Pierce was too smart by half to think this daft lad in the photo was the genius behind Mr. McGee's death.

I caught Pierce, while the family were putting on their cloaks and bonnets for the march to the funeral Mass.

"Pierce, you've seen the picture?" I said.

"I'm the one who put the papers by the fire for burning," he said.

"Whelan—he's that Sullivan fellow."

"Devil take him by whatever name he uses," Pierce said.

"But this man tried to help the McGees."

"How'd you figure that, Clara?"

"He warned us of the plan to bomb the house."

"But not the police," Pierce said. "So much for his word or his character. A right four-flusher—it seems the man's as flim-flam as the name. Of course, any idiot can shoot a gun."

"It may be Sullivan—"

"Whelan," Pierce corrected me. "He took the name of his mother's people, back in Ireland."

"It may be," I said, "that—Whelan—moved to Ottawa, then, to avoid the Fenians whose bombing he'd spoiled?"

From Pierce's frown, I shouldn't be speaking my thoughts so freely.

"His wife didn't move with him," I said, pushing him anyway. "It says so in the story. Even during the election, Mr. McGee thought he was just a lad wanting to be a part of the high jinks."

"McGee knew the lad? D'you know his wife?" Pierce said.

There'd been a woman next to Sullivan at the election hall, but . . . "no— maybe . . . if so, only by sight," I said. "And I saw her, if I saw her, months ago. Anyway, why would the man warn Mr. McGee against harm, then three months later shoot him dead?"

"Clara, it makes no sense to say D'Arcy's fallen to a bullet," he said. "I've known people to make deadly judgements, for the merest of trifles—what passes in their minds for a reason. And if others did put this Whelan up to the murder, they'll all hang high."

"You promise—"

"Clara . . .." Miss Frasa was in deepest black, her veil was folded over the back of her mourner's cap.

Pierce took off his hat.

"I'm sorry you can't stay working here at the house, Clara," Miss Frasa said.

I looked up.

"I know you've been helpful with Peggy," she said. "Mother, she's beside herself and—"

"I'll be right enough at Mrs. Trotter's, Miss McGee. Nothing the family should be worrying about at such a time," I said, looking her right in the eye.

"You're coming with the house servants to the funeral?" Miss Frasa asked.

"I'll be praying for you all, Miss Frasa."

She crossed herself, and unfurled her veil. As soon as she was gone, Pierce set his hat back on, and sat himself down on the liquor box.

"I suppose you want permission to take this along?" he said. "At least it will take up less room at your feet than the casket." He kicked the box, but it didn't budge. "What do you have in this box, girl?" Pierce said. "Maybe a foundation stone, or one of the shamrocks from the lintel?"

"Just a book. I'm allowed a book," I said.

"One book?"

"It's a Holy Bible—"

"Heavy with judgement, then," Pierce said. "You're sure you don't happen to actually know Mrs. Whelan as well, even by some other name?"

"No," I said.

"You said you could point her out."

"Pierce, when I pointed out Sullivan, I had no idea—did you?"

He pulled a jackknife from his pants pocket. Cut the twine, lifted the box's lid.

"You can't—Pierce—"

"I knew he was Whelan five minutes after you fingered him, Clara. People were happy enough to tell me that. We didn't catch him then, though—the *Times* was right about that."

I picked up the *Times*.

"What was Mr. Lacey wrong about?" I said, scanning the story.

"Oh, no, Clara, you're not that cute," he said. "though you're of a size, and I'm thinking may share your nature with, a fox. And I bloody well can take a look, Clara, wherever I may choose."

Maybe Pierce would see it was indeed the Word of God in there, and leave it well alone . . ..

He lifted out the bible, though. "What's stuck inside this tome?" He pulled out one notebook page, and looked up, sharp. "The McGees didn't hand all this over to you."

I didn't reply.

"You looking for clues, Clara?" he said.

I said nothing.

"There's no point kidding a kidder, Clara."

"Mr. McGee made notes nightly," I said. "I thought, as his *Apologia*'s on a ship . . .."

"His private scribblings are more valuable to me than a book D'Arcy wrote to burnish his own reputation," Pierce said. "This is Property of the Crown, as of this moment, Clara. And I'll tell Mrs. McGee we're taking D'Arcy's diary—you can read this gibberish?"

I nodded.

"It's good you've admitted you know McGee's codes, Clara. I'd read that fact in the sergeant's notes," Pierce said. "You're altogether more of a slyboots than I imagined, girl. In fact—as you want to help. There is Whelan's wife."

"I said I don't know her. I can have Mr. McGee's diary notes, then?"

"You can write them out in plain English for me. And the government will pay you for the time you spend doing it. Though we may not want to tell Mrs. Trotter."

"I don't see as I can fool her—"

"You were going to do exactly that, Clara," Pierce said.

I waited.

"Whelan's lady-wife—she's weathered our best men's strong-arming," Pierce said. "After the week she's had, though, she may relax and say something to a young *cailín*. You'll miss the funeral Mass."

"Fine," I said.

"I'll drop you off a short way from Victoria Bridge then. Whelan's bride Bridie—an easy enough name to remember?—is going to the Wishing Tree by the Black Rock, I've been told. I thought perhaps Hannah . . . but women don't take to her so much."

"I don't know how to do such a thing, Pierce."

"Be straight with her—tell her you saw Jimmy in Ottawa, and here at the house. See what a bit of honest talk shakes loose."

"So I've permission to not lie, and to not hide my mourning for Mr. McGee."

He smiled. "She may just be looking for a friendly face, right now. You know, people often tell strange truths to a kind stranger."

If Jimmy Whelan killed Mr. McGee, I didn't want to be his wife's friend. If he didn't—and 'twas my fault in part he was a suspect—she shouldn't want to be mine.

"Pierce, here—" I handed him what I'd composed that morning. "My memories of Devlin, and some thoughts..."

"You are eager, I'll say that. If you can winkle information from Bridie, Clara, you may be good for more than mere copying . . .. I'll have to see."

When I hesitated, though, Pierce was clear.

"I see you've brain enough to be of use, Clara," he said. "But only if you're willing to take on the work, girl. It's bound to have some foul bent to it, given the circumstances."

XI

The hawthorn Wishing Tree had been planted at the base of Victoria Bridge by the Irish who built it. As I hurried away from Pierce's expectant gaze, I thought of the tragic, yet proud tale that Mr. McGee had told me about the bridge, the Wishing Tree, the black rock set in place by true giants, and the grand river that was the closest the Irish of Montreal could find to a sacred well.

Shortly after I'd arrived in Canada, I had asked Mr. McGee where to find the closest sacred well in Griffintown.

"Is there a well dedicated to St. Ann?" I asked him. If so, 'twould be near the church bearing her name . . . .

"Clara, now you've come to it," Mr. McGee said. "The most foreign thing about Canada. There are no sacred wells."

"No wells?" I could hardly credit the thought. "We have nowhere to ask for a special blessing from any of the saints? How do we worship?"

"There is one such place," he said. "It's not the site of a saint's miracle, mind. But it has been sanctified by Irish blood. And the people of Griffintown have planted a hawthorn Wishing Tree there. Griffintown treats the place as if St. Ann herself is watching out for all of us. In its own way, what happened there is a strange kind of epiphany all on its own."

Then he cleared his throat, in such a way that I knew a tale was to follow.

"Clara," he said, "I must begin by telling you of a catastrophic loss for our people. Six thousand Irish immigrants died of typhus in fever sheds, on the shores of the St. Lawrence, twenty years gone by. Their bodies were buried by the City of Montreal, unmarked and unsanctified, in one polluted pit.

A decade passed. Then some Englishmen, who either hadn't been told, or hadn't cared about the bodies under the river's banks, chose that exact spot to build a marvel of engineering, a bridge which would span the mighty St. Lawrence. To do the work, the English, naturally enough, hired a fresh new wave of Irishmen, for who else would do such heavy lifting?

And so the shameful truth of the desecration of these poor souls came to light—as desecration is invariably exposed, be it soon or late.

For who do you think uncovered these bones, Clara? All unsuspecting? Why, they were dug up by the honest Irish immigrant workers, the very brethren of those earlier doomed sons and daughters of Éireann.

The Irish bridge builders were heart-sore to learn of this fate of their brothers and sisters in spirit. They cried and they raged. 'Twas terrible indeed, to find the remains of those poor souls who, in the wake of the terrible famine at home, had travelled across an ocean—only to fall ill on the very shore of their Promised Land. And they were horrified that these Irish had yet never made the final passage, to the Catholic churchyard.

As you can well believe, Clara, the Irishmen did the job they were paid to do. The bridge rose in place, as marvelous as its engineers had envisioned it. And still, the workers were not allowed to rebury their countrymen—for even though the Englishmen building the bridge had no trouble letting Irish workers turn what could be plague-ridden soil, the City of Montreal still feared contamination from the dear departeds' very bones.

The Irish instead ensured those bones were reburied, on the spot, with a proper Catholic ceremony. And then they rolled to that very spot a black stone so large, it looked like it could only have been set there by giants. Yes, I tell you true, Clara. Our honest countrymen, those who made Montreal mark these graves, they were giants indeed.

And the community of Griffintown had a proper inscription carved upon this great Irish Commemorative Stone—a monument the height of a cathedral and the width of two bishops, laid end-to-end. They made sure it said that it was the Irish who suffered the loss, and the Irish who built the bridge, and the Irish who told the truth of the matter."

Mr. McGee smiled, as he always did when he'd handed me a tale well told.

"And that's when they planted a Wishing Tree there?" I said.

"Indeed it was. The hawthorn has already weathered a full decade of wishes tied on its branches," he said. "Though the bishop frowns upon it. You do understand we must learn to worship alongside our French countrymen, Clara. In the Canadian way."

Miss Keough told me, when I quizzed her later, that Mr. McGee himself had been one of the forces behind the raising of the Black Rock. She'd said that on the day of the stone's commemoration, Mr. McGee had made a speech she didn't think people would soon forget—as it had scorched the hides of a few English Montreal politicians.

So it seemed to me the Wishing Tree by the Black Rock would be a fine place to make my own personal goodbye to Mr. McGee. I'd already sat, stunned through the requiem service in Ottawa. This would be better than kneeling in the servants' pew behind Mrs. McGee, no doubt of that.

I couldn't countenance, though, that I would gain any information here through a so-called chance encounter with Jimmy Whelan's wife.

By whatever means he knew, though, Pierce was right on the mark about one thing—I wasn't the only Irish woman in Montreal not at Mr. McGee's birthday funeral Mass.

Someone not much bigger than me was reaching up high into the tree to pull at a rotting rag. She was wearing woollen gloves with the fingertips cut out, the way I did sometimes—to keep the chill from my fingers while still allowing me to properly perform my tasks.

I thought again of what I'd witnessed being done to the lads in custody—and what I'd had done to me. I didn't like to think about soldiers or coppers strong-arming any other woman, or beating her like they would a man.

This lady didn't have a mark on her, though. Wrinkles I didn't expect, having met her husband. Bags under her eyes, too. Still, she was fair enough for a middle-aged matron.

"*Beannachtaí na Cásca ort.*" She shaded her eyes to get a look at my black arm band. "Ah, sorry, dear—you've suffered a loss?"

"Aye," I said.

She was wishing the blessings of Easter upon me? Even if she and Whelan were both Fenians, how could she greet me so—like she was the only being in Montreal who didn't know it was a black week for the entire country?

"Clara Swift," I said. "I believe we may have met in passing." Should I say I'd met her good husband?

"With a loss, you've need of the tree, Clara." She pulled again at the rag, then wiped her fingers on a fine linen hankie. "I tied that on two years ago."

"Have you had your wish?"

"Yes, I have." She pulled out a strip of navy-blue suiting wool from her cape pocket. "Bridie Boyle, I was, when I tied that. Now that I've married, I'm here to trouble St. Ann with another mighty wish." She pursed her lips. "Go ahead, girl, you needn't stand and wait for me."

"Thank you kindly, Bridie." I pulled out my rosary and a black hair ribbon and circled the tree, avoiding the hanging cloths and the branch she was standing under.

I spotted a bare, sturdy limb.

Mr. McGee had given me the rosary last Easter, shortly after I arrived at the house. Plain wooden beads, but blessed by the Holy Father in Rome. I knew Mr. McGee had a whole box of beads so blessed when he visited with the Pope, and he'd been generous with them during the election. Still, this would be the only rosary offered up to St. Ann, our Lord's own grandmother, in his name.

I wrapped the black ribbon three times around the rosary, securing it tight to the tree branch with a sailor's knot. I closed my eyes, made the Sign of the Cross, and prayed for the saint, and her daughter the Madonna, to watch over Mr. McGee's soul. I breathed in the river and the soil and held the cold air within me for a long moment.

It wasn't that I expected my prayers to rise higher than the bishop's in the cathedral. But now Mr. McGee was remembered here, along with the other dead Irishmen.

When I opened my eyes she was staring at me, the dark-blue cloth still in her hands. "So it's a prayer to our Lord then? For your dear one's soul?"

"And—let's make it a prayer for Mr. McGee."

"Did you know Mr. McGee?" she asked.

"A—little," I said. "And you?"

"No, I never had that particular pleasure." She reached for the limb again, and looped her fresh cloth next to her rag. "I'll include him in my prayer, and you too—"

"Clara," I repeated.

"Would you listen to that, Clara?" the woman said. The bells had begun to knell. First at St. Patrick's Church, then at Notre-Dame, then at the Anglican's Christ Church Cathedral. "Catholic and Protestant are as one today. The English and the French uniting to ring out the man beside the Irish."

"Thanks for your prayer, Mrs.—Boyle? What's your married name?"

She let the limb go, her rag hanging untied. "You shouldn't ask questions, dearie, when you know the answer," she said.

"I—"

She placed a hand on my arm.

"God love you, *a cailín*, don't you know that what you're thinking's written all over your face?" she said. "You'll never be a trickster. Or maybe you just came for curiosity? I won't hold that against you—I'm very popular right now."

"I do know. But you call yourself Boyle, and he calls himself Sullivan, and—I'm not the only one who wears my feelings on my collar, missus."

"You know my Jimmy?"

"Not well at all, Ma'am. Yet I've seen him rabble-rouse here in Montreal. I've seen him warn the McGees off, like he knew of a bomb plot. I've seen him in Ottawa—"

"—plying his trade there, girlie. My Jimmy never did harm to Mr. McGee. He's a gallivanter, sure, but no warrior. He hasn't the stomach for it. Nor the head, either. Now, be off with you. I'll tie a wish that you'll still have as honest a face when you're full grown."

I left her standing with her hands shielding her eyes again, and a soft smile on her own face.

Hannah hurried past the stragglers outside Notre-Dame Cathedral.

"Clara, where were you during Mass?" she said. "I thought you lost in the crush here. Though I wouldn't fault you for daring to shun Mrs. McGee, after her firing you."

And indeed, Hannah did have a glimmer of admiration in her eyes.

"So, did you say your goodbye to Mr. McGee at the Irish service, at St. Ann's Church?" she said.

"I was off visiting Mr. McGee's rock, and the tree by our bridge." I stepped double-time to keep up with her.

"How did you make it that far, Clara? People are fainting in the street, and nowhere to lie them down, we're so mobbed in this city. And why, in the Lord's name? That frozen river can never replace a sacred well."

"It's the bodies of those who died and are buried there, by the bridge, that give the tree its power, Hannah."

"Enough of faery stories, Clara. Why, I'd never think of wasting my time tying on a wish. I'm going to spring Mike from his hellhole, I swear I am, and this very day. We Irish women should do things, rather than pray for them to be done for us," Hannah said.

She grabbed me by one shoulder. "C'mon. I was told during the service that if we cut through the alley—here—we'll be at the jail."

Somehow, while attending a Funeral Mass, in a church crammed with mourners, with the streets almost unpassable, Hannah had found out about a short-cut, and it was an alley that turned out to be almost empty. Maybe she could free her Mike. Although—

"Pierce is allowing this?" I said.

"He's there waiting, and already smoothing the way. *Déan deitneas*, Clara."

"I *am* hurrying."

Hannah ran up the stone steps to the jail and threw open the iron-grilled door.

Pierce waved off a couple of guards, who looked interested at the prospect of Hannah. "It turns out Mike went home to Ottawa," Pierce said. "The day before the shooting."

"He never did," she said.

"That's where he's been scooped up. In Ottawa, the morning D'Arcy died," Pierce told Hannah.

She wasn't having any of it. "How could you not know this, Mr. Prime Minister's Man? Didn't that rogue Paddy Buckley tell you Mike was in jail with him?"

"What a Buckley may say is no concern of yours, Hannah," Pierce said.

Hannah's face flushed red. "Sonofabitch."

I'd never heard a female swear in English, it made me shiver. Somehow it was so much worse than if she'd yelled *Mallact Cromail ort*, and simply called down the curse of Cromwell upon Pierce.

"You'll see Mike, never fear. In time, and if it's right for you to do so," Pierce said. "Why are you acting so twisty, Hannah?"

"I've lost almost a week's wages helping you with a dead body, and squeezed lads for 'information' on your behalf. Now you're acting like Mike being jailed is a laughing matter. Who's the twisted one?"

"Oh, there's no laughing about Mike's knowing Jimmy Whelan, Hannah. Why d'you think I got you away from there?" Pierce said. "Those two used to have a fine time together here in Montreal, didn't they?"

"Your Mike knows Jimmy Whelan?" I said. "Hannah?"

Pierce looked Hannah over. "Didn't Jimmy wind up Mike when he first came to Ottawa, as well?"

"Mike was smart enough to cut ties with Jimmy," Hannah said.

"Why didn't you tell me any of this?" I asked her.

"Jimmy Whelan marched right next to Chief Marshall Patrick Buckley in the Ottawa St. Patrick's Day parade, down our own Elgin Street, last month," Hannah said. "Every Paddy in Montreal and Ottawa both—but you, Clara, it seems—knew him by name at least."

"That was last month," Pierce said. "Nobody's going to be claiming any acquaintance with Whelan now. The boys here"—he nodded to the jail guards, "are placing bets on how long it'll take before the noose is round his neck." He looked at me. "Clara, I suppose Mrs. Whelan painted her man as a saint reborn?"

"She said he'd never do Mr. McGee harm."

"Is that what you were doing at the tree, Clara?" Hannah said. "Pierce, that makes you every bit as much the fool as she is. What could you hope to gain by sending a hare to charm a fox? Clara's the least likely creature. . .."

"For anyone to suspect," Pierce said. "You must admit, Hannah, 'twas neatly done."

"Clara, I'm sorry I let you anywhere near my cousin," Hannah said. "Or told him anything about you either."

"'Twasn't your doing, Hannah," I said.

"Pierce, you bastard," Hannah said, "you knew where Mike was all along, didn't you?"

"Hannah, if I knew as much as I wanted to know, as soon as I wanted to know it, I'd have all Whelan's confederates locked up already."

"I was such a fool, to place all my trust in you, Pierce," Hannah said. "I know you're not one to stand with me when it matters."

Didn't Hannah see that Pierce had been protecting her, by bringing her with him? What did Hannah mean?

Your friends will cheer you on, Clara," Mr. McGee had told me one night, as we walked home from an election speech. *"But have no doubt—they won't all stand with you."*

"Enough, Hannah. Clara here's an orphan too, and she doesn't carry on like a banshee," Pierce said. "Christ on fish-hooks, be still or—"

Pierce raised his hand. He was flashing a temper that made me wince, for how she would hurt if he hit her.

I had to help. "Bridie Boyle Whelan could read my face," I blurted out.

"A babe could read your face, Clara," Hannah said. "What of it?"

Pierce lowered his hand, and placed it in his pocket. "So Bridie Whelan smoked you out, and bested you, Clara?" he said, looking at me now.

"She did."

"And you're not keeping anything back from me?" Pierce asked me.

"Not a thing, Pierce. I swear by St. Ann and St. Bridget too, and she Mrs. Whelan's namesake."

I had never kept my da and his new family a secret . . .. I just hadn't talked about him any to folks I met in Ottawa. Or in Montreal, either, other than that one time, to Mr. McGee. Let them all think me an orphan, I may as well be. That didn't make me a liar . . . except by omission.

"If you look in the right light, though, you may catch the truth in even a trickster's eyes," Mr. McGee had said that night.

I knew whoever was doing the looking, my horror at Mr. McGee's murder must surely be the message they read from my own gaze.

Maybe I hadn't seen Mrs. Whelan in the right light. She'd shown no fear, despite her Jimmy's arrest . . .. What about Hannah and Pierce?

They'd just about come to blows, yet Pierce's eyes were once again taking me in, but giving away nothing. If I hadn't seen that one moment of true anger . . .. And this was the man whose bidding I would now be doing.

As for Hannah . . . the girl just looked plain scared.

She was right to be. Those as had her man were in a frenzy.

And this past Lenten week, Mr. McGee's death had proven once again that a man could be executed by his enemies, for his very innocence.

XII

"Clara? Ma doesn't want—

"Willy—" Mrs. Trotter said.

"Ma, you told me—"

"Of course we want Clara here," Mrs. Trotter said. "We'll just—find her something to pay her way."

"I'm grand, Mrs. Trotter," I said, parroting the words I'd rehearsed with Pierce. "I've a cleaning job lined up at Parliament itself."

"Girls aren't allowed—"

"—I'll be cleaning in the brand-new Security Service's office—"

"—It's called the Constabulary, Clara—"

"The gate's just being built. And I'm to work there." Willy kept cutting in, but I kept on talking, until he let me be. "It's part-time, so I can work here like I used to?" I looked at Mrs. Trotter.

"You can share Willy's food basket," Mrs. Trotter said.

"I'd have to go to him then—Willy isn't allowed in this new office," I said. "Nobody is, unless Pierce says so."

"And you're not allowed on the House of Commons floor, Clara," Willy said. "So smoke that."

Pierce was right. Provoking Willy had taken both mother's and son's minds off the strange nature of my new employment.

Misdirection, he called that.

Hannah worked on Pierce, until by week's end she was allowed to see Mike in jail.

When I met her on her return, I didn't know how to ask, so I just looked my question.

"He's cut up bad, Clara," Hannah said.

"Like the lads we saw?"

"Worse." She wiped her eyes. "I don't know about your Gram, Clara, but I learned a lesson from my mother's parents, those as brought me up. Don't get hot mad, Clara. Get cold mad," she said. "My Docherty side's good at cold, and I'm taking my pattern from Uncle Eamonn."

After that, Hannah's smile was different.

Even Willy commented on it. "She doesn't light up the same way," he said.

Willy had been jailed overnight himself, and was going all 'round town bragging—to some lads, that he was a jailbird, to others, that he'd been cleared right away, and received an apology to boot.

That last item had happened after Mrs. Trotter had gone to the jail.

The coppers who'd pulled him in didn't know him from Adam, Willy admitted to Hannah—and Willy was sprung as soon as Sergeant O'Neill found out about it from his mother. Willy wouldn't tell me what happened, but Hannah did.

"His ma was ever so grateful," Hannah said. "I would be too, if a guard would help Mike . . .."

Willy didn't say anything to me, either, about how much time Sergeant O'Neill began spending at the boarding house.

I was as happy as Willy now, to head off to Parliament Hill.

At first I felt like I'd wandered into a warrior's camp . . . and I had my own memory to fight every time I passed through the gate. Still, once Pierce's men became used to my puzzling over squiggles and loops at a desk by the window, they assumed I was one of their own, and not old enough to be interesting.

And once the redcoats and militiamen learned the little girl was cleaning up for those fellows in the Prime Minister's personal Constabulary, they figured it best to forget about me.

I didn't see the Saxon soldier again.

By Pentecost—fifty days on the Catholic calendar—I had all fifty-two pages of Mr. McGee's diaries decoded.

After the holiday, I returned to Parliament and spread all the papers out on my desk, so no-one would guess how much I'd really done.

I wasn't ready to give the words up yet. This was his final story. Mr. McGee had left a picture of what had been going through his mind through the election fight and his illness. Through not being put in the country's first Cabinet, then coming here to sit in its first Parliament.

The words were darker than the man I'd known. 'Twas as if after he put his fears and upsets on the page, then he could be brave and bright in his life.

His writing codes were a bit different for the diaries than for his speeches, as well. I had to work the words, this way and that, until they made sense. In the first weeks, when I was so undone by his passing, this helped me.

I'd asked for scrap paper to try out phrasing. Mr. McGee often played with the Latin, and the English, and the Gaelic meanings of the same word, so I had to guess whether he'd used a word to mean, say, a heart's pulse or a river's flow. I knew not every phrase I'd managed to write down was exactly his . . . indeed, Mr. McGee would have laughed at some of them, and enjoyed the private joke. And then he'd have taught me the right words, showed me how an uptick in his cursive script meant *ing* or a printed S at the beginning of a word meant *sp*, not *st*.

Without him there to school me, I also had to make out when the letters meant someone's name. I hadn't known all the politics, even with reading the newspapers, so I'd questioned Pierce and Monsieur Robitaille about the Americans. Monsieur Robitaille was impressed with the interest I was taking in all the doings south of the border.

By the time I was pretty sure I'd matched the people to Mr. McGee's notations about them, the nib pen I'd been given by Mr. McGee had broken twice from its holder.

Pierce had brought me a new steel pen, and told me not to bother about returning it, but he'd balked when he had to refill my inkwell. He told me he hardly needed to spend that much for what amounted to a pot of soot and jelly, and that McGee must've been mad to buy the best India ink, and then leave so few funds for his widow and daughters. It was the longest speech I'd heard from him.

Yet the ink bottle arrived, before I did, the following morning.

I knew some of this writing would never be in his new book. The parts about his family, their fights, his worries about the children at home, and his prayers for those children he'd lost.

I also hadn't known of his daily struggle with his loyalty to his fellow Irish. He'd written here that our past and present are tied in a knot with two strands, our religion and our land; and about how he had to try to weave in a third, for this new country, where the same laws applied to all.

He'd confessed to himself how, at the worst, when he'd been called upon for judgement, this twist of loyalties had pulled him back to the bottle.

There was some nastiness in the politics, too. This private Mr. McGee had enmities, and feelings of being hard-done-by and passed over. And I was truly shocked by the venom in his writings about America.

And then there was what Pierce was looking for. Mr. McGee had made lists of names. Names of men he knew for certain were Fenians—though he didn't say how. Names of men he suspected, and the reasons why. Between the two, they totalled ninety-seven names.

Those lists I gave to Pierce right away.

I'd been so pleased to see Mr. McGee had not mentioned Hannah's Mike. And I felt righteous, when I read that he truly didn't believe the worst of Jimmy Whelan either . . . though he did suspect Devlin.

As for the rest . . . with each page I pushed against my sin of trespass. I slowed down, pretending to have trouble with the shifts in his word codes—until Pierce told me either I could do the work, or I couldn't, and that was that.

The best part of me wanted to give it up altogether, to honour Mr. McGee's instruction that I not read his diaries.

Yet every time I set the pages aside, I was drawn back.

This puzzle was one blessed thing that belonged to me, only to me.

And I could find him again, in these lines. To copy his words meant my very hand gave stuff to his spirit. As though he was just out somewhere, and I was preparing his next speech.

Once in a while, I felt 'twas spookier—like he was guiding my very hand. The Bible calls that inspiration.

Then there was one phrase he'd penned the first week in January. It was the last entry before he'd brought me to Ottawa.

> *I've had nightmares, and no wonder. Of going over the Falls again. Threats and high tempers all around me. But now, a more peaceful dream. A reaching, a sending. I'm as mortal as any man. Feeling more so. Steady in my belief in the beyond. Will my thoughts go with me? Or die with me?*

I didn't know if the words did travel with Mr. McGee. But they'd stayed to be passed on to me, for sure. And if they weighed me down . . . well, Mr. McGee had warned me not to touch them.

For all he'd railed about the Fenians, and despite the lists of names, there was nothing in these diary pages that pointed to a Fenian conspiracy to kill Mr. McGee. He had dismissed the threats he'd received, as the baggage that came with having a vision and standing up for it.

Mr. McGee had made mention of the false alarm in Montreal when Jimmy came to warn about the house bomb. The strangeness of being moved in the middle of the night while so sick, and for nothing.

I was mentioned in that New Year's entry too.

> *Clara said the lad who came was polite, but excitable. Jumpy. And not the brightest on the block. Clara may look too much at how much intelligence a body has, rather than how much heart. Talk to her about that.*

I did worry that when the Prime Minister read Mr. McGee's real thoughts about Mr. Macdonald's knighthood, and about the Prime Minister listening to others, and not supporting Mr. McGee much during the election—or giving him a big position in running the new country . . . well, Mr. Macdonald might think less of his friend.

But whether this was the case, or no, I had to hand something in.

Oh, Pierce had laughed on the train trip back here, when he'd read the notes I'd written about Devlin. He'd said it was interesting, certainly, to figure out how my mind approached a problem. And that I had to start reading some authors who were neither Irish, nor Mr. Shakespeare.

"You mean Italians, like you do?" I'd asked.

"No, but I'll think of a few books for you," he'd said.

And he had been lending me books on a regular basis since then. He'd been wicked impressed at how quickly I returned them, and how I could argue with him on the finer points of the plot.

But despite this tutelage, Pierce wouldn't tell me if Mr. McGee's naming Fenians had helped in the investigation.

"You remember the thousand islands?" he'd said. "There are really a lot more than a thousand of them . . .. Some people counted from one end, and some people counted from the other, and in the end they all settled on a number."

And now the days were lengthening into June's summer, Whit Monday had come and gone, and that Easter Monday train trip was just a memory.

Pierce had become impatient for me to finish up and clear out.

He hadn't told me so straight, either. Mrs. Trotter had arranged for me to clean in the *Times* office, and when I'd protested, she'd said the Prime Minister's Secretary had decided that Parliamentary policy should apply. So no girls could clean at Parliament—no offence to me, and Pierce had told Mrs. Trotter that he'd already been dragging his feet on the matter for my sake—but I did need to line up other work.

"I'm sorry, Mr. McGee, I truly am," I whispered, into folded hands.

Then I offered up the *Our Father.*

Sed libera nos a malo, I prayed. Mr. McGee's desire, after all, had been to deliver us all from the evil of Fenianism. But . . . I couldn't lead myself away from this temptation.

I crossed myself. Then I stacked the pages.

TRIAL

Saturday September 5th, 1868

XIII

In late August, I tagged along with Hannah to the farm of one of her many Doyle cousins, in a place called Brewer's Mills. We were to help thresh corn.

We travelled by boat down the canal, which was so different than my ocean journey that I actually enjoyed myself.

For one thing, the trip took only took two days. There was a good breeze, so the black flies and mosquitos weren't as wicked as I feared they would be. Willy had twitted me that I'd die of disease from a bite. But I arrived without more than a bit of welting in various spots, both mentionable and otherwise.

For another, I had Hannah to protect me from the other kind of bug, once we arrived. She did try to matchmake me with three of her male Doyle relatives. But 'twas all in fun. And they soon told her they were looking for a woman, not a girl.

I saw that Hannah was the favourite cousin amongst the dozens of Doyles. When I said as much to her, she scoffed at this notion.

"None of them stepped up to take me six years ago, when I wasn't so pretty," she said. "I had to go work for Eamonn, didn't I."

I sympathised. After I'd finished with Mr. McGee's diaries, Pierce had sent me some additional copying work, public documents that could be openly copied by me at Trotter's, and delivered by Willy to Parliament. But with summer's Parliamentary recess, that had petered out. Now, in addition to my chores at the *Times*, I had to hie off, at a moment's notice, wherever else Mrs. Trotter heard someone needed a hand—just to make up my wages.

That was why I was glad of even this job.

Hannah, of course, thought she'd done me the best of favours. While she much preferred Niagara, where she'd grown up with her grandparents on the other side of the family, Hannah thought any farm was better than a tavern in town—especially in August.

I wasn't so sure about that. My skin burned to blisters from the days of fieldwork. I snuffled constantly, and could hardly breathe bytimes around the ragweed—let alone when I went too near the horses.

And Hannah did quiz me about the work I'd done for Pierce. Was I sure it was just cleaning? And while I was in Pierce's office, had I heard anything—anything at all—about Mike?

I reassured her, on both counts.

Pierce showed up for the final days of the corn harvest. It turned out the Prime Minister, his wife, and her brother, had gone to a village in eastern Ontario called Portland. They were enjoying Big Rideau Lake for the month of August. As Pierce had gone with them, he didn't have far to travel.

He raised his eyebrows at my weeping skin and snotty nose. He put his hand in front of his mouth to hide a smile when he saw me beating the grain with a flail.

They both had a big laugh, though, when they caught me rolling in the field with the piglets.

"'Tis clean grass, and these sweetlings smell like heather," I protested. "They're ever so much more interesting to play with than a mewling kitten."

"Clara," Hannah said, "didn't your Gram teach you not to make a pet of a farm animal?"

But neither of the cousins could deny I'd worked my full days, the skin on my forearms peeling, then settling to a mottled tan.

Come September, Pierce dropped us off to catch a boat in Portland, and hied off to transport the Macdonalds. We all needed to be back in the city, and for the worst of reasons.

Jimmy's trial was set to begin.

On my return, Mrs. Trotter told me I'd have to work in the parlour bar of an evening. She didn't like it, and neither did I, but neither of us had any choice.

Mrs. Trotter had been spending a lot of time lamenting to Sergeant O'Neill, that she didn't know whether she'd ever be able to rent out Mr. McGee's room. How nobody wanted to take the place of a murdered man. How the house may as well be haunted.

Woodmouse, Hedgehog and Bat had all made noises about finding more 'suitable' accommodation for the next Parliamentary session. She'd had to cut their rent by a third, to keep them as reluctant occupants of what they insisted on calling *D'Arcy's death-house*.

My first night serving in the bar was Saturday, September 5th. It didn't matter that the evening was hot as Hades, every chancer in Ottawa wanted to lift a few at the site of the shooting that night. They were determined to drink enough that it would carry them through Sunday, as they were hoping to enter the courtroom on Monday morning, for Jimmy's trial, with a shine still on.

The lads could talk of nothing else, as they hung off the bar. They started to joke, about how the bullet that knocked out Mr. McGee's denture was the best thing to ever come out of his loud mouth.

Then they decided they needed a break from the heat inside. They went out on Sparks Street, in front of the parlour bar entryway, and danced a treble jig. They stomped and clicked and called out rude words, while one of them whistled the tune *The Night Before Larry Was Stretched*. Some lads began to yell out the lyrics, chanting *Jimmy* in place of the original dead Dubliner.

"Buggers," I cursed—but below my breath. I dared not curse aloud, even though Mrs. Trotter was at this moment all the way through the connecting doors, in the dining room.

To top all this grief, she had ushered Sergeant O'Neill in there a few moments earlier, and they were hardly whispering.

The sergeant had grown so comfortable about dropping by in the mornings. This was the first time he'd shown up at this time of day, though. And while it wasn't unusual for them to go off alone, they didn't ever chat in that room.

"The Whelan woman can't very well be housed at the jail, now can she, Nancy?" Sergeant O'Neill said.

I'd never heard them argue before.

"Will no one else have the murderer's wife in their establishment?" Mrs. Trotter's voice rose with each word. "What about your own cousins at Docherty's Tavern, Major Doyle?"

So Pierce was in there too? He must've arrived by the back way, while I was throwing slop water into the street—and maybe hitting a dancer or two in the process. I tucked the bucket under the bar.

"Eamonn would've taken the money," Pierce said.

"Hannah wouldn't have it," Sergeant O'Neill told Mrs. Trotter, with a hint of derision. "I never knew Eamonn Docherty would put up with such nonsense, and from his nitwit of a niece."

"My cousin's still tough as a witch's tit," Pierce said. "But Eamonn needs Hannah's hand in the kitchen—and all her charms in the bar room."

"Watch your English," Sergeant O'Neill told Pierce.

Mrs. Trotter wasn't having any of it. "I'm to step in and house the murderer's wife? You're no more my boss than you are young Hannah's, Major Doyle. And you, Tommy—" Mrs. Trotter said. "You're both daft, to think I'll board the wife of the man who shot Mr. McGee on my own doorstep."

"It'd be some sort of justice," Pierce said, "if old D'Arcy disturbed her sleep."

There was a silence.

"Your Willy could profit from notice on Parliament Hill," Pierce said.

"Come on, Nancy," Sergeant O'Neill said. "Accept the Prime Minister's patronage."

"Tommy, it's blasphemy to suggest that Whelan's wife should sleep in Mr. McGee's place," she said.

"Then move one of the other boarders in there," Pierce said.

"I've told you Tommy," Mrs. Trotter said, "the others, saving Monsieur Robitaille, are nigh unto moving right on out."

"Your Parliamentary boarders won't argue with any arrangements they understand have a nod and a wink from Mr. Macdonald," Pierce said. "I'm going to have a walk with my cigar, Mrs. Trotter."

I heard him step out the boarders' door.

Everybody but me used that door again, had done so for months, as soon as the militia had replaced the bloody sidewalk boards. I still couldn't cross the threshold.

As soon as Pierce left, Mrs. Trotter said, "Tommy, how could you even—"

"Nancy, you don't like what this place has become," Sergeant O'Neill said.

"How would that woman's presence ease any of my trouble?" Mrs. Trotter said.

Was I wrong, to hope she'd be upset that the sergeant had his nose poked too far into her business.

"Tommy, you know I'm not proud of making money from the ruination of my own home." She was speaking lower now. "You want to take me further into the pit."

"I won't defend Bridie Whelan," Sergeant O'Neill said, "but she's not the first woman who's married a rotter."

I scratched my arm. The sergeant could look to home to see a man who was no prize husband.

"You might even find her better to have around than yet another politician," he went on, as if to make her laugh. Creeping, he was, softening her up, and it always worked.

This time I heard Pierce's entry. I eased over to the connecting door, and took a peek.

Mrs. Trotter was pulling a key off her *châtelaine*. She set it on the sideboard and pushed it away slightly. "Tell her she can't be in here, with the gentlemen," she said.

"Right enough," Pierce said, scooping the key. "The room's ready, for when she arrives?"

"Oh, it's sparkling clean. Clara's in that room, every day," Mrs. Trotter said. "Treats it like a shrine."

Pierce stopped. "What's Clara up to in there?"

"What do you mean, 'up to'?" Mrs. Trotter said. "She prays, and reads her family Bible."

"The girl has time to waste while you're slaving, Nancy?" Sergeant O'Neill said.

"Just a few moments now and again—Clara does her part and more," said Mrs. Trotter.

"We all know Clara's too high-falutin' to be happy cleaning bedpans her whole life long," the sergeant said. "It's McGee's fault," he added. "He gave Clara expectations."

"How about this," Pierce said. "Tell Clara I want regular written reports on Mrs. Whelan's days here. That should keep her chuffed with herself."

"You can't be serious," said Mrs. Trotter.

"Sure, she'll be grand at it." Pierce glanced over. "You can come in here now, Clara."

I ran through, landing so close to Pierce he stepped back.

"You want notes—?" I asked.

"A list of everything you see—or find to read—while you're tidying up after the woman," Pierce said. "She liked you well enough that one time you met . . .."

"She thought me honest, is all."

Pierce caught Mrs. Trotter's glare, and ignored her. "No question, she'll be in need of a friend here, Clara. And she thinks you an easy touch. Show us you're not," he said. "If you could be open to offering up a little honest sympathy. . .."

XIV

I smoothed my new good dress. I was lucky. Mrs. Trotter's Maisie had been taller than me, but every bit as skinny. Maisie had sewn this blue muslin with lace on the cuffs and at the hem for a cousin's wedding. She'd tatted the lace herself, a pattern of roses.

At least she'd had her chance to dance that night, so Hannah said. It was only two weeks later the typhoid took her. The hem lace had to go when we turned it up. Mrs. Trotter had placed it in the box where she keeps all her memories of Maisie.

On the inside of the left sleeve, just above the elbow, there was a stain the size of my fist, in the shape of a half moon. Nothing I tried could work it out.

"Quit fiddling with that sleeve, Clara," Mrs. Trotter said. "The mark's hardly enough to stop a galloping horse, and you'll make the dress look worse if you wrinkle it." I couldn't help but poke at it, though. Sitting here waiting for the trial to start. I'd no apron pockets in which to stick my fingers.

Nothing but Mrs. Trotter would take Sergeant O'Neill up on his offer of a buggy ride, and he had to be here well ahead of the start of the day's session.

The sergeant had special use of a four-in-hand brougham carriage, with a glazed front window and the copper named Pat doing the driving, all courtesy of the Ottawa Police. Mrs. Trotter was proud to sit inside beside him, and Willy was incensed that he had to work that morning, instead of having such a fine ride and watching what he was calling 'the trial of the century'.

I'd rather have walked the short distance to the Carleton County Court House on the corner of Daly Avenue and Nicholas Street. Instead I'd sat on a fold-down corner seat, coughing at being so near to four horses at once, while bumping knees with Hannah. And both of us opposite a coupling about which I didn't want to know, let alone be seen with in public as a member of their party.

127

On top of it all, we'd arrived so early we could've sat through a High Mass by now.

By nine o'clock, though, the angels and the devils had gathered in the courtroom.

The judge was a Mr. Richards. He used to be a politician. Like Mr. McGee, he'd started out on the other side of the floor of the pre-Confederation legislature from Mr. Macdonald. And, in time, he too was won over, by the man Mr. McGee joked should be called *Machiavelli*.

The Prime Minister entered from a private door alongside the judge now, with Mr. Macdonald's new English wife on his other side. Mr. Macdonald climbed right up and into the catbird seat—on the platform, next to the judge.

Sergeant O'Neill had to squeeze another seat onto the dais for M'Lady.

She was wearing a rich green velvet dress, with a cap to match. Lady Macdonald, she wanted folks to call her. Mr. Macdonald was John A. to the men on the street as well as in Parliament. And him the one who had been granted the knighthood. Some said that's why she married him. Though I thought any woman would be proud to marry the Prime Minister, even such an elegant lady.

"She'd be finding it hot in here today," I said, "in that outfit."

"Ladies call that a glow," Hannah said.

"Shush," Mrs. Trotter said.

Mr. Macdonald's tan was as freckled as mine. M'Lady must've kept out of the sun on her sojourn to Big Rideau . . . her face was smooth as ivory.

She began to fan herself.

"She looks to be in a family way," Mrs. Trotter said.

I looked M'Lady over again. I couldn't see any baby shape under her velvet folds. Mr. Macdonald a father?

Mr. McGee told me Mr. Macdonald's son had been long since moved out West, while his first wife had gone to Heaven. People said Mr. Macdonald wouldn't be Prime Minister if he hadn't worked so hard—rather than having to go home and hear her long suffering.

Then he up and married this Englishwoman, his personal secretary's sister. He'd signed us all up for a new country at the same time he'd signed up a new wife over there in London. Now there was to be a new family, too?

"What makes you think so?" I said.

Mrs. Trotter nodded. "She has the brooding look about her."

Hannah leaned across me. "How far along do you think she is, then?"

"Four, maybe five months," Mrs. Trotter said. "That's why she's wearing such a high waist."

Hannah nodded like she saw something, though I was closer to the lady and it was still a mystery to me.

"She's a tiny thing, so she's showing all the sooner," Mrs. Trotter said.

"April . . ." I said. "When we lost Mr. McGee."

"A birth's a special blessing after the death of a loved one." Mrs. Trotter shifted her hankie from her sweaty forehead to swipe at her eyes.

Hannah patted Mrs. Trotter's hand.

I straightened, looking at the empty prisoner's chair that had been placed to the judge's left, just below the Macdonalds.

When it came time for their baby to be born, 'twould be full winter again.

To think, the land had all been under snow, back when Mr. McGee was shot dead. Now Mr. McGee had been under ground these five months. He'd expected his *Apologia* to arrive from the London publishers, come this harvest. He'd joked with me about the germ of an idea having a cycle, like the plants we set in the earth. He had to ensure his own seedling was in High Commissioner Tupper's nurturing hands, he'd said, in time for the book editors' spring planting season.

"When the apples ripen and fall," he'd said the day I packed the *Apologia, "so will my book land, fully ripened and polished, in my readers' homes. I like to think on it, Clara, as my own small grafting onto the fruit of the Tree of Knowledge, if I may be so immodest. And we won't leave that one up on a high shelf, Clara. No, I want my Apologia to be changing hands and changing minds."*

At a nod from the judge, the guards grabbed poles and swung open the upper windows by their hinges. The breeze that blew into the courtroom was as hot and heavy as the air weighing us all down.

As grand as this room was, with its fine plasterwork and leaded glass, I felt the stones of the building pressing down upon me. 'Twas as I were sitting in the shadow of a cairn.

The door that led to the jail opened, and Jimmy Whelan was ushered in.

From his months locked up, Jimmy came out looking like what folks thought of when they cursed the Irish. His beard long, red and a lot more unkempt than it had been last New Year's Eve. His eyes wild. Even his black frockcoat picked up a sheen of green in the light of the courtroom.

He was clearly happy to be out among us all, despite the circumstances. His hands were clasped together behind his back, so he looked like he might as soon break into a jig, as take his seat between the coppers. He breathed the stale, humid air deeply, like he was facing a clean sea wind.

It wasn't only my shame that an Irishman was charged with killing Mr. McGee that made me worry over his fey manner. Hannah had been visiting her Mike at the jail. He'd told her it was as if the faeries had addled Jimmy's brain. He'd been living too close to the world yet to come, she'd said.

Of course, Hannah said the cells were hardly large enough to lay out a body, the stench such that the men may as well be breathing from a midden.

In that place, she said, there was no need for a faery curse to turn a man barmy. Especially if he were a bit daft at the start.

Bridie Boyle Whelan hurried in, just in time.

The day of Mr. McGee's funeral, she'd worn a grey cape and no arm band to show we were a country in mourning. Today she wore grey satin, as fine as any cloth that could be purchased by Lady Macdonald herself.

Her nostrils were red, and her eyes were creased and puffy. Maybe she suffered from the ragweed too. Her hair was pinned up under a lilac scarf, one silver streak showing.

She looked around for a seat.

"There's room on this bench," I called. I shuffled over to make room for one more. "Mrs. Wh— Bridie?"

"'Mrs. Patrick James Whelan, and I don't mind who knows it."

The crowd leaned toward her for a good look, even while they all spread out to make sure she didn't try to sit next to any of them.

"To think that you're the friendliest face in this Godforsaken room, girl," she said.

But she placed a flowered tapestry bag, with leather handles, on the empty seat. She must've come right from the station.

"You'll watch my kitbag?" she said. "Many thanks—I've only a moment to speak to my husband's barrister, before today's travesty begins. I've hired Jimmy the best in the country—can you imagine, he's being defended by an Orangeman?"

She headed to the table where Whelan's defence attorney sat.

"Hannah," I said, "did you see how Mr. Lacey wrote that Jimmy's lawyer, Mr. John Hillyard Cameron, is grand master of the Orange Order?"

"Never mind that, Clara, we've more to worry about right now than a Catholic killer being represented here by a Proddie," Mrs. Trotter said. "What are you thinking—giving up a seat to Whelan's wife. I'll not have it, that's what."

More than a few heads turned to us.

"It's enough that she's to stay—" Mrs. Trotter started to say.

"Shhhh," Hannah said, as people around us whispered about our goings-on. "Best not to spread news of her lodging, Mrs. Trotter. And Mrs. Trotter's right, Clara."

"She needed a seat," I said. "And Pierce—"

"I don't care what Major Doyle told you to do, Clara, we don't want anyone thinking we're here in support of that joker Jimmy Whelan," Mrs. Trotter protested.

At the front of the courtroom, Bridie shook her head at the lawyer.

Behind us, a girl whispered, "Is she Whelan's mother?"

Hannah laughed.

"You shouldn't be mixing with Jimmy Whelan's wife any more than is needed, Clara," Mrs. Trotter said. She poked my rib. "How can you sit there like butter wouldn't melt in your mouth?"

"I told you there was no good to come from a Wishing Tree," Hannah said.

I shifted away from Mrs. Trotter's elbow. Two years, Bridie had said, and then her wish came true. I didn't think being married could have made her happy, though.

The butcher was waving to Hannah from the doorway.

"There's a blessing." Mrs. Trotter motioned the man over and lifted Bridie's bag off the bench.

Bridie walked back toward us.

"Tell that one there's no room, Clara," Mrs. Trotter said, shoving the bag at me.

There was no need. Bridie looked past me, at someone sitting in the spot she'd marked as her own. She was a foot away when she held out her hand for her bag.

I stood up, and stepped to her. "I'm sorry—"

Her nostrils pinched, but no other message showed on Bridie's face. She didn't look at Mrs. Trotter, or the others glaring all around us.

"I see those as know me won't be offering a welcome," she said, clear enough for the room to take in. "No reason to expect matters would be different here than in Montreal."

She turned and made her way to the front once more. Her husband's defender called over a guard and gestured to the bench right behind him. The guards seated there rose as one and, with filthy glances toward Bridie, took places standing along the side wall.

Bridie settled onto one end of the seat, plopping down her bag in the space beside her.

XV

Barney Devlin made his testimony, on that first morning of the trial, into another platform speech. Jimmy Whelan, he said like an accusation, had yelled wild Fenian threats at last year's St. Patrick's Day procession in Montreal.

Hadn't Whelan near as led this year's parade here in Ottawa, Devlin asked? How did he become so prominent in the Irish-Canadian community, so quickly?

Devlin didn't credit Jimmy's helping in Devlin's own election campaign, as being part and parcel of the lad's sudden popularity.

Bridie's gaze was fixed on her husband. She hadn't made a sound or so much as twitched her lip. The tower bell had rung the hour, and then the half-hour, but her gaze had not wavered.

Devlin went on so long that Mrs. Trotter had to step out for a break.

Hannah shimmied over. "She's older than Mrs. Trotter, you know," Hannah muttered. "What would a boyo like Jimmy Whelan see in the likes of her?"

"What does she be wanting with him?" I said. "He's no smarter than he's born to be."

"It's not about his brain, Clara," Hannah said. "Not when a woman moves from maid to old lady without having a husband. Look at you blush," she said. "You're a laugh and a half, Clara."

Jimmy's wife arrived at Trotter's on Monday night, with Sergeant O'Neill, in the brougham carriage. She looked at me strangely when she entered by the kitchen door. But I was soon forgotten when Bridie Whelan found out that her new landlady was the very biddy who'd denied her a seat in court that morning. And that this biddy was no happier to give her a seat at the dining table.

The two ladies had quite the to-do.

Bridie demanded all three keys to her room, saying she wanted no help and she'd have the only right of entry.

Mrs. Trotter was adamant she'd allow no such thing, this was her own boarding house, that not even the landlord had keys to the new locks she'd installed. But, in this, Bridie had prevailed. Mrs. Trotter handled her defeat with bad grace, and would only allow Sergeant O'Neill to have her key and mine. Bridie had to trust that arrangement, the Sergeant said, and pocketed both.

I was fairly sure the sergeant would've handed both keys back to Mrs. Trotter, right after that show for Bridie, although I hadn't been given mine. I hadn't had a chance to ask Mrs. Trotter for it either. After they'd settled the key business, the sergeant and Mrs. Trotter had a private chat. In fact, yesterday, he'd been in the house when I'd stepped out of my room at dawn, already slopping up three fried eggs and sausages.

Mrs. Trotter had never been one to nurse a grudge, but her bad mood carried through to the carriage ride the next morning. The sergeant had debated about actually offering Bridie a ride as well. To keep an eye on her, he said.

I was happy to say that she'd been locked in her room since she arrived. Then, by dawn, she had left her pot in the hall, and was gone, without her breakfast.

But Mrs. Trotter was offended that he thought she'd sit in the same carriage as the woman, and be tainted by association.

At court, Mrs. Trotter was almost as disgusted by the first witness who appeared that Tuesday morning. 'Twas a middle-aged man named Enright—who Sergeant O'Neill told us on the way to court had been locked up himself for the week after the assassination, and would be lying on Jimmy's behalf. Sure enough, Enright had only good things to say for Jimmy, but said he hadn't been anywhere near Jimmy for two days prior to Mr. McGee's murder.

Mrs. Trotter told me she had a matter of private business, and left me with both of our lunches.

She returned from the noon break at the last possible moment, with Sergeant O'Neill rushing in the door a moment after her, and neither of them looking at all composed. A few of the guards nodded at the sergeant in a knowing way, which I did not like at all.

"Hannah," Mrs. Trotter said, plopping down between us. "I saw your Michael outside."

Hannah jumped up, her eyes fixed on the jail door, not caring who saw her.

The judge didn't even bother to signal she sit down, he just nodded at the prosecution desk.

"The Crown calls Michael Walsh to the stand," the Crown Attorney said.

So this was Hannah's Mike.

From all Hannah's talk I'd pictured a strapping farm boy, all muscles and chest. Here he was a proper lad, with the sage blue eyes and goldenrod curls of a cherub on the church wall. His bottom lip jutted out ever so slightly, drawing my gaze to his neatly clipped goatee. He was almost as pretty as Hannah. And for all the horrors of the jail, he'd managed to clean up well enough. Hannah had dropped off a starched white shirt and a black string tie, which he'd looped into a bow. The brown felt coat Hannah had brushed so carefully hung wide on his shoulders. She'd been dropping off meals regular but he hadn't escaped the jailhouse diet.

"Don't make a spectacle of yourself, girl." Mrs. Trotter pulled hard on Hannah's dress, until she settled on the edge of the bench.

Bridie shifted at last, nodding to Mike in greeting.

Hannah pulled a face at Bridie.

Mike grabbed a large white cotton hankie out of his breast pocket and wiped his face.

Hannah tilted on the edge of the bench, head in hands, elbows resting on her knees. "I wish I were in the front row. Whelan's wife will be spooking my Mike. Look at her. Staring at him like she's throwing a curse his way."

"Why would she?" I said.

"They'll have to let Mike out after this," Hannah said. "Don't gawk so, Clara."

"If I must call for quiet again, I'll clear out this place." The judge was looking straight at us. Mrs. Trotter elbowed Hannah, who finally slipped back in her seat.

"Michael Frances Walsh, place your hand on the bible." He was sworn to tell a true tale, then ordered to sit. The Crown's attorney walked toward him until they were eye-to-eye. Mike was looking to the side, though, at the judge and, beyond him, the Prime Minister and Lady Macdonald. He squinted in the light from the window.

"He hasn't seen day in six months," Hannah whispered. "And all these people, so fancy, here to weigh his words."

"You know the accused, Patrick James Whelan," the Crown Attorney said.

Mike pulled out his hankie again and twisted it into a ball. "I never knew him as Patrick. He's always gone by Jimmy."

"Mr. Walsh. You recognise the defendant, Patrick James Whelan?"

"Aye, that's Jimmy there. Though Whelan's not what he called himself when I knew him first."

The Crown Attorney nodded. "What name was he using then?"

"Sullivan—James Sullivan."

"So he was using his late mother's surname?"

"Sullivan he was, that's all I knew then." Mike cleared his throat. "I never asked whether his father had made his mother an honest woman." He ventured a small grin.

"And where was this?"

"In Montreal—at Starr's boarding house. We were living there, and half a dozen lads besides."

"Was there a pub in this boarding house, Mr. Walsh?"

"Nothing open to the public, but Mrs. Starr would serve us and our guests."

"Did Mr. Whelan ever have any particular guests, Mr. Walsh?"

"Jimmy'd barely arrived from Ireland." Mike tugged at his goatee. "He did bring home a Yank one Saturday night."

"When was that, Mr. Walsh?"

"It was after the election—a year gone by. Right before Jimmy married the Missus here"—this last with a nod to Bridie.

"Were he and this Yank talking privately?"

"For a time, yes. Then more of the lads came home, so they had to share their table."

"Do you recall any of this conversation?"

"I couldn't forget such talk, now could I? They were making plans to—do away with McGee."

The murmur of voices in the room dropped dead silent at those words. Jimmy Whelan went to jump up. His guard stepped forward.

Whelan looked at Bridie, who had stopped looking at Mike, to once again gaze at her husband. He settled back.

"To do away with—you mean Mr. Whelan spoke of a plan to assassinate Mr. D'Arcy McGee? Is that what he said?"

"'Tis so, yes. What you and I talked about."

"Please be clear, Mr. Walsh. What did Mr. Whelan say that night?" The lawyer was leading Mike like he had a ring in his nose.

"Jimmy was talking about a bomb. The two of them were hot about it. They were to plant a bomb in Mr. McGee's house. Mr. McGee had been sick in bed ever since the election, he hadn't so much as stepped outside, so—"

"And how did Mr. Whelan here—" He pointed at Jimmy. "How did *this man* say he would bring a bomb into the McGee home?"

"Neither Jimmy nor the Yank said particularly. Though one night in his cups, Jimmy was mewling over a picture of a girl a mite younger than the one he married—begging your pardon, Ma'am."

He bobbed his head at Bridie.

Hannah poked me. "He didn't mean to suggest you, Clara, I swear."

But a number of people were looking at me. They knew I'd worked for Mr. McGee in Montreal. Everyone in the court had seen Whelan's wife coming to sit by me.

"Did they talk of any other plans?" The Crown Attorney asked.

"What d'you mean?" Mike said.

The lawyer waited.

"Oh, Jimmy said if the bomb didn't work, he'd have no trouble tracking down Mr. McGee and shooting him dead."

The attorney had turned toward the jury before Mike answered. He was expecting this. He kept his eyes on them as he posed his next question. "To shoot him dead. Do you know whether Mr. Whelan carried a firearm in Montreal, Mr. Walsh?"

"I believe he did, Sir."

"Thank you, Mr. Walsh." The lawyer nodded to the judge, the Prime Minister, and the jury in turn. Then he turned to face Hannah's Mike once more. "Oh, Mr. Walsh. Have you been offered any reward for your testimony today?"

"Money? Not at all, Sir. Not a bloody cent."

A man's voice rose behind me. "And bloody it would be, Mike Walsh—blood money, you lying bastard." That was a Galway lilt, same as Whelan's.

The judge's gavel came down again, right sharp. "Haul that man out of the court," he said.

Two guards caught the lad as he reached the door.

The lawyer turned to Mike again. "Thank you for your illuminating testimony, Mr. Walsh. You may go."

Mike made to walk down the aisle and out of the courtroom himself. The same jail keeps who'd brought him in stepped up and motioned him toward the jailhouse door instead.

He had a panicked look cross his face then. And well he should worry. The last place Mike Walsh would have wanted to land after those tales was in the rebel-filled holding tank.

The judge called for a break and the benches cleared. As Mrs. Trotter left I grabbed Hannah's arm.

"You said your Mike and Whelan were friends?"

"Mike doesn't know you worked at the McGee house." Hannah said. "But—Jimmy Whelan will hang, Clara. Now Mike won't be up there swinging beside him."

She peeled my hand away.

"It doesn't matter what anyone says here. It's just like an English court, with Mr. Macdonald seated as Lord of the Manor," she said. "We all know how they treat the Irish in English courts."

"I believe this may have been the Irish mistreating the Irish here today, Hannah," I said. "Aren't we here to learn the truth of who shot Mr. McGee? And your man as good as saying someone in the McGee house would plant a bomb. That's a lie, 'tis. Is every Irishman in the jail to lie when he's brought out on the stand, then?"

Hannah took a step away from me. "The best any of us can do is to stop this hunt before it's at the door of our own home."

"Mr. McGee landed at the door of my home, Hannah. Mrs. Trotter's and Willy's and mine."

"Yes, your Mr. McGee's dead. He's long gone, Clara. And his murder's not taking my Mike from me." She moved to the door. "I'll make sure Pierce knows—that Mike didn't mean you."

That wasn't much to leave me with.

XVI

Hannah had told Mrs. Trotter, after Mike's testimony on Tuesday, that she wouldn't need a ride to the trial again. Why bother going to goggle? Hannah said. 'Twas clear, she said, that the English would roast Jimmy until he was done. Then his poor old wife would only have the blackened Whelan name to hold onto. Hannah said she'd spend the time instead making arrangements for Mike's release. With the banns already having been read, they could be married right away.

Then she had flounced off toward Pierce.

Sergeant O'Neill had said that Hannah would have to make some very pretty arrangements, in order to see Mike released by the end of the day. And that he didn't think Pierce would want to know anything about those particular negotiations.

On the drive back to Trotter's, the sergeant revealed to us that the third court day would be given over to lawyers arguing points in the morning, and only one witness in the afternoon. None other than Patrick Buckley, jailbird, St. Patrick's Day grand marshall, and possible government spy.

Patrick Buckley could hardly be called a spy, now could he, I'd said. Why, Willy had observed Buckley's brother John once again driving Mr. Macdonald to and from his Parliamentary offices, bytimes.

The sergeant sent me a quelling look.

He and I had both seen Willy riding in the cab of that carriage about a month ago. And jumping out in the alley, down by Docherty's. I hadn't known who Willy's friend was. The sergeant, though, had given Willy a right talking to—about how Willy shouldn't upset his mother by chumming around with those Buckley brothers.

The sergeant assured Mrs. Trotter that Buckley was a patriot, and would testify about everything he heard when Pierce had him planted in the jail. Buckley would tell the court that Jimmy had been bragging, in Irish, about the brother who was jailed over in *Éireann*. And how their mother would be proud to have two heroes for sons.

The sergeant phrased this news in a strange way, however. He didn't tell us that Jimmy had said this. He said that Buckley was going to tell the court that these thoughts came from Jimmy's unguarded, Gaelic tongue.

But it was no matter that Buckley was now known to be a true government man. Mrs. Trotter still felt the sting of her rumoured association with a man who'd posed as a traitor.

Mrs. Trotter decided, then and there, that we'd be better off at the boarding house on Wednesday, catching up on our work.

It was just after four o'clock on Wednesday afternoon that she went out to the back garden to weed. "Pulling up a few of the overgrowth invading my plot is just what I need," she said, "to take my mind off that scalawag Buckley, and worse, that woman soon returning here from her husband's jail cell."

I thought she might also be looking out for the sergeant, by the look on her face, though he didn't come around in the afternoons.

He'd been here again this morning. He didn't even pretend he was hanging around on police business anymore, even after Bridie Whelan came in to sit at the end of the table.

Mrs. Trotter just kept frying up eggs, and me serving the two of them—sergeant of the police and jailbird's wife. And nobody saying a word, until they'd both used their bread to sop up the grease from their plates.

Bridie had wiped her mouth with Mrs. Trotter's linen, risen, and placed the napkin on her chair.

Then Bridie had looked at me, a smirk right across her face, and said "Bless you, child."

And she'd left for court. So early she must've had plenty of time to talk to the defence attorney, to make up for the day before.

She hadn't returned, as far as I had heard, anyway. So I took the chance to scoot upstairs, and try Mr. McGee's—Bridie Whelan's door. 'Twas locked tight, no surprise there. I needed that key back. Or, barring that, to figure out another way to learn something for Pierce—anything—about Bridie's most private life.

So far, the only secrets I'd managed to secure had been my own.

Bridie's arrival meant I'd had to relocate the McGee Bible from under the bed she was now occupying. I'd squirreled it away, in the place where I hid myself to cry.

With a few free minutes still, I made my way there.

The Holy Bible only fit under Mrs. Trotter's extra linens, in this storage closet in the laundry room, if I left it lying open. Last night I'd sewn a sack to keep it from harm's way, using the remaining scraps from Mr. McGee's old boiled-wool pants.

I had left it agape at the story of Queen Esther. I didn't have time to think about her, though, nor any other bible lesson—excepting at Sunday Mass. Nor did I have ample time for any other reading. Now that I was working in the bar, as well as elsewhere on the street bytimes, I only had a snatched hour or two each week to myself, during daylight. Mrs. Trotter didn't mind me reading in the parlour with her at evening's end. But she didn't allow a candle, or any lamp, to burn late in my room. Lest I fall asleep, and knock it over.

There was a reason the bible was so fat. I had hidden my own sin within it.

I could hardly believe I'd managed to make a complete second copy of Mr. McGee's diary pages while sitting in the spy room at Parliament, without anyone noticing—especially Pierce. After a while, I didn't even sweat or have palpitations while doing it, either. It became clear the new government hadn't yet learned to keep track of its paper supplies; I'd only handed in the fifty-two pages, but I'd used up a hundred and twenty-four. Surely, they couldn't believe I'd wasted so much good paper on mistakes and do-overs?

I had layered these secret copies into the McGee Bible, the way I'd once layered the originals.

I was right to keep my own copy of Mr. McGee's precious words, I told myself. Look what had happened with his *Apologia*. Though Pierce had told me back in Montreal that Mr. Tupper would look after the book, nobody had spoken of it since, in all these months. So much for Mr. McGee's apples of wisdom taking seed here, or in America.

Willy insisted he'd heard nothing of it from the Members of Parliament, and finally told me 'what of it', and I should stop bothering him. Mrs. Trotter said that Mrs. McGee had never so much as sent her a line in reply to her condolence letter, let alone written to inquire if there was a copy of her husband's unpublished book lying somewhere about the boarding house. The newspapers had written nothing about its upcoming publication, for all their gossip of the manhunt and the murder trial.

When we were eating roasted corn of an evening at the farm, and Pierce seemed to be at his most relaxed, I asked him whether Mr. Macdonald had heard from Mr. Tupper when the publishers would be sending Mr. McGee's *Apologia* our way.

He only shook his head at me and said, *"you're persistent, Clara, I'll give you that."*

It niggled at me, like an itch, that the *Apologia*, which that man had spent his last months crafting—to help shape this new country—had so far remained unheard.

Meantime, the public and the papers were shifting the shape of the tale of Mr. McGee's shooting, until it sounded more like an Irish myth than an Irishman's tragedy.

And now, even my thoughts of Mr. McGee were being pushed aside. By the questions I had about Jimmy's guilt. And my anger, that even I was being looked at askance.

Well, at least I'd preserved these few private musings, to visit with, and to remind me of what I was capable of . . . and who most mattered.

There was a knock on the laundry-room door. Nobody ever looked for me here.

I pulled the grey flannel sheathing over the bible, and piled on linens.

The laundry room door opened, ever so slightly.

"Mademoiselle Clara? I tried your door . . . then I heard a rustling in here . . .. *Excusez-moi*—"

"Monsieur Robitaille?" He never knocked on my door for special service, unlike Woodmouse, Hedgehog and Bat. Thank goodness those three were still back in their constituencies.

I pushed the closet door shut, but it was sticking . . ..

"I have visitors, you see," Mr. Robitaille said. "Could we have tea in the parlour? Six cups, *s'il vous plaît.*"

"In a trice, Monsieur. Sandwiches?" He'd never had a single visitor, these nine months.

"Shortbreads will be fine."

I found a bit of foolscap, lodged into the bottom hinge. I'd stuck a few scrap papers, on which I'd figured out Mr. McGee's coding, in the bible as well. For sentiment's sake . . . but didn't think I'd dropped any . . ..

I shut the closet firmly, shoving the misplaced paper into my apron pocket as I left the room. In the kitchen, I set water on the boil above the hearth, then ran in and collected the silver tea service from the dining room sideboard.

The mantle clock there read five minutes to five o'clock. It was still as bright inside as a winter noon.

I hefted the laden tray back into the kitchen, and plated a few biscuits. When I poured the heated water into the pot, I felt heartened just sniffing the Assam black tea from India.

Monsieur Robitaille had brought the tea from Montreal for Mrs. Trotter. 'Twas only right his guests be served it.

Out the open window, I saw Mrs. Trotter in the vegetable garden with Sergeant O'Neill. It must be late enough that the trial had ended for the day. So I'd been right, she'd been expecting the sergeant. Why did he have to show up for tea, wasn't breakfast enough?

The tower bell rang five o'clock.

After the last peal died down, their voices came inside, loud and clear.

"The whole Ottawa Valley's in town today, setting up for the fall fair," Sergeant O'Neill said, as Mrs. Trotter rose from the potato patch. "I spoke with a farmer who's brought in some piglets—you mentioned raising up a gilt and breeding her, Nancy. After all the good food you've given me . . .."

"That's ever so thoughtful, Tommy."

"Willy and I can knock up a pen for you," the sergeant suggested, as I carried the tray on through.

When Monsieur Robitaille held the parlour door open for me, I was thrown to see who was inside.

I knew why the sergeant was in the back yard. Was it because of Bridie Whelan that Pierce was one of the party sitting pretty in here? Did he expect me to know something about her, already?

For some reason, Monsieur Desbarats was there as well. Mrs. Trotter's landlord and Monsieur Robitaille were both Quebecers, sure, but I didn't think them friends.

One of the other men I knew by sight. He was Mr. Macdonald's secretary, and now brother-in-law, Mr. Bernard. The fourth man . . . I didn't know. I may have served him, in that crowded room at Parliament. He wasn't a man you'd take note of. Brown hair, brown suit, neatly clipped moustache.

"I can pour that, Clara," Pierce said.

Mrs. Trotter and Sergeant O'Neill were now in the kitchen together. If I made my way into my own room, or went back into the laundry . . . I'd have to step in the middle of those two.

Of course, I'd need to go into the kitchen soon anyway, to help prepare supper. Maybe the sergeant would have taken himself off by then. For now, I took a well-thumbed novel from my apron pocket, and leaned against the archway, Pierce-Doyle style.

Pierce had lent the novel to me on Monday morning.

We'd all been waiting for Jimmy's trial to start. I'd leaned forward to see what he was reading, and he'd laughed, and handed it right over.

He'd said I should enjoy it, being as one of the characters was as touched as me.

Miguel de Cervantes, I'd said, reading the author's name from the cover. *That's grand, I'd like to read about someone as close to God as me.*

I'd been proud that I knew how to pronounce the author's name. He was no Mr. Shakespeare, Mr. McGee had told me, but Signor Cervantes had been a noted author of that day.

It was quite possible that Mr. Shakespeare had read this book. That was recommendation enough for me.

Still, I wondered how Pierce read while pushing up against a wall; it wasn't at all comfortable. After another few minutes of not being able to concentrate, I relocated to the dining room. I sat in Hedgehog's seat, at the far end of the table. From there, I had a partial view of the archway.

It was so strange, though, to sit in a boarder's place.

'Twas no use even trying to read. I lay the book on the table.

It was Pierce who came out, jumped up on the bottom stair, and let in the latest guest.

Pierce backed up another step. The man who joined him on the staircase was the Crown Attorney himself. Mr. James O'Reilly by name. He was a Queen's Counsel, from Mr. Macdonald's own riding of Kingston. A most impressive Irishman. He'd been in the front row at last Sunday's Mass, with every eye upon him.

"I understand the Prime Minister has a goodly representation here," the attorney said, as he slammed the boarders' door shut. "Am I to be intimidated?" He made it sound like that possibility was a good joke.

"I've asked to have this conversation, sir, because Monsieur Lacroix can't," Monsieur Robitaille had clearly been hovering inside the entry. "Desbarats is having trouble with the heat," their host continued. "So we'll leave the door open, in the hope of a little ventilation."

Lacroix.

'Twas about the Frenchie lumberjack, then. The one who Sergeant O'Neill was so proud to have ferreted out.

People said Lacroix was walking down our street, right when Mr. McGee was shot. I thought it passing strange that we hadn't seen him. He hadn't come forward, neither, not until someone told Sergeant O'Neill which drunk had told such a story down in Lowertown.

His name, Sergeant O'Neill had said, means *Christ's own cross*. And that Jimmy would be carrying that Frenchie's testimony on his back, no question.

Monsieur Robitaille was speaking on that man Lacroix's behalf?

"Poor D'Arcy can't talk to us, either," said the Crown Attorney.

"That new constitution we all worked so hard to sign just last year," Monsieur Robitaille said, "states clearly we're to conduct our trials in both languages."

"That's not how the judge ruled," said Mr. Bernard.

"It's our law." Monsieur Robitaille wasn't backing down. "Macdonald knows that well. He was there when the Queen signed it."

"So was D'Arcy," said the Crown Attorney.

"You know how close D'Arcy and I were," said Monsieur Robitaille. "We chose to board here together. I'm hoping that here, at his very place of his death, you might all remember what D'Arcy stood for. Freedom to live Catholic, or Protestant, Irish or English—or French."

What would Monsieur Robitaille think of my saying 'Frenchie'? What I felt when people said 'Dogan'.

"You never saw D'Arcy going around speaking Gaelic, did you?" said the Prime Minister's brother-in-law. "Unless he was well in his cups—and then only in song."

Monsieur Robitaille didn't laugh with the others.

Bridie Whelan chose that moment to tromp in the boarders' door. She looked sharp when she heard the voices.

I scurried to close the parlour door, despite the heat.

Bridie stopped a moment, listened. "Is Major Doyle here to check up on me?" Bridie said.

"No," I replied.

"And the Sergeant?" Bridie motioned to the kitchen. "Does he have a wife at home?" she asked.

"He brought over Mrs. O'Neill to help us the night—someone—shot Mr. McGee."

"Does Mrs. O'Neill mind?" She nodded again. "That?"

I scratched my arm. "I've no idea what you mean, Mrs. Whelan."

She looked sideways then, at the parlour door. "You've a full house here today, Clara, that's sure. Was it that devil Doyle who set you on me, at the Wishing Tree?" She smiled. "I see you haven't grown out of your honest Irish face."

"If you could wait but a moment, Mrs. Whelan—I'll fetch your tea," I said.

'Twas what Pierce wanted, that I feed her sympathy. And with the way I'd seen people treat her in court—I found I wanted to handle her properly.

"I'll just rest my bones a moment?" Bridie said.

I motioned her into the dining room, and plumped down across the table from her. In Mr. McGee's old chair.

"This is a nice enough room," she said, taking it all in—the mahogany dining set and matching sideboard; the painting of the Quebec townships that Monsieur Desbarats had rented to Mrs. Trotter along with the building.

Bridie had been given a choice for meals, her room—Mr. McGee's room— or the kitchen. Mrs. Trotter regretted offering the choice, when Bridie chose the kitchen.

"I appreciated your attempt to share your seat with me on Monday," Mrs. Whelan said. "Jimmy said he knew you in Montreal, and that I'm right to think you're a rare, honest soul. You know, you may as well call me Bridie, even if I am a paying customer. Don't think the government's paying for this—I look after my own money."

I pulled out my scrap paper and a pencil from my apron and made busy, to let her talk on.

She looked at my paper, upside-down. "I've always wanted to learn my letters."

"You can't—you do?"

"In the back of my mind, like. I know my numbers, mind, I've always been powerful good with numbers. Don't keep track of figures by writing them out, I like to keep all my nuts in my own noggin." Bridie tapped her forehead. "It struck me hard, though, when I had to sign my marriage paper 'X'."

"You could still learn how," I said.

"Copy out my name for me?"

"I haven't paper here, it's in my room—" I motioned to the kitchen.

"Another time's fine . . .." she said. "Will you be testifying, Clara?"

"I—yes, I mean—I haven't been told when, but . . .."

"About knowing Jimmy?" she asked.

I was ever so thankful that the men filed out right then. We both turned to listen, but none of them spoke as they left, and Monsieur Robitaille went straight upstairs. Huffing.

I moved into the parlour to clear. None of the tea had been touched.

"I'm not too proud to drink one of those," Bridie said, right behind me. "Cold tea's better than none. You know, there isn't a single Irishman on the jury."

"I did read that," I said. I handed her a cup for herself, and took a cup for me.

"That lot of Saxons and Scots sitting in judgement are bound to think this is just another Irish feud, hardly worth their bother." She sipped the cold tea like it was fresh-brewed ambrosia. "Why was the Crown Attorney here, dear?"

"They'll think Mr. McGee worth the bother." There was nothing else for it but to take the tea set into the kitchen, to wash it up. Wouldn't the sergeant ever leave? "I'll be back in a moment," I said. "With some paper."

"I'll hold the door for you, dear," Bridie said.

So we both witnessed Sergeant O'Neill, bent over Mrs. Trotter's chair at the kitchen table.

A sweet piglet was squealing in Mrs. Trotter's arms.

"Would you look at her, Clara?" she said. "A pig for luck, as we say over home."

"What will you call her?" I asked. "Should I pour this good tea in the slops bucket?"

"*Nac ar muin na muice a beid sí?*" Bridie said, from the kitchen doorway. "Riding on that *muc*'s back, you'll be doing well—oh 'tis your good luck, indeed."

The door swung shut on Bridie's laugh.

"Don't go naming the pig, mind, Clara," Sergeant O'Neill told me. "She's a gilt—we're all meant to be eating her bacon, after she has a litter or two."

Still, he looked soft on the piglet himself.

XVII

"That's your testimony, Mrs. Trotter?" Jimmy Whelan's lawyer said. "You went out to the street, right after the shooting. And you saw nothing, and nobody?"

"The street was empty, sir."

Mrs. Trotter's hands were busy, pleating her stiff black silk skirt.

She had led off the Thursday testimony, telling the Crown Attorney at great length about the no-good fellows who'd scared her—asking after Mr. McGee. She'd said how she was sure, now, that one of them was the defendant. Then she'd wandered into a story about how she was no relation of anyone connected to the trial, until the Crown's barrister had cut her short.

Jimmy's lawyer had asked only about the street—which she had just assured him had been empty from the time she'd gotten herself outside, until all the gawkers arrived.

"Thank you, Ma'am." The lawyer's eyes swept past Mrs. Trotter, toward the jury.

Sergeant O'Neill offered his arm as she stepped down from the dais, and she leaned on him until she regained her seat beside me. He looked as relieved as Mrs. Trotter did, that they were done with her. I'd notice him becoming progressively uneasy as she blathered on.

The sergeant hadn't been at all worried, before she started talking, though. He'd talked a bit about how she should present her testimony, between bites of breakfast and during the ride here, but more about how hard he was working, and did she have any of that liniment she'd learned to make back in Tipperary.

I straightened my back. It would be my turn next. And I had seen something.

Mrs. Trotter didn't remember the night of Mr. McGee's shooting as clearly as I did, it seemed. When I'd reminded her, on the way to court, how only I had seen that buggy turning the corner, she'd said, *"A buggy, Clara? How be I missed that?"*

Sergeant O'Neill was back to driving himself in an open-top rig with a tandem team. He'd hawed the horses, and asked why I would even look to the corner, with Mr. McGee dead at our feet.

Mrs. Trotter had whispered to him, *"Sure, nobody could have seen a buggy at that distance."*

"Don't I know it," he'd whispered back, then jogged her foot with his own.

He didn't need to sit so close. His leather bench was poorly sprung, but it could seat three more than comfortably—when one of them was only me.

I was ticked off on more than that account, though.

I'd told Mrs. Trotter more than once how my eyes are sharp, without saying that half my job was to follow behind her, and sweep the dirt she'd missed.

And while the sergeant might be fuming that he'd lost the brougham, once the powers that be had realised he was transporting Nancy Trotter to the trial, and not Bridie Whelan, I didn't need him jawing at me. I knew that they'd put out an alarm to stop all buggies that night, as a matter of course. They'd caught up to a few, including one leaving town.

Sergeant O'Neill reminded me anyways, as we entered the courthouse, that neither the alarm nor Pierce's telegraphs to near and far had amounted to anything.

Still, I'd seen what I'd seen.

With Mrs. Trotter seated, the judge rose. "Court will re-adjourn at two o'clock, we've a few legal matters to review at that time . . .."

"Clara, thanks be that's over." Mrs. Trotter patted my arm. "I was ever so nervous. I haven't been addressed as 'Mary Ann Trotter', rather than just plain Nancy, since my wedding day. Now I need to step out to the chandler, once Tommy's run us home. Remember the potatoes need peeling, and—"

"I'm to give my testimony after lunch," I cut in. "Surely."

Sergeant O'Neill motioned us into the aisle. "No worries there," he said. "We've heard from Nancy, and from Robitaille. He was first to view McGee that night, after all."

"You said the street was clear," I said to Mrs. Trotter.

She looked at me, like she didn't understand any of my fussing.

"It may make all the difference," I said, "that there was a buggy going down the road. Monsieur Robitaille never looked beyond Mr. McGee's body, Mrs. Trotter. And you didn't see the street at all, not until we went out the back way."

"I'm only saving you trouble, girl." Sergeant O'Neill said.

"'Tis the plain truth, not some phantom like everyone tells me," I said. My throat tightened in anger, so my voice came out weak.

"'Tis a figment of your over-active mind, child," the sergeant's words were a dismissal. He folded his arms across his ample chest.

Mrs. Trotter leaned close. "Clara, the Crown Attorney won't be calling you," she said. "Leave well enough be."

I looked back and forth.

We all knew they were too close by half. A married copper. And the woman who paid my wages.

I nodded, and almost ran down the aisle.

"Clara—" Mrs. Trotter called.

Well, she'd have to peel her own potatoes today.

And Sergeant O'Neill would rue having told us that the lawyers took their lunch at the Russell House.

The *maître d'* left me in the Russell House boot room.

There was only the one houseman's stool, and a chest I didn't have to open to smell polish, clothes, and scraper-brushes. The houseman did his job well, three shelves bare and the table scrubbed clean. Boot-cleaning was a night-time chore; maybe he did double duty in the dining room. No, they'd never have a waiter at such a fancy establishment with shoe-black under his nails.

I couldn't see out of the high-set window. At least it let in some light. It must've been a hundred degrees in there. Why didn't he leave the door open to let the air circulate? I felt a desperate need for a cup of tea, and to clear my throat of this place.

The next best thing was to distract myself, as only a book would. I reached into my apron pocket, for that beat-up copy of my borrowed novel.

The doorknob turned, clockwise. The heat-swollen door fought back. I was relieved it swung open.

And shocked, when Pierce walked in.

Before I could say a word, he'd closed the door and leaned against it. "They've put you to work here now, Clara?" Pierce said.

I made a face. "There's hardly room for both of us," I said.

Pierce stroked his fat lip with his thumb. "We've both been in tighter spots." He looked me up and down and up again. "D'you have news for me about Jimmy's Bridie?" he said.

"I've neither seen nor heard anything worth repeating, yet," I said. "That's not why I'm here."

"You found nothing when rooting about her things, nothing about her money, or her fine Fenian friends?" he persisted. "No word's arrived for her?"

"She can't read or write, Pierce. You must know that."

He sniffed. "She claims she can't."

"I said I'd give you notes, and I promise I will. I can't do any better than the truth."

"'Tis the truth you're dealing in, is it?" Pierce said. "I praised you up to the woman who gives you a home and wages, Clara, and that wasn't done lightly. Next thing, you're acting the child, I hear. You want to tell me how, six months gone, you've only now discovered something you must tell the court?"

I held my back straight.

"Oh, it's the phantom buggy. Yes, O'Neill told me. Was it a sulky you saw, Clara? A Democrat? The butcher's wagon? Give it up, girl. I'm doing what I can for you, as well you know. Let's face it Clara—you've lost your pony. D'Arcy died, I know it's rough, but you're out of the limelight. And here you are, trying to scrape an acquaintanceship with the Crown Attorney. Well, I've given you a chance—now get back to Trotter's, and make yourself feel important by decoding the puzzle that is Bridie Whelan. That'll make us both happy."

"Mr. McGee's murder is the most important matter, not Mrs. Whelan's eating habits. Which is all I have to tell you about her so far—she prefers fried potatoes, to those baked in the jacket. Right now, the Crown Attorney needs to know I saw a carriage at the corner that dreadful night."

"You're not saying the shooter wasn't Jimmy." He shook his head, mocking sorrow. "Did I make the same mistake twice—Jimmy's wife's gotten to you again? You, who still think so much of McGee? Well, if she's played so on your sympathies, you'll be needing to take whatever tale you've imagined to your boyo's defender, Clara. There's no point trying it on with the Crown."

"Bridie—Mrs. Whelan— has not gotten to me in any way, shape, or manner," I said. "I just want all the men behind Mr. McGee's death to be found and then found guilty."

"All the men," Pierce said. Judging from the sudden colour on Pierce's face, I'd hit the nub of his problem. "We have a country that's barely a year old, Clara. And that's a miracle, with Yankee soldiers looking north for land."

Pierce edged forward, so I was forced to look in his face, or face his nether parts.

The air pressed heavy between us.

"We have Maritimers wanting to pull out of our deal," he said. "And savages about to stand, armed, between us and a rail link to the West."

I blinked sweat from my eyes. "What of it?" I said.

"The country's future was D'Arcy's fight on his last night alive, Clara," Pierce said. "And you want to muddy the jurors' minds—" he coughed. "Goddamned shoe-black."

I wasn't just sweating from the heat now.

"If Our Lord remembers we're the new Chosen People," Pierce said, "Jimmy might tell the priest about any other bastards who've been hiding behind him. During his Last Confession."

"Jimmy saving his soul through the Last Rites is the only way to find out who conspired to murder Mr. McGee?" I said. "And you won't let facts get in the way of that. Here, have your book back. I'm finished with it."

"Oh, give it up, Clara." Pierce said, pocketing the novel. "A mad dog, you are. Well, you've got your Irish up—there's nothing else for it, I see."

Pierce swung open the door at last.

"I can't talk sense into you," he said. "We'll see who can."

It was the Prime Minister who rose as I entered the private dining room. Neither the Crown Attorney nor Jimmy's lawyer were in the room.

Any food had been cleared from the table. The tea service was by the wall. I wouldn't be offered a cup, but with my throat so rheumy, I couldn't help looking that way.

Mr. Macdonald glanced down at a pile of papers. Then up at me.

I felt like he'd pecked me.

"The McGee family servant . . ." he said.

"Yes sir, Mr. Macdonald. Sir."

"Please sit, my girl."

Pierce pulled out the chair. I started at such treatment, then sat and let him push the chair forward until I was tucked under the table.

"And you're here now . . .?" He glanced at Pierce, who was holding up the wall with one shoulder, in his customary way.

Pierce's jacket shifted open, and I saw the curled edges of the book he'd lent me. Pierce had clearly read it a few times himself.

"Sir, that terrible night, I saw a buggy, I did. Turning d—"

"You believe this is significant."

"I can't say what it means. Sir. But I can say . . . Mr. McGee would want me to tell of it. *"Give the truth light,"* he used to say."

"That he did." He thought on that. "You were fond of D'Arcy, Miss?"

"He was a kind man as well as a great man, Mr. Macdonald." I stopped pulling at my sleeve, and set my hands on my lap like a lady, though I hadn't any gloves. "Uncommon kind to me, he was."

"Uncommon. That was our D'Arcy. A man with great charm about him . . . naturally, you'd want to help." He nodded. "And then there's this."

Mr. Macdonald pushed a poster across the table, turned so I could read it. It was the notice they'd sent around the country, last April. The print had pretty much worn off the ones that were still up around town, on posts and wooden palings.

This one was fresh paper, the ink still heavy on the board. REWARD $2000 FOR THE APPREHENSION . . ..

I looked at him, straight. "I don't want that. Sir."

"Ah . . .." He looked at his papers again. "You support yourself, I see, without great resources?"

"Mr. Prime Minister—Sir. I don't want that money."

I was glad I hadn't been offered the tea. My bladder felt about to burst.

His finger ran down the page. "Mrs. Trotter hired you . . . as a personal favour to McGee?"

"Mr. McGee wanted me to better myself."

He nodded, like my entire life was all written down there. Did it say Mrs. McGee thought me not made for service?

"Sir, I don't understand," I said. "Those notes—why would you care about me?"

"I have an open mind, Miss Swift. An open mind."

154

I was a bit damp now, below. I shifted. I'd never been so uneasy in a conversation . . . .. Hadn't Pierce told the Prime Minister that I'd worked for him, for the Constabulary, in the past? That I was supposed to be helping Pierce now? Had Pierce written down that I'd been the one to point out Jimmy, at the inquest, in Parliament?

Could the papers suggest I had something to do with Jimmy myself?

"It's not because of what Mike Walsh claimed, surely," I said. "No one at the McGee house would have helped place a bomb."

"How can you be so certain, miss?" Mr. Macdonald asked. "The other staff— and you—are all Irish, born and bred."

Miss Keough? Bonnie? "I—they'd have risked being killed themselves, if a bomb had burst," I said.

"You really didn't know them very long," he said. "Nor they you, Miss Swift."

Had one of those ladies pointed at me?

"Is there aught else you have to tell me?" he said. "What other—special knowledge—might you have, Miss Swift?"

Well, here's for it. I might be red as a rutabaga and leaking my own well water, but I'd have my say.

"There was planning behind Mr. McGee's murder . . . I understand that, Sir. Some of the answers may be in the *Apologia*. That Mr. McGee sent to High Commissioner Tupper."

That showed I knew something.

"Indeed."

"And he said too—he may publish it with another name. '*Nom de plume*', he said. Has High Commissioner Tupper arranged for publication?"

"The book will have its day," Mr. Macdonald said. "Of course, publishers have their own ideas. But I believe you can help us, Miss Clara."

"I can?"

"You're right, of course, Miss. Until we find everyone—everyone—behind this damned conspiracy of evil, we can't be complacent."

"Yes, that's why—" I said.

"I understand you enjoy writing? And you're skilled at it," The Prime Minister stood as he said this.

I knew my manners well enough to stand too.

And then I was on the outside, my audience with the Prime Minister finished, with Pierce staring at me and the clock, and how far it had moved since I went in.

"You may as well embroider your reports on Bridie with a few of your own musings," he said.

"And I'll tell the Crown Attorney to have you say your piece tomorrow."

He looked—proud of me? Despite himself.

"Tight lips, mind," Pierce said. "I wouldn't want anyone troubling themselves about you. And do not forget—I'm expecting you, *Don Quixote*, to elicit a bit of blessed truth from Bridie Whelan."

I scurried down into the Ladies Retiring Room, where I had to use one of their fancy linen finger cloths to pad my knickers.

I was so overset, that I walked halfway to Trotter's before I realised the Prime Minister hadn't told me the publication plans for the *Apologia*. Or if Mr. McGee's unpublished book had been of any help in catching Fenians. At least Mr. Macdonald had said it was safe in London . . .. He had said that, hadn't he?

XVIII

I tried to boost myself in my own window, but Mrs. Trotter caught me in the alley. She gave me what-for. For disappearing, and leaving her all the work to do and the piglet to feed beside, and all in this unseasonable heat. Then she told me I stank like the dickens, I was so bad I'd need to fill a tub and use soap all over my body.

I didn't say a word, and she was so hot and overwhelmed, she didn't remark on my sudden silence. I was fit to burst, what with the Prime Minister knowing so much about me, and Pierce saying that if I helped keep track of Bridie, he'd help me in return. And I was just smart enough not to tell Mrs. Trotter a thing about any of that.

As I bathed in the cool water, in the quiet of the laundry room, I turned my mind to how I was going to finagle my way to the trial the next day—while keeping Mrs. Trotter at the boarding house. So I'd be safe from her trying to protect me from myself.

In the morning, I was aided by fortune.

Sergeant O'Neill wasn't there when I awakened, and he didn't arrive at Trotter's in time for breakfast.

I took it as a sign.

As I was peeking out the parlour window, to catch the sergeant before he could come inside, Monsieur Robitaille walked out the front door, to Monsieur Cartier's waiting carriage.

Another sign.

I went into the kitchen and told Mrs. Trotter that Monsieur Robitaille had a problem, he didn't say what, just that it was important.

I said that he'd gone up to wash, and he wanted to talk to her when he came down—and that I'd go outside and be on the lookout for the sergeant. That if he arrived, I'd tell the sergeant that she'd be but a moment.

Mrs. Trotter was over yesterday's snit, which was both a blessing and a sign.

She said she might as well go upstairs right away, she could collect the boarders' laundry while she waited for the Monsieur.

"And then I'm going to lie down until Tommy comes," she said. "I'm suffering something terrible from this heat."

Three affirmations. The Lord above meant me to be telling these lies, so that I could tell my truth.

Unless the sergeant, for some reason, wasn't going to show up at all . . ..

But he did.

So I'd guessed right. I'd counted on his being eager to show off his star witness, LaCroix.

I climbed up onto the leather seat before the sergeant even had a chance to settle the horses. "Mrs. Trotter can't come to court this morning," I said. "She's down with one of her headaches, made worse by this heat."

"I guess I shouldn't check on her?" he said, scanning the front windows.

"She has her curtains drawn against the light," I said, "and a cold cloth on her temple."

"You should stay and tend Nancy," he said.

I doubted he was this solicitous with Mrs. O'Neill.

"She said we should both just go, Sergeant. She knows how excited I am, to hear from that Frenchie you found. We don't want to be late."

He wasn't happy, but he set the horses to a trot.

I pinched my arm. This could be my last day at Trotter's. I'd never acted so rash. And I'd lied to a copper to boot.

Ahead of us, walking proud down the dusty street, was Bridie, in her stiff grey satin and a straw sunhat.

"Here's a bit of fun, Clara," Sergeant O'Neill said. "Let's see if we can convince the Widow Whelan to take a ride, as she's late starting off today. We'll take the mickey out of her."

"The Widow—"

"Well, the name may be anticipating events," he said. "That's what they all call her at the jailhouse."

He pulled over, startling Bridie. She lifted her head to see beyond the shade of her bonnet. Wary, checking who had stopped, and what they might do to her.

"You're needing a lift to the courthouse?" The sergeant was ever so pleasant. "We have a free seat today."

"Free, is it?" She looked from one of us to the other.

I shook my head, ever so slightly.

"I'll be fine on my own," Bridie said.

Sergeant O'Neill glared at me, then at her. "So it's no thanks, then?"

"That's right." She shaded her eyes. "No thanks to the Ottawa Police."

Sergeant O'Neill led the horses through a dust pile as we passed her. The last I saw, she was heading into the post house to hire her own transport.

If I'd been secure that I had steady work in my future, I'd have stopped the sergeant's carriage and done the same.

There was a man already in the witness seat. His chin was set back, so that his upper teeth showed. He was hunched for flight.

Monsieur Robitaille had taken a prominent seat in the courtroom. He waved me over, and I perched on the end of the bench. I'd rather have been seated near the back, like the other days.

There weren't any other young girls there that morning, and I didn't know any of the matrons. I suddenly wished for Mrs. Trotter to be there, no matter her reaction to what I was planning to say.

Mr. Lacey muttered for his colleagues, loud enough for Monsieur Robitaille and me to hear, "Frenchie's testimony will nail the bugger."

The Crown Attorney stood. Mr. O'Reilly was a dapper man. Today he wore a royal-blue, three-piece suit, and boots that might have been polished at the Russell House.

"Your name, Sir?" the attorney said.

"Jean-Baptiste Lacroix. *Je m'appelle Jean-Baptiste Lacroix.*"

The court secretary repeated the Oath.

"*Qu'est-ce que vous dites? Comment?*" Monsieur Lacroix interrupted. "*Monsieur, je ne comprends pas.*" He didn't straighten to look the lawyer in the eye.

"May I speak, Your Honour?"

'Twas the priest from the French church. St. Vincent de Paul. Père André, they called him.

The judge waved down both lawyers. "I'll allow it."

"Monsieur Lacroix's ancestors have been settled in the Gaspé for close to two hundred years. He lives in Hull, Quebec, when he's not in the woods logging."

"That's all fine, Father, but—"

"I have been his Confessor here in Ottawa." Père André wouldn't be gainsaid. "In Christian charity, let me act as his interpreter."

"I've ruled on this, Father. This is a British system—a trial in English Canada, and we'll have no French in the courtroom."

"It wouldn't be French anyhow, it would be that *Joual* they use," an Irishman yelled out.

The judge rapped his gavel and looked at the Prime Minister.

Mr. Macdonald made no sign. I noticed M'Lady hadn't come today.

"Thank you for that Father," the judge said.

It was the Crown Attorney who really gave the testimony, and he never even had to raise his voice to do it.

Monsieur Lacroix mainly just said "Yes" and "As you say." It was far less believable than even Mike's testimony. At least Mike had made up his own words.

Yet the story Monsieur Lacroix agreed to—that he saw both Mr. McGee and Jimmy on Sparks Street and was there when and where the shot was fired—felt like less of a lie to me. It could have happened. Lacroix could have been gone down the alley across the street before we opened the door. The murderer was gone by then, why not Lacroix too?

For the first time, I thought Jimmy might have been there. What had Pierce said? *Any idiot can shoot a gun.*

Then Jimmy's lawyer turned Lacroix's words on their ear.

He walked soft up to Monsieur Lacroix. Mild as milk he was.

"You say Mr. McGee wore a top hat made of beaver felt, Mr. Lacroix."

"*Un haut-de-forme*—top hat."

"Made of beaver felt?"

"*Le castor*—What you say."

"What I say? No, what you say, Sir."

"*La même chose.*"

"Your Honour."

The judge rapped his gavel. "English, Mr. Lacroix."

"Yes."

Jimmy's lawyer raised a hand toward the judge.

"Could you ask Sergeant O'Neill to show us all Mr. McGee's hat again, Your Honour?"

The judge turned to the jury. "Let the court stipulate that Mr. McGee's hat was white."

Now I felt sorry for Monsieur Lacroix. Such a small thing, the colour of the hat, in the middle of a murder.

The lawyer looked at the jury while he spoke even more quickly to Mr. Lacroix.

"Was Mr. McGee a tall man, Sir."

"*Oui*—Yessir."

"And Mr. Whelan, was he a tiny lad?"

"'Sright."

The lawyer turned. "Mr. Whelan, will you please stand?"

Jimmy unwound himself from behind the desk. He needn't have, the judge and jury had seen all six feet of him on a daily basis. But he stood, staring, almost even with Monsieur Lacroix up in the box.

"Thank you, Mr. Whelan." Jimmy looked to make a bow on his way back down into his seat. There was a hoot from one of the lads behind me.

"You recognise Mr. Whelan today, Mr. Lacroix?

Monsieur Lacroix was silent.

The lawyer pointed at Jimmy. "Is that Jimmy Whelan?"

"Yes."

"Are you certain?"

"Yes. *Je suis sûr.*"

"Yet you did not recognise him when you first saw him at the jail, did you?"

"When I saw *l'homme*—the man—in his coat. Yes."

"You didn't identify him in the jail, did you? The guards had to have Jimmy paraded by you a second time before you said he was 'the man'—did they not?"

"I saw him. Yes."

Jimmy's lawyer pointed at Jimmy.

"You didn't, and then you did?"

Monsieur Lacroix sat, unsure of the question hidden in there.

"Am I wearing a green cravat, Mr. Lacroix?"

"Yes."

"No, Mr. Lacroix, I am not. My cravat is purple. *Aubergine*. And thank you for your service to the Crown, Mr. Lacroix."

"Step down, Mr. Lacroix. Step down—oh, show him," the judge said to his assistant.

The assistant led Monsieur Lacroix from the chair.

The lawyer returned to his desk and sat by Jimmy.

"I wouldn't want to hang a man on that testimony," Mr. Lacey said.

The newspaperman beside him said, "The frog's been gutted."

Monsieur Robitaille up and left, clearly angered by the whole proceedings. I wished that I'd told him I'd be appearing. I'd hoped for his support, at least.

Many spectators followed, sure they'd seen today's big show. Most everyone who stayed looked like they wondered what was for dinner.

Monsieur Lacroix took a freed-up seat between Monsieur Desbarats and a young lady. Lacroix was in a daze. He leaned his elbows on his thighs, put his head down into his hands.

The Prime Minister, from on high, exchanged a slight nod with Monsieur Desbarats.

I didn't have a chance to wonder what that was about.

I was up next. With my mind turned every which way.

"One more witness, your Honour," the court assistant said.

"Fine." The judge looked to the lawyers at both tables. "I'll have your summations on Monday."

The assistant motioned me forward.

Sergeant O'Neill looked gobsmacked as I walked past.

A guard set out a stool and I scuttled up to the high seat. Glanced over at Mr. Macdonald. He barely nodded. I took it as encouragement.

The room looked different from up here.

Jimmy stared at me like who was I, and friend or foe?

Bridie was smiling at Jimmy's lawyer.

"You saw a buggy—no, the outline of a buggy—or did you say the shadow of a buggy?" From up here, the Crown Attorney sounded like a preacher bellowing in the park.

"With your beloved employer lying right in front of you, half his head blown off, blood everywhere—you took the time to glance all the way down the street?"

He pulled at his lapels, as he paced and delivered this speech to the audience.

"Thank you, Miss, for telling us about this apparition that turned the corner to nowhere. Seen only by you, the one person who was somehow staring into the distance, not down at the greatest horror of your life. At a man whom you claim to, and certainly had reason to, admire."

I'd never felt a look more unnerving, not even Pierce's. Pierce—thank the Lord, he wasn't in the room.

". . . and, heaven help us," the attorney said, finally, "may I assume that's all you claim to have seen, the day Mr. D'Arcy McGee was murdered?"

He wasn't even facing me. And while he was pretending to ask me a question, no one believed that. Any more than they believed me.

I answered anyway.

"No."

He pounced. "You didn't see this ghost buggy, is that what you're saying now?"

"I did see it."

"Miss Swift, do you have any reason to think that anyone other than Jimmy Whelan was on the street that night?"

"I didn't say any such—"

"Precisely. You saw nothing."

"No. I saw that buggy drive round the corner of O'Connor . . ."

At that, Bridie fixated on me. And she was smiling.

". . . and later, that the manuscript was missing."

Monsieur Lacroix had raised his head, to give me a nod in sympathy. It may be the man couldn't make out my meaning, but he understood the feeling in my voice.

"What story can you possibly be claiming at this point, Miss Swift?"

"I believe Mr. McGee would've kept a copy. I've been thinking about it . . .. There were twice as many pages on his desk, as were in the package he sent off in the London pouch."

The attorney gestured toward the jury. "A book. The man was murdered—a cold-blooded assassination—and you want to tell these good men about a piece of literature? Your Honour—"

He was stopped by a slight cough, emanating from the dais on the other side of the judge.

I was shamed that the Prime Minister had seen me so reduced.

His cough made the difference, though. The judge leaned toward me, and the attorney had to as well.

"We'll hear out this witness, Counsellor," the judge said.

The attorney stood. "Very well, Miss Swift. Mr. McGee was missing one of his books, as well as the back side of his head. Is that it, then?"

"A book he'd written all about himself, and politics."

The judge looked over at Mr. Macdonald, then leaned toward me. "Do you know what was in the book, Miss?" the judge asked.

The Crown Attorney choked back a laugh. "With all due respect, Your Honour. How would a housemaid have any idea—"

"My housekeeper knows every inch of my home, down to when I need to order new writing paper," the judge said in reply. "Let's hear from the girl. Little lady, how does this book have a bearing on McGee's shooting?"

So, it counted even here to be a good housemaid.

"He told me he was very het up against the States in the book, Your Honour, Sir," I told the judge. "That it would cause a stir. *Hot*, he kept saying."

"Did you happen to read any of this book?"

Mr. Macdonald tilted his head.

"Nobody in Canada had a chance—"

"So there's nothing." The Crown Attorney jumped in. "Nothing to see, nothing to read, nothing you can tell us. Step down now, girl."

The judge hit his gavel at that. "That's for me to—"

Pierce walked in, Willy and a few others behind him.

Willy stopped cold when he saw me. Then he went over and whispered something to Mr. Lacey.

With a wave of a hand at the judge, Mr. Macdonald stood, stepped down from the dais and crossed quickly to Pierce.

As they conferred in low tones, the judge noticed I was standing on the stool that had been put there to help me in and out of the witness seat.

The judge waved me off. "Oh, you may as well go now, Miss."

The Crown Attorney looked at his notes. He put up a hand to stay me. "Your Honour, she's still under oath, for all that's worth. May I?"

The judge frowned. He was more interested in why the Prime Minister was off chatting to Pierce.

"Fine, fine, Counsellor," he said.

"Miss Swift, you were also a maid at the McGee house last New Year's Eve?" He turned toward the jury. "The night we've been told that Jimmy Whelan tried to bomb that house?"

The crowd stirred.

"In point of fact, you answered the door to him that night?"

I was still standing on the step stool, arms braced against the witness chair to keep my balance.

I started to boost myself back up.

"Miss. There will be no need for you to sit." I stumbled at his condemning tone. "We now know all we need to."

Jimmy's counsel had no questions for me, once he'd canvassed the jurors' faces. The Crown Attorney, connecting me to the bomb scare, must've made them all think I'd been spinning a roaring good yarn.

That, and Bridie's smile.

"No. Thank you, Sergeant," I said. "I'll walk. I need some air."

"I'll bet you do. But Nancy needs you back at the house. Along the way, I need an explanation for this"—he motioned to the witness box.

"O'Neill," Pierce called.

Thank our Lord Jesus, Pierce was waving the sergeant over to a gathering of coppers and militia.

"Hold on then, Clara," Sergeant O'Neill said. "Don't go anywhere."

"I'll walk home, Sergeant." But I said it too low for him to hear.

Home. That was a laugh and a half.

"Don't you set off without me," he called back.

I followed the laggards out onto Daly Street.

Willy was there, listening to his hero, Mr. Lacey. The editor nodded toward me, like Willy was to fish out the real story behind my testimony.

I scurried past them—but Willy soon caught me up.

"Where is Ma, then?" Willy said.

"I imagine you'll find her at your home."

"Doing your work?" Willy said. "Mr. Lacey says the judge and jury weren't buying your words, Clara. You'll have people thinking you slammed the door on McGee on purpose."

"'Twas your mother who told me to do so."

"Ma's too soft on you by half."

"I earn my keep."

"What about the time you spend holed up—first in McGee's old room, now in your own?"

"Go keep the sergeant company, Willy," I said. "As your ma's not here."

"What'd you say?" Willy grabbed for my elbow.

"She enjoys his visits often enough."

"She's taken you in." He strained to keep his voice low. "You're her—our servant, Clara." Willy slapped my cheek.

I stepped back, eyes tearing. When I raised my face, Willy slapped my other cheek.

"Leave my mother be," he said. "Or—"

I jerked away from him, and ran.

XIX

I'd lose my job. My place. I'd been likely to anyway. But now—

I never should have said it of his mother, no matter the consequence to me. He was right. She'd kept me when it wasn't easy.

It was too much to go and face her. Not yet.

I kept moving. North on Nicholas Street, away from the courthouse. Away from Trotter's. Across Rideau Street and west. Out of Sandy Hill, over to the Byward Market Square near French Lowertown. It was still early enough—the market was safe, but I had been warned never to go walking in Lowertown after dark.

At the market, I landed straight in the midst of the Fall Fair. Ottawa was doing it up big this weekend, with booths and games of chance at the market, sport competitions, even an archery championship over at Major's Hill, to the west above the canal. People in the courtroom had been talking of the fun to be had, come Friday night—spectators, that is, whose lives didn't rotate around the trial.

Lady Macdonald stood a ways off, with a young miss and a cow. The girl must have won Dairy Princess. Must Lady Macdonald watch her do the milking before she gave her the prize?

"Imagine M'Lady on the three-legged stool, pulling on those udders." A loud woman was laughing at her own joke, at M'Lady's expense. People shifted around where she stood and I could see the face that matched her familiar voice.

Hannah, walking arm in arm with her Mike. So he did get sprung after he testified against Jimmy.

She had a rash on her cheeks and chin.

"Clara, quit with your staring," she said. "It's only beard burn." She stroked Mike's arm. "From too much kissing, you gosling." The way Hannah was smiling, she didn't choose to remember the words we'd had in court. "Don't look like that, Clara, we did it—we're married. Mike, this is my young chum Clara Swift—the girl I've mentioned."

"You married already?" So Hannah had managed it.

"Mike got out night before last, thanks be," she said.

Of course, right after that testimony of his.

"Like I said," Hannah said, "I had something better to do than be sitting in court. After Mike had the chance of a good wash and a good eat, we married. Yesterday morning."

Hannah was the cat who'd claimed the cream, all right.

"Nobody knows but the priest," she said. "Oh, and Mike's sister and brother, they were the witnesses. We even convinced them to give over their place to stay, and bunk with the neigbours. Now I've sent a note of warning to Uncle Eamonn—if he wants me back there and working, he'd best move a bigger bed into my room."

Mike didn't look any too happy, for a man just wed. He took out a hankie, and wiped a runny nose.

"Can you believe he's come down with jailhouse flu just as he was released?" Hannah said. "And not a sick day in all those months locked up. We'll have a *céilide* once my husband's better—Tuesday, after the fair. How's that, Mike?"

After the trial, she meant. After the sentencing.

"Let's wait until some other lads are out of lockup, Hannah." Mike looked around then, as if it may not be good news to see some lads he knew.

"Come with us then," Hannah said. "Don't lag along, Clara. Be happy for me."

Mike pulled Hannah toward a tintype portrait-maker, who was handing out his cards.

"We should make a date with him, Hannah. I need a new photograph of my girl, after 'losing' that, and almost everything else, in that jail. Just in case."

"You don't need to go anywhere, Mike."

"That's not what I'm hearing from the St. Patrick's Society. I may have to go to the States. For a while at least." There was sweat on Mike's forehead.

"All right," Hannah soothed him, "though I don't have that sweet hat with the ribbon streamers anymore."

At that moment, a collie dog ran toward us at top speed. A chalk sandwich board had been tied to his neck, and he was dragging it behind him. The dog was crazed that he couldn't shed the sign.

"Hannah," I called.

The collie veered left. The sign hit a man in the back of both knees. The man, in quick succession, hit the ground, hard, landing on his backside. The dog kept running, sign in tow.

Hannah pulled Mike in the opposite direction.

"C'mon, Clara," she called.

I hurried to the man instead.

"Oh, she's in one of her moods," Hannah said, her voice now coming from behind me. "Well, she's not dragging us down tonight, Mike." She called to me as she walked away. "You need to be smiling at our *céilidh*, Clara."

Another man was ahead of me, already bent down to help the dog's victim.

The downed man leaned on his helper. Rose, and dusted himself off.

I shivered from the dog's speed, the man's fall, the fact that fate had felled him . . . and yet saved him from serious harm. I shivered from what I'd seen that day. From what I'd done. From what I'd find at the place that had been my home these nine months.

The men stepped around me, and were off. Together, talking like old friends.

I looked around, to find that I'd moved into the middle of the fair vendors. Rows of booths lined half of the square.

In the midst of this rumpus, I saw Monsieur Lacroix. A group of lads and Frenchies were plying him with drink. Lacroix already looked ready to fall back without the aid of any collie. He grabbed a water jug from the booth, and tipped it over his own head.

The man doing the pouring came around from behind at that. "You lot shouldn't have bought him all that strong whiskey. He's used to watered-down *vin de table*."

"*Il buvait comme un trou.*" One of them raised a glass and curled his lips like a fat fish and they all laughed.

"Someone take Lacroix to his wife before he lands in my lap. Or knocks over my booth."

None of the lads was willing.

"Lacroix?" said another. "Forget him. *Il ne sait rien faire de ses dix doigts, celui-là.* Useless, even when he isn't drunk. Now his wife, her I have time for."

"You'll get nowhere with her," said the pie-man. "She's too loyal to him by half."

I moved toward Monsieur Lacroix and asked the crowd, "Where is she, Madame Lacroix?"

"Métis," the meat pie man said. "Selling the beaded hides. Her booth's behind us, a few down." He pointed wildly. "She's the only one in that aisle with skins. Makes clothing from them, and moccasin slippers."

"You're going to let the girl do it?" a feeble old man asked the younger lads.

"I think I saw them in court together—this one and Lacroix," one of the lads said.

"Then she won't want to meet his wife," another said, and earned a big whooping laugh from the bunch of them. I had made myself the object of these jokers' amusement.

I put one of Monsieur Lacroix's arms around my shoulder. "Is your wife this way then, Monsieur?"

He squinted. *"Vous êtes un ange."*

He managed to balance himself as we turned into the aisle the pie man had pointed to, which was for the best. Small as he was, he still outsized me, and he could have taken us both down.

I spotted a beaded pair of moccasin boots hanging from a pole.

A young woman's eyes, though, were what captured me. 'Twas uncanny. They were just that peculiar shade of sea blue that I thought I'd seen the last of when Gram died.

Her dress and apron were made of a fine, unbleached cotton, and she had a long, beautiful black braid, hanging over one shoulder. That plait put me in mind of Miss Frasa McGee's thick black hair. Miss Frasa, she always kept her braids tightly pinned up—even that one time I'd seen her at night.

The young lady hurried forward. She eased her husband from my shoulder to her own. "Jean-Baptiste, *Mon Dieu,* you were to buy me a pie. *Merci—Mademoiselle?"*

"I'm Clara. You're Madame Lacroix?"

"They let you do this alone?" she said. "They're know-nothings, those men." She eased him around the chair and to the back of the booth. *"Je m'appelle Suzanne.* You're Irish, *oui?* Could you spread this hide, Mademoiselle Clara?"

I tossed it to the ground. Mr. McGee had spoken of the *Métis* people as living out West.

"Jean-Baptiste, aide-moi."

Lacroix smiled a wet smile at his wife, and stumbled to his knees. Then he rolled onto his back. Like he slept on a hide in public every evening.

"Mon pauvre mari. They should have let him tell his truth *en Française."* Suzanne said. "You know that," she turned to me. "You spoke after Jean-Baptiste."

"I didn't—it wasn't the way the barrister made it sound—"

"Nous comprenons tout," she said. "That's exactly what happened to Jean-Baptiste."

"But your husband said the wrong colour clothing. He didn't describe anything right," I said. "Mr. McGee's clothing, nor Whelan's."

"Would you notice a man's clothing when there was a *coup de feu?"*

What had Mr. Macdonald worn, when I looked out of Mr. McGee's window that night? A hat? A topcoat?

"Not so well, Suzanne," I said.

"And Jean-Baptiste is always saying *aubergine* is *vert.* His colours aren't the same as yours or mine."

Lacroix spoke up, without opening his eyes. *"Dîtes l'histoire de l'ange—le petit agneau."*

Suzanne Lacroix smiled. "He's right; you did look like a little lamb walking, all unknowing, to a slaughter. Both of you did. *Tu en es sûr, Jean-Baptiste?"*

He raised an arm. *"Dîtes-lui."*

She looked around; nobody was anywhere near the front of her booth. "Jean-Baptiste saw that Irishman," she said.

"He saw Jimmy Whelan?"

"Oui. Then there was a shot. He ran, as any sensible man would."

"And he didn't tell anyone?"

"Aside from me? Any sensible man wouldn't," she said. "And then he went out and he drank. Everyone was talking of the murder. And so he told. To be sorry ever since, for having done so. And today, *c'était incroyable*—what they asked of him."

She reached to pat his belly. "It's no wonder he's this way tonight. To not be able to speak it the way he wanted. Jean-Baptiste's English is not like mine. Maybe it's because I already have two other languages and he only the one."

"What would he have said, in French?"

From the ground, her husband answered. *"Il était là, dans la rue. Qui a tiré le pistolet, je ne sais pas."*

"He never saw," she said.

"Was Jimmy Whelan alone?" I said.

"He was alone," Madame Lacroix replied. "But Whelan wasn't holding a gun when Jean-Baptiste saw him. And the shot, it came a few minutes later."

"So he doesn't know," I said.

"Non. Jean-Baptiste told me the lawyers, they were tinged brown when they spoke to you. When they talked to him, they were smoky black. What could he do in that *atmosphère.* He knew they didn't want to hear him."

I looked at him, then her. He had no reason to think me anything but a servant. A servant who had been disgraced in court, same as he had. I was not someone whom he needed to lie to.

So Monsieur Lacroix had seen a man he believed to be Jimmy.

"What did he look like—Jimmy?" I said. "I mean—not the way he was dressed. Did he look angry?"

"Il était plein de peur," he said.

"He told me the man was sweating fear," Suzanne told me. "Not anger." She turned to stroke one of her hides. "My husband needs rest, *ma belle.* As do you and I."

Lacroix had passed out.

"Doubtless," I said.

A couple almost stopped to look at the moccasins. Lacroix groaned from the rug and they backed away.

She had dresses, vests, all hanging for show. All sewn inside-out, with beading on the skin. I ran my fingers over a pair of gloves. Squirrel. Decorated with lilies and green leaves. "Beautiful," I said.

"The nuns teach us when our fingers are big enough to hold a needle," Suzanne said. "Try them."

"I couldn't—and gloves are always too large for me."

"Put your hand against mine." She raised her right hand in the air—I didn't want to be rude. I raised mine, and pressed.

"No, *de rien* in your size," she said. "I'll trace your fingers, and make up a pair for you. No money."

"I can pay." I'd done every other careless thing today, why not spend money?

"You know your letters?" She nodded. "Monsieur Robitaille told us in court that you write things out."

"I used to."

"I would like to write a letter *en vrai anglais*. I have a niece in a school with the nuns near the Red River. I want her to live with us." She tossed a shoulder. "As you see, I'm not so busy. I'll finish your gloves by Sunday afternoon."

"I don't know if I can come back here this weekend," I said. "I could bring my writing tools Tuesday." After the court decision . . .. If I still had my few things. I could be out of a job, my trunk seized, if Willy told . . ..

"I like to work outside," Suzanne said. "I'll be by the canal, if the weather allows. At the lock below Major's Hill. You want the beading to be *les fleurs de lis, comme ca?*"

"Could you make a Celtic knot?" I said.

"*Bien sûr.* We'll trade."

"You're sure you've no Irish in you at all, Suzanne? You've got an uncommon resemblance . . . to our old folk."

"I know my mother's story better than *mon pere's. Maman* always said that he was *pure laine.*" She shrugged. "With French and Irish tribes settling in Catholic Quebec, *c'est possible . . ..*"

"Suzanne, I'm mixed-up too; half-Protestant, and that half really English at heart. And I'm not an angel—or a lamb."

"You're a lamb of God's flock, dear."

Be that as it may, at least I wasn't walking into the next slaughter blind. I knew what I had coming to me.

XX

I left the fair while the streets were still safe for a girl, and spent the rest of my evening hours sitting by the canal. I wouldn't have thought of it as a place to linger but for Suzanne Lacroix. The drunks and hobos stayed at the fair, and I was blessedly alone. When the tower bell rang half past one o'clock in the morning, I crept back to Trotter's. I'd left my window open a crack because of the heat, so I was able to tumble into my bed.

Five hours later, when I heard Mrs. Trotter stirring overhead, I grabbed a roll and cheese, and headed over to clean up the *Times*. It would be a chore for me to do any work today. Yet when you've no choice, your body rises with the sun even if it hasn't rested with the moon.

The scribes wrote the words for the *Times* upstairs, then walked their pages downstairs to be set on paper by a devil of a printing machine. Six engineers manned the machine, polishing all around as they inked and oiled, leaving only a bit of sweeping and the privy for me to deal with down below. Upstairs I mopped and dusted, then set straight the rats' nests the writers made of their desks. I dared not touch Mr. Lacey's desk, as that could get me fired.

Out-of-town reporters had been dropping in evenings all this past week. They came to chew over the characters of those who'd turned up in the witness chair at Whelan's trial. Mr. Lacey poured his liquor for all and sundry. He hoped one of them would spill some news, but the best they served up in return was speculation. They all laughed over the testimony, the lawyers' antics and the judge's rulings. This past Tuesday night, even me scrubbing the floor had turned into a bit of amusement. The reporters teased me about taking up a seat on the court benches when bigger folks were in need of it.

As I climbed the stairs, I thought of Mr. Lacey's face after I'd said my piece on the stand yesterday. I must have provided entertaining material for last night's commentary. Perhaps I'd even be trashed in today's big weekend edition of the paper.

It was so much harder to clean here than at Trotter's. The printer's ink inched in everywhere. Not even lye soap would lift it, and my fingers raw from trying. To think Willy was jealous of my spending time here.

I'd laughed when he protested to his mother that I shouldn't be hearing the newsmen talk. Once a maid's dealt with one man's sheets, bathwater, and chamber pot, there's little any man can do to shock or shame her. Short of touching her person.

Whereas to know a man's mind, you look to his bookshelf. And listen closely while serving at table. Or dust his desk, and you've got him sorted. That was why Mr. Lacey didn't want me touching his.

Mr. Lacey was smooth as sealing wax, always. He started in asking little questions whenever I crossed his path. *"Did old D'Arcy ever tell you . . ."* or *"I wonder whether D'Arcy had any thoughts on . . .?"*

"Not that I'd chance to know, Sir," I always said in reply. I kept my head down, mop in hand. Nothing to see but the scrub maid.

I was doing my final polish, when a cane came tapping up the stairs. Mr. Lacey loved his blackthorn walking stick. "Make way for my *shillelagh*," he'd say. "My own little piece of *Éireann*." He had no need of it that I could see. Unless he'd used it as a weapon, on occasion, during his late-night journeys home.

"Ah, Clara. Quite the show you put on yesterday," he greeted me. "Never knew you for an actress."

As he crossed the room, his grey woollen satchel bumped against his belly. "Not that it was anything other than what we heard the night D'Arcy died. People had all sorts of stories that night, as you'll recall. But they've all boiled down to Whelan."

I didn't look up from my work.

"Give it over, girl." Mr. Lacey walked past me to his desk. "How is a man to work, with this fussing?" He knocked ashes out of his pipe into the cold tea in his mug.

"Sorry, Sir. It's my chance for a clean-up . . .."

"What do you have to tell me about your hijinks yesterday?"

"I said what I saw, sir."

He waited.

"Do you think it was only one man, sir?"

"That's all you've got to say about yourself?" he said.

"The men who killed Mr. McGee deserve the devil's own justice," I said.

"Willy does say you worshipped old D'Arcy," Mr. Lacey said. "D'Arcy was a saint to rights, was he?"

I didn't join in his smile. Mr. Lacey didn't respect anybody properly. It was always "Old D'Arcy"—and "The Old Man" for Mr. Macdonald, even, not John A. And politicians he didn't care for, they were "that idiot Howe" or "that old coot Cartier" or "the Yank Johnston" when speaking about the American president. Sly, it was. Laughing at better men and all they'd done in the world. I couldn't see him saying such to their faces. At the trial this week he'd had his pencil down scribbling every move Mr. Macdonald made.

I picked up my rags and moved to the near windowsill.

"Here's a story about Saint D'Arcy," he said.

I swiped at the window dust.

"Clara. Look over here." Mr. Lacey nodded, satisfied. "D'Arcy knew my desk well enough. Why one night, 'twasn't more than a year ago, he slept here."

I slid a look over to the settee near the door. It was big enough for me, but no man, not even Mr. McGee, could have a comfortable laydown there.

"Oh, no, Clara, not over on the settee." Mr. Lacey followed my eyes. "He wasn't so high and mighty as that, our D'Arcy." He stopped smiling. "Our fine orator was on a spree that night. With our Prime Minister. Of course, they had heavy matters to ponder, such as signing us all away from the Crown."

Mr. Lacey looked down at the desk. "Ah, but D'Arcy wouldn't let a fine story get away from him like this. He'd spin it to a gossamer shine. He never had a good word for my style of telling tales."

"He never said a word about you, I swear, Mr. Lacey."

His face didn't like that fact, either. He patted the oak wood. "Does this look like a downy bed for our fine Parliamentarian? Not a bit of leather on top to soften it. Yet our man D'Arcy tossed up here one night—one morning, sure it was—and laid himself out here as stiff as a marble effigy."

I lowered my eyes and raised two fingers to my forehead, then above my heart.

"Oh, she's Signing the Cross at me now. I shouldn't have phrased the truth so plainly, Clara. Yet the truth 'tis. You do know he liked a tipple."

I busied myself folding my rags, ready to stow them away.

"None more at home with a drink, excepting of course old Macdonald. When they were on the town, D'Arcy would sing to John A.'s tunes on the piano—no matter if anyone wanted to listen. The only difference between them when they were rousting about was John A. always made it home to his own bed. Come over, girl."

This last was an order.

"You've been wanting to neaten this pile," he said. "Now's the moment. Come over."

I walked to his desk, head down. Tossed the ash-filled tea in my slop bucket. Pulled out his top middle drawer and swept in chewed-down pencils and pen nibs. "Should I deal with your papers, Sir?"

"You can put them on the floor while you polish the desk." He patted his satchel. "I'll need a clean space to pile these papers."

I shifted his papers to the floor, and dug into my basket for my hemp wax. I polished with a circular motion to bring up the wood grain until the dry oak shone.

Mr. Lacey watched, as closely as he watched Mr. Macdonald in court.

Suddenly, he'd had enough. "Pack up, girl," he said. "With this heat, my papers could soak up that much wax, and be ruined."

I shuffled his books and notes and old newsprint pages back on top of the desk, arranged in neat piles.

"Leave room, Clara," he said. He sat his satchel on the chair. "Here we go."

The pages he pulled out of his bag were handwritten, on lined foolscap, with a sharp-nibbed pen that had pierced the paper in a few places.

There was a tear in the page, where I had—"How did you come by my papers?"

I knew the answer, though. Willy.

My hand darted out. Mr. Lacey beat me to it. He flipped the satchel shut, and pulled it all the way over his shoulder, to rest on his backside.

"Your papers, is it?" Mr. Lacey was enjoying this. "Your handwriting, so I've been told. D'Arcy's words. And well worth publishing. He's telling tales on himself here, and on others. Big men. No wonder he wrote the originals in code. I've rarely read the like. Not since reading St. Augustine's *Confessions*. Or the new book by that British priest, Newman."

"*Apologia Pro Vita Sua*," I said.

"Apology for a man's life, indeed. 'Tis a chronicle of all the mistakes of D'Arcy's youth, before he came back to the church at the last. What was D'Arcy about, writing this? He's set himself up in these pages to be a saint in the making.

Doomed, like the Irish heroes he eulogised so well. A prophet of his own tragic ending. Is there a whole book of this malarky?"

"That's not his book." Mr. Lacey had six inches and a hundred pounds on me. I couldn't see how to rush him.

"With what he's said here about Brown, Howe, and Johnston—calling the President the money behind the Fenians—D'Arcy built up quite a heat against President Johnston, before he was killed." Mr. Lacey stepped backward and moved to the doorway, watching me.

"That's not his book," I repeated. "That's only from his—private— notebooks."

"If they're so private, how'd you come by them?" He patted his satchel. "You can take down my words now, Clara, if you want. Nobody in London is talking about D'Arcy's book being published. I've checked. If John A. has a copy, he's not flashing it about anywhere. And I've eyes very close to the government."

He picked up his walking stick. "These papers are as close as we're going to get to hearing from him beyond the grave. I'm going to publish on Tuesday. With the verdict coming down, it gives us the best chance for a big print run. And if you have any more of D'Arcy's work, Clara . . .." He shook the stick at me. "Remember, he's not the one who's employing you now."

I lifted my eyes to meet his. I worked for the man, yes. And I needed the work. More than I did yesterday.

But he wasn't my Lord and Master.

XXI

I was becoming good at this tumbling onto the bed—I'd left the window open wider, which helped. And I was just in time. Only a tick after I made it inside, I heard Sergeant O'Neill's knock on the kitchen door.

Mrs. Trotter hurried into the room and across to answer it.

"I'm glad you're so much better, Nancy," the sergeant said.

But she didn't invite him in.

"What the dickens do you mean, Tommy O'Neill?" she said instead. "I've been het up all day and night. Clara's gone missing, and it turns out Hannah disappeared as well, she's been missing for three days. Follow me down to Docherty's, I need see if Eamonn's managed to find out anything—"

"No, Nancy, you need to hear this—"

"Then you'll have to tell me as we walk, Tommy."

The door slammed.

The flannel sack from the laundry room closet was now bunched up on my pillow, empty. So Willy had taken the McGee Bible too.

No, not quite empty, I found when I picked it up. My single page of thoughts and memories was still inside the sack. I'd composed it on Thursday, after my conversation with Mr. Macdonald. While plotting how to get out of the house to testify . . . .. I'd been stunned by how hard it was to write my own truth, so it was just a few notes . . ..

At the bottom of the page, Willy had written a note of his own. *"Thanks for the scoop, and my first newspaper story."*

I'd go to Father Clement, and see if anyone needed help—on a farm, maybe even at the nunnery. I pulled my kitbag from my shelf, my clothing from the knobs on the wall.

Out in the alley, Sergeant O'Neill was relaying the sad tale of my sins against him, her, and the memory of Mr. McGee. "When Clara Swift does show her face here, she'll have to be let go, Nancy," he concluded.

"Maisie acted out at this age too," Mrs. Trotter said.

"She's not your own, Nancy."

"Don't I know that?"

Their voices were fading, as they walked away. They were about to find out about Hannah's marriage.

There was nothing for it. I'd best catch Mrs. Trotter, and use this moment to apologise. I pushed aside my kitbag and few belongings, and leaned right back out the window. "Mrs. Trotter," I called.

She stopped in the alley, and whirled round. "Why I never—Tommy, look."

I pulled my head back in, and sat on the edge of the bed, legs crossed. I didn't unpack, though.

Sergeant O'Neill didn't return, but Mrs. Trotter soon filled the doorway. Her eyes were on the kitbag. Her hands held the bible.

"Clara, you treat me as you did yesterday, that will get you dismissed."

"I'm just packing up now, Ma'am."

"You lie to the police, that can land you in jail."

"Is Sergeant O'Neill waiting for me now?" I reached for the bag.

"Clara, what is this about?"

I looked up. "I needed to tell my truth up there, on the stand. I couldn't have you stop me again."

"Tommy said you went on and on about that buggy nobody saw. And then that book. What do you mean with all this, girl?" She stroked the bible's leather cover. "Major Doyle thinks you worthy of bettering yourself—"

"Pierce is making me into a spy. I can't do it, I'm not cold like him—" My last words came out of my throat thick, like sobs.

Mrs. Trotter mistook my rage for weakness. She came and sat next to me on the bed, placing the bible between us. "No need for packing yet. But Clara—why have you stolen this sacred book?"

"Mr. McGee left me a book of my choice."

"Mr. McGee would never have given you leave to take the family's holy record. And well you know it," she said. She patted my hand, then opened the bible. "I know you've not had much family, Clara. But you must know. This holds the McGees' memories." She started to read, her finger running below the names listed.

> Dorcas, died at age three. Our Rose, taken from us by scarlet fever.
> Our son Tommy.

"She had to leave three children in Yankee graves, Clara. Three babes she could never visit. You can't imagine." She paused. "And she has one name still to write in here."

My tears ran, as it hit me that I had done a great wrong to Mrs. McGee, and to her girls.

"It must be weighing on you, Clara," Mrs. Trotter said. "Taking what belongs to another family."

"I'm sorry about what I said to Willy yesterday, too."

She shushed me. "Times like these make people forget themselves, lose track of what's right. Lord forgive all us sinners."

She closed the bible. "Mrs. McGee's coming to hear the judge announce Whelan's hanging, Tommy says."

I sniffled.

"It's providential," she said. "The Lord's given you your chance, Clara. To return this to the McGees. At little cost to yourself." She picked up the bible, and stood. "Now go feed the pig."

After supper, Mrs. Trotter posted a sign in the parlour bar window. CLOSED UNTIL MONDAY.

"I've made enough money this week from gawkers dancing on Mr. McGee's grave," she said. "This one Saturday night, I'm going to enjoy myself." And she went out with a few neighbourhood biddies, for an evening at the fair.

She'd planned to go with Willy, but he'd made himself scarce all day. He'd finally poked his head in for a minute, only to put her off. "Mr. Lacey's letting me work on a story—yes, I've eaten," he said. Willy didn't look my way. I didn't have nerve enough to challenge him, either. Not in front of her.

Monsieur Robitaille was dining out, and Bridie had asked for a tray delivered to her room. Mrs. Trotter and I had agreed that tonight was a chance for me to do a thorough cleaning. A small penance.

Though I feared that, barring Willy's forgiveness, a larger punishment was soon to come.

Still, I wanted to do my best job for Mrs. Trotter. And the room certainly needed a going-over. All this past week, dust had been blowing in the windows something fierce, and sticking where it landed.

The weather had turned the day the trial started. Muggy, and yet so windy bytimes. Indian summer, Mrs. Trotter called it. 'Twasn't anything like autumn weather in Ireland, for sure. Or even what I'd experienced the year before in Montreal.

Mrs. Trotter didn't have to worry about gawkers tonight, it turned out. The street was as quiet as I could remember. I didn't see or hear a soul as I made the room shine, every window, table, stool and floorboard.

I left the bar for last. Polished the counter, the stools, the brass hat hooks screwed below the lip by the barstools. Then moved the bottles and wiped down the mirror that helped the bottles catch the light, and the customers' eyes.

The bottles had a sweaty film, a grit made from ash and horse droppings. As I set them in place I ran my finger across each one, as if they were holy wine and me in charge of the blessing.

A waning moon appeared in the sky as I rubbed each bottle clean.

Tomorrow I'd have to beg Willy for mercy. Eat his dirt if need be.

I opened the boarders' cupboard, where their private bottles were kept. The only one shiny clean was Mr. McGee's brandy wine. He'd kept it here for guests. Since his death I'd been drinking from this bottle, refilling it from the cask in the root cellar that Mrs. Trotter hadn't bothered to return to Mrs. McGee.

I needed to think, but first I needed to sleep. I lifted Mr. McGee's bottle of sin onto the bar. Uncorked it. Raised it to my nostrils, and inhaled. I no longer choked at the strong sweetness, like I had back in April.

My head tilted and I let it pour straight into my gullet, not caring that it trickled outside my lips. I sank to my knees behind the bar and put the bottle on the floor between them.

I welcomed the heat, and a harsh tang of metal. A lick of honey, and blackberry, and the sourness of rising bread dough. The magic that let me sleep without dreams. My Gram had said liquor was a sorcerer's poison that let you live only if you kept on drinking it. I couldn't feel its power yet, so I lifted my elbows for another long, burning gulp.

Gram must be wrong about this as well as about Catholics marrying Protestants. A jug of yeast and rotted fruit couldn't be able to swallow a person's will and hold it captive.

I set the bottle back in the cradle of my knees. Dusk had set in and my sense of where my body pressed against the floor was blurring.

What was clear: I was a thief, if not yet a drunkard. I'd unearthed Mr. McGee's words, but they weren't mine to resurrect any more than they were Mr. Lacey's. If he published the worst of them, I couldn't make that mess clean.

I supposed there was a grand justice to this. But I didn't think Pierce would laugh at the joke. The very thought of Pierce, right now, made it hard for me to breathe.

The wood floor was sticky with heat and the residue of spilt spirits. I corked the still-heavy brandy bottle. Mr. McGee had birthed the idea for this country while on the bottle. He'd written that down, proud. He'd confessed to taking a nip on his way to meet the Pope. And when he couldn't face his problems, he'd written, well, the drink helped then too.

I'd poured drink on my problems, but the sick feeling was still there.

If I could stand on a chair, and reach all the way up to Mr. McGee's volumes of works, there was one where he wrote about how to stop drinking . . .. I pulled myself along the floor, then up the side of the bar. I even managed to place one stool on top of the other.

But when I tried to climb on top the both of them, to reach Mrs. Trotter's display shelf, I fell flat. The stools fell beside me. I was lucky one of them didn't bean me.

As it was, I had to sit still a while, before I could move without retching.

Then I went back behind the bar, scooped up Mr. McGee's bottle, and carried it with me out to visit the piglet.

She looked even sweeter, in the gloaming. Her tail curled three, no . . . four times round my little finger. She was the colour of . . . a red brick? No, this little lady piglet was of softer stuff, and the shade of her coat shifted with the light . . . and the movement of the muscles underneath. She was as lovely as linen, dyed with madder root.

She bit at my finger, I had to pull it back quick.

"Oh sweetling, I know you'd like a treat," I cooed at her. "But I'm not sharing any more of myself today."

Sunday was a blur of fear, and headache, and Mass, and preparing for Sunday dinner. Then serving it, and scraping it, and washing dishes, all on a sick stomach.

Willy went to the newspaper before Mass and didn't come out all day. Or night. I tried to let myself into the *Times*, but they'd double-locked the door on me.

I finally caught him on Monday morning, as he made his way across the street to the boarding house.

"Let me go inside my own home, Clara," Willy said.

I followed him in, and up to his bedroom door. I waited until he came back ten minutes later. He'd put on clean clothing without bathing. His eyes were as red as I felt mine must be.

He pushed past me, but I stayed close, down the stairs and out the door.

He re-crossed the street, and rapped on the *Times* door.

"Willy, I'm sorry for what I said. I never should have," I said, keeping a respectful distance.

"Say it's not true."

"It's not true."

"You say that 'cause you want the papers back."

"Mr. McGee wrote them for himself," I said, "—not even his family."

"You've no more right to them than I do, then."

"You're right."

Mr. Lacey unlocked the door, then headed up the stairs without a word.

Willy had his hand on the knob. "Step away, Clara."

"Did you tell your ma, Willy?"

"She knows I've a big story." He turned the knob. "It's a Special Edition, we're printing it extra to sell at the courthouse tomorrow."

"Did you tell her what I said?"

He went inside.

"Willy."

I grabbed for the door. But even at thirteen, he was the stronger one.

Mr. Lacey should've gone to court on Monday for the lawyers' talk to the jury. If he did, I didn't catch him going.

And when I did see him, I thought, as I watched the building from the street
. . .. I didn't know how I could wear that man down. Now, if I could get to Willy
again . . ..

No, I'd tell Pierce, as soon as we arrived at court.

"Clara?" Mrs. Trotter found me outside, staring at the newspaper window,
while Sergeant O'Neill finished breakfast. "I told Tommy I'll not waste a day
listening to those legal men repeat themselves."

"We're not going to the trial today?"

"We'll be there tomorrow, for the sentencing."

Bridie came out the front door, to walk to the post house for her ride. She
stared over, like she knew something was going on between me and Mrs. Trotter.

For a moment, I had a wild thought that I could summon Pierce to the newspaper, by sending a note by way of Bridie Whelan.

Then I realised how wrong my thinking was. As if Bridie would run an errand
for me. To help me contact the man she'd already figured out was my spymaster.
Even if I explained it wasn't about her, Bridie would hardly care. What was the
McGee family's embarrassment compared to her husband's fate?

And even if Bridie didn't toss such a note to the side of the road with a laugh .
. . Pierce, he'd think me such a fool . . ..

And then Bridie was gone.

My only hope lay, at it had for two days, with Willy.

I did my work as best I could, until noon, with one eye out the front window.

Mrs. Trotter didn't understand why I was so anxious about her son, even if he
was staying out night and day.

"Do you want me to fetch him for lunch?" I asked.

"No, leave him be. He said it's only until the trial's over."

"I'll take him some food then."

"All right . . .. I know you two have argued over something again, Clara.
Something you said, this time. But I'm sure he's forgotten about it, now he has
this chance to write a story."

So I went and stood outside the *Times* door yet again.

This time with a steak and kidney pie, and ginger beer in a jug.

Willy came to the window.

"Leave the food," he yelled. Then he drew down the blind.

I set both jug and pie plate, ever so carefully, on the sidewalk plank. Just in case. . ... And waited. And waited a little longer. While the food sat in the sun, and yet another blast of wind blew dust right at my face.

This stand-off meant Willy won.

It was down to Pierce, then.

I'd have to defy or lie to Mrs. Trotter again. And run all the way to court, and just hope that Pierce was there. No matter what Pierce said or did to me, he could stop them printing. . .

I heard the whirr of rollers pressing paper. It was too late for even a desperate measure.

XXII

Tuesday morning, Mrs. Trotter carried out the bible, wrapped in unbleached cotton, as she hadn't wanted to use the sack made from Mr. McGee's old flannel pants. She had it tucked into her largest wicker hamper.

Sergeant O'Neill took the basket from her cart and dropped it on my seat. I pushed my writing kit alongside it. There was no room for me.

Mrs. Trotter moved the kit to the floor, lifted the basket into her own lap, and pretended everything was fine.

"Why do you have your kit with you, Clara?" she said.

"A lady I met at the fair is to trade me—for gloves—if I copy out a letter."

"The fair's over, girl," Sergeant O'Neill said. "You've work enough to do— and lucky to have it."

"I won't take long. Promise, Mrs. Trotter."

"For what that's worth." Sergeant O'Neill steered his team onto Nicholas Street.

"Would you look at the rubberneckers?" Mrs. Trotter said, as we pulled closer to the courthouse.

People were gathering outside, to be among the first to hear the news. A lot of them were holding fresh copies of the *Ottawa Times*.

I jumped out as Mrs. Trotter asked Sergeant O'Neill to keep hold of the bible, as the hamper was too large to fit under the spectator benches.

After I heard him reply that she shouldn't let me go trotting off after the verdict. How I was above my place, passing myself off as a scribe of some kind. And I didn't deserve such attention.

I supposed he was in the right of it.

All the talk in the courthouse anteroom was how the McGees must feel. I heard how 'that lovely Miss Frasa' had made the journey here with her mother.

They had both sat yesterday, listening to those lawyers hammer away at all the details of Mr. McGee's death. All day, making sure the jury saw them.

And today, they would see the gallery judging them by the newspaper gossip, and by their reaction to that gossip, even as they awaited the jury's judgment of Jimmy.

I both wanted and didn't want to look at the *Times*.

I saw Pierce, and knew I didn't have a choice in the matter.

His copy was tucked under his arm.

"Did you see your old boss made a fool of in here?" He tossed the rolled paper at me. It fell to the ground between us. "It's worth reading."

"Pierce—

"Read it all, Clara. Then you and I will have our talk."

Mr. Lacey had two stories. Together they took up the whole first page.

The first story was all about *McGee's secret, anti-American manuscript*. Mr. Lacey may have heard me mutter after all, because it was referred to as *McGee's Apologia*.

Mr. Lacey linked the book to the so-called *discovered diaries*. He detailed Mr. McGee's money troubles, his having so many fights with Mrs. McGee, his wife wanting him to leave politics, her angry he didn't spend time with their girls.

Mr. Lacey had written about the time Mr. McGee fell off the wagon, too—the lie Miss Frasa had told in front of the Prime Minister.

All the worst of Mr. McGee was there.

The second story I wasn't expecting. It suggested Mr. Macdonald wanted to convict Jimmy so he could let the McGee investigation slide.

Both stories said they were written only by Mr. Lacey. I found no consolation in the fact that Willy didn't garner any credit.

As I read, Pierce gained us early entry to the courtroom.

"I'm mad at myself," he said, once he had me alone. "For not seeing this coming. It's who you are, Clara. A pack rat. A Peeping Tom. The peeping I can use. The secreting of information for your own pleasure . . .. That's criminal behaviour, Clara."

"I just couldn't –"

"Couldn't let it go. Could you?"

I rubbed my eyes with my fist.

"None of that. Look at me," he said. "Look at me."

His eyes held no anger, no light in them at all. 'Twas the way he'd looked at Hannah, when they fought over Mike.

"I've let myself be fooled too many times by your learning," Pierce said. "You're little more than a child, to be taken in by a *cailleach* like Bridie, even while puffing up your own importance."

I was scared to bits, but I held his gaze, until he finally nodded that I could look away.

"Well, your precious McGee's diary's done its damage, girl," Pierce finally said. "I'll tell those who need to know how this bit of scandal got loose. For God's sake, don't go confessing to your priest, Mrs. McGee, or any other likely party. Those who don't need to know shouldn't be told, especially not to make yourself feel better."

I nodded, face to the floor.

"You should feel badly, Clara," he added. "And don't let that feeling fade any time soon. You little idiot, today of all days, you must have something to tell me about Bridie?"

I held out my single page of script. It was all I had to offer him, though it was only about Bridie laughing over the pig.

"That's all?" I asked.

Pierce pocketed the note. "Take a lesson from Mr. Macdonald, Clara—leave the spilt liquor on the floor, and look for the next watering hole."

"Then . . . that second story—?"

Pierce looked at the judge's dais. "Mr. Macdonald would string up as many rebels as he could, if any could be found responsible," he said. "You notice how nobody's talking about Whelan or Fenians today?"

He was right, all the talk outside had been of the McGees.

"They all know it won't take long," Pierce said, "for that jury to send Jimmy to the Ever After."

Pierce sounded like this was a Mystery Play, where an actor would be nailed up, then come out for his bows.

"Why?"

"'Tis simple enough," he said. "Trial law says they're to have no food or drink until they agree on his fate."

"They've had to sit up overnight?"

"No, they've had cots, and candles and kerosene lamps as needed. But with no food or drink to wet their tongues, we'll have a verdict. So they can have their breakfast."

And so we did. They let as many as they could in for the sentencing. My luck, a big boyo plopped in front of me. I had to lean way over the end of the bench, to see the whole of it.

The jury shuffled in; the judge and Mr. Macdonald took their places, Bridie took hers. Mrs. McGee came in last of all, with Miss Frasa following. They were guided to seats behind the Crown, which placed them in a strange alignment with Bridie.

The McGee women needed the guidance; both had the same black veils, hanging from the bonnets they'd worn to the funeral, still covering their faces and half of their silk dresses.

At least these dresses were summer-weight. I thought how black would hold in all the worst of the heat. Then I thought how silly I was to consider such a thing, at such a time.

Jimmy was brought in, a constable posted on either side of him, and one between him and the door.

For the first time, Jimmy didn't fix his eyes on Bridie. His eyes swept over Mrs. McGee, paused on Miss Frasa.

Then he fixed on the judge.

The juryman handed the piece of paper to the guard, who delivered it with all ceremony to the dais.

"James Whelan, you've been found guilty of the murder of D'Arcy McGee." The judge stared right back at Jimmy. "You will be held in the jail here until you are hanged by the neck until dead. Will you be wanting a priest?"

"Always happy to visit with a good Irishman like Father Clement," Jimmy said.

"Do you have something to say to Mr. McGee's family, Jimmy, before you make your peace with the Lord?"

"Wishing you and yours all the best, Ma'am, as ever I have." Jimmy's eyes shifted over to Miss Frasa again, though, not to Mrs. McGee.

Miss Frasa crossed herself, and clasped her hands in prayer.

Jimmy fixed his stare on the judge again. His look turned so wild, the judge motioned to the biggest of the guards. Then the judge shook his head, as if to clear it of Jimmy's menace.

"Take him to his cell, boys," the judge said.

The biggest guard pushed his kneecap into the back of Jimmy's right thigh. "March, laddie," the guard said.

"In my own time." Jimmy pulled out a heather-green woollen cap from his pants pocket, and placed it on with some ceremony.

Nobody dared cheer.

When Jimmy did start walking, his breath went quick and shallow. He stopped, and turned once more to the bench.

His words came in a loud rush. "Just because you say it, Judge, doesn't make it true."

Mrs. Trotter motioned me over to where she was listening to Sergeant O'Neill complain. "And we're not to get the extra bit of pay we've petitioned for," he told her. "After all the work we've done. . . .."

Mrs. Trotter looked as sorry as she would be if the money would have been coming to her own household.

I lifted the heavy hamper with both hands.

"Take your chance to apologise, Clara," said Mrs. Trotter. "You'll be glad of it, after."

Sergeant O'Neill escorted me to Mrs. McGee and Miss Frasa.

"Clara?" Mrs. McGee sounded like she wasn't sure 'twas me.

"I'm sorry," I said. "I brought you back your B—"

"Fine, thank you." She motioned for me to leave the hamper. If I did, I'd have to buy another for Mrs. Trotter.

Mrs. McGee looked over my head.

"Done is done," she said, addressing the Crown Attorney, who had stepped up behind me. "Thank you for justice. As for that other matter—at least now all of Parliament knows I'm close to losing the house," she told the lawyer. "They may make my widow's pension more generous—Excuse me, sir?"

She was addressing another gentleman now, the first of a line-up had formed to condole with her.

Miss Frasa lifted the lid of the hamper, and peeled off the flannel sack. She stared, suddenly struck, at the gilt lettering on the cover of the Holy Bible.

"Clara?" she said. "When I couldn't find this anywhere, I thought—I'd never be able to add Da's name. Thank you."

"Frasa, I'd like you to—" Mrs. McGee called, and motioned for her daughter to pay proper attention.

"Miss Frasa," I said. Curtseying, though no-one was looking.

XXIII

I was a block from the canal when Bridie called out for me from a fancy two-horse barouche.

"Clara—Clara. I saw you pack your kit today."

The driver had hopped out to check on his horses, but Bridie spoke to me from the window. "I need to deliver personal letters of appeal, today," she said. "To the courthouse. And to Parliament."

"I'm meeting up with—a friend," I said.

Suzanne Lacroix had her goods laid out on the canal bank's grassy slope.

"She's a friend of yours?" Bridie said. "The drunk's wife." Bridie wiped the sweat above her lip with her good lace hankie. "Well, aren't you a piece of work, after all?" she said.

The horses began to frisk and pull on the harness. "Hold over," Bridie called. She shook her head at me. "How can I trust what you write down?"

There were plenty of passers-by on this sunny late morning, enjoying the path that wound along the water route through town. But like at the fair, nobody was stopping to buy Suzanne Lacroix's goods.

"*C'est finis?*" she said as I reached her. "No—you're upset. We need not speak of it." She reached over, untied a hide purse, and showed me her handiwork. "Clara . . . try these on."

They were the first pair of gloves I'd ever had to fit. The Celtic knot was done in three colours of beading, each one looped back on itself in the triple knot of the Trinity. Green, blue, and purple.

"I've never had something—perfect," I said.

"They'll *gardent tes mains au chaud*. Even in an Ottawa winter."

I unpacked my writing things.

"Suzanne, what does *Métis* mean, exactly?"

"That my mother was Algonquin. This is her people's land we stand on. Ottawa is an Algonquin word, for 'the place where we trade'."

"How can Canada's capital city belong to a tribe?"

"French and English soldiers stuck their flags in our land. It's no less our land for their occupation. You should understand, you lost your land to the English."

"My da's family only arrived in Ireland two hundred years ago."

"Like you've arrived here now, to stake a place on my mother's soil," Suzanne said. There was a tease in her voice, and an edge to the tease.

"And like your own father's grandfather did, or his grandfather before him?"

"This is not my day to fight." She glanced down the canal.

Bridie sat on a rock on the bank.

"She wants letters written too," I said.

"Tant pis," Suzanne said. "Quickly then."

As I finished Suzanne's petition, I wondered if the nuns would have heard about her husband's behaviour at the trial. If so, even her fine sentiments may not bring her niece home.

When I gave her the envelope, she held onto my hand. "The gloves were a trade. I want to give you something more—for helping *mon mari* the other night."

"It's not necessary—"

"De rien," she said.

I chose a blue table runner with red beading. "I'm off to a wedding party," I said. "This will be grand."

"Non, I wanted to give you something for yourself."

"And so 'tis. Now I won't be blushing, to be the only one without a gift."

"You Irish have too much pride," said Suzanne. "Voila— "

A lad came cycling along the edge of a canal on a velocipede. The vehicle looked just like I'd seen pictures of in the *Times*. And he was grinning to beat all.

"What *métiers* will *les étrangers* use next, to invade?" she said.

I appreciated the laugh, even as I wondered how any grown man could be so light-hearted. He must be English, I thought. To have so few troubles. . . and the necessary bank notes.

Bridie's hack driver was drinking from a flask on the road, where Elgin Street bent back to meet Sparks. I never passed it, without thinking 'twas the last corner Mr. McGee had ever turned.

"Clara, I've no time to parse words," Bridie said. "I'm off for Montreal tomorrow."

She was giving up.

"I'll be back to see Jimmy, but—I need a rest from all of this. Once I've applied to the higher powers to save him."

Again, I helped a woman beg for succour for her kin. Bridie's letters were all the same—the witnesses had been bribed, Lacroix hadn't understood, the judge had been out to get Jimmy, there'd been no Irish Catholic jurors. Even that the defence attorney was a big Orangeman, which hadn't bothered her a whit until now. Particularly after he'd torn apart Monsieur Lacroix.

She sent a plea for a new trial to a Court of Appeal, and to the Attorney General—who happened to also be the Prime Minister.

"I've no faith in that man, of course," Bridie said. "But a new set of judges may see the truth—and the lies told."

"Do you want envelopes?"

"No, I'll have Jimmy's counsel read these over."

I realised at that moment that she was smart, not to trust me with the final words.

I'd written what she said.

But if I had to choose, I believed Lacroix.

I was in no mood for a party. So I walked slowly, stopping to pick up maple leaves from the grass along the canal. The colours were starting to turn. Last year I'd stared at the trees turning so red and orange in Montreal. Mr. McGee and I had talked about the wonder of them, of how back in County Louth, our old trees would just be gaining their full green after the summer rains.

Not that either of us had much time to enjoy the sights outside last fall. Mr. McGee had barely won the election—a year ago now—when he'd taken sick with the gout. I'd worked even more for him after that, while he'd done all he could from his sickbed. Occasionally, he'd nod off, then start awake after only a few moments.

He told me he dreamed over and over about the great Falls he'd visited, where Lake Ontario met Lake Erie. *"They're a sight that, once seen, can never be forgotten,"* he said.

I'd listened to his description, rapt—every word he said had such import.

Suddenly, it was a long time ago.

The wedding *céilide* was too quiet as I walked up to Docherty's tavern. There were voices, but no fiddle or singing. And lads hurrying in the opposite direction.

I added my table runner to the pile of presents at the door of the bar.

Sergeant O'Neill was at the entrance. "Is Nancy with you?" he asked.

Hannah saw me, and came running. "Clara," she said. "Mike's slipped away on me."

"To the States?" I said.

"I wish 'twere so," Hannah said. "He wanted to go to the U.S. but he didn't feel well enough to argue with me about it. And now he's gone and died on me—"

"He took a bad punch," Sergeant O'Neill spit in his hankie. "Twenty lads in this local and nobody saw a thing."

"I didn't know the man who hit him," Hannah said. "I thought him a chum of Mike's. Until he started in calling Mike a liar and a rat. He knocked Mike over, and was for the door."

"I'd never have thought Mike to be such a lightweight," said Hannah's Uncle Eamonn. "He fell back so quick. Had he already been into my liquor?"

Dr. Gillivray emerged from the back room.

"Your husband didn't die from the fall, Mrs. Walsh. He died from the fever, I'm afraid."

Hannah's uncle Eamonn looked sharp at that. "Fever?"

"You must have seen the rash, Mrs. Walsh?" Dr. Gillivray said to Hannah. "Your husband's all scabbed, where he'd been scratching."

"I knew he was sick—he didn't want to lie with me because of it. I was short with him about it too. So he did—but he wouldn't take his clothes off. So I didn't see him." I blushed for her, but she was beyond any shame in talking about the marriage act.

The doctor turned to the rest of us. "You need to go, and stay clear of here for a while. The tavern's closed until I say different."

"What kind of damnable plague is it?" said Eamonn Docherty. He seemed more distraught about losing business, than about Hannah's husband having passed away.

Hannah, however, was nigh on to collapsing.

I pulled her to me.

"Measles," said the doctor. "It's all over the jailhouse. Jimmy Whelan's one of the few who hasn't caught it." Dr. Gillivray patted Hannah's back. "Your husband will need to be buried quickly."

Sergeant O'Neill nudged me. "Take her to Nancy."

"You can have my room tonight," I said. "I'll sleep in the parlour. Tomorrow we'll have a room for you."

Mrs. Trotter and Willy were at Mass when Bridie Whelan took her leave that Wednesday morning. They'd gone special, to pray on Mike's account, while I'd stayed behind with Hannah. She was sleeping, but she'd been wailing and keening much of the night, and we had all agreed she shouldn't be left alone.

It was clear, when Bridie entered the kitchen, that she'd heard us all from her room, and knew well enough what had happened. And that she wasn't mourning Mike Walsh's passing.

I shouldn't have been at all surprised, but . . . she was so disdainful.

"We'll both be widows then," she said, with a nod to my bedroom door. "Mrs. Mike Walsh and me. Oh, I know what you all call me, the Widow Whelan."

"Not I."

"Well, that friend of yours has been calling me that," Bridie said. "She who's lost her lying man. And before I've lost my sweet Jimmy. That's some rough justice."

"Mrs. McGee's a widow too, Bridie," I said.

"And I have sympathy for Mary McGee," Bridie said. "Though neither she, nor your friend Hannah, either, have had any to spare for me."

Bridie left by way of the kitchen door. And I headed up to clean Mr. McGee's old room, yet again.

When I stepped out with the piglet's afternoon bucket of mash, Sergeant O'Neill and Mrs. Trotter were visiting down the garden path again.

"That little gilt needs branding," Sergeant O'Neill said. "What d'you want inked on her, Nancy? Your initials?"

"A cross?" Mrs. Trotter said.

"Ink her with a knot," I broke in. "Like this—" I pulled my gloves from my apron pocket.

"Fine beadwork," Mrs. Trotter said. "I've never seen any so fine, on squirrel skin."

"Clara shouldn't be inserting her opinion—"

Mrs. Trotter gave Sergeant O'Neill a big-eyed stare.

"All right, Nancy," he said. "I'll have the brander drop over next week and ink an Irish knot on the gilt's shoulder."

"I'll take the gloves in, Clara—lest you soil them with pig mash," Mrs. Trotter said.

They left me to the feeding.

"No, don't try to push your way out, you," I told the piglet. She bent her head to the bucket. Sergeant O'Neill was right. She'd grow to be a sow soon enough.

"I'll call you Sow." She grunted over her meal as I patted the smooth, russet hair along her pink spine. "That way, no one will know I've blessed you with a pet name."

HANGING

Sunday January 31st, 1869

XXIV

With Jimmy set to hang, Ottawa forgot about Mr. McGee.

Parliament was in session until November. Then Ottawa hollowed out again, as politicians headed for their families and their voters. Monsieur Robitaille kept his room and paid 'half-board' for that privilege. Woodmouse, Hedgehog and Bat packed their belongings, and made Willy lug their trunks up to the attic, so as to pay only a storage fee until they returned in April. Mrs. Trotter rented out those empty rooms for a few weeks at a time over the winter to logging foremen from the Valley, who came to town to spend their year's earnings. They weren't the kind Mrs. Trotter liked to house, but even four-flushers and lumberjacks could be customers as long as Father Clement vouched for them—and they paid in advance.

And even the lumberjacks wouldn't sleep in Mr. McGee's room.

So she also accepted Bridie's monthly visits, though she didn't welcome her. And even with the other rooms empty, Mrs. Trotter always directed Bridie to what everyone now called 'The McGee Room'.

I'd been writing regular reports for Pierce, noting everything Bridie said and did, for the little that it was worth.

I now wrote at the dining room table, with Mrs. Trotter's permission, though Willy carped about my having such a chance.

And I enjoyed the opportunity to get to know Jimmy's wife. I'm sure that shone through, when I repeated all Bridie's stories, faithfully.

In October, she told me how such an unlikely couple met—through a cousin, who'd known Jimmy's mother when they were girls back in Ireland; what a good tailor he was, how he'd sewn lace her late mother had tatted onto the most beautiful pearl gown for their wedding; how she'd cried like never before when Jimmy went for a visit to Ottawa and didn't come right home, and how he had assured her he'd be back by spring; how she was proud of him for marching next to Buckley in the St. Patrick's parade, as it showed how popular her lad had become in only a few months' time.

"He makes me happy, Clara," she told me during one of her trips. Then she thought a moment, and placed her joy in the past. *"I was happy."*

She had me read her all the letters Jimmy's mother had sent her, since before they'd even married. And I did start to teach her how to write her letters. It was funny, how Bridie couldn't make a proper little *d*, no matter how often she tried. It always came out backwards, so her name looked like it was spelled Bri*b*ie.

But she was ever so smart when it came to figures. Bridie could tote up any line of numbers quick as a flash. And count backwards, seven by seven and nine by nine, starting with 1869, all the way back to one. Like a party trick. When I wrote the numbers out long-hand and added them up, she was proved right.

These games cheered her up a bit, that first visit after the trial.

But the next month, Bridie told me how Jimmy's mother in Ireland had stopped writing to her. The elder Mrs. Whelan blamed Bridie for Jimmy's jailing. Bridie said that she understood. The poor woman must be beside herself, she said. One son imprisoned at home, and the other gone so far away, and now to lose his life.

She handed over the latest letter from her mother-in-law.

"Read this out, Clara," she said.

She pointed to the middle of the page, where it said,

> *I'll never see either of my sons again . . ..*

"But Bridie," I said, "how did you know which line on this page I should read?"

"Clara, I've had a different person read it to me every day since I received it," Bridie said. *"It's important folk know Jimmy's the son of a grieving mother, as well as a grieving wife."*

Every few weeks, Hannah would let me know Pierce was to drop by Docherty's. I'd go over and visit with her, until he arrived, so I could give him my written offering.

I always felt small when Pierce and I met, and the feeling had nothing to do with my size. Pierce never said boo about whether anything I'd heard from or noticed about Bridie, or my ideas about her, were of any value. Let alone if he'd shared them with Mr. Macdonald.

Once or twice he made the odd remark. When I'd recorded the story about their wedding, he said, *"Two big Fenians stood as their witnesses."*

Mostly, Pierce just shoved my notes in his pocket, and downed his ale or whiskey.

He didn't ever say he wanted me to report in more regularly. Mrs. Trotter did once mention, though, how Major Doyle was sending her small payments to add to my wages, every now and then.

Mrs. Trotter and Willy didn't take their long-planned winter visit to her sister's family in Toronto. Mrs. Trotter had her own reason for staying in town, but I was so grateful for the job I didn't so much as look askance at Sergeant O'Neill's visits. I needed to keep my place at Trotter's, clean at the blasted newspaper, and hope for more chances to work elsewhere. Some days I despaired of ever fulfilling my pledge to sponsor a younger girl.

Willy took credit, when the landlord gave me some overnight cleaning work at his printer's shop next door. The Prime Minister had clearly forgiven Monsieur Desbarats for owning the property where Mr. McGee had met his end—he'd appointed Desbarats as Queen's Printer.

Perhaps that had something to do with the plaque the landlord had cast and mounted outside the house, marking Mr. McGee's last moment and listing his life accomplishments.

It certainly meant that Monsieur Desbarats was the only one on the street who could afford to pay for such a monument. Pierce thought it provocative, but I thought it patriotic. I read it over in silent homage every time I stepped between the two buildings.

Parliament's closure had left Willy out of work. Being Willy, he finagled a better deal with the landlord for himself than he did for me. In return for Willy doing odd jobs, Monsieur Desbarats was now giving Willy regular French lessons. The trial had convinced Willy that he needed to understand French.

Willy told Mrs. Trotter it would help him rise at Parliament.

"Why, I'll understand Monsieur Robitaille when he speaks in the House, Ma."

Mrs. Trotter could believe what she liked. Willy wasn't planning to return to Parliament as a page. He wanted to be sitting on the press bench. Mr. Lacey hadn't helped Willy into a reporter's job yet, but Willy was sure he'd have his chance.

I agreed with Willy. After what had happened to Monsieur Lacroix in the courtroom, it would be best if as many Canadians as possible could tell their truths in both languages.

So in the afternoons, Willy went next door to the print shop and learned a new language. While the street slept, I traipsed over there and dealt with machine grease that no amount of effort could lift from the floor.

My pattern, on my return in the morning, was to visit with Sow, and listen for Sergeant O'Neill's voice. If I heard him, I headed for my bedroom window; if not, for the breakfast table.

Sergeant O'Neill didn't show on Christmas Day, though I saw his wife in her regular pew at Mass. He left his family home on Boxing Day, though, and ate his evening meal at Mrs. Trotter's table.

Bridie didn't come for her Christmas visit with Jimmy, either, and Mrs. Trotter was put out she had no word of a cancellation. The Trotters and I headed to Docherty's for New Year's. Hannah fed me a few drinks, under the counter, so Mrs. Trotter wouldn't see. And when I finally saw Pierce that night, I finally blurted out that I shouldn't bother giving him notes anymore. And that, if Pierce didn't think my words worth commenting on, then he should feed these into the fire right then and there. He could stop giving Mrs. Trotter the little bit of coin, I said, I had another job now anyway.

He rolled his eyes, like he knew I'd been drinking, and walked away.

I did catch him glancing at my script in the midst of the celebration, but I didn't see whether he pocketed it.

Then we were snowed in solid the first two weeks of January. With no boarders, the three of us ate dried beef—and potatoes with the black spots cut away, same as Sow. Mrs. Trotter and Willy were both so glum, I looked forward to going outside at the end of each meal, to see my secret pet.

Sow was no piglet anymore, of course. At five months, she had to weigh almost what I did. I had to be careful she didn't knock me down flat when I brought her mash or water, she was that happy to see me. I still loved to stroke her back, though, and watch her curly red tail wiggle.

Willy didn't bother me in the back garden, he was too busy watching out front, in case there was a light at the newspaper. As soon as he spied one, he'd plough his way across the street for a visit with Mr. Lacey.

That's how we heard, mid-month, that two out of three high court judges had ruled against Jimmy, on the appeal Bridie had demanded.

One of these higher judges was the same Justice Richards who'd called Jimmy a liar at the trial.

I'd like the man for his treatment of me, but I had to wonder why that judge in particular been promoted to the higher court, right after sentencing Jimmy. Justice Richards had just been given the job of Chief Justice of Ontario—by Mr. Macdonald, in fact.

And now he had cast the deciding vote against Jimmy, and the highest court had announced that Jimmy must, upon reflection, hang.

It was on a Sunday, the last day in January, when Jimmy had no hope and only ten more days to live, that Bridie's letter arrived.

That afternoon, I let Willy win at draughts.

While he was crowing about it, I packed up the board and stones, and asked if I could start listening in on his French lessons.

"You know Ma's struggling to keep you on here, even part-time." Willy pushed himself up from the kitchen table. "You could be grateful for once. I won't sit here listening to your caterwauling, that's for sure. Tell Ma I'm off to Lowertown."

"Don't be an idiot, Willy," I said. "You can't go out in this."

"Why not—we just played a game of checkers on the Sabbath, and the Lord hasn't struck us down. Besides, here's the sergeant himself, coming up the alley. And just so you understand how things stand, Clara—right before Christmas, Ma sold Monsieur Robitaille those books of McGee's."

"She—"

"She wrote and asked Robitaille to find a buyer, made sure he knew she wouldn't take any charity off him neither. Monsieur Robitaille, he wrote back to say he'd buy the books, and not to sell them to Monsieur Desbarats. He sent a letter to his banker here too. They're only up there on the shelf on loan now. Ma's already run through that money. I've something to fetch, before I head out."

Willy left me sitting with that, as Sergeant O'Neill tramped up to the kitchen door. I couldn't understand how the sergeant had ploughed through the snow drifts—until I saw the native walking shoes strapped on the bottom of his boots.

They looked like giant warped embroidery hoops, with a cross-thatch of sinew strings. He needed help unstrapping them.

Mrs. Trotter rushed into the room, like she'd been in her room by the window on the lookout for her Tommy.

I looked away while they greeted one another, with their smiles and almost-hugs.

"Have you ever seen the like of these snowshoes, Clara?" Mrs. Trotter kneeled by the chair near the entry, and unwound the cords holding the contraptions onto the sergeant's legs. She passed me the first hoop. "Hang that on a hook, while I deal with the knot in this other lace," she said.

I ran my finger along the fine woodwork and plucked snow off one of the strings.

"'Tis whale gut," Sergeant O'Neill said. "From Hudson's Bay. The city ordered them for the whole force." He pulled off his coat. "Macdonald's outfitting his Constabulary with them, so the city ordered some up as well. I'd as soon the money went to pay us, for all our extra work last year. But I might as well make use of whatever the Mayor chooses to hand out."

Through the window, I could see how the shoes had left diamond patterns all along the alley. "Mrs. Trotter, that's just like what I saw in the snow outside my window the other morning."

"You see, Clara, 'twas only an officer of the law out there. Nothing to worry about."

"Someone's bothering you, Nancy?"

She leaned close. "Clara's on edge, 'tis all," she told him. "I think she may be finally having her time—you know."

I flushed. I was past the age to show signs that I was a woman, but so far I'd had none. And now Mrs. Trotter was speculating—with Sergeant O'Neill—that women's problems were causing me to see footsteps in the snow.

"You're in luck, Tommy. I've made a shepherd's pie for lunch. It'll be out of the oven in a tick." The best meal we've had all month, and he somehow shows up.

I made to leave the room.

"Hold on, Clara." He handed me an envelope with a Montreal postal stamp. *Mrs. James Whelan* was printed on the back.

Sergeant O'Neill nodded to Mrs. Trotter. "It would be best if she read that here—with us."

I examined the seal as I lifted it. It didn't quite fit over the wax stain underneath it. "Haven't you already read it? And taken it to Pierce for approval?"

I sat on the far side of the table, so they couldn't look over my shoulder while I scanned the two pages.

"She'll be back for the hanging. She's been ill."

"If she's looking to stay, surely she'd write *me* for permission?" Mrs. Trotter didn't want the woman here, but she reserved the right to be put out about not being consulted.

I scanned the page without replying.

She looked sharp at me. "It's your age, I know it more than you do. But it's no excuse right now. Tell us what Bridie Whelan has written."

I cleared my throat, and read it out.

> *My neighbour is writing this. She's writing one to the prison too, and Jimmy's so-called lawyer. And Father Clement. I'm giving them all your name, Clara, in the hope you'll be a good Catholic and visit Jimmy. You can bring someone with you if you fear going to the prison alone, I've told them that too. My Jimmy's got no more appeals but to the Lord now, and I'm laid up. First with influenza and now neuralgia, like the devil wants to keep us apart. I won't be there until his life is almost run through, Clara.*

> *Will you visit? If not for Jimmy, then for my peace of mind. His last letter is worrying me so. Bring him hot food and some comfort, there's a lamb. My boyo needs human kindness now. None of the lads has been there, not a visitor but Father Clement. You're the only one in that jumped-up town I can think to ask. At least you spoke in his favour*

I had not. I spoke in favour of the truth. Why did everyone judge me for that, one way or t'other?

> *I'm telling you true, Clara. He didn't do it. Jimmy couldn't kill any man.*

Sergeant O'Neill picked up the letter from where I laid it down. He stared at the backwards *b*, that read like a *d*. Where Bridie had written her own name. Then he stared at me, like I shouldn't have taught her even that much, like it was better when she could only sign *X*.

"Imagine her asking a girl like you to go to the jail," Sergeant O'Neill said.

"She's got nerve, trying to dictate what happens in this house," Mrs. Trotter agreed.

So Mrs. Trotter wasn't having it.

"Hannah went to see Mike," I said.

"It's not the same and you know it, Clara. Hannah's older—and she has family to protect her. And because Hannah does a tom-foolish thing doesn't mean you should. Look where she landed from consorting with jailbirds. Why, you'd be risking your good name all over again." Mrs. Trotter shook her head. "What would people say?"

"They don't have to know, do they?" I said.

"One thing's for sure," Sergeant O'Neill said. "If this bull-headed girl does take it upon herself to go, Nancy, you can't be going with her. Not after those old rumours that you're connected to the plotters."

"Plotters, Sergeant?" I straightened. "You still think there are others to be brought to justice?"

"Never mind that, Clara. This"—he waved the letter at me—"is the trouble, right here and now."

I wasn't sure whether Sergeant O'Neill was speaking as a copper now or as Mrs. Trotter's man. Either way, I didn't know if I could go against him again and keep my place here.

Willy clomped into the kitchen at that moment. Spied the snowshoes, and grabbed one. "Let's have a try, no harm, Sergeant?" The shoe was way too big for his boot. "I've got to get me some of these." He looked at us, around the table. "So it's come to this? Things are bad enough you've let Clara go?"

"What gave you that idea, son?"

"Why, Clara's face." He laughed, chuffed with his joke.

"Clara's going nowhere—certainly not to that jail."

"What's this?"

Sergeant O'Neill handed Willy the letter, and he whistled as he read it.

I snatched the letter from Willy. "Bridie's sick—"

"What's best for Bridie isn't best for you, Clara," Mrs. Trotter said. "A young girl visiting a murderer in a jail full of filthy animals. And I don't mean the rats, I mean the ones locked behind bars for good reason."

"Don't worry, Ma, I'll take her."

We all looked at Willy.

"Why?" I said.

"I'd be helping you help old Bridie." He smiled. "Mr. Lacey would have to put my name on top of my own story of the assassin's last days."

"Now, Willy." How often had Mrs. Trotter said those words, and to what end? "It's dangerous to set your face out front around those rebels."

"Ma, it's not like Clara isn't going to run to Pierce, which is just as dangerous."

I'd have to write Bridie that I couldn't keep Jimmy's secrets. Surely she didn't expect that of me?

"This one interview, and I could secure a proper trade, Ma." When he used that tone, she always gave in.

"Besides, Sergeant O'Neill here's been in the jail scores of times. Hasn't hurt him any."

Now that was a shift in the wind. Willy treating the sergeant as an ally.

"It is a chance for the boy, Nancy." The sergeant could read the lay of the land, all right. He rose and reached for his snowshoes. "I'm off to the station."

"Not without your shepherd's pie?" Mrs. Trotter said.

Her pleading made my cheeks burn, but he didn't stay.

When Mrs. Trotter had put together his snack in a cloth-covered pail and his snowshoes were tied tight, Sergeant O'Neill called out from the door. "Let the lad do you the favour, Clara. You may have need of a man in that jail. And it's not like Whelan would say a good word to you, if you were to be escorted by me or the Prime Minister's driver."

I doubted Willy would ever be my saviour. It was sure, however, that I wouldn't be going alone.

XXV

The stone walls were dripping ice water. The windows were set high enough I couldn't see out and were cut narrow as castle arrow slits. The floorboards were stained with years of abuse. I'd stepped in many a horse pat and my boots hadn't stuck this way. And 'twas as rank as butcher's slaughter. I pulled up my scarf to cover my mouth.

The warden walked us down the hall past doorways so small a man would have to walk in sideways. Even I had to stoop in order to peek in. There was a wooden pallet against the wall, and a chamber pot in the corner.

"A cot and a pot, that's our accommodation," the warden said to Willy.

He hadn't spoken to me; he'd looked askance at my being there. Sergeant O'Neill had made the arrangements the day before, so I shouldn't have been surprised.

I did make my way through the drifts down to Docherty's, on the Monday, to send a note to Pierce, by way of Hannah. Now I finally had something to tell him about Bridie, and where was he?

I didn't want to spell out why I needed to speak to him. I was worried, lest Hannah hand the letter on for delivery to one of the useless lads who'd been hanging around her, ever since Mike's death. None of those jokers could be trusted to carry so much as a sack of potatoes, in my judgement. But most of them did have buggies, and she might not have a better chance.

Hannah said Pierce had made himself scarce all month, she didn't know quite what was up with him. All I knew was, this Tuesday morning Pierce was surely nowhere to be seen here at the Carleton County Jail.

"Who cleans these cells?" I said.

"The boys do it themselves," the warden said. "When we want to cheer them up, we let them run a mop around and toss their business into a bucket. And they should be glad of that much, the buggers."

The warden opened the door to a room with a wooden table, four chairs, and two window slits. A low fire burned, with no logs or kindling set aside to build it up. "There'll be enough morning light in here so you won't need a lamp," the warden said to Willy. "You're writing up an article? I've stories for you. Girl, you wait and we'll be back with Whelan in two winks."

I set my basket on the table. A guard had rooted through it at the entrance, confiscating the meat tarts and sticking one in his mouth as I stood there. But there was still milk and mash and a bit of cake left.

I'd barely seated myself when the door swung in, and there was a man I barely recognised as Jimmy.

He was all bones. There was a sheen to his skin, like his layers of muscle and gut had been all but dissolved by the jail's dank chill.

Jimmy's sandy mop of hair was dark with grease. A few of his teeth were missing. He was sucking at a sore on his lower lip. His hands were both fisted.

"I'm Clara. Bridie asked me to come in her stead."

"Thank you, Miss Clara." He eyed the food, then bent to the table and opened his fists, laying a pair of tiny wooden boxes between us.

Then Jimmy set to. The milk went down his throat in one steady stream. He choked on the mash—he was swallowing without chewing. He still had mash in his mouth when he began to stuff in cake. He took in air along with the food and wheezed until I was afraid he'd upchuck, but he squirreled what he'd yet to chew until he could breathe again. And then he was running his tongue around his mouth, sucking the inside of his cheeks for aftertaste.

He rose and knocked on the door twice.

A guard looked in. "I'll take that milk bottle. For safekeeping."

"Don't worry yourself, man. February promises to be short enough for me," Jimmy said. "I'm not going to make it easy for the bastards, and slit my throat on the first day of the month."

That caught the guard's attention. Jimmy kept his gaze locked onto his captor's, as he handed over the glass bottle.

"Water?" Jimmy said.

The guard handed in a long-handled dipper.

Jimmy tilted his face and downed the liquid in one gulp, caught a few drops with his fingers.

The guard reached for the spoon. "A quarter hour now, no more," he said. "Here's the young journalist."

Willy stepped in, his hand thrust out. "Willy Trotter, Sir. Your good wife Bridie and Clara here thought I should come to set down your words for the public."

I gave him a look. The liar.

"Bridie wants me to talk to you?"

"I'm going to write your story, Jimmy. For the newspaper. Maybe even a book. You'll be as famous as the heroes of '48."

Jimmy smiled. "It's good of you to come, lad." Yes, he'd lost most of his teeth. His words came out all muffled. "I do have a story."

Willy set a black-bound pad on the table, a page flipped open, a pencil lying on top. "If you had to choose one word to describe yourself, Mr. Whelan, what would it be?"

Where did Willy come up with that?

"Jimmy. Please be you call me Jimmy. Clara—and what's your name again, lad?"

"Willy."

"William's the worst sort of Orange handle to have. It marks you as a Saxon, boyo, and the spawn of worthless invaders."

"I'm Wilfred, Jimmy. My mother's a Corcoran from County Tipperary."

"There's a proud Irish name."

I hid my smile. Jimmy would have himself a visit, and Willy no story at all.

Jimmy eyed my gloves, and that made me feel like they may already have picked up the smell of this infernal place.

I peeled them off and shoved them into my cape.

"I see you're fond of knots too, Miss," Jimmy said, nodding at my pockets, then pointing at his carved boxes. They were walnut, finely worked. He'd carved our Irish eternal circle, with its loops to honour the Trinity, into the centre of each.

Willy ceased his attempt at notetaking and pried open one box, then the other. Each contained its own curl of sandy hair.

Willy wrapped a curl around a pinkie finger. "Are you a lover or a fighter, Jimmy?"

"A romantic it is," Jimmy said.

Willy replaced the lock of hair, and reached once again for his writing tools. "You don't mind if I write that down?"

"Would it matter?" Jimmy said.

Willy started scribbling.

"Miss, I made those for my ladies." Jimmy swiped the boxes from where Willy had placed them, back over to me—double-quick, like he was used to having to make a grab for things. "I couldn't send Bridie a Christmas present, but I'd plenty of time to whittle and carve. Will you see she gets them both?"

"How'd you lay your hands on a knife that sharp in here?" Willy said.

"I guess the guards know I'm no danger, don't they, Orange?" Jimmy said. "You know, Miss . . . you can keep one. In the Holy Bible, a man often had a wife and a sweetheart, didn't he? My sweetheart's turned a cold cheek lately. And my wife's been ailing."

"I couldn't do any such thing," I said.

Jimmy drummed blackened fingernails on the table. Most of his nails were missing now too; a couple of the scabs were clearly infected.

"I hear you're quite the artist as well, Jimmy," Willy said. "Are you still drawing pictures of your lady?"

At that, with a sly smile, Jimmy pulled a pencil drawing from under his shirt.

With only a few lines he'd shaped a face, from the side. She wore a scarf, and he'd shaded in hair along her forehead. She had a proud nose, strong cheekbones, full lips. Her eye held a hint of trouble—I don't know how he managed that; it might have been the way he'd lined her lids. He was no portrait maker, though. She looked more like a faery than a colleen. Fey, and young.

Willy sat up. "Mike Walsh testified you had a sweetheart."

What had Mike said? *"Jimmy was mewling like a babe over a girl's picture. And him married to that old woman."*

"Mike's where he deserves to be," Jimmy said. He ran an infected nail along his edge of the paper, wiping off some pus. "A liar and a thief into the bargain, Mike. Bridie saw right through that lad. Ma was right when she told me to marry a steady woman, one I could see was soft on me. To look after me in rough country."

"And that girl you've drawn?" Willy asked.

Jimmy shook his head. "I never thought to be struck by a love curse, did I? How was I to know?" Jimmy turned and spit on the floor.

Willy scraped back his chair to avoid the hoark.

"Ma was right; it's better when she's soft on you, than the other."

"She's beautiful, Jimmy," I said. "What's her name?"

"*Fódla*, I like to call her."

"The lady of the land?" I said.

"Smart girl," Jimmy said. "That's my name for her—my Lady *Éireann*."

"Jimmy, do you still say you didn't shoot Mr. McGee?" Willy broke in. "You've nothing to lose now by claiming credit."

"I never did," Jimmy answered Willy, still looking in my eye. "I do know the killer."

Willy dropped his pencil.

While Willy was scrambling on the floor, Jimmy stretched out his legs. "Well, you think I've nothing left, but I can still choose to die a hero. Why should I tell you the tale, Orange? I'll never be a rat, no matter how small the hole they place me in."

Willy was breathing through his mouth when he crawled back on the stool. I saw that Willy's pencil was now wedged under Jimmy's foot.

Jimmy leaned back so his chair balanced against the wall. "What would Bridie be thinking of me, speaking so in front of a girl who brought me dinner?" He flexed his hands. "Tell me, dear, I don't hear the news. Has M'Lady Macdonald birthed her bairn yet?"

What . . . where did Jimmy come up with that?

Jimmy locked eyes on me. "No? It doesn't always go well when an old man like Macdonald decides to spawn again."

He began to rock the chair. "I guess D'Arcy's death made Macdonald feel his own mortality. So he set out one more time to leave a little something behind. 'Course, Macdonald married a young thing. Bridie and I didn't have such luck. I'm not blaming Bridie, though at the first I did think her younger. And maybe Bridie's the one who's been blessed, and not M'Lady Macdonald. After all, every birth is a pass through the valley of death for a woman."

The chair legs hit the floor. "I've a feeling. Maybe because I'm so close to the other side of life myself. Lad, are you getting this down?"

Willy shrugged, knowing he'd been bested.

"Root out Pierce Doyle for me, Miss. It won't be hard for you to do, from what Bridie tells me. Unless he hasn't had need of you recently? And he's done one of his disappearing acts? Ah, I see how it is."

I cursed my eyes.

"Why, lift a few rocks and you'll find him sure enough, dear. When you do, tell Doyle to pass on this message: Jimmy Whelan's praying for M'Lady's delivery."

"Don't you have better reasons to be praying, Jimmy?" I said.

He spit in his hands, and clasped them together, in a mockery of a sinner's petition.

There were two raps on the door.

Jimmy scooped up his drawing and stuffed it back inside his shirt. "As for Macdonald and Doyle, I'll be right welcoming when McGee and I meet them in Hell. Now you give my Bridie all my love, and set aside one of those boxes as your own keepsake of our visit. I remember you at New Year's, of course, and I'd seen you before in my meanderings. A doll, playing at learning with a big Bible, out in the garden."

"The McGees' garden?" I said.

"*Fódla*, now she's never been so easy to watch from afar. . . .. There's a good girl, be a friend to my wife Bridie."

The door swung open.

The guard put up a hand. "The warden will be along for you two," he said.

Jimmy walked out of the room without another word. When he was a ways down the corridor, we heard him call out Éirinn *Go Brac*.

"I'm afraid he's singing the wrong tune," Willy said. "He's soon going to meet his Forever. And he won't be doing so in Ireland."

I slipped on the icy jailhouse steps.

Willy caught me. "You should quit wearing that old cape, Clara, It's too long for you," he said.

"'Twas my Gram's. Good Irish wool lasts a lifetime or more."

"C'mon, Clara. I'm hieing home. What a tale. He didn't shoot McGee, but he knows who did the deed." Willy strode ahead. "And threatening the Prime Minister to boot."

"I don't like it," I said.

Willy glanced at me. "You going to start up again about my writing a story, Clara?"

"I don't care what you write anymore, Willy. I don't like Jimmy Whelan calling out curses."

"It could be Jimmy was putting on a show for your benefit. He likes the colleens all right," Willy said. "Or Whelan's wife may've told Jimmy you're a gullible girl, and one who can't help snitching. Maybe he wanted to wind you up, Clara, and Pierce Doyle in the bargain."

Willy sped up. "I have to jot down all his very words. 'I know the killer.' What a way to spin a story."

I tripped, trying to keep up, then tripped again trying to right myself. "The man's about to meet his maker, Willy."

"Clara, choose a side," Willy said, stalling until I had a foothold, then walking on ahead again. "You can't be suspecting the man of sorcery, and wailing for him at the same time."

"What he said about Lady Macdonald gave me the creeps, no doubt. He may have gone bad and mad in jail," I said. "But I don't believe he shot Mr. McGee, Willy. And he's to die for it. That's what I'll tell Pierce, as I am a snitch. But go on with you. You've scooped up your story, then. And you're welcome."

He glanced back, but not enough to meet my eyes. "Maybe I'll have you copy it out for me when I'm done," he said. "Look it over."

"Don't be doing me any favours, Willy," I said. "Can you not consider someone besides yourself?" My cheeks burned with more than the cold wind. "I've long since trusted Pierce Doyle more than I do you, Willy Trotter."

"Best I don't let anyone see this until the story's in print, then," Willy said. He ran away from me, full tilt. Down the road aways he jumped in the sky, his arms a Vee, his legs kicking up snow. Like a child who's been promised a prized toy.

Pierce actually showed up at Trotter's parlour bar the next night.

He looked almost impatient, so I'd guessed he got my note, and just hadn't been able to come on Monday.

I pulled his copy of *Paradise Lost* from my apron, and held it out. The report was tucked inside. It listed everything Jimmy had said, as close as I could recall it all. I'd left out that he'd made two small presents for his wife.

"You have a regular lending library going, Mrs. Trotter," one of the lads in the bar joked.

"What are you going to read next, Clara?" she asked me.

"I'd like to try something in French," I said.

"Oh, Mrs. Trotter, you won't be allowing that," the lad said. "French books are either revolutionary, or they're smut. In either case, they're teaching lessons no proper maiden should know."

"That's just what my Willy says," Mrs Trotter told him.

I slammed the lad's ale down in front of him, so it slopped. I was wishing that rotten Willy were sitting there instead, so I could spill it all over him.

When I looked over to see whether Pierce would speak up in my favour, he'd already slipped away.

Around midnight, I finished up and went to my room. There, I found my kitbag sitting on my bed, with a new book inside. *A Tale of Two Cities*.

So Pierce had been looking for the two tokens from Jimmy. He must've known about the boxes from the prison guards. He'd certainly made sure I'd note his search, and that he knew what I didn't tell him.

I was still glad I'd stuffed the boxes inside my gloves. Which were tucked in my cape pockets, safe on the hook in the kitchen. Ready to give to Bridie, when she arrived at Trotter's.

Late Friday afternoon, I found Mrs. Trotter standing with the boarders' door open, staring out. She held a folded newspaper in her right hand and an open letter in her left.

I touched her shoulder. "Is anything the matter?"

She started. "Clara. Read this."

It wasn't Mr. Lacey's *Ottawa Times* in her hand but yesterday's Toronto newspaper. THURSDAY, FEBRUARY 4, it read.

WHELAN CONFESSES ALL TO GLOBE REPORTER. The wind blasted us as I took in the name directly underneath. BY WILFRED TROTTER. SPECIAL CORRESPONDENT.

"Jimmy didn't confess a thing," I said. "We talked about Bridie, and the woman whose picture he keeps sketching. And—"

"Read it all first, Clara."

The story didn't quite match the headline. Willy wrote how Jimmy had told us he knew who the killer was. He wrote that while Jimmy said he was innocent, even having knowledge of the killer was a hanging offence. He had that bit straight from the Crown Attorney, with lots of quotes about how Jimmy had run out of luck and time and had changed his story too often to be telling any truths. That must've been where Willy ran to from the jail.

Willy wrote how Jimmy looked near to death already, a week before his hanging. His words caught the dirty poverty of the jail. There were more big headlines further down the page about how Jimmy's spirit rose when he cursed Mr. McGee and Mr. Macdonald. How Jimmy expected to go to Hell.

Willy left out Jimmy talking ill of Lady Macdonald, and his own wish for a baby. Pierce's name wasn't there. Or else the editor didn't think that was worth the print.

Willy ended the story with Whelan being led to his cell, shouting *Éirinn Go Brac*.

> *For the reader who may not speak Gaelic, this is a rallying cry for rebels: 'Ireland Forever.' Whelan also referred to the mysterious female in his drawings as 'lady of the land of Ireland', and spoke of a 'love curse'.*

As I read, I felt better about Willy having his chance. He'd copied down Jimmy's words fair. And he could lay down a sentence so you wanted to read it.

"Why is it in the *Globe*?"

Mrs. Trotter lay the letter on top of the news page. "It's all in here."

> *Mr. Lacey wouldn't help me after all, so I went right to his competition. The Globe editor telegraphed that he liked my writing—and if I came to town right away there was a fellow off sick and I could fill in. I'm taking the next train as far as Prescott, and I'll find my way along the river to Kingston and on west. You can reach me at Auntie's, Ma. Sure, and she'll be wanting you for a visit. Oh, and tell Clara not to worry. I didn't mention she was there with me.*
>
> *Your favorite son*

Mrs. Trotter closed the door. "My boy's gone. I'm sorry I ever let you take him to see that Whelan."

"He's written it well," I said.

She pulled out a hankie and blew her nose. "At least my sister's in Toronto to look out for him."

"It may be for the best, Ma'am."

"What do you mean?"

"What he said, about not telling the editor I was there. From this headline, somebody may think Jimmy did give us the killer's name."

She took back both pieces of paper. "A Fenian rebel who plotted with Whelan—such a devil thinks Willy knows his name?"

I nodded.

"Then you're right, Clara," she said. "It is better my boy's gone from here."

XXVI

The long-suffering husband of a biddy who was popular in the parish passed away that same day. "We could both use some company," Mrs. Trotter said.

So when the weather warmed up a bit the next day, we took it as a sign.

At the Saturday evening wake, Mrs. Trotter saw many of the friends she'd made in the two years since she'd moved to Ottawa from Toronto—after her own husband's death. And she was indeed buoyed by the song and dance. Until Sergeant O'Neill dropped in late in the evening, his own Mrs. Polly O'Neill on his arm.

Mrs. O'Neill stayed close to Mrs. Trotter from then on. And she insisted that she and her husband deliver us home. So we all squeezed into Sergeant O'Neill's familiar buggy.

"You and Tommy being such friends, Nancy, we should be too," Mrs. O'Neill said. The woman seemed to think she could set the friendship up fast, if she talked the whole way to Sparks Street.

Which was a blessing, because neither her husband nor Mrs. Trotter had anything to say for themselves.

"A good old biddy, the lads were calling our friend Patsy tonight," Mrs. O'Neill said. "I suppose that lot think me an old woman too, at forty-eight. Wait until you get there, dear."

I looked up at that. But Mrs. O'Neill had addressed that remark to Mrs. Trotter, not to me. How old was Mrs. Trotter? She once told me she'd married at seventeen . . . that made her what, thirty-six?

"They were all talking about your son Willy, too." Mrs. O'Neill hadn't slowed down with her switch in topic. "And his story that Whelan two-timed his wife. Men can be fools, sure."

I filled in the silence. "You're ten years younger than Bridie Whelan, Ma'am," I told her. In case she needed reassurance.

I didn't say that Mrs. Trotter looked more than a dozen years Mrs. O'Neill's junior, now I thought on it.

"Some are saying Bridie Whelan's a Fenian herself," Mrs. O'Neill said. "Of course, we've all heard she has some coin—Tommy?"

"Polly, it's police business," he said.

"And to think, the murderer's wife stays with you, whenever she's in town, Nancy," Mrs. O'Neill said. "Tommy had to check on her regular, I know."

Sergeant O'Neill whipped the horses.

When we arrived at the boarding house, Mrs. Trotter helped herself out of the carriage. The sergeant barely waited for me to land on the street before he pulled away.

Mrs. O'Neill called goodnight, as Mrs. Trotter double-timed it to the boarders' door.

"Mrs. Trotter, slow up," I said. "I hear something. From the alleyway."

"Girl, you've been hearing and seeing 'something' since last spring—Christ on a crutch, there *is* a joker coming out—Clara—"

I ran to the stoop and Mrs. Trotter pulled me to her, though the man was already across the street.

"You—where are you rushing to, scaring a decent woman and a girl?" she called out.

"It's a public alley, lady," he called back, as he ducked behind the *Times'* building. The man spoke with the flat, nasal tones of the English who'd been settled here for generations. His scarf was wrapped high and his hat pulled low. The lad couldn't hide his height, though he'd bent his head.

"Gone before I could mark his face."

Mrs. Trotter turned, and set her key in the boarder's door. "He was as big as my own Bill, bless his memory."

As she walked inside, I realised how rarely she spoke of Mr. Trotter.

Then Sow ran out of the alley, squealing and making for the road. For all the world like she was hunting down the Saxon herself.

I bunched my cape under my arms and raced in front of Sow. I thought, suddenly, of how to make Gram's cape work for me. I eased my arms out of the sleeves, and closed in on Sow. Then I untied the cape, and threw it on top of her.

221

Blinded, Sow circled, madly. Tripping, like I always did, on the long gathers of wool.

I pulled at the corners of the cape. Of course, I couldn't budge her. Sow had gained even more weight, she must have been six stone already. All of it fighting against me.

I was wheezing, and Sow was wriggling and pawing, until suddenly, she was free of her cloth cage, and off.

I was left holding only a cape that reeked of Sow's pee and wet wool. I couldn't even give chase. I was that winded, and chilled through.

I had a sudden thought, and felt the pockets. Somehow, those boxes of Jimmy's had stayed inside through that melee.

The kitchen door opened. "Clara?" Mrs. Trotter called down the alley.

"Sow's gone," I yelled back.

"That blasted pig's chosen tonight, of all nights, to run off?" she said. "From the sounds I heard, I thought that thief had a confederate—and you were waging war with him."

"She'll find her way home, come daylight, Mrs. Trotter," I said. didn't believe a word of what I said. I was merely trying to stave off what came next.

"If we do find that pig, I'll sell her to someone who wants to breed her," Mrs. Trotter said. "Or I might just forget about breeding her, and have her bacon. I'll see. . . what Tommy advises . . ..." Mrs. Trotter sounded more miserable with every word.

I couldn't sleep. After Mrs. Trotter had been upstairs half an hour, by the tower bell's tolling, I pulled on a second pair of stockings for warmth. Then I lit a candle and crept into the laundry room.

I held up my cape. It smelled nice enough, after the scrubbing I'd given it. Better than the tallow candle. And the cape might even have shrunk a bit, which would be to the good. But it could use some close heat, to dry completely.

I donned the cape, over my nightie. Then I grabbed the gloves from where they'd been drying on the mangle, and once again tucked the boxes in the pockets beneath them.

Once in the kitchen, I stoked the fire, and placed my candle on the hob. I curled up on the hearth, with *A Tale of Two Cities*.

"Maybe you'll read some of that to me, of an evening, Clara," Mrs. Trotter had told me, when she spied it in my apron pocket earlier that day. *"It hurts my eyes, to look at such small print. And I do enjoy that Mr. Dickens. He writes about people we might know."*

She was right about that. As I read the tale of a different country's rebellion, my worries about Sow's fate, Mrs. Trotter and the sergeant, Willy going off to Toronto, Bridie, Jimmy . . .. were all pushed aside. I began to nod off . . ..

That wouldn't do. Mrs. Trotter would have a conniption fit if she found me asleep, with a candle lit, and with that burning smell . . ..

It wasn't the candle. It wasn't the fireplace, that was drawing nicely. But there was a faint, definite charred aroma in the air.

I unrolled myself from my cocoon.

I couldn't see a thing out the kitchen window, for smoke. Then, as I hesitated to open the door, there was an explosion of light and colour. Coming from the Queen's Printers.

Mrs. Trotter feared a fire, more than anything. Her room faced the street, though. She might not have smelled or seen a blessed thing . . .. "Mrs. Trotter," I screamed as I ran through the house. "Nancy."

Mrs. Trotter wasn't in any of the upstairs rooms, or anywhere downstairs either.

The boarder's door, when I tried it, was unlocked. She'd gone out without me, then.

For the first time since the shooting, I stepped out that door.

Neighbours were rushing over to the printer's, with buckets of snow.

Someone ran to the firebox bell, only recently placed on a post at the corner of O'Connor.

'Twasn't long after that little bell began to peal, that the church bells, then the Parliamentary bell joined in.

All alerting the entire town of Ottawa to the danger of spreading flames.

Hannah and her uncle ran up the alley in tandem, carrying a ladder. At the front of the building they stopped, set the ladder on the ground, and just stared.

I could see now, too, that there was no place to safely prop up a ladder against Monsieur Desbarats' printshop building.

And the roof had started to burn at Trotter's.

"Hannah, Hannah—" I ran to her. "Hannah, help me find Mrs. Trotter."

"She went for help?" Hannah said.

"She left me inside," I said. "She wouldn't do that." I suddenly couldn't breathe.

"Clara, you're choking—c'mon." Hannah dragged me into the road.

Everyone else was retreating, too. There was no other choice. People carried their empty buckets to safety, and just stood on the far side of Sparks St., staring, helpless.

Then the Ottawa Fire Department arrived, and the Chief confirmed all of Mr. Desbarats' buildings were as good as gone. They looked on Trotter's Boarding House only as a tenant of the Queen's Printer, no more salvageable than his own business.

"Give over, you can't fight a bomb with snow," the butcher shouted.

He'd manoeuvred his way next to Hannah in the spectators' line.

"A bomb?" I said.

"It only stands to reason the Fenians would strike, sooner or later," Hannah's Uncle Eamonn said. "A warning. In advance of the hanging."

"Desbarats did just put up that plaque in praise of McGee . . . ." Hannah added.

"What the hell—" said the butcher. "Look, up there—"

Mr. Lacey had stuck his head and torso out one of the print shop's second-storey windows.

There was a crackling, and the room lit up behind him.

A flagpole was masted secure against the wall, about three feet below Mr. Lacey's window. Then there was a drop of about five feet, to a canopy. Below that, it was a ten-foot plunge, to the wooden walkway.

Mr. Lacey hoisted one leg over the sill. He was half in the room and half in the air. Seeming to lose his balance, along with his nerve. He swung his other leg out, though, and managed to right himself, seated on the sill. Then he twisted sideways and stretched his feet forward until they rested on the flagpole. He eased his body out and around, and flattened himself, facing the building. His hands found purchase between its planking.

He had the wisdom, in that moment, not to look down again.

The flames licked out the window. They caught his silver hair, then his black jacket. "Jesus," he cried. Then there was just a high call of agony. Like that made by an animal in a trap.

Mr. Lacey fell to the canopy, setting the tarp alight. It ripped away from its moorings and they both landed, curling and sparking, on the ground in front of us.

The smell of death by burning had come too close to the crowd.

"Go clear," the butcher called.

There was no need, we were all shoving each other to be furthest away, quickest.

As we scattered, I felt like the whole town was screaming. And there was someone unexpected, standing across the street.

"Suzanne." I ran to Madame Lacroix.

"*Le pauvre homme*," she said.

The entire print shop suddenly collapsed into itself. The crowd surged toward us again, in panic. Suzanne and I grabbed onto each other, just to stay put.

Everyone was saying, *Trotter's, Trotter's, Trotter's,* as the Desbarats building stoked the boarding house fire until Trotter's was completely ablaze as well. *Cursed, haunted, death house.* The words swirled round me, with the smoke. But the only ones that I breathed in from the air were *no hope.*

I put my hands over my ears. "Suzanne," I said, "tell me about your niece, or Monsieur Lacroix. So I don't have to look over there, at the fire, or listen to these fools. For just a moment."

"*On se casse,*" Suzanne said. "I'll be so happy when we've left this town. If only *ils paieraient.*"

"Pay?" I said, pulling back from her.

"*Rien.* That's how much reward money we've received, for all Jean-Baptiste's trouble. Those *flaneurs.* You should be paid too, Clara," Suzanne said. "You told them what you knew."

"Suzanne—"

"I want only that Jean-Baptiste and I are able to leave my land, Clara. We'll head West, and the nuns won't be able to deny me my niece when I show up on their door. " Suzanne said. "*Et vous?* Where will you go?"

"I don't know," I said. "I've lost Mrs. Trotter." Then the smoke lifted, for a moment. "I can see my other friend again," I said. "Over by the *Times* building with the butcher. And the sergeant too—thanks be."

"Girls, where's Nancy?"

I was so happy to see Sergeant O'Neill.

"She's not here, Sergeant," Hannah said. "Clara checked every room, before she got herself out."

"Except the attic," I said.

"You what—" he said, as I panicked.

"No—Nancy must be around back, she won't have gone far from her home." The sergeant began pushing through the crowd, swinging his billy stick and lamp.

I ran after him. Down Sparks St., around and down O'Connor, to Queen Street, and up the alleyway to Mrs. Trotter's back garden.

And, to the sergeant's credit, he was right. For there we found his Nancy. Lying, as if dead to the world, beside Sow's empty pen.

Mrs. Trotter had a deep cut in her temple, and a goose-egg bruise on the back of her head. The sergeant lifted her from the snow, like she was no weight at all, and ran with her to Docherty's.

Hannah's uncle had returned to his pub. In fact, Eamonn was doing a steady business, pouring for customers. The neighbours were all taking their jars of ale or shots of whiskey outside. To nurse, as they stared through the smoke at the minute-by-minute destruction of Trotter's Boarding House.

I didn't have so much as a chance to look, as my home flamed to ash. Nor a thought to give to that fact. Instead, I trailed the sergeant into Eamonn Docherty's office.

Sergeant O'Neill let me take his lantern, and plumped down on the settee, Mrs. Trotter still in his arms.

His billy stick was half hanging out of his coat pocket by that point. And Sergeant O'Neill was neither to hold nor bind. He wanted answers, and he wanted them from me.

When I had none, he cursed me up and down and sideways. Never mind that I was sobbing, and begging to see to Mrs. Trotter.

"I swear, sergeant—I looked for Mrs. Trotter, I ran for her. With the print shop burning—" I said. "What was I to do?"

When Hannah rushed in, with a pile of blankets, Dr. Gillivray hurried after her. It turned out he had arrived to treat some lads who'd gotten too close to the printer's, on a dare. And ended up with pretty bad burns.

After the doctor examined Mrs. Trotter's brow—and once he hadn't been able to awaken her by waving spirits under her nose—he said her injury couldn't have been an accident.

"Of course not, man," Sergeant O'Neill said. "Nancy's been coshed, hard."

"She's going to need watching," Dr. Gillivray said.

"You're lucky she's alive, Clara," Sergeant O'Neill said. "Now I'll take Nancy home."

Hannah and I shared her bed that night, drinking from a bottle of brandy until we finally slept.

"I still think it was a bomb, as well as arson," Hannah said—not for the first time. "I've seen a regular fire before. It didn't send all those colours into the air, with a bang."

We each had another draw from the bottle. I let Hannah talk on, without taking in much of her chatter. I kept imagining Mrs. Trotter, lying in Sergeant O'Neill's arms.

And Mr. McGee, laying outside on the stoop.

Mr. McGee was the reason I'd come to Trotter's. But it was Mrs. Trotter who'd given me the place in her home. Handed me those keys, that first day.

I'd arrived more than a year ago; another cold January. The train had broken down at Brockville. So once Mr. McGee had introduced me, he'd hurried straight to Parliament.

I was so afraid this woman, Mrs. Trotter, wouldn't want me once she'd met me.

She opened the door sharp, before Mr. McGee could insert his key in the lock. An icicle on the eave cracked from the sudden movement, and fell beside us. But Mrs. Trotter was sweating like it were August.

She had the hack driver deposit my trunk in a tiny room just off the kitchen. Then she led me into the laundry room, where she'd clearly been doing battle with the mangle.

"You understand, girl, it's room and board and a proper set of clothing. And two dollars at each month's end," she said.

Two dollars. I tightened my right hand over my left wrist behind my back, so as to hold myself tall. A woman's wages.

"Not that I'd pay that much for a house girl like you, mind. Mr. McGee said he'd chip in half, for your secretarial services."

She pulled a linen hankie with a green T embroidered on the corner from her apron pocket, and rubbed the back of her neck.

"And I'm not to tell his wife about that, should she come to town."

She eyed me. Not like she was thinking something she shouldn't, thanks be. More like she couldn't make out Mr. McGee at all, or me either.

I stood quiet and let her take her measure.

"I'd wonder, but—you're thirteen?" She looked me up and down again. "I saw hungry days myself as a girl, but I was never so scrawny as you."

I could see that. For my part, I couldn't imagine ever being as buxom as Mrs. Trotter. My Gram was a sprite too. Gram's legs were about as long as Mrs. Trotter's arms, and not so round about.

"I'm fourteen next week, Ma'am. And I can do a powerful amount of work on any day," I said. "Mrs. McGee would tell you I'm fast with polishing and all kinds of cleaning. I can even handle that upright mangle, Mrs. Trotter."

"By yourself, you say?" We both stared at the giant machine.

"There are a powerful lot of sheets that need doing. With regularity, you understand." She patted her forehead next, but the linen didn't do a proper job and she still glistened. "You can tackle a load in the morning, Clara. And all credit to you, if you can bring that mangle to heel."

She showed me back through to the kitchen. There, she lowered herself onto an oak pressed-back chair, and motioned to me to do the same. "We'll see, soon enough."

And then she reached over to the matching sideboard and pulled out an extra key ring from the drawer. She made sure to show me the key for my own room, first. There was also a key for each of the boarder's rooms, so I could go in and tidy as needed. A larger key for the front door, another like it for the back. She'd let me right in, then and there.

Hannah finished her breathless recital, finally. And noticed that I had been scratching my arm, again and again, until the wound had reopened.

"Itchy, Clara? What, are the goose feathers giving you hives?" Hannah said. "Maybe it's these blankets from Hudson's Bay, I don't know why Uncle Eamonn's so careful about them. Or it's the soot—we both smell of the fire."

She rose, and went over to the pitcher and bowl set on her dresser.

I settled my head against the unfamiliar lumps in the pillow, brandy in hand. "When did you scoop this bottle from our boarders' stock?"

Hannah poured water in her ewer, and pulled off her shift. The candlelight flickered as she scattered dried petals and seeds in the water, dipped her cloth and washed under her arms.

Her breasts plumped out higher on the chest than mine would sit even once they bloomed. *"Barmaid's breasts,"* she'd often joked. *"Docherty women have hardly any neck to scrub, but our shelving draws lots of crumbs."*

Hannah shrugged on a clean shift, sat down beside me, and fluffed her pillow.

"We were running out of rye whiskey. He'd some Valley boys in town to hoot it up, lumber money falling from their pockets. I went over for a bottle, while you two were out."

"How did you get in?" I asked.

"I kept the boarders' door key. From when Mike passed away, and I stayed there those few days."

"Mrs. Trotter let you keep a key?" I said.

"Get off your high horse, Clara. And I know your next question, of course I locked up proper," Hannah said. "Don't look so green about her trusting me, either. I've never fussed about you taking Maisie's place."

"I'm sorry, Hannah. It's just—"

"I know Clara. Look, I'm as worried about her as you are. I know you've lost everything, and you haven't even a stitch to wear, either. The sight of you earlier, in your cape and your gloves, and no boots, only stockings—and then with only your nightie on underneath. And now—it's too bad you can't wear any of my things. Not without some major adjustments . . .."

"Father Clement said the Sisters will fix me up," I said. "He'll make sure they drop off a dress, and boots too, come morning."

"I can imagine what that will look like," Hannah said. "Just be careful they don't try to recruit you."

"It wouldn't be so bad," I said. "They're all educated, you know."

"Well, they can send up a *novena* of thanks on my behalf," Hannah said. "If I'd been a bit later going in tonight for this—" she took the bottle from me, and knocked back a tot. "I might have been the one who was attacked."

"I'll have to find a new place," I said.

"And think how Willy will feel. His hero dead, and his ma—" Hannah said. "I guess O'Neill will telegraph Toronto."

"I don't think Mrs. Trotter would want Willy to come back here."

"He'll have to come, won't he?" Hannah said. "To think that fool Lacey's nose was out of joint, because of Willy's story. He was in earlier for his supper and pint, nattering on about how he'd have a bigger scoop in the next edition of the *Times*. And then, to stand and see him fall—"

"Stop, Hannah." I grabbed the bottle. "How'd you end up with brandy," I said. "You went in for rye."

"I was brave enough, to go in, but then I got spooked. I don't know how you lived in D'Arcy's Death House, Clara. When I stayed there, it creeped me out more than this place does. And Mike died here."

"Well, I won't be living there now, will I? And don't be calling it that, he was a great man." I held the brandy out in front of Hannah. "See that mark? Those are Mr. McGee's initials."

"So he kept a private stock, even though he'd become a tea-totaller?" Hannah yawned. "His guests must've been happy; that brandy's smooth enough."

I swallowed. I'd fetched this bottle from the root cellar just the other day.

Hannah lay back on the bed. "Put that bottle aside now, and try to sleep, Clara. You take the inside." She curled her legs and I crawled over to the wall. "You know, I'd have no room for you here, except I had this bigger bed brought in for Mike."

I was to lie in her late husband's place. Where they'd lain together. I rolled, until I was pressed right against the plaster.

"I miss Mike something terrible for himself, you know that. But I'll tell you now and blush tomorrow—I miss him making me feel good at night. Have you gone through the change, Clara?"

I curled tight. "You can see I'm still flat as a board."

"You know there's more than that to it. Don't you ever feel the itch and want to scratch it?"

I flushed. "How old were you? When you first had the *Cursai*?"

"Twelve; two years younger than you are now. I was still living on our farm, then."

Hannah always talked about her grandfolks, never any other family. "Do you remember your parents, at all, Hannah. . .?"

"No, I was a tot when they were both taken."

'Twas influenza, I knew that much.

"Grannie and Gramp brought me along fine enough though."

"And they died of . . .?"

"Being Irish . . .. Clara, we've had enough of tears tonight." She spooned toward me. "I own the farm, still. It's been let out. I've no Aylward cousins, and none of my Doyle or Docherty cousins want to live anywhere near the border raids. Uncle Eamonn says he won't till ground where there was blood and sweat spent, for no gain. But I've a plan to go back to Grimsby . . . except now I don't have Mike. Maybe you'll come with me, Clara."

The offer made me feel a different sort of funny than taking Mike's place in their bed. Nice, to be wanted. Shy to say it was not where I wanted to end up. And not sure what she wanted of me in asking such a thing.

"I could help out here. If your uncle—?" I could feel Hannah breathing on my back. She shifted; Lord save me, what was going to happen now?

She brushed against me, but it was only to roll to her other side, to face the window.

"My uncle's not an easy man," she said. "He'll want you to help, sure enough, while you stay here with me. So what's your secret, Clara?"

"Secret?"

"You've been through enough, for your age—what pokes at you, when you think how your life could have been different?"

"Sometimes I get so angry, I'm afraid of what I'll do," I said.

"Well, you're Irish," she said.

"I think it's more about who I'm becoming, than where I come from. I didn't feel this way until this past year."

A bit of Mr. McGee's brandy made its way up the back of my throat.

"And there's—I never really knew my father."

"Where was he then?"

I was in for it now. "Kilkenny." I bit my tongue. "He's a Proddie. My stepmother and their sons too."

She said nothing for a few minutes. Then—"you're English?"

"Anglo-Irish," I said. "The family's been settled there a long while."

"Planted, you mean. In our land. And you've family, living there still."

She rolled away from me and pulled at the blanket. "I can see that in you, y'know."

"What're you saying, Hannah?"

"If there's a chance to get ahead, Clara, you don't let being Irish get in the way. Like your sainted arsy D'Arcy McGee."

"I've never been disloyal—no more was Mr. McGee, either." I was half uncovered now, but I felt the heat of lying beside her body. "How can you say such?"

"What's all your copying about? And writing notes of your own devising, for Pierce? You do see yourself as a step above, Clara. You're just looking for a way to take that step. Up and away from the Irish inside you." Hannah shoved her rump back into me. "Give me a bit of breathing room, will you, Clara?"

XXVII

I set the last of the chairs upside-down on their tables in preparation for mopping the pub floor. Hannah's uncle had given me bread and board for three days and nights. I'd taken every opportunity to make myself useful.

Hannah had found me a sleeping pallet for the floor, after the first night, and she'd come into the bedroom late and left early. Each day she wanted me there less.

But thanks be, it was Shrove Tuesday, and there would be plenty of beer spilled before Lenten fasting began. I asked Eamonn Docherty at lunch whether I could mop up the pub floor before the supper hour—and I was chuffed that he'd said he'd use my extra hands in the pub tonight too.

I dipped the rag mop into the pail of soapy suds, then splashed my face on purpose. I'd had so little rest of late. I'd taken the early shift today at the O'Neills' house. Keeping watch, lest Mrs. Trotter awakened . . . and in case she didn't.

There'd been no chance of me nodding off this morning. Church bells all over town had rung out for hours, harmonizing with Parliament's tower bell, in celebration of the birth of the Macdonalds' daughter.

After a while they were nigh to driving me mad. Yet the constant ringing didn't cause even a ripple to stir across Mrs. Trotter's still face.

Dr. Gillivray had come to check on her, walking over after Mass, with Father Clement.

The doctor had stroked his chin, and said the more time passed her by, the less likely she'd be coming back to us.

The more likely she'd be meeting with Our Lord on high, Father Clement added, as he blessed her.

After they left, I knelt beside the bed and prayed Mrs. Trotter had made her confession. I offered up all my troubles to the Lord. My thoughts rose and fell in time with the bells . . . a birth and a death, a wave in, a wave out. I couldn't help but believe it—'twas so often the way.

Watching Polly O'Neill tend Mrs. Trotter, shame had washed over me, to suspect the sergeant's wife may do Mrs. Trotter a bad turn. She only treated Mrs. Trotter with the respect due to a damaged woman brought to her home to be nursed. She was as gentle as I was when we stripped Mrs. Trotter, bathed her, and changed her shift. She clucked with sympathy as she smoothed the sheets over this mere acquaintance . . . .. A woman who'd been laying with her own husband, on the wrong side of the blanket, these past many months.

She couldn't know.

As for Sergeant O'Neill, he'd been every bit as affectionate to his wife as I had seen him be with Mrs. Trotter.

And as willing to share police business. That's how I learned that Mr. Lacey's death was deemed to be an accident, caused by misadventure.

"Desbarats' beyond distraught," Sergeant O'Neill told Polly. *"Lacey had been all over him, trying to wheedle out government documents that hadn't yet gone to press. Lacey was fit to be tied, being bested by young Trotter like that."*

"So it wasn't a bombing?" she'd asked

He'd looked at me. *"Some things are best not talked about, right now,"* he said.

"Is Nancy's son coming home?" his wife had asked next.

"He'd better look out for me when he does. The no-good son-of-an-Orangeman, running off and leaving his mother without protection."

I felt worried for Willy, remembering the way Sergeant O'Neill had looked right then.

I wrung out the well-soaped rags and wiped my hands on my apron. The O'Neills' home life was not my puzzle to piece together. I had enough to do, keeping a solid shelter over my own body and soul.

I moved the mop handle across the floor, beginning at the bar and working my way to the swinging kitchen door. I pushed hard at the spills and stains under each table. The water lost its froth, then blackened, with the grime of horse droppings mixed with sanded slush.

I needed to run over and feed Sow. Thank goodness she'd been spotted by one of Sergeant O'Neill's coppers right after the fire. Happily rooting, in a backyard two blocks over.

The sergeant had cursed out the pig to me, using the occasion to also ream me out me all over again. As if either poor Sow or I had somehow caused Mrs. Trotter's coshing.

But he'd had his copper cart Sow home. 'Twas amazing, how both the pen and the root cellar had been untouched.

And every other part of Trotter's Boarding House, like the adjoining print shop, had burned clean to the ground.

I turned my thoughts away from that black pile of ashes.

To how, after all that fussing, the sergeant had made sure there was enough mash stored in the cellar. So Sow could be kept happy for quite some time.

She did seem sorry to have run off, the way she tried to cuddle with me on her return. Like she was a piglet again. I crouched close. But I knew I had to be careful, now she was almost full-size.

I was a couple of hard pushes short of finishing the job, when Pierce walked through from the kitchen. With snow on his greatcoat, and his boots dripping. Even the hollows of his cowboy hat were shiny with hoarfrost.

My entire being was sharp with sudden madness, at the mess he'd brought in. It was made worse, because I couldn't tell him to watch where he was walking, to take off his blessed boots when he first came inside, to stay out of my way. This was *his* family's establishment too. Hannah'd said Pierce had more say here than she did. She'd said it in such a way as to make me think that Pierce might even be a partner of Eamonn's.

I bit inside my cheek, to keep myself mute.

"Tooth aching, Clara?"

"I'm fine."

"You haven't been sick with the influenza, have you?" he said.

"No—thank you." I needed to sound more cordial. Like I was a welcome guest here, comfortable greeting a family member. "I'm as well as ever, thank you."

"That's good to hear." He coughed. "If you're looking to be taken on here —"

"I'm to work tonight."

"Tonight, Eamonn needs all the help he can lay his hands on. But what with Lent . . .." Pierce shook his head "From what I was just hearing," he nodded at the kitchen, "there's just no call for another barmaid. And even if there were —"

He looked me up and down in a way I couldn't answer. I was wearing a nun's shift. In any case, I just couldn't fill out a barmaid's blouse. Though I could do the work as well as any more pleasing woman.

"You don't want this, Clara," Pierce said. "What would your Mr. McGee think of you cleaning every Dogan's spittle, after listening to their cursing?"

This last bit of humiliation I had to answer.

"Mr. McGee made the best of what he could find in life," I said. "He'd know I'm doing the same."

"They'd only be taking you on for charity, Clara." He nodded to the kitchen again. "They were happy enough just now, to learn that I've a use for you."

A use for me. "They want me here tonight," I repeated.

"They'll do grand enough without you," Pierce said.

Charity . . . I saw it now. Hannah had made a funny face when her uncle gave me the work tonight. I was Eamonn Docherty's Lenten offering. My grip tightened around the mop. If Pierce had a job for me, at least I knew he didn't offer charity.

"What do you need from me?" I said.

I knew what I needed. I'd made my pact with Our Lord, after Hannah and I knocked off Mr. McGee's brandy. Not a drink would I take if He kept this roof above me.

The brandy was on the top shelf over behind the bar. Across my clean floor.

"You'll like where I'm taking you, Clara."

What kind of girl was I, when only Pierce saw value in me.

"There's no place finer than the Prime Minister's residence," he said. "Now is there?"

"The Macdonalds'?" Nonsense. All the help in town would be lining up if there were work at the Prime Minister's, even if M'Lady was so high and mighty.

"Now that Miss Macdonald is born, they're in need of another maid."

Pierce lifted his hat, knocked the rime into my bucket. He took care with it, like there was nothing more important than his finger circling snow from the thick felt. "For the nursery. You'll be sitting with the baby as much as cleaning."

"Surely they've long since hired the help they'll be needing," I said.

"A maid didn't—she wasn't found to be suitable," he said.

"A maid was dismissed on the day of the little miss's birth?"

"The girl let her lips run loose." He raised his eyes to mine. "At least I know you'll keep your thoughts to yourself, Clara. This other girl was like our Hannah—sharing the customers' secrets with the neighbourhood."

Hannah and Pierce and their secrets. He told nothing to nobody, and she . . .. What a family.

"You'll have room and board and two dollars a month. Same wage you earned at Trotter's." His boot toe flicked at the puddle he'd created. "I need you to come now."

I hadn't made that much money at Trotter's since Mr. McGee died . . .. All these months of working odd jobs to make up the shortfall, and never quite managing. Now I was to be paid a woman's wage again—at the Prime Minister's house. No matter that I didn't understand this luck. Or Pierce's part in making the luck happen for me. As I'd no choice, it was a good choice to be handed.

"But—Sow—"

"I've left word for Hannah to take care of your pig," Pierce said.

"I'll just finish up . . .."

He set his hat back on. "I'll be waiting in the buggy."

My thoughts pushed and pulled me as my arms drove the mop across the floor's final inches.

Hannah hadn't been the same since I'd admitted I was part Proddie . . .. I must send a note to Polly O'Neill . . .. I mightn't have time to watch over Mrs. Trotter . . .. I needed to tamp down the fear of what was to come.

I dropped the rag mop into the slopping water, leaning the handle against the wall.

Someone else would have to set the chairs in place.

I ran to the bar. Right across the clean wet floor, my new boots clomping even more than the old ones had. Then I felt along the shelf above me, with my fingertips, guiding the brandy bottle to the edge. It dropped into my left hand.

Hannah's uncle was a careful man. He'd marked a line with candle wax to show how much he'd poured.

I set down the bottle and grabbed a shot glass. Pulled the cork, tilted the liquid, righted the bottle on the bar. Shut my eyes and set the glass to my lips.

Happy fifteenth birthday to me. I gargled the burn around my mouth and let it slide down my throat. My nose tingled, but I had no time to enjoy the spread of fire through my body. The madness in me eased, settled.

Glass in hand, I skipped lightly to the bucket and scooped a shot of the water. Then back to the bar, a quick tilt of my wrist . . . the level of the liquid rose to the waxed line.

I wiped the glass dry with my apron and set it in place.

Pierce was sitting inside Mr. Macdonald's Clarence carriage, facing the rear. The Indian driving it wore a skin-side out coat. I thought of Suzanne Lacroix, and her niece being so unhappy living with the nuns.

Pierce opened the door from the inside.

"What kept you, Clara?" He held out his hand, for a boost.

"I looked to thank Hannah."

Pierce was silent, as I leaned forward to swing the door shut.

The cabman geed up the horses.

"But she'd stepped out," I added.

"You'd never want to make a fool of me again, Clara?"

The padded leather seat could hold three of me, and the glass window gave me a clear view of the road ahead. We were moving along O'Connor Street at a clip. It wouldn't be long until we reached the Macdonald residence on Daly Street.

"Never say never," I said.

"Giving me back a bit of my own, are you now?" Pierce surprised me with a short, soft laugh. "You are a sharp tool to have in my drawer."

Ah, here it was, the sticking point. "I'm not to spy on the family for you, am I?"

"You'll be working on the Macdonalds' behalf. And that includes keeping an eye out." He pushed at the brim of his blessed hat. "A dollar a month will be paid to you from the Macdonald household accounts, and a dollar a month from Mr. Macdonald's security budget. Like how Mrs. Trotter shared your payment with McGee."

"How could I 'secure' anything?"

"You'll be doing just like you used to, for McGee. Only instead of writing words down for him, you'll be writing things for me again. Different kinds of things, though. Who approaches Lady Macdonald when she's out with the babe; how visitors act. Some other particulars, as I may need them. Lady Macdonald needs canny eyes around her. Especially now."

"I was never a spy for Mr. McGee," I said. "Only for you."

"Then you should take it my level of trust in you is even higher."

"Mr. Macdonald knows?" I said.

"Mr. Macdonald follows the accounts for the security service closely, Clara. You wouldn't be here without his knowledge. When I suggested—he said he recalled the Russell House, how you were loyal to D'Arcy's memory, and not so easily cowed. The Prime Minister values both those qualities."

"Will I be carrying a firearm too?"

"You think it's a joke? There'd be no harm knowing how to use one, Clara. After all, girls younger than you have fired shots for the rebels. There's no time to train you though, so not to worry."

"I'll be looking after the baby's laundry and such?"

"No, the downstairs staff will wash the clouts."

The Clarence carriage turned down a lane, and pulled up slightly beyond the Macdonald's grand house.

After we'd both descended, Pierce stood between me and the house. He waited for the driver to pull into the stables.

"Before we go inside," Pierce said. He looked at me, straight on. "There's something wrong with the babe."

"What's the matter with the little girl?" I asked.

"A problem with the birth. It's made the whole house jumpy." Pierce held my gaze. "The Prime Minister is nigh to beside himself, and nothing gets to the man."

"And M'Lady?"

He shook his head. "That's the first thing you'll need to make note of."

Pierce pulled a small cloth bag from an inside coat pocket. Out came a slice of rum cake, rich with prunes, raisins, and a marzipan glaze.

"Here. Miss Stewart, who's both cook and housekeeper, left this soaking in rum for two months. I often carry a bit, as I know it won't spoil easily." He cleared his throat. "It's as much liquor as cake. Have a bite."

I took a big bite, and savoured the rare bit of cake.

"If you walk in with a crumb still in your hand, and a compliment for her, that'll set you up proper. Nothing better than for a cook to smell her cooking on your breath. And Clara," Pierce said. "You'll need to stay on your toes around here."

Pierce was serving me notice—he knew I hadn't been fare-welling anyone. And If I wanted to keep this job, the comforts of the house wouldn't be liquid in nature.

The Macdonald house was the finest I'd ever entered. Even the back entrance had a veranda big enough for a gathering, with carved oak railings. A wooden gliding chair sat on it. Greying from the weather but with all the snow dusted off.

"Shouldn't that be stored for winter?" I asked.

"Lady Macdonald turned against tobacco, around her third month. She can't stop Sir John, but as for the rest of us. . .. This chair is for Miss Stewart's use."

"How many are there, working here?"

"Eight, including the nurse and you," Pierce said. "Two all-purpose maids. They're twin sisters, though they don't look alike. The stable man, Mr. Macdonald's man, Miss Stewart I've mentioned. Hortense is the nurse, she'll be the one teaching you. There's someone who comes in for laundry as well. The names will sort themselves out later. And the brother-in-law, of course."

"Mr. Bernard," I said. Mr. McGee had told me Mr. Macdonald's assistant was a very capable man himself.

"Bernard's Secretary of the Cabinet now," Pierce said. "Almost too big for the house to hold him. You needn't concern yourself with him much."

"Are they all Proddies, Pierce?"

"Don't worry about that, Clara." Pierce shrugged. "Macdonald's a proud Presbyterian, but he doesn't mind that his wife's Anglican, and devout. The staff . . . they were all born in Canada, come to think of it."

"So nobody but us speaks Irish—"

"Lady Macdonald won't want you crooning to the babe in Gaelic. Mind you, Macdonald may himself sing in Scots, of an evening."

We stepped into a large mud room. I hung my cape on a peg by its hood, then sank to a bench to unlace my borrowed boots.

An older woman walked over, with a pair of grey woollen slippers in her hands.

"Clara, this is Miss Stewart."

"Clara. Pierce here said you'd be just the thing." She looked me over. "We've a yellow dress that will fit you close enough. These slippers were Lady Macdonald's. You're almost her size. Everything's been cleaned with boiling water, mind.

She moved to the far side of the kitchen, and pulled a grey checked apron wrapper from a shelf below the baking table. "You'd best tie this on, right away. You'll be changing your apron daily. You'll need to wash your hands before you go any further as well, Clara. Over here, at the basin. The water's just cooled."

Miss Stewart handed me a bar of lye soap. She and Pierce watched while I rubbed it onto both of my palms.

"Always rinse well, and you're to use only these cloths," she said. "And only one use for each, then it's into the wash." She looked to Pierce. "She's ready to work?"

"I'm ready, Ma'am."

Miss Stewart nodded. "Right, then. I've left you some personal items, on the bed in your room. We'll work out all your clothing needs once you're settled. Right now, Hortense is anxious to have you in the nursery. I'll send up dinner, and that yellow dress," she said. "You can make your way upstairs and along the hall, it's the second door on the left. Do not knock. You might disturb the babe."

The staircase wound round itself up from the back of the kitchen. It had been cast out of iron, and was such a tight fit that I felt dazed looking up. I grasped the rail. My heel missed the first step; my feet were just slightly too small for Her Ladyship's cast-off slippers.

Second door on the left. Don't disturb the babe. I lifted the latch.

"Stop there."

The nurse was rocking in a chair without armrests. Her hair was stuffed under a cowl. A copy of the King James Bible sat on the table. "You haven't a cold, no illness?" She looked me over as if she might find a dirty handkerchief hanging from my pocket. I couldn't place her accent.

"No, Miss Hortense."

"It's just Hortense. Miss Macdonald's sleeping at last, bless her. Don't touch the young miss, or go nearer than necessary. Be sure her chest is rising and falling."

She rose, and rushed past. "Don't—breathe on her. I must go," she said. "We're not allowed commodes in the little miss's room." Hortense ran out.

Not knowing what else to do, I took her place in the rocker.

Watch the babe's breath, she'd said. But don't breathe anywhere nearby. Even craning forward, I couldn't see the bundle in the tiny bed. I reached for the candle holder. Knelt, and crept until I could peek over the cradle's edge. My hand shook. Wax bled onto the floor, burning my fingers.

Her head was twice the size of any baby's I'd seen. Misshapen, like she'd been whacked with an anvil. A deep red, and all puffy. Her veins shone through their casing . . . such thin skin.

All the baby's weight seemed settled at her swollen head. Her body didn't equal it, even with the thick blanket.

I placed a hand above her bow lips, and felt the merest puff of air . . . then another.

It was full dark when the nurse named Hortense returned. My questions were too big for me to give them voice.

"Water on the brain," she said. "They don't usually last."

"How—"

"Lady Macdonald—" Hortense nodded to another door, which blended into the wallpaper— "insisted on doing her public duties. She came down with measles, just after the fall fair."

Just after the trial.

"Come, Clara, I'll show you how to change her clout." Hortense picked up the tightly-bound baby girl. "And you can help to give her a sponge bath."

"Hortense, I've never—"

"You're not going to walk out too?" she said.

"No."

She smiled down at the baby and said, as if soothing her, "The Macdonalds shouldn't have to suffer through this affliction."

XXVIII

Sunlight lifted the shadows behind Miss Macdonald's cradle. I leaned over and snuffed the lamp. Then the door out into the hall opened, with a kick.

Mr. Macdonald himself carried in a breakfast tray. He nodded to the tilt-top table. "Hoist that up, would you?" he said. "I hear you left your supper tray almost uneaten."

I stood up from the rocker, in a rush. "Thank you, Sir. You needn't have—"

"Nonsense. Thought we should have a chat, as you're looking after my baboo."

Miss Stewart had sent up cutlery wrapped in a pea-green napkin. The blue plate was heaped. Four pieces of buttered toast, two rashers of bacon, with coddled eggs, potato hash, beans. I'd rarely eaten so much in a day.

Mr. Macdonald lifted a half-full glass from the tray, then sat on a straight-backed chair. "Nothing like a good spread first thing, is there?" he said. "Take your seat, don't be shy."

I balanced myself with my toes, poised at the edge of the rocker. "I'm not much of a breakfast eater, Sir."

"That won't do at all," he said. "You need to stoke your own fire before you can provide comfort to others. Matter of fact—" He lifted a rasher of bacon from my plate. "Aggie bats my fingers for this," he said. He knocked the lids off the poached eggs. One swipe of my knife for each, no shell left hanging.

"We need soldiers for these—you do the honours." He held out the knife, blunt end toward me. Mr. Macdonald certainly had a gentleman's hand; half-moons shining, no ridges on his nails, and a writer's callus. Just like Mr. McGee.

I cut the toast.

He pushed an egg cup toward me. "Let's dip together," he said.

I held my hand under a soggy soldier, and sucked up the warm liquid mix of butter and egg.

Mr. Macdonald ate his soldiers, used my teaspoon to scoop the remaining egg, then tucked into the potato hash.

Almost emptied, the plate showed off a thistle pattern. 'Twas so pretty, the way it was painted on under the glaze, in bluish-purple, deep green, and warm brown tones.

"You see? Everything's better once we've eaten." Mr. Macdonald downed his drink. "You can pour my tea in here. Wait—" He licked the spoon and dropped it in the glass. "To catch the heat," he said.

"I've never seen tea drunk that way," I said.

"Russians protect their pinkies with a silver holder. A Glaswegian has no need for such a nicety." He took a sip. "You're forgetting your own tea, Clara."

Little Miss Macdonald whimpered.

"You eat that rasher of bacon I've left you," Mr. Macdonald told me. "And the potatoes. I'll look after the baboo."

He dragged his chair over to the cradle, and reached for her waving hand. "Now, my baboo." His Scots accent suddenly came on thick. "There's my girl. How're you today, my loo?"

I couldn't help but think he hadn't washed after the bacon and soldiers.

"Are you awake, my loo, my sweet baboo?" he crooned. "You'd like a song, would you?"

And just like that, Mr. Macdonald was serenading us.

> *Did you ever see a lassie, a lassie, a lassie . . . go this way and*
> *that . . ..*

His voice wasn't powerful and low as Mr. McGee's had been, but a sweet tenor fit for a lullaby.

"D'you know this one, Clara?" he asked, still looking at his daughter. "She likes this song," he said. "Look how she's settled."

"I've heard it, Sir."

"Good, hum it even if you can't sing. Then you'll be able to soothe Margaret Mary Theodora." He ran his roughened pen finger around the ruffles on Miss Macdonald's blanket. "I'm afraid my baboo's been a great source of anxiety for us all," he said. "Thank the Lord that Aggie survived the birth. I wasn't here, you see—a matter of Parliamentary business . . ... But they're both with us now."

Mr. Macdonald straightened. "And my lass, she can grow past this." He reached into his pocket, and held a piece of jotting paper toward the window light to read it. Then waved it at the breakfast. "You haven't finished."

"I've eaten all I can, Sir."

"You're as mule-headed as D'Arcy himself." He waved the paper. "You've strong voices in your favour, Miss Swift. Pierce is one, and that's most unusual." Mr. Macdonald focused on the paper again. "And D'Arcy's voice the most powerful, coming from beyond the grave."

"What do you mean, Sir?"

"I've been looking at poor D'Arcy's letters," he said. "This is from last autumn."

> *The speech has been copied by my most faithful servant, Miss Clara Swift.*
> *Were she a boy, she'd be me at fifteen. Brimming with possibility, anxious to make her way. Though a bit prettier.*

"You can't get better praise than that ," he said.

A bit pretty? "There isn't better than Mr. McGee," I said.

"Thanks be we've a devil to hang," Mr. Macdonald said. "Though it doesn't even the balance."

I took a breath. Dare I?

"Do you think, Sir—with more time—Jimmy Whelan would lead you to others behind Mr. McGee's shooting?"

"Whelan thought that would be his saving—to tell that young reporter he knew the real killer." He stood. "I made sure to roust Whelan's lawyer, and have him explain the law to the rebel."

I looked at the cradle. He'd raised his voice, but his daughter didn't stir.

"You see, Clara, if you're party to the murder but you don't pull the trigger, that's still a hanging offence," he said.

"It seems a hard law—no offence, Mr. Macdonald."

"You're a reader. D'you know Shakespeare's story about the Moor who strangled his young wife?" Mr. Macdonald said.

"*Othello*," I said.

"Then you know that bugger Iago was as guilty as the Moor? And twice as dangerous." He placed the paper in his breast pocket. "A right blatherskite, Whelan. Pierce has had you stay close to his wife, I know."

His words nipped at me now, the way they had at the Russell House.

I cleared my throat. "She believes Jimmy wouldn't have the wit to be so evil."

"He may be witless, or too clever by half. He may have been listening to rebels' whispers, or to Satan himself."

"John?" A voice called from the dressing room.

"I can trust you to look after my womenfolk, Clara?" he said.

Pierce had told him about Jimmy's curse, then.

"Understand, Clara, I have many lives in my hands." He bent over the cradle. "Your mother and I will be right here, baboo."

"John?" Lady Macdonald called again. "Is everything all right?" Lady Macdonald stepped through the dressing room door. She was wearing a loose silk dressing gown, a lilac shade. I'd never seen one so rich. Her hair was plaited and pinned back. She was every bit as elegant as she'd been last fall, and she had only just given birth.

"John, you've a line-up of people," she said.

"The baboo's asleep, Aggie." He answered the question she didn't ask. "I was having a chat with our new junior nursemaid. Clara."

I stood as straight as I could without looking daft.

"Miss Swift, isn't it?" she said.

"Yes, M'Lady?"

"Thank you for stepping in," she said.

"Thank you, M'Lady—for the honour."

"There are birth presents piled in there. Could you sort them, make a list, see what we could use?"

"Yes'm."

Lady Macdonald lowered herself into the rocker. "Set our girl in my arms, John."

Mr. Macdonald picked up his daughter, pulled her blanket tight, kissed her forehead. He ever so gently set her in her mother's arms. Neither parent seemed to notice anything wrong.

Mr. Macdonald winked at me. The man who stole my breakfast was back. "You've eaten, Clara, now it's feeding time for my baboo," he said. "Aggie wants us to be off. There's a collection of D'Arcy's published works in the library, both his poetry and his attempts at political history. You're free to borrow any of them, if you've need of something to put you to sleep."

Once we were in the dressing room, he tapped my arm. "Clara, you're to pick up my girl, and hold her," he whispered. "Let her feel the warmth of a loving touch. She's not a china doll, Clara. She's not going to break."

I folded all the dresses and nighties and even baby-sized short-alls that had been sent. I wrote careful notes on the back of each letter or card about the present. Lady Macdonald hadn't yet called me back to the baby's room, so I pulled out the armless, low-set mahogany chair tucked into Lady Macdonald's dressing table.

When I sat, my legs fit just right to the ground. I plumped the grey silk pillow that rested against the chair's back. The table was full of potions and perfumes. Lady Macdonald's hairpins were in a glass bowl; her hairbrush was silver, with a curly SAM inscribed into its back. I'd read that stood for Susan Agnes. I lifted the stopper out of a cut-crystal bottle and sniffed ammonia. Ladies said it made their faces whiter. She had a pot of white face paint as well. She must despair of her pink blush. I pulled out another stopper. Rosewater. I went to dab a bit on my wrists, then thought better of it—Miss Stewart seemed the type who would catch me, if I went downstairs with any scent on.

The chair was padded, the pillow downy, and the air sweet. I'd stepped up. Like Hannah had said I would, given half a chance.

This new world may never fit me like my old one had.

And higher didn't mean easier. Mr. Macdonald ran everyone and everything. But even he couldn't make this small world right.

Hortense opened the baby's door. "M'Lady's fed Miss Macdonald, but she wants to help me bathe her," she said in a low tone. "You'd best return your breakfast tray. Miss Stewart will show you to your room."

I went down the front stairs this time, to get the lay of the house.

Mr. Macdonald was in his study, with Pierce and Mr. Bernard. And a fourth man.

"So we're no closer to arresting the Fenian leaders?" said Mr. Macdonald, as I passed by. He sounded so tired, now. "Nothing on the bombing that destroyed the Desbarats block? And Devlin?"

"Not a whisker out of place." That was an English voice.

"No rebel money flowing through Whelan's wife?"

"None we can find," Pierce said. "The money's dried up, since the uproar about McGee. Though it doesn't mean the Green Ghost won't be blowing back across the border at some future time."

"If they do," said the English voice, "I'll put an end to them. I'm more worried about the Red River Territory."

"Well, at least D'Arcy's war with the Fenian Brotherhood ends with Whelan," Mr. Macdonald said. "Tomorrow."

Miss Stewart was kneading bread dough on a wooden board. She brushed her forehead, leaving a flour mark. "Are you off to Mass for Ash Wednesday?" she said, as I placed the dishes down.

Mary Mother of God, I'd gone and eaten.

"Pierce is to drive the other girls and go himself as well," Miss Stewart said.

"Girls?" I said.

"The twins are Roman as well."

Hadn't Pierce said there were no Catholics here but we two? No. He'd said the other house staff were all born here in Canada. And not to talk about religion.

Miss Stewart set the dough on a plate, under a cloth. "I don't know why you Romans make such a fuss of the Lenten weeks."

I started, at such a description. "I mean no disrespect, Clara," she said. "As I'm an Anglican, that makes me an English Catholic. You're being a Roman Catholic—it's not that big a difference, from what I can tell."

She couldn't mean that. She must know what being true Catholics has cost us Irish.

"Pierce says you're from a mixed marriage. The woman has her say in matters of religion, of course. Did your father mind, though?"

Pierce was right, Hannah couldn't keep a secret. Or she didn't care enough to keep mine.

Miss Stewart wiped her hands on her apron cloth. "Of course, you won't be able to go up to Miss Macdonald with ashes on your forehead."

"We're not allowed to rub them away, ma'am." I'd broken my fast. How many more sins would I have to commit today?

"Then you'd best wash your hair as soon as you're back here." She picked up my plate from the tray and scraped it clean, before setting it in a washtub.

"Lather well, and use lots of water to rinse. I'm sure you understand now why we must have no dirt around Miss Macdonald. Were you comfortable sitting with her during the night?"

"She mostly slept." I crossed over to the mud room. "I'm fine to work tonight, Miss Stewart. Is it all right if I'm out tomorrow during the day?"

"You're not going to the hanging."

I didn't let her catch my eye.

"I just need to drop off a present." I tied the hood of my cape tight.

As I followed twins who didn't look remotely like sisters up the stone steps outside St. Patrick's Church, I made my plea to Pierce. The boxes being in my cape pockets, and thus being saved from the fire, I told him, meant it was ordained that Bridie should have them from me.

"So you see," I said. "I need to meet up with Bridie tomorrow."

"I happen to think that would be a good idea, Clara," Pierce said.

I stared at him.

One of the twins tapped my shoulder. "You're keeping us out in the cold, Miss Clara."

We all entered the church, but I lingered as he and I wet our fingers in the font, and blessed ourselves. "Clara, no one cares whether his widow holds a few locks of Jimmy's hair in her hand," he said. "What Bridie says, when she realizes he'd been carving two boxes—that's what interests me."

I took a seat in a back pew. Three people had already filed into the row between the twins and me. Pierce moved to a back corner, from whence he could survey the entire church.

I knelt. Who should I pray for first?

At the altar, Father Clement blessed the ashes, then anointed them. The march of sinners began.

Cinis in cinerem and pulvis in pulverem,

Father Clement chanted. You are dust, and to dust you must return. The row in front of me rose, then it was our turn. At the railing, I knelt again. All the altar statues were shrouded in purple cloth. Father Clement made the Sign of the Cross on my forehead.

A terra usque ad pulverem.

Father Clement intoned, as he pressed his thumb into my skin. Ashes to ashes, as ever was and will be.

I felt like my allegiance was stamped on my face now. I was a Paddy, and proud of it.

As I walked in single file back to my seat, though, my first prayer was for the Protestant little Miss Macdonald.

After Mass, the twins stepped to the side altar to light votive candles. Pierce and I shuffled outside to a day made grey by sleet.

Over in the church cemetery, Hannah stood by Mike's footstone.

Pierce tented his hands over his head. He'd left the cowboy hat at home today, of all days. "I'll wait here, but only until the twins come out," he said.

When I reached her, Hannah was laying down a bouquet of dried lavender, tied with a braid of lace. I could think of nothing but what she'd said a widow missed.

She spoke without looking up. "Are you enjoying the big house?" she said.

"Please thank your Uncle Eamonn for me—"

"'Twas nothing." She brushed at the stone.

> MICHAEL WALSH 1840-1868
> NO CROSS NO CROWN

"There." She pushed herself up. "Mike sang *Lavender's Blue* to me, the night I met him in the bar. Did you know he was a fine tenor?"

"Do you want me to leave you be?"

"No, I've had too much of death." She walked toward the church. "There's a man in Grimsby," Hannah said. "His family was friendly with my grandparents."

"You're to marry a stranger?"

"I had hot blood with Mike, and my fun before him," she said. "Now I want to go home. And a man who has no loyalty but to me."

"I don't understand."

"Of course you don't. You're such a gosling." As we neared the steps the twins emerged, arm in arm. "Your new girlfriends?" Hannah said. "And how's the sweet baby?"

I stamped my boots against the cold.

"Will the proud Da leave the nursery, to see Jimmy swing?"

Hannah saw Pierce waving, and waved back.

But the signal was for me, not for her.

I touched her arm. "I'm so sorry you lost Mike, Hannah."

"'Tis the right day to offer it up, at least." Hannah swiped one of her gloves across her eyes. "Do leave me be now."

There was a good view of the street from the nursery. As I rocked the baboo's cradle, the sun rose on Jimmy's last day. I could now see that while the snow was packed hard against the houses, there was sand enough on the road to reassure the public. There'd be a crowd at the hanging.

For the next hour, the baboo slept, and I took peeks at one of Mr. McGee's books of poesie.

As soon as we'd returned from Mass the previous day, I'd rushed to the library. It'd been such a comfort to run a finger across the row of bound volumes, straighten their spines, and pluck out one or two. To think, they were there to be read. Not out of reach, but available to be touched. I had chosen *Canadian Ballads, and Occasional Verses* to borrow, after I'd read the inscription by Mr. McGee.

> *John, you're too smart by half, but a fine enough fellow nonetheless. You'll have to do.*
>
> *—D'Arcy*

One of his poems was called *Our Ladye of the Snow*.

As I read it, I hoped that Bridie was able to comfort Jimmy, at the last.

I wondered, though, if Jimmy would search among those there to witness his death, for the lady in his drawing.

The heavenly being Mr. McGee wrote of in his poem sounded a bit like Jimmy's lady of Ireland.

> *Oh! lovelier, lovelier far than pen,*
> *Or tongue, or art, or fancy's ken...*

Mr. McGee had written, and

> *So the warm radiance from her hands*
> *Unbind for him Death's icy bands,*

And nerve the sinking heart—
Her presences make a perfect path.
Ah! he who such a helper hath
May anywhere depart.

M'Lady Macdonald strolled into the baboo's room. She caught Mr. Macdonald eating my breakfast once again.

"M'Lady?" I closed the book, and stood.

'Twas a vain hope, that even these laments would take my mind off the scene about to unfold.

Pierce, and M'Lady's brother Mr. Bernard, each came looking for the Prime Minister as well.

"Leave me alone with my daughter, the lot of you." M'Lady took little Miss Macdonald from my arms. "I know you all want to go and watch that devil hang."

"Aggie, you know I must—"

"John—go." M'Lady kissed the air, just above her baby's forehead, lest she hurt her. "Make sure John wears his fur coat," she told her brother. "You know he doesn't like to dress so well in a crowd, but he'll need it today."

"I'm Cabinet Secretary, Aggie, not John's valet."

She pretended not to hear. Did brothers and sisters act like that, when they'd grown up?

"Will this be your first, Clara?" M'Lady asked.

"Yes'm."

Lady Macdonald looked over at her husband. "The girl could catch a cold there, or worse, and bring it back here . . . should Clara go near all those people? John?"

"I would like to honour Mr. McGee's memory, M'Lady." I said.

Mr. Macdonald wiped grease off his lips and hands, with a sizable white linen hankie. "Miss Clara went to church yesterday, Aggie. Plenty of chance to get sick in a church."

Pierce smiled at that. "And I'd like Clara along, M'Lady," he said. "In case the widow needs soothing."

Of course Bridie would need soothing. Standing with a crowd of strangers while her husband met the noose. And after today, she would finally be the Widow Whelan.

"That isn't appropriate for a young girl, either . . . .. We must have you properly outfitted, Clara." The way M'Lady looked at Mr. Macdonald, then changed the subject . . . she knew she'd lost.

In that moment, I felt for her. Men so often get their way . . . and her husband more than anyone.

The hanging was to be held in the jail courtyard.

Mr. Macdonald went into the warden's office. Pierce motioned for the household staff to come ahead.

The snow hit my face straight on. I stepped in Pierce's boot prints as he walked to the cordoned-off stands, guarded by coppers.

Sergeant O'Neill was already positioned at the far end of the benches, with what looked like the entire Ottawa Police force ranged around nearby. Militiamen were standing in line on the opposite side of the field.

"It was a good choice to come here on an empty stomach," Pierce said.

"You're the apostate, Pierce," I said. "I'm observing the fast."

The way his lips curled, ever so slightly, he knew about my slip at breakfast the previous day.

"What we're about to experience is a real dose of ritual sacrifice, Clara." Pierce said. "I've been to many hangings, and none of them left me with a good taste. I advise you to look away at the moment of truth."

Sergeant O'Neill let all the Macdonald staff past the barrier, though he gave me the fisheye.

"Perch in these seats," Pierce told us. "Keep them warm for the dignitaries. You can step over to the front of that crowd when you see Mr. Macdonald leading the parade out the door."

Parliament's tower bell rang the hour. Ten in the morning, and nobody in Ottawa was at work once again. It looked to be as big a crowd as had turned out for the procession to the train, with Mr. McGee. The day I'd learned what thousands really looked like. Only instead of mourning a death, they were gathered together in expectation of one.

They kept coming, through the snowstorm. Merchants' wives and their well-dressed daughters stepped out of carriages. A man boosted his young girl onto his shoulders. Then a group of Orangemen marched up, holding banners. One of them read NO DOGS OR CATHOLICS.

There was no doubt, though, that Jimmy's own had shown up to see him out as well. It looked like every lad who'd been at yesterday's Mass was in the crowd. The ashes on their foreheads had been smeared by sleep.

You had to know the thumbprint of the Lenten season's onset, to identify the grey smudges on their brows now. A few more minutes in this storm and they'd be cleansed of the most obvious marking of their Catholicism. Yet having been forced to remove my own ash-mark, I felt somewhat a stranger to my tribe.

It began to snow harder then. Those without the sense to have them in place already pulled their caps out of their pockets.

A cry went up. *"Clann na Gaedeal."*

The coppers and militia were going to need to move with all speed, if the Orange began mixing with the Green.

The big men began to appear, guided over in groups of three and four. One group included the coroner, and Dr. Gillivray.

As Mr. Macdonald walked across the grounds, Pierce and a number of his men at the Prime Minister's side, a chant rang out.

> *"Where's Devlin and Enright and Buckley, Oh Boys?*
> *Where's Devlin and Enright and Buckley, Oh Boys?*
> *They're not for the noose, John A. let them loose,*
> *For Jimmy's to hang and it gives John A. joy."*

Joy. So the crowd didn't yet know about Mr. Macdonald's private sorrow. The Prime Minister's right glove flicked across his coat pocket. I'd filled the flask for him.

I hadn't taken a swig.

We moved off the dignitaries' seats. Hortense, the twins, Miss Stewart, and I were let right in front, to some grumbling from those who'd come early for a good spot. The stableman moved to the back; no way they'd make way for an Indian, even one who was Mr. Macdonald's man.

My fingers curled into the squirrel skin of the inside-out gloves I'd traded for with Suzanne Lacroix. The stableman's coat must be warm, with fur in the lining. I pushed Jimmy's boxes further into the pockets of my cape.

Following after Mr. Macdonald, and his Constabulary guard, were those Cabinet ministers and Parliamentarians who'd made a special trip for this.

Monsieur Robitaille was among them. I wondered where he was staying now, and if he'd shaken himself loose of Mrs. Trotter's trio of troublesome boarders.

The trial judge walked over, ahead of the lawyers for both sides of the story. Even the bunch of other journalists who had always hung off Mr. Lacey were guided to a seat in the higher-ups' stands.

Then everyone was looking at Mrs. McGee, still shrouded in widow's weeds, and protected under an umbrella by Miss Frasa.

Mr. McGee's daughter's dress and veil were also the same she'd worn at the funeral and the trial, though she was allowed to wear grey now.

The McGee women sat next to Mr. Macdonald.

Pierce showed up again, from behind, pulling Hannah forward with a stiff hand on her elbow. Men grumbled, but they made way.

"Are you satisfied?" Pierce asked Hannah.

'Twas so like Hannah. She scorned my working for the Macdonalds, but she never minded taking advantage of Pierce's position, or her own beauty.

The jail door opened again. Bridie stepped out.

Miss Frasa startled the crowd by rising, and raising her veil. Tears were flowing down Miss Frasa's cheeks, and for a moment I wasn't sure whether Miss Frasa might be planning to confront Bridie, or perhaps even to comfort her.

Mr. Macdonald reached for the umbrella. The Prime Minister opened it, at such an angle that only a few of us saw Mrs. McGee whisper to her daughter. Then clasp hands with Miss Frasa, in such a way that their hands were fisted together. Mr. Macdonald kept the umbrella unfurled, until, after a few moments, Mrs. McGee released her daughter's hands.

Miss Frasa lowered her veil.

Bridie had ideas of her own as well, no surprise. As prison guards steered her toward the special benches, Bridie pointed to the crowd. Then she looked Sergeant O'Neill up and down, and stepped past the barrier. As close as possible to the scaffold.

People cleared away from her, while Sergeant O'Neill moved to stand beside her. Was he there to protect her, or to stop her from running up and throwing herself at Jimmy as he walked his last?

Despite her bold move, Bridie didn't look like she'd be making a holy show of herself today. She looked turned into herself. Shriveled. Not big enough for her coat. Not the woman she had been in court.

Pierce elbowed his way over to me. He lay a glove on my sleeve. "Let Mrs. Whelan have her patch of land," he said. "Later, you'll come over to her with me."

The crowd and the officials all waited a long minute. Bridie stared across the yard.

Then the warden and four guards flanked Jimmy as he stepped high through the powder, across to the platform.

A fifth man followed behind. His face was hooded.

A whisper passed from man to man. The guards had played dice, they said. The loser had to act as the hangman.

The men who'd been leading the chant pulled their hats off and placed them over their hearts as Jimmy climbed up the makeshift steps of the wooden scaffold.

He faced the scaffold's crossbeam. The rope was looped, and hanging from a hook attached to one of the scaffold's side beams.

"Standing here on the brink of the grave, I wish to declare to you and to my God that I am innocent." Jimmy was hoarse, our view of him blocked by the guards.

Bridie began to weep, and Pierce to cough. They both kept it up as Whelan described his service in Her Majesty's army, his desire to settle down. I wasn't sure if Pierce was trying to draw attention away from Whelan, or from Bridie.

"My dear wife Bridget was to join me here in Ottawa," Jimmy said. "To make a new home together."

I knew that was a straight-out lie. I had it from Bridie's own mouth that she'd always wanted her Jimmy in Montreal.

"I'm only standing here, to be sent to hang, because I'm a good Irish Catholic."

There was a cheer at that, and a chorus of boos. The men were all calling out and shushing one another so loudly, I missed the warden's call to move Jimmy forward.

"What did Jimmy say?" An elderly man asked.

"Whatever the man said or didn't say is of no matter," said his son. "He's going to our Lord and there'll be a proper judgment of him yet."

The crowd settled, though, so that when Jimmy Whelan spoke his last, his words carried through the crisp, cold air.

"God save my soul, and God save Ireland."

The winter light jumped bright off the snow. My eyes watered from it. My lips tasted the wool of my scarf, and the damp of my breath ran through its threads. My cheeks burned from the air's sharp dryness. I pulled my scarf higher, tied the hood of my cape tighter. I shifted my weight, pushing my stiff toes into the ground for purchase. The snow under my boots scraped like fine chalk powder on a board. I shivered. The powder began to blow then, so that I couldn't tell which snow was being carried with the wind and which was falling from the heavens above. I rubbed the skin of one gloved palm across the beading on the back of the other.

Jimmy's wrists were tied behind his back, his hands bare. He wore no coat, and the collar of his grey prison shirt was unbuttoned. His shirt billowed where it was tucked into black trousers. He'd been allowed his boots. Perhaps for the weight.

Father Clement anointed Jimmy with oil, on his forehead and lips, and each cheek. Then the priest touched a wooden crucifix to each side of Jimmy's throat in blessing. Finally, Father stepped to one side and bent his head in silent prayer.

Jimmy didn't bend his head. Two guards had to restrain him, while another two helped the hangman place the noose. He tried to kick the stool away.

One of the Orangemen shouted, "be a man about it, you Dogan."

Jimmy closed his eyes at that, and gave himself over to the guards. They guided him up onto a stool. The hangman tightened the cord, and tucked it behind Jimmy's left ear.

I wanted to close my eyes as well, but I granted Jimmy my full attention.

The hangman kicked the stool.

Jimmy hung, suspended from the crossbeam. His face turned a deep red. He choked, spittle ran from his open mouth.

"God in heaven, but they're making a botched job of it," said the man who'd brought the young girl. He swung his daughter back to the ground.

The tower bell rang the half hour. The rope was taking the Lord's own time to do its job. Jimmy's face turned grey; his tongue hung out; his body swung the smallest bit.

Finally, the call came. "Cut him down."

Jimmy's body dropped to the wooden stage. Blood flowing, his head almost severed from his body by twisting.

"Turn away Clara, for the love of Jesus," Pierce said, as his gaze swept the scene.

Hannah's tawny-hazel eyes were set on Bridie, with a mix of empathy and disdain. They were two women, as Bridie had said last September, who each believed the other's husband deserved to die.

All around us, there was a wiping of eyes with hankies, men loosening their scarves to spit in the snow. Turning to one another.

"You got to give it to Jimmy. He didn't die easy."

"He didn't die calling out names. He was no weasel, Jimmy."

"A bad death for a good enough lad."

"I've been to twenty hangings," said the old man who couldn't hear. The only one still looking at the scaffold. "And I've never seen one. My eyes look right past the man. Can't take him in."

And then, from more than one mouth, "I need a drink."

As if to order, one of the men who'd chanted pulled out a fiddle from a burlap bag and set it under his chin. Another placed his hands behind his back and began to dance to the dirge. Boots clicking and kicking up the snow as if he were wearing the finest, lightest slippers.

"Hanging is a thirsty business," the old man agreed.

A young man eyeing Hannah called out, "There's our beauty. She'll be handing out the drinks at Docherty's."

Hannah gave him her barmaid smile. She'd told me it kept the lads happy while holding them off. "I'll see you there, all night," she called.

"Aye, we'll take the party to the pub, and wake Jimmy in right style," said the old man's son.

Like that would make what happened any better. Only these men would say it had to.

It was our way.

Then a man's voice rose in the air to match the fiddle, and another and another joined in with a rebel song of love and death, and the cycle between sinking into the land and rising up from it. They sang about the barley every Irishman carries in his pocket, in case he needs to eat on the march. How when an Irishman is in the ground, the barley grows over him, until the breeze blows and the Irish rise again.

The Orangemen tore the banners from their planks and started to swing the wood at the singers. From their separate flanks, the coppers and militia both rushed into the fight.

Pierce motioned. "Step over, Clara."

We left Hannah amidst a mess of men who were singing, and dancing, and fighting.

And made our way over to Bridie's island of sorrow.

"O'Neill, we're getting Mrs. Whelan out of this," Pierce ordered. "It's like St. Paddy's and the July Twelfth Orangeman's Parade, out there, all at once."

In a lower voice, he told me, "We can't make martyrs of Jimmy and his wife both today. You'll let her talk of her loss. Even if you can't sympathise, after seeing what the man really was."

But I could; I did. And yet, I would also do my job.

"Jimmy said he knew the killer," I replied. "Did he let slip a name, in the end?"

Pierce pushed me toward Bridie. "Maybe she'll tell you."

LIFE AFTER DEATH

Thursday February 11th, 1869

XXIX

It took but a few minutes to reach the hotel. Pierce and Sergeant O'Neill both rode outside on the driver's cab of the Macdonalds' carriage. Inside, Bridie let me hug her and whisper my condolence. But her shock flashed at me as anger, not tears. I was happy for it. This was a bit more the woman she'd been six months ago.

"The Orange bastards," she said.

Pierce came around to fetch her out of the carriage.

"The Russell House, of all places, Clara," Bridie said. "Where Jimmy's lawyer used to lunch with the Crown Attorney between trial sessions. I had trouble gaining admittance here to talk to the man standing up for my own husband. Now the hotel's taken me for the two nights, if you can believe it. By courtesy of the government's persuasion, of course. I'll be off in the morning."

I didn't mention my time in their boot closet. But I felt the faces turn to us, with their silks and their superior eyebrows. Surveying the whole room from behind a cushy corner table, there of all people was Barney Devlin. Holding court, as we entered the tearoom, like he was already a Parliamentarian.

We were ushered to the far side of the room. Pierce motioned, and an ebony screen inset with bits of ivory was lugged over by three waiters. Pierce arranged the screen so we were shielded from the room, but he could see us. When the *maître d'* took Bridie's cloak, Pierce motioned him to lay it on the extra chair at his table. Meanwhile I took my own cape off, so I could extract the boxes. I laid it over Bridie's.

The tea that arrived was Chinese, like the screen. A strong black, with a perfume that put me off a bit. I couldn't fault all the fancy fixings. There was a three-tiered china tray with tiny ham or egg sandwiches, scones with raisins and clotted cream on the side, jams and jellies, and slices of apple pound cake. I reached for the cake. Stopped, thought about Lent. Decided I'd confess it on Saturday, and who cared if Pierce saw me eat. For the first time in days, I craved food.

Then I hefted the silver teapot. "Your people will come to sit with you when you're back in Montreal," I said.

"No," she said. "I just want to be behind my own doors, without anyone watching me."

I put my hand over hers.

"I worry that I'll live a long life—years, living with *this*," she said. "I can't think of that—what of you, Clara? Mrs. Trotter's not taking boarders? How's that left you?"

"I'm training as a nursemaid—"

"You've a proper job again, then. Was that your wish at the tree?" she asked. "After being turned out by the McGee family?"

"I wished for Mr. McGee's killers to be brought to justice."

"Then your wish hasn't ripened." The thought hung between us. Even if my wish did come to pass now, it couldn't help Jimmy.

Pierce coughed.

"What was your wish that day, Bridie?" I said.

"My old wish was to be a married woman. The one I tied the day we met— that one was for Jimmy to come back to me."

"Why did he move here, Bridie?"

"Oh, Jimmy was a born wanderer. I took him as I found him," she said. "I let him go off, thinking he'd find his way home to where the money was soon enough. I never thought—"

"I've something for you, Bridie. From Jimmy." I pulled the boxes from where I'd set them on my seat.

She picked up one in each hand. Fingered the knot carved on one, then the other.

"There's a lock of his hair inside each," I said.

Bridie placed them on the table.

"Thank you, Clara. I've precious little from Jimmy's own hand, aside from the clothing he tailored and left behind in Montreal. I saw him only for a few minutes today, and he was far past thinking of a gift for me. I trashed the rubbish the warden saw fit to give me . . .." She sipped her tea. "Jimmy'd time enough on his hands . . ." she said. "But it's strange he made two boxes with the same pattern."

"He asked that you send one to his mother," I said. "Would you like me to freshen your cup, Bridie?"

I poured the red-black brew into the bone-white china.

"Jimmy loved his mother, no mistake, Clara." Bridie said. She wrapped her hands around the cup, rather than stuffing her finger into the dainty handle, and gulped her second cup of tea. "He may have come around to that idea, of sending her the box. But when he cut off that lock of his hair, he may have had someone different in mind."

She turned the empty cup, as if reading the leaves. "I'm thinking maybe he told you a yarn, Clara. But you're old enough to understand? I was happy enough, just to have Jimmy as my husband, for those moments when I did have the boon of his full attention."

"Was there a sketch of a girl, in the belongings you trashed?" I asked.

"No picture there, no. Yet that was the only bit of truth buried in all Mike Walsh's lies." Bridie said. "There was a girl, Clara. A young woman he met after we married. A colleen who didn't care about that fact. I have to think she was a real beauty, for Jimmy to stray so soon."

She set the cup down so hard the leavings sloshed across her saucer and onto the white linen cloth. "I didn't care how many knots he carved, or how often. Whether he drew pictures of Lady *Éireann* or worshipped the moon. As long as he came home to me."

Bridie's tears had come. She picked up the napkin and swiped at them. "I know I'm an old woman, and his blood was still up. Nancy Trotter would say I shouldn't be talking like this to a girl. You should twig to this now, though, Clara. It's the hardest thing in the world to love a man, bytimes. When the madness hits you, you do it anyway. When it hits him—it's not uncommon for a man of any age to be gone from home of a night. Even if it's just around the corner. You've seen that close-up, goodness knows."

"Mrs. Trotter's not well—" I said.

"I know there's been a fire and brimstone judgement on her house. Though I can't read the newspapers, my neighbours rushed to tell me. Whether well or sick, Mrs. Trotter's no better than she should be, you know that, Clara. Just like that other one," Bridie said. "Oh, I hate the judge, and the jury, and every man who told a tale on Jimmy for cash in his pocket," Bridie said. "But more than any, I hate this sweetheart. Whoever she was, she never visited him once."

"Bridie—Jimmy said he was at Trotter's. At the shooting."

Bridie blew her nose in the Russell House napkin. "He swore to me he didn't know the shooting was to happen."

"So you knew."

"I don't know who was with him, Clara. Or why he was on the street." She shook her head. "Jimmy would tell me anything. Even about that woman." She sighed. "But not about the shooter. He said, 'Mother Ireland loves me, but *Fódla* is a cruel mistress.' And if I knew, I'd die too."

"Bridie?" I said. "He wouldn't tell you how many were behind it?"

She looked at the screen, her eyes tracing the ivory inlay, like she was reading a story in the patterns. "Only the daft would talk against the Fenians, Clara." Then Bridie glanced over at Pierce, and raised her voice. "There's nothing for me now but to go home and mourn Jimmy in my own way." She grabbed for my hand. "I want to take Jimmy with me, Clara. The warden won't even tell me where he's to be buried." She squeezed. "You can ask your Mr. Macdonald for this boon, Clara."

"How do you know that's where I'm working?" I said.

"Clara. All I want now is my husband's dead body. Can you ask the big man for that much? He's hanged his Fenian bogeyman high, for all to see. Let me have the remains."

"Mr. Macdonald's not the devil, Bridie. And Mr. McGee was shot dead by a man, not a hobgoblin."

"Macdonald's an Orangeman himself, a Mason through and through," she said.

"Even at the trial, the Prime Minister tamped down tempers. You know 'twas so." She held my hand fast. "Can you offer Mr. Macdonald a name, Bridie? A name, for Jimmy's body?"

"Jimmy told me no more, in our last talk together as man and wife," she said, "than he had already told you, from the sound of it."

Bridie was smarter than Jimmy, though she hadn't been smart about him. Could she really know nothing more?

Pierce folded back the screen. His look said I was a maid, there to calm Bridie, lest she think to march out on the street and hold up Jimmy's image as a holy relic of rebellion. Offer comfort and solace, he'd instructed me earlier. Don't ask questions.

"How do you know I'm working for Mr. Macdonald, Bridie?"

My hand grew hot under hers. I pulled it out. But before I could quiz her, Barney Devlin's face appeared next to Pierce's.

My stomach cramped. After the sudden pain I felt a strong, clean flow of hate, directed at Devlin.

"Mrs. Whelan," Devlin leaned between us. "My profound sympathies, from all of our community in Montreal—"

A look shifted between Devlin and Bridie. Each probing the other, shielding themselves.

"Mrs. Whelan doesn't want sympathy, Mr. Devlin," I said. "She wants Jimmy's body."

He looked startled that I could speak.

"For burial," I said. "You're in the running to be her Member of Parliament. Surely you can arrange that for her?"

"Jimmy was one of your boys in the election fight," I said. When Devlin had called Mr. McGee a traitor, stirred up so much heat against Mr. McGee. "You repay loyalty, don't you?"

Devlin looked at Pierce, as if I were Pierce's problem, and he should remove me forthwith.

The people across the tearoom stopped their polite conversations. I didn't realise my voice had gone so high.

Another cramp, and I felt my own tears welling. 'Twas as if I was hearing Devlin at the wake all over again, claiming he wasn't an enemy.

"I must go, Bridie." I pushed myself up.

"Clara, dear," she said. She took my hand again, and pressed one of the boxes into my palm. "Life cuts to the quick. Be careful."

Then she turned to Devlin. "If you could help, Barney, I'd be ever so grateful—as you said during the election, *beid lá eile ag an bPaorac*."

'We shall have another chance'? Those had been Jimmy's words, when he came to warn us . . . .

Was Bridie threatening Devlin, invoking the Fenian cry like that in front of Pierce?

Or reminding Devlin of a planned bombing, and a successful assassination, and what was owed her?

I felt a clammy rush of shame. For losing track—behind Jimmy's death and Bridie's sorrow, today, like every day, was about my doing right by Mr. McGee.

My gut cramped again, sharp, lower than a stomach pain. I stepped around Pierce, and grabbed my cape from his extra chair.

XXX

Sergeant O'Neill was standing guard at the Russell House front door. "Clara," he called as I rushed by. "About Nancy."

"Sergeant?" Another cramp hit me.

"Now you've this job——" he said. "Nancy could catch something from that baby."

"I'm not to come then?" I pushed my hands against my knees.

"We'll send over a note, if you can come by. D'you care to know how Nancy is?"

"There's been a change?" I said.

"She's awake. She has no idea about her attacker, so——"

"Thanks be to God," I said. I felt a moment's joy, then another great pain.

"You'll freeze yourself sick, girl, walking. You look sick already," he said. "And what good will you be for anyone then?"

I made it to the next street before I doubled over. I crouched into the wind, and reached under my cape and apron. And lay my fur-lined hands against my dress, to shield my private parts.

Mrs. Trotter was awake, and I couldn't see her. Because of the baboo.

Or were they afraid I'd bring danger with me?

It had been eating at me, just at the edge of my thoughts.

Was she coshed because Willy and I had gone to the jail?

If talking to Jimmy had been that dangerous, Bridie should have been dead by now. Unless Bridie was the reason Jimmy was dangerous?

I thought I'd wet myself again, worse than I had the last time I'd been at the Russell House. When I'd made it safely into my room at the Macdonalds', I peeled off my new tights and dress, and the under-shift from the nunnery. There

269

were stains on my thighs. Some of the blood was dark, and stiff on my knickers. But more was light red, and fresh.

The dresser had a tray with a brush, a comb and a hand mirror, for my own use. I picked up the mirror to try and see myself down there. Should I have known this was coming? Was that why Hannah had talked that way—had she seen my breasts were budding, despite what I'd said? I had hair where a woman would, now . . . I had to get clouts to staunch this.

Hortense was enjoying a scotch egg, in the kitchen. "Clara, you're bent in half. Are you all right?" she said, when I hobbled in.

"Who's with the baboo?" I asked, inching toward the laundry room.

"The Macdonalds . . .." Hortense was looking at me like she knew something was off.

"How could the girl be, Hortense, with what she saw today?" Miss Stewart was turned to her pastry board.

"Could I boil water?" I asked. "I thought I'd take a sponge bath."

Hortense nodded. "A good thought, that," she said. "What do you have wrapped up there?"

"It's for the rubbish bin," I said.

"Is that blood, Clara?" Hortense said.

Miss Stewart wheeled around at that. "Is Miss Macdonald bleeding?" she asked.

"'Tis—it's my knickers," I whispered to them.

Hortense pushed my legs apart. I stared at the thistle emblem embedded into the wall, a proud symbol of the Scots. What was I doing here, in this fancy mahogany bed, in the home of a knighted Scottish Presbyterian married to an English Anglican, with a Proddie nurse, who I barely knew, staring at my body?

"Dr. Gillivray's in with Lady Macdonald and Miss Macdonald now," she said.

"No, please. No. I've never had a doctor see—me."

"Is there any chance that you're breeding, Clara?" Hortense's hand knocked my thigh.

"I've never—bled before today," I said.

"We won't need to have Dr. Gillivray step in, then. Nothing but the march of life going on down here." She straightened and turned to pour water in the ewer on the nightstand. "So it's your first visit from Auntie Flow."

"In Irish, we say the *Cursai*—the course of life, you know," I said, though I was shy of the subject. "I guess that's the same as the *ban-dortad*. A womanly overflowing."

"And I always thought you Irish women were saying the Curse."

I cramped again then. "It's that too, isn't it? From Eve?"

"You're a quick learner." She dried her hands. "We've plenty of flannel here, at least. I'll bring you some to cut up. You'll have to have a full bath in the tub, Clara. You've even blood under your fingernails."

I knew Lady Macdonald had an early evening caller. But I was ever so startled when Mrs. McGee stepped through, from Lady Macdonald's dressing room.

I rose from the rocker.

"So this is where you've landed." Mrs. McGee took it all in. The polished wood, the carpet from Turkey, the chair with the view of the garden.

"Ma'am." Had Lady Macdonald said Mrs. McGee could see the baboo? "Is M'Lady—?"

"She's resting." Mrs. McGee looked past me, to the cradle. "It was a blasphemy to sneak off with our Holy Bible, Clara Swift. 'Twas blessed by the Archbishop of Boston as a wedding gift."

I bowed my head. "I know I did wrong, Ma'am."

"My daughter said she's sure you're rueing your—mistake, she called it. We both know a body can't mistake such a matter."

She'd have me fired. I rubbed my belly. So be it. "I hope today has given you some relief. Ma'am."

"The devil's gone to Hell. Doesn't bring D'Arcy back to me." She squeezed the handkerchief she held in her right fist. "He's left me to deal with a pile of trouble."

This last was said as if I weren't there. And sure, there was nothing I could say to be of help.

"The babe's asleep?" She stepped around me, in a rush. "Margaret Mary Theodora—I believe the Mary's after me. Aggie did say how if the babe had been a boy, he'd've been named D'Arcy."

She bent to Miss Macdonald. "My Lord save her," she said, signing the Cross.

"Mr. Macdonald is sure she'll recover," I said.

She straightened. "Poor lamb. To think Aggie never said a word—" She shook her head. "I'll mention her in my prayers."

Mrs. McGee walked away from the baboo just as quickly as she'd hurried over. At the threshold of the hall door, she turned and looked right at me. "When a child's born sickly, you can't become too attached, Clara."

"Yes'm."

The names recorded on the McGee family Bible's frontispiece were in her hand, not Mr. McGee's.

"It might be better for Aggie if—" Mrs. McGee stopped herself. "You be sure to show *her* proper respect, Clara."

"I will, Mrs. McGee," I said. "Miss McGee, and Miss Peggy, they're well?" I said.

"As well as can be expected." Her lips turned down. "Frasa's . . . resting, at the Cartiers' house. Overwrought, and no wonder . . . Peggy's growing into a young lady herself," she said, sounding like she was on surer ground. "You've not changed at all."

"But I have—"

"Clara," she said. "I'll say nothing about your past behaviour to Lady Macdonald."

"I appreciate that, Ma'am. Thank you."

"Pray for D'Arcy's soul. While you're praying over your own sins." Mrs. McGee nodded. "I'll mention to the girls I saw you."

From Mrs. McGee, that was as close to a benediction as I could hope for.

The pain came back on me, right after Mrs. McGee left. Holding the baboo helped, somehow.

Pierce found me rocking her in the late evening.

"Are these weepies about the babe, or Bridie?" he said.

"No."

"And you know Mrs. Trotter's on the mend . . . .."

"Yes."

"What've you been reading?"

"I was reading your copy of *A Tale Of Two Cities* in Trotter's kitchen. . . .."

"'Tis replaceable. Lucky for you, there's a lending library here," he said. In fact, I saw that this morning, you'd already found your favourite author's poems. Crying around Miss Macdonald means you're caring for yourself, Clara, not her."

He was right. Somehow, I still couldn't stop.

"I guess you were too young for the hanging, after all."

"It's not that either," I said.

"Well, don't be crying for Bridie Whelan, Clara. She had to know what Jimmy was, when he took off with a wad of her money."

Bridie had mentioned money. "How'd she have money?"

"Her folks left her a tidy packet, and a farm that she sold besides. Why d'you think Jimmy married her? Or maybe it's why she married him. Maybe the rebels gave him a rich wife as a payoff. To sweeten his having to do the deed—kill McGee, I mean."

"You mean you don't know what to believe either."

I set Miss Macdonald back in her cradle.

"So you're coming round to it," he said. "You see the Widow Whelan's a Fenian, you just can't admit it yet."

"If that's your version, Pierce," I said, "then you believe it." Yet . . . .." Bridie pretended she didn't know I'm working here. But she knew."

"A lot of people are interested in what's happening in the Prime Minister's house." Pierce smiled. "Best if they fear you, isn't it?"

"There," I picked up my report. "I've written up our conversation. Nothing's missing. Thank you for leaving me the paper and pen."

Pierce leafed through the pages. "And I notice that, once again, more than half of this is your own opinion. Well, I've a present for you too, Clara." He held out an envelope. "From O'Neill's wife."

This letter was still sealed. I tore it open.

> *Clara dear,*
> *Nancy's to join family in Toronto, though my husband and I don't think she's well enough. She's asked me to thank you for all your help, and to say, God bless,*
>
> *Mrs. Thomas O'Neill (Polly)*

"I can hardly believe it," I said. "Mrs. Trotter's truly well enough to travel? She'll be fine?"

"The doc thinks she may be . . . given time. He can't say for certain. And she says she doesn't recall a blessed thing, except going out to look for that pig."

"What if Mrs. Trotter was coshed because of me, Pierce?" I said, finally speaking my fear. "Because Willy and I spoke with Jimmy?"

"I won't mollycoddle you, Clara," he said. "It's possible."

"Wouldn't they as soon cosh me?" I asked.

He raised an eyebrow. "You're under Mr. Macdonald's protection here, Clara."

"So was Mr. McGee," I said.

"In Montreal, he was." Pierce said. "Not when he came back to Ottawa."

"What?"

"It was D'Arcy—he called us off the watch," Pierce said. "Macdonald's been carrying that fact close to him, worrying over it. Macdonald let D'Arcy convince him that the threats were nothing but talk," Pierce said. "That man was fierce to have no guard trailing him. Always cocky, leprechaun that he was. And he prevailed. I wonder, now . . . whether D'Arcy thought he could flush out his enemies. Or whether he saw a way out of this life that would give him a martyr's glory."

"You're not suggesting Mr. McGee brought on his own shooting?"

"I could argue that he courted the risk."

"He was a religious man, Pierce," I said. "Not like you."

"He was ailing, in pain, broke, not likely to be re-elected, Clara. Down about it all, with reason," Pierce said. "Still, you have the right of it, D'Arcy was one religious son of Ireland. And he'd engineered his own resurrection more than once. No," Pierce said, "I think D'Arcy loved himself too much to imagine his own end."

"Pierce," I said, slowly, working it out even as I spoke the words. "There's something else . . . .. When Jimmy told me that he was watching the house in Montreal, he said he'd been watching the young ladies. And on New Year's Eve, Jimmy said to get the girls out of the house–he meant both McGee girls, not we staff. Of course, Miss Frasa wasn't there, but anyone may expect she'd be with the family, for the holiday."

"You think he was sweet on the nun?" Pierce said.

"Miss Frasa's not going to be a nun anymore." I said. "And she came home when she wasn't expected, during the election–when Mrs. McGee was away, now that I think on it . . . .."

"Jimmy'd no right to even think along those lines," Pierce said. "A lady like her . . . .. Though it's more than possible Bridie Whelan sent Jimmy to Ottawa to get him clean away from some young thing in MontreaL. Miss Frasa McGee, of all people. The girl does take after her mother in looks, she drew the lucky straw on that." He smiled at his own joke, or at Miss Frasa's fine looks. "Well, if Bridie did send Jimmy away for that purpose, she's been punished for her jealousy."

"And Mr. Macdonald thinks Mr. McGee's murder is *his* fault?"

"It looks like I'm to wear it, though. He's liking the English lad for the top job now," Pierce said. "Oh, Macdonald will find me something. He's straight that way."

"So we both lost our futures that night." I crumpled up the letter. "Is that why you brought me here, Pierce?" I asked. "For my own safety?"

Pierce already looked sorry he'd told me this much.

"Our needs dovetailed." He pocketed my note. "You're like me. You can put your hand to a lot of jobs, Clara. You'll be grand. As long as you're tough enough."

XXXI

Sow had gone missing again.

From the looks of the sty, she'd gotten out recently.

I ran down to Docherty's.

"Hannah's not here," Eamonn Docherty said in greeting. He was, as usual, in his little office by the entry. He was counting his receipts.

"Do you know where Sow, I mean the pig, is at, Mr. Docherty?" I said.

"Hannah may have left the pen door open." He looked back down at his precious records. "Yesterday, before she left for the hanging. She says not, but that's what happens when you count on a flibbertigibbit."

So Hannah had been careless, or she'd tired of looking out for Sow—or someone had been poking around, and taken her for himself. This last thought chilled me through.

"I guess I'll go, then," I said.

"You could take something to Pierce for me," Eamonn Docherty said. He wrote like a leftie, his hand curled so I couldn't see what he was marking down. It could only have been a single letter, though, or a number . . . .. He folded the paper, sealed the envelope, and waved me off.

I had no need to retrace my steps down the alley. There was nothing there for me at all now.

I did anyway.

The only part of Trotter's that hadn't been destroyed by the fire was the root cellar. It was set deep into the ground, with rock walls that had always made me think it must've been a cave that was there before the building had been set atop it.

And it was set deep under the part of the wreckage of Trotter's that had been furthest from the printer.

As I drew closer, I saw that even the hatch door had survived, intact. There a smudge of snow outside that entry to the cellar, and a track of ashy footprints. The door was almost, but not quite, shut.

I leapt forward, and slid the bar across, before I could think about the wisdom of that action.

"Wait—" Such a familiar yell, and I was ever so glad to hear it.

"Willy," I swung open the doors. "Here, take a boost then."

"Back away, Clara, I'm man enough to get myself out."

I stepped into a snow drift, and waited.

A grey knitted toque like the Frenchies wore came into view.

Willy had the start of a moustache. It must've been coming on, and I hadn't noticed. Now that he'd been away for more than a week, it lay across his upper lip. Just a dusting, darker than his hair. It made his nose look more like his father's did, in the hall picture. There were razor cuts below his cheekbones, too.

And he'd bought a new pea coat in Toronto, cut larger across the shoulders.

My changes had all been inside. Blood, clouts, and cramping. As usual, Willy came out the better of any matchup between us.

He boosted himself out of the cellar. He had a bottle of whiskey in his hand. "For protection," he said.

"Willy, where's Sow?"

"The sow? That's your first question, Clara? Before, 'Willy, I'm sorry about your ma' or 'Isn't it terrible that Mr. Lacey died, and you lost your home,' or even 'What in hell's half-acre are you doing down there, Trotter?' You ask about the pig?"

He set down the bottle, and pulled two potatoes out of his pockets. "Darned if I know where she is. Probably bacon by now. I could use a rasher or two, myself."

"I'm ever so sorry about your Ma, Willy. You must know—"

"I know, Clara," he said. He looked down at the potatoes, overset.

"And Mr. Lacey, of course."

Willy swiped at his eyes. "I'm not so sure about that," he said.

"Willy—"

"C'mon, Clara, let me have my joke."

"Such a blessing's your ma's awake, though," I said. "Is she doing better today?"

"Well," he said. "Soon as I heard, I made my way back," he said. "I've been hired to work the agriculture beat. The telegram just caught me, packing to go all the way off to Niagara. The *Globe* was decent about it, but I'd have come anyway . . .. I got back here night before last."

"How is your ma really, Willy?" I said. "All I've heard is she doesn't remember—"

"I thought if I laid low here, I might figure out who coshed her," Willy said.

He never did such a foolish thing—"You haven't been to see her?"

"I walked by, while the whole town was at the hanging," he said. "Thought you might be there to let me in. But it was only O'Neill's wife I saw through the window."

"They're not letting me see her," I said.

"I can't like O'Neill's wife having charge of Ma."

He looked like he was waiting for a smart remark. But I was well beyond that.

"I'll have to show my face though," Willy said. "No help for it. May be best. The idea of snooping around seemed smarter before I'd spent two nights here shivering under a pile of blankets I lifted from Eamonn Docherty's storeroom."

"Hannah gave them to you?" I said. She'd said that Eamonn Docherty was almost as close with those blankets from Hudson's Bay, as he was with his money.

"No, I haven't even asked her for help. I waited for a likely moment, is all," he said.

"You're risking Eamonn's wrath."

"If he finds out," Willy said. "I was about to go see Hannah, though. I couldn't hold out any longer. I've had nothing to eat but pickles, preserves, and blackened praties. And I'm about out of those . . .. Don't suppose you brought food?"

"Bread and cheddar, a regular ploughman's lunch. Here." I pulled the roll from my pocket.

"You sure?" He eyed the cheesecloth wrapping like he might eat it as well.

"Don't worry, Willy. They're not stingy with food at the Macdonalds'—that's where I'm at."

"I figured that one out yesterday, Clara. I was trying to give you something, matter of fact. C'mon, let's get out of this snow."

So I followed him underground. We left the hatch wide open this time, though.

Willy set down the food on the earth floor. Then he pulled over a sack. I didn't need the bit of sunlight seeping in. I knew just from the feel of it, 'twas was the first grey flannel sack I'd sewn. With Mr. McGee's missing manuscript still inside.

And 'twas right back at Trotter's—this bit that was left of Trotter's—more than ten months after Willy carried it to Parliament for Mr. McGee.

I hefted it. Ran my fingers along its length. Then I handed it right back to Willy. "I don't understand," I said.

"Which part?" Willy had already downed the loaf and the cheddar slice.

"Every part. First off—how long have you had it?"

"I happened upon it last month—before we went to the jail," he said.

"What do you mean?"

"The day before we visited Jimmy, I trudged up to Parliament to see if they had any odd jobs," Willy said. "A mail packet had come in, they had me sort it. Until I saw that funny old sack, when it popped up in that incoming London pouch, part of me thought the *Apologia* had never left the building. Every pouch has to make a stop at Macdonald's office, you see," Willy said. "I wasn't at all sure it hadn't been pulled out and read—and that had been the end of it. If it were as bad as Mr. McGee said."

"Mr. McGee speaking his mind wasn't bad."

"The Prime Minister sent the book on, to give him all credit. The publishers balked. There's a letter from Tupper. Too anti-Brit, they thought. Though I'd say it's too anti-Yankee."

"You've read it?"

"I thought to make a story of it. My boss has me writing on crop rotation and foaling—I'm no farmer. This book would be bigger than Mr. McGee's diary," Willy said. "So I took it along with me, to Toronto."

"Then why is it here?"

"I aimed to leave it in Doyle's carriage yesterday," Willy said. "Doyle was bound to show up wherever Bridie Whelan had been lodged, sooner or later. Then you ran out of the Russell House—with O'Neill behind you. I didn't see that twist coming," Willy said. "So I tracked you to Macdonald's. Were you sick to your stomach or something?"

I shook my head. "I'm fine."

"Well, I saw how matters had tumbled in your favour, Clara. You know, you might drop it off to Macdonald on the sly, like—"

"The night your ma was attacked." I poked at the sack. "And the fire, or the bombing, or whatever really happened. D'you think the Fenians were looking for this book, Willy?"

"So you're turning it on me?" He grabbed the sack, and scrambled up the ladder.

I found him kicking at the charred planks and ash that were the parlour. Willy spit into the ashes. "Will you take the book to Macdonald, Clara? Or not?" Willy said.

"I'll take the book." I ran my finger down my cape sleeve. "Willy—I'm spooked."

Willy turned. "Honest truth, Clara, I'm spooked too. That's why I'm not writing anything," he said. "On account of Ma. I even stopped reading it. Show me—just where did you find Ma?"

We circled around the remnants of the building. I stopped, at Sow's pen. "She was coshed just here," I said.

"It is my fault," Willy said.

"No," I said, though neither of us believed it. "Do you have any idea who attacked her, Willy?"

"I've been hiding here, not an idea, not even sure where to look," he said. "So I'm shouting to the hills that I know nothing," Willy said. "I've a story in the *Globe* tomorrow that makes it clear I can't follow Jimmy's trail further than the grave. And I'll take care of Ma."

Willy picked up the bottle of whiskey, which he'd set down when he saw my food. "You know, Clara, the boarder's brandy kegs are still in the root cellar as well... Sergeant O'Neill will end up with it all, like as not. So why not have our first drink together—a tipple to Ma's recovery?"

"I have to work." I licked my lips. "And whiskey's strong, Willy. You toast for both of us."

"You'll never know what's good," Willy said. "You have to have something wet to knock back, as well, for a goodbye toast. But I'll go first, as the man. Ma's health," Willy said.

Willy choked as the whiskey worked its way down. "Damn stuff must be off," he said.

I didn't tell him that's what a first drink was always like, and he should never have gulped it.

Instead, I took the whiskey bottle, and touched my tongue to the liquor. "Your Ma," I said. "May she live long."

His ma. However Mrs. Trotter and I may have fooled ourselves, these many months, Willy's big sister was dead, and Mrs. Trotter had only one child.

He poured the remaining whiskey out all over the garden, then tossed the empty bottle at the ruins. "Living with the Macdonalds, Clara," Willy said. "You're practically gentry now."

"It's fine that I'm a maid, Willy."

"I hear the baby's not right."

"Best to leave that as well."

"You won't help a lad make a dollar then? Oh, I'm just trying you on again, Clara. But you know that."

He belched, and I swallowed the smell of sharp cheddar.

I had to ask, now, or I wouldn't have the chance.

"Willy, I—Willy. Can you sneak me in to see her, please?" I said. "If you could, I'd be ever so grateful."

"I have no bloody idea, Clara, I—I'll have to see her first myself, you know? And I wouldn't want her catching any germs from—"

"I won't be transporting any contagion from Miss Macdonald. I swear, Willy."

"I don't . . . if—I'll send for you, Clara."

XXXII

All those months I'd wondered about Mr. McGee's manuscript. Now, I was almost sorry it had turned up. Scared I'd be fired. Guilty from just holding it in my hands.

I stared at the manuscript all day. Started to read it, then stopped myself. Picked up the book to take it to Mr. Macdonald. Set it back down.

Mr. McGee believed his book would turn heads on both sides of the Atlantic. But the High Commissioner, Mr. Tupper, who had always been Mr. McGee's friend, wrote differently.

> *Publisher says neither Brits nor Americans are interested in D'Arcy's 'message'. Hope Mrs. McGee is compensated. To think you were about to set up D'Arcy and his family nicely. That postal appointment would have granted him the creative time he craved. Poor D'Arcy had better books still to write, once he'd left politics behind him.*
>
> *—Tupper*

The people at the publishing house had made markings all over. So many pages scrawled with questions, pages slashed so I hurt my eyes reading under the heavy ink to the original lines. More than one hand had been at work. One jotted note at the front said Mr. McGee's death would increase sales, but they couldn't see a way to make it ready without his help. And at the end, another had written that it was more of an idea for a book than a book.

That evening, Lady Macdonald cast up to Mr. Macdonald that Mrs. McGee hadn't been given enough pension money.

"Aggie, like everything else in Parliament, it's a compromise in the end," Mr. Macdonald said. "To keep the wheels turning."

"Mary McGee will suffer for the rest of her life, without money to keep house or marry off her girls."

I'd moved the rocker to the window. Lady Macdonald left the dressing room door open so she could look on the baboo, safe in my arms. So I could see Mr. Macdonald in profile, sitting at M'Lady's vanity table.

The *Apologia* was right there on the floor by his foot. In my sewing basket.

Breathe.

Give the truth light.

"You can't make me feel guiltier than I already do about D'Arcy, dear Aggie. If I had the money myself—"

"I know you can't, what with the Commercial Bank failure, John. Is there no way to raise more for her?" M'Lady said.

"I could canvass the Montreal merchants . . . Lord knows their new steamship-rail venture is profitable enough . . . ."

"It's the right thing to do, John,' said M'Lady.

Soon after, Mr. Macdonald toddled in, glass in hand, to visit his girl.

M'Lady followed him. "I wish you wouldn't drink this early, John," she said. "Can't you control yourself right now?"

"I am controlling myself, Aggie." He winked at me. "Don't worry, alcohol's a cleanser."

"Clara, there's water on the boil in my dressing room," she said. "Could you make Sir John a cup of tea? I'm sure you could use one too."

"Come on, Clara , we've been given our orders."

"Off with you, then." Lady Macdonald took the baboo to breast. She looked like a stained-glass Madonna. Only the poor baboo looked nothing like Baby Jesus.

The Prime Minister closed the dressing-room door behind us. "I'll pass on that tea, Clara," he said, "though you should make yourself some."

"No Sir, thank you. I've something for you, though—"

I lifted the manuscript from the basket and thrust it forward.

"It's Mr. McGee's."

Mr. Bernard stuck in his head. "You're needed in the study, John."

"Follow me, Clara." He called out to Lady Macdonald, "I'll send the girl right back to you, sweetheart."

To me, he said only, "Bring that with you."

I followed them down the front steps. The Englishman was inside the study.

"Stay here." Mr. Macdonald gestured to the chairs lined up outside his door.

A moment later, Pierce showed up. "Shouldn't you be sleeping, Clara?"

"I'm waiting for a word with him."

"As am I. Is that McMicken inside?"

"The silent man?" I said.

"That about captures the Englishman. He's the coming man for sure." He eased himself down into the chair beside me. "I know when I've been bested."

"Beaten for what?"

"For top job. Of the new Canadian Police."

The door opened. "It's over, then," Mr. Macdonald said. "We've enough new enemies to deal with."

The silent Englishman came out. Glanced at Pierce, ignored me. Set off down the hall.

Mr. Bernard came to the door. Nodded to Pierce. Stared at me.

"Clara? I'll have the girl in, brother Bernard." Mr. Macdonald came up behind. "You may as well come in while we're at it, Pierce. Brother, could you tell your sister I may delay Clara's return?"

Lady Macdonald's brother looked askance at delivering such a message about the nursemaid. But he went.

By the time we'd taken our seats Mr. Macdonald was standing behind his desk. He held up the manuscript in one hand and Mr. Tupper's letter in the other.

"Where did all this spring from?" This was not the baboo's father speaking. This was the Prime Minister, like he'd been at The Russell House.

Pierce straightened. "I'll be damned."

I perched on the edge of the chair.

"And you didn't know she had it, Pierce?" Mr. Macdonald set down the papers.

"She didn't have anything at all when she first came here."

"I found it in the root cellar at Trotter's," I broke in. "Today."

"The whole story, Clara," Mr. Macdonald said.

So I told them about Willy.

"He wanted you to know, Sir. Willy, he thought better of writing a story about the *Apologia*. And it would have been a big scoop. He won't be punished, will he?"

"Far be it from me to jail a member of the press. But we'll be having a talk, he and I, before he leaves these environs."

"Another member of the press in your pocket," Pierce said.

"Have you ever read any of the *Apologia*?" said Pierce.

"Mr. McGee put the book together all by himself," I said. "He was driven by it."

"It shows in the writing," Pierce said.

That stopped me cold. I looked from Pierce, to Mr. Macdonald.

"Pierce reviewed the book, before it went off," said Mr. Macdonald.

"I'm hoping the book can help support Mrs. McGee and the girls?" I said.

"You read Tupper's letter."

"Yes, but—Mr. McGee, he was convinced the *Apologia* would be a big seller," I said.

"And his widow's left with a pittance and a heavy memory," said Pierce.

"Pierce." Mr. Macdonald had heard enough about the pension.

"Could I copy it for you, Sir? On my own time, I mean. There should be a second copy," I said. "There was, in Mr. McGee's room. And then there wasn't."

"I'll read poor D'Arcy's book, now it's here again finally," said Mr. Macdonald. "Once I'm done—we'll see what's what."

I was surprised that Willy didn't take the chance to turn up at the Prime Minister's house. He was clearly more afraid of Mr. Macdonald's wrath about his stealing the *Apologia*, than he was attracted by the possibility of benefitting from the overall connection.

Or his ma had taken a turn for the worse.

Three days later, Pierce found me swabbing Miss Macdonald's cradle, with a strange mixture of boiled water and a Russian alcohol called vodka.

"Is that one of Gillivray's potions?" Pierce asked.

"If it will help Miss Macdonald . . ." I said.

"Well, finish up, Clara. It's good M'Lady and Miss Stewart have fitted you out in a few new things," he said. "We're going to make a call." Pierce said. "To O'Neill's."

"You're dropping me off?" I said, as we headed to the sergeant's house.

"No, I'll be staying with you."

"You don't trust I'd tell you, Pierce? If Mrs. Trotter said aught?"

"Nonetheless," he replied. "She's not making a lot of sense, I understand. Goes in and out. And who's to say you'll know what matters? As for O'Neill, he has a habit of not being truthful where Nancy Trotter's concerned."

I felt sorry for Sergeant O'Neill, though, when I saw him.

Here he was, in his own home, and not able to say what he was really feeling. Instead, he began ranting on about Willy.

"Pierce—Nancy's in no shape to leave town," the sergeant said. "I can't talk sense into that son of hers—". He nodded at the room where Mrs. Trotter lay.

"She's the lad's mother, Tommy." Mrs. O'Neill said, "Clara, dear—it's a good time to see Nancy, she's just been bathed and—"

"Yes, Polly, we don't need all the details," Sergeant O'Neill said.

"You men aren't crowding in there as well?"

"Polly—"

"You can just listen from out here, you two?" Mrs. O'Neill said, taking both her husband and Pierce to task. "You'll all be the death of Nancy."

When I went on through myself, I saw Mrs. O'Neill had reason to fear. Any of us could be bringing in a bug . . . I thought it possible it might not even take that much. Mrs. Trotter had lost weight, and her colour was too grey for comfort.

Polly O'Neill had been doing her job all right, though. Mrs. Trotter was half-sitting up, pillows tucked behind her, and she smelled like soap and lavender water.

I was struck hard, in that moment, to think I'd always thought of Mrs. Trotter as old—but she hadn't been. And now she was.

Willy nodded at me from a seat by the bed. "Here, Clara, you can have the chair." He walked to the open door and leaned back against a post, blocking Sergeant O'Neill's view.

"Clara?" Mrs. Trotter said. "Could you lay a cloth over my eyes? And shut the curtains—my head. You smell like a bar room."

I'd been nowhere near liquor. Well, nowhere closer than the seat next to Mr. Macdonald's. Except there was that vodka solution, to clean the cradle.

"I'm sorry, Mrs.—"

"I'm glad to hear your voice, Clara, but I can't stand the light."

I dipped the cloth in the bowl of water that Mrs. O'Neill had on the nightstand, wrung it out, and carefully laid it in place over Mrs. Trotter's shaded lids.

"I'm so thankful you're doing well, Mrs. Trotter."

"We'll see," she whispered. "Don't tell Willy, but—"

"Don't talk, Ma'am, if it's too much."

"No, I want to tell Clara—don't wear that scent."

"Ma'am?" I was always scrubbed clean these days.

"That scent—I can't stand it now. I never liked it . . . .. Is that really you, Clara?"

Willy rolled his eyes. This must be her mind wandering.

"I'll be sure to go home and scrub myself proper, Mrs. Trotter."

"Take that cloth off me, it's weighing on my eyes. And don't forget to feed the pig, mind," she said. "It'll be time soon—I must ask Tommy . . . ."

"Clara," Willy cut in. "Best we leave it at that?"

I removed the cloth though, as Mrs. Trotter had asked.

She opened her eyes, just for a moment. "You're a good girl, Clara. I wish you were one of my own. Now give us a kiss. I need that cloth, though."

I kissed her forehead. Careful to hold back my tears, I secured her blindfold once again.

Willy trailed Pierce and me out to the carriage.

"I can't wait to be shed of this place," he said.

"I'll miss you, Willy."

He gave me a rare smile. "Never think you've seen the back of me. I'm going to write my own book about all this one day, Clara. And you'll be in it."

"Or maybe I'll write the book, Willy."

He swiped a forefinger along the side of his nose, like we had made a pact.

A week after I'd handed over Mr. McGee's book to Mr. Macdonald, the Prime Minister brought the manuscript back to me.

"Clara, tell my brother Bernard your needs regarding paper and ink," he said. "You can work on the desk in the library, and I'll have one put in the nursery for you. All out in the open, as it were. No more than an hour a day of copying, mind. I want you to have your proper rest when you're looking after my baboo."

So it was close to St. Patrick's Day, by the time I'd completed the copy.

As I worked, a bit each day after breakfast and before my sleep, I saw Mr. McGee's book was not written like his other books had been. Of course, they were all about Ireland's history, or collections of poesie.

This book was more like his diary.

He'd always cautioned me about self-aggrandizement.

"Let others give you glory, Clara. If you paint yourself golden you'll find the glitter washes off with the first rain of public opinion."

Some of it was good reading, though. One story in particular caught at me.

Back in 1862, Mr. McGee had been president of the Executive Council of colonial Canada, as Ontario and Quebec were then called. It was the burden of being in charge of justice, he wrote, that made him stop thinking like an Irish immigrant, and begin to think like a Canadian. That's when he approached the colony's co-premier, Mr. Macdonald, with the idea to make a new country.

One particular choice he'd had to make, in 1862, had set them both off on the road to London and our Confederation.

An elderly couple had killed a Protestant neighbor named Munro, after feuding with him a while. The unfortunate Munro had earned his end, they'd said, as he'd hung a dog in the old folks' well. And after being warned off, Munro still ventured onto the *scothaosta* couple's plot of earth—to complain that they'd shot one of his straying hens.

The pair were Aylward, by name, Catholic by faith, Irish, by birth, from County Donegal.

The woman had struck the fatal blow, with a scythe. But they were both convicted of Munro's slaying. And by law, a murder conviction meant death by hanging.

Yet the jury recommended mercy, and the judge agreed he would pass on that tender plea.

For the final decision rested with the province's Executive Council.

Of course, all of the Irish, in all of the colony, wanted Mr. McGee to show the old farmer and his biddie the Lord's sweet mercy.

But he said that he couldn't.

Hanging was the right verdict, he wrote in the *Apologia*. The fair end for all. The way he had to act. Not as an Irishman living in Canada West, not as a Catholic even. But as a settler acting for the best of the community.

The new land, before the old.

He said it a number of times and ways, and him always in the right of the story. Like writing it would settle his own soul about his hard, cold choice.

That was when Irish immigrants started to look Mr. McGee askance, he admitted. And the rebel Fenians to call out his name in anger.

And Mr. McGee had, in turn, stepped up his crusade against the real threat of danger posed by the Fenians. He had become their fiercest opponent, years before their first border attack.

Mr. Macdonald had also found the history about Mr. McGee and the Fenians of interest. He'd underlined a large number of sentences in this part of the *Apologia*. And he'd made a note in the margin, beside the Aylwards' story—*Talk to Pierce.*

After I copied those pages, I went to bed and dreamed of Sow, and then of the dog who had run wild at the fall fair. Bowling the man over with his chalkboard. Hannah and Mike walking away, to arrange a new photograph. Mike lying dead of jailhouse measles.

I awoke in a sweat. Imagine, killing a neighbour over a dog.

Then I arose, and dug out Jimmy's carved box from where I'd hidden it under the mattress. I placed it right out on the dresser, next to the mirror. No more secrets, Mr. Macdonald had said.

I finished the book copy on March 15th. *The Ides of March*, the calendar on the library desk said. Irish houses would be preparing to mark St. Patrick's Day, two days hence, before contemplating the Lord's death and rebirth—and the post-Lenten Easter feasting to come on the 27th.

I leafed through the original *Apologia*, taking a last look at Mr. McGee's intense scrawl. There was Mr. Macdonald's hand too; by the passage where Mr. McGee had let the old folks hang.

Mr. McGee had been marked by his ruling. In the way he thought, in the way others thought of him.

I must ask Pierce what he'd made of it all.

The trial for the Aylwards had been at a place called Thorold, it said in Mr. McGee's story. Mr. Macdonald had ordered that giant maps be mounted of all the provinces, and Rupert's Land to the west. The map labelled Ontario had only arrived last week.

I went over, and studied it. Niagara was well west of Toronto . . . and then south. Where Lake Ontario ended, and Canada curved south to meet Lake Erie. The Fenians had attacked there from the States three years ago—Mr. McGee often spoke of it during the election.

I ran my fingernail along the line of the lake. To me, this was the edge of beyond. Yet this was the Niagara farmland to which Willy was supposed to travel, for his new Toronto employer. To whence Hannah was so anxious to return.

The place-names were in such tiny print.

I picked up the looking glass kept on the bookshelf. Thorold was one of a number of names, all dotted close together.

Thorold . . . Pelham . . . Wainfleet . . . Lincoln . . . Grimsby.

Grimsby.

XXXIII

I waited, until Pierce left for his rendezvous with the tobacconist. Then I ran outside with my bootlaces dragging—like I'd seen him by chance, and thought to take advantage of that happy accident.

"Can I ride the few blocks to the market?" I called out.

"Why not," Pierce replied. "Though you know you should be sleeping, Clara."

"I'll be grand," I said. "Being as you're going nearby, I'll visit Hannah first. I can stop by the market on my way back."

Pierce had a way of knowing when a body needed quiet. As he reached the stable near Docherty's, though, he caught my eyes.

"Tell her I'll be by for a pint," he said.

I nodded as I jumped, using my lace-tying as an excuse to keep my head down until he'd pulled away.

There'd been a sudden thaw, and my boots sloshed in a mud puddle outside Docherty's door. I pushed down the hood of my cape, and tucked away my gloves.

Hannah's uncle barely nodded as I passed by his office.

The bar room, as ever, smelled of spilt beer and sick stomachs. And there was another odour, as I neared the kitchen.

Offal.

I swung open the door with my backside, as I had the day I'd left there.

Hannah was standing, facing me, at the far end of the long, wooden table set in the centre of the kitchen.

"Clara?" Hannah said. "You can stay if you want, but you can see what I'm in the middle of here."

She was working on a carcass with a bristle scraper. Beside the pig sat a butcher's saw and a six-inch kitchen knife. Organs were soaking in a variety of dishes. The head had been severed, and was boiling in a pot on the hearth.

"So is it true?" Hannah said. "I heard at the market the other boys will be released soon, and no more charges. Macdonald has ended the search for Jimmy's fellow fighters?"

She went back to her scraping. "Can you believe the butcher wouldn't help me, once I finally turned him down? Anyway, you've missed the worst; it's been stuck and scalded. Once I strip the hair and scurf, Uncle Eamonn will round up enough lads to hang the carcass."

I walked over to the table. I needed to see the pig's left shoulder.

Hannah just kept talking, double-time. "Uncle thinks me barmy to take this on. Clara?" She smiled. "You need to put your head between your legs, girl. I knew you'd be no good on a farm."

There was still a pattern of blue ink dots. In stripping the bristles, Hannah had cut into the circles of the knot.

"You've killed Sow," I said.

"Willy said I could have it."

"I don't believe you."

"Well, really the butcher snagged it, all those weeks ago. 'Twas a present, though. Can you imagine? He thought I'd have him, along with the gilt."

"Sow hadn't had a litter."

"It was raised to be cut down—like we Irish." She saw I wasn't going to let this go. "I know it was a sweet piglet at first, but girl . . .."

"Would it be different if it were someone's dog whom you'd slaughtered, Hannah? Would you understand my being in a rage over a dead dog?"

"As if I'd ever—a pig is no dog, Clara. Have you ever had a dog?"

"I imagine you've had one, Hannah. A pet dog, at your grandparents' farm? Will you have another dog there? When you move back to Grimsby to be with your farmer correspondent?"

"That farmer hasn't come to the point—yet. And yes, we may have a dog. They're useful around a farm. Look, I've work to do here, Clara," she said. "Why don't you hie back to the Orangeman's den? Rock the cradle, take tea with M'Lady? I'm sure you come by it all naturally. You'll make your father proud yet, Miss Swift."

She dipped a bow, waving the scraper. It shed bristles all over the floor.

"And your kin—they went by the name Aylward?" I said. "I'm sure that's a proud old Irish handle, back in County Donegal. Not so proud in Grimsby?"

She stood still at that.

"Were you at the hanging?" I said.

"Wasn't I there beside you?" said Hannah.

"Not that hanging, Hannah," I said. "It must have knocked you over, to see your own grandparents hanged. You'd have been only twelve then. I imagine you're not over it yet."

"What's Pierce been saying?"

"Pierce is no part of this. I have the story from Mr. McGee's own hand," I said. "Your Grannie and Gramp carried on quite the Irish feud."

"Trust the great man, to be twisting stories from beyond his grave. And you still to be playing his handmaiden," Hannah said. "There's plenty of true Irish who agree that McGee could have saved my grandparents. *Muintir na hÉireann* saw McGee, even then, for the creeper he was. How I laughed, when the *Times* wrote he died just before he could collect that sweet government job from his lord and master Macdonald."

"'Twas you all along, Hannah," I said. "You're *Fódla*. Jimmy's goddess of the land."

She set down the scraper on the table, and picked up the kitchen knife. "Jimmy was soft on me, sure. Married to the old lady, and sorry enough soon after."

"You played those two lads one against each other?" I asked.

"We all saw eye to eye about the Irish sticking together. Jimmy was full of big talk . . . but he'd yet to prove himself."

"To the Fenians."

"To the other patriots. Jimmy was a joke to us all, no matter how much money his wife siphoned to the cause."

She took a step toward me.

"You and Bridie, Fenian rebels both."

"Mike was checking up on me that night, if you can believe it," she said. "To see if I was going off on a tryst with Jimmy. Then Mike hightailed it so fast . . . . I don't know how you saw him, Clara, I didn't even know he was there myself at that moment. But he knew I was in for it. Mike saw it could be me and Jimmy, or just Jimmy."

"Mike saw that truth," I said. "Once you'd visited him in jail, and laid out the law?"

"Mike could've been hanged himself, just for being on the spot," Hannah said. "Jimmy did buy the bullets for me. He should've known I would have my *díol greise*. Revenge was an Irish idea that my Grannie made sure I understood. Why couldn't Mike and Jimmy both stay clear, that one night?"

Hannah, with her gift for bewitching men. Now, I saw the enchantment came with a curse.

"The fool went to Parliament that night to warn McGee once again," Hannah said. "But McGee was last to speak. As Jimmy paced in the gallery, he found he couldn't bring himself to betray me. His bad luck he came to me, instead. That alerted me McGee would soon be home."

She looked at the knife.

"When McGee did toddle up, Jimmy stood back—so McGee and I could talk, he thought. Talk. And me with the gun in my hand. Jimmy ran across Sparks Street, after. And ducked behind the *Times* building."

And Hannah had only to go back down the alley to the pub.

"'Twas bad luck twice over," she said, "that Jimmy ran into that Frenchie on his way to me."

"Jimmy must've loved you something awful, Hannah. To never tell."

I took a step away from her, guided backward by the table's long edge.

"Rat on a Fenian and face sure death and a shaming besides. Or die a hero, for Ireland. That's an easy choice."

"You didn't choose to be a hero."

She said nothing.

"All this time . . ..“ I said. "You felt you were safe?"

"I was. Until Jimmy told Willy something about me. I heard Willy recounting a tale to his ma. About Jimmy, and his *Fódla*. Did Willy tell you too?"

"And so you struck that loving woman down? For nothing?"

"She'd have told her man O'Neill—"

"Willy was only at the jail because I went. In Bridie's stead," I said. "And Jimmy made no hint to us that it was you he was worshipping."

I took a second step backward.

"He wanted to leave you with a lock of his hair," I said.

"He was mad to think I cared."

"I do believe he was mad, by the end," I said. "Did Jimmy realise you weren't acting on behalf of the Fenian Brotherhood?"

"D'Arcy McGee killed my own. I returned the favour. For myself, and for Ireland."

"And what did Mrs. Trotter do, but treat you like her own daughter?" I said. "She smelled your lavender, Hannah. She tried to warn me . . . she said she never liked your scent."

The door to the bar creaked behind me. "Are you not ready to go, Clara?" Pierce said.

I'd never been so glad to hear any person.

"How long—" Hannah turned the knife in her hand.

"Long enough, cousin," Pierce said.

As if Pierce and I had planned it, I stepped backward once again, along the long table. And Pierce, quick as a flash, moved in front of me.

"Then you know Clara needs to rest here, cousin," Hannah said.

"A girl like her can be in a room and no one notices," Pierce had told Mr. Macdonald the night of Mr. McGee's death.

I had to count on that now.

That, and my being so small that Pierce could shield my movements.

"Clara won't be resting here today, Hannah," Pierce said.

Hannah was keyed on Pierce now. She saw him as the threat.

I crouched, and crawled under the table. I came up to a crouch again, just below the table's rim, on the other side. I was now closer to Hannah than Pierce was.

I was almost behind her.

I slowly peeked above the table.

Pierce leaned down and grabbed the gun from his boot holster.

"Leave off, cousin," Hannah said, as he aimed it at her.

I snatched up the butcher's saw, and rose.

"Sonofabitch, you've never helped me—" Hannah lunged at Pierce, her knife cutting air as Pierce arced away from her, just out of reach, but unable to fire his weapon.

I sprang up, caught Hannah's knife-arm with my free hand, and twisted. She couldn't wield the knife properly. But she didn't let go of it.

I shifted my weight forward, wrapping both my arms around her. Trapping the knife in front of her while I set the saw edge up against her neck.

"We'll have no more, Hannah," I said. "You leave go."

Pierce, who'd righted himself, froze.

Hannah did let go of the knife, saying "I won't be taken—" She jerked her neck, hard, down against the saw.

"For Christ's sake, Hannah—Clara . . ." Pierce called out, even as Hannah's blood spurted out over her chest.

She'd sliced herself right open.

Hannah was suddenly limp, and so heavy. I was rocked, as her body slid down mine, and we tumbled to the floor.

How could she lose her lifeblood so quickly?

"What's this racket?" Eamonn Docherty ran in. When he saw Hannah, his face registered only mild surprise. "I told her it would come to this." Eamonn spat, then swiped his mouth with the back of his arm.

Pierce pointed his gun at the ground. But he didn't reholster the gun.

Eamonn picked up Hannah's knife, took the butcher's saw from my hand, and placed both blades on the counter.

"You knew, Eamonn?" said Pierce.

"I've known for seven years McGee deserved to die," Eamonn answered. "I'd no proof Hannah exacted the forfeit. No more do you, even now."

"You *bastaird*."

"I'll call you a liar and worse, Pierce, if you say any different," Eamonn said. "The girl had a long shadow, swinging above her. We're best clear of both."

XXXIV

Pierce and Eamonn rolled Hannah's body in one of Eamonn's treasured blankets, and carried her from my sight.

"Clara?" Pierce had come back, to find me carving out the tattoo from Sow's skin.

"Clara," he said again. Gently, then sharply. "Clara."

I wrapped the bit of skin in a dishtowel, and carried it close all the way home. Shivering, and thinking it was amazing how little blood there was on Gram's cape.

Pierce took me right upstairs. To the nursery.

The Macdonalds were inside, and Hortense as well.

While Pierce explained what had happened, Hortense removed my cape. Lady Macdonald placed the baboo in my arms. They both smelled so fresh.

"No, M'Lady, I—"

"Come. My bath water's not been let out yet," said M'Lady. So I followed her. Feeling able to walk only because of the burden in my arms. The comfort in my arms. Stepping so carefully, lest I drop the baboo.

Hortense followed, carrying in the wicker bassinet we had just lined and out-fitted in Easter colours. Lilac for sorrow, yellow for spring.

Lady Macdonald took the baboo from me, securing her wee body in clean bunting. The baboo cooed when she was all tucked in by her mother.

Hortense untied my apron, letting it drop onto the wooden floor. At least it didn't dirty the Turkish rug.

Together, she and M'Lady unbuttoned my dress, lifted it and my shift off, untied my shoes, pulled down my knickers. They supported me as I dropped into the tub.

"The water's lovely," I said.

M'Lady knelt on the carpet. "Hortense, fetch that clean cloth. Hortense liked you immediately, you know, Clara. Even Mary McGee had a good word. That poor woman never was one to look on others with kindness."

M'Lady untied my bun, shook out my braids, soaped my scalp. Hortense poured more water for the rinse.

"Step out then, Clara."

As I rose, I noticed the water had pinked up, with patches of deeper pink where the soap scum had gathered.

Hortense and M'Lady grabbed my shoulders to steady me.

"Lift your arms, Clara." M'Lady wrapped a towel around me. "You're such a tiny thing. I don't notice that about you when you're working. This scratch on your arm—we'll have to see to that. Tomorrow."

Hortense spoke up. "You're fine now, Clara. It was mainly your clothing."

Fine. I was fine. Only a scratch, and that of my own making.

M'Lady took one of her own silk dressing gowns from a hook. I shook my head at that.

"It's only a wrap to keep you decent, Clara," M'Lady said.

Hortense led me back through, to the rocker by the nursery window. A few minutes later Lady Macdonald again set her daughter in my arms

"It's all right to kiss her head, Clara," Lady Macdonald said. "I do."

The baboo and I rocked together for quite some time. The day darkened, but Lady Macdonald didn't allow Hortense to light any candles.

Then Pierce was standing in the doorway. Wearing a white linen shirt hanging out over his pants, feet bare.

"We'll leave this for tonight, Pierce," M'Lady said.

He stood looking at me another minute. Then he left.

When Hortense gentled me to my own bedroom, I noticed my feet were bare too.

I lay down, still wrapped in Lady Macdonald's silk. Hortense pulled up the covers and laid on an extra blanket.

The shakes started up again once I was alone with the dark.

I arose to a strong April sun. Shrugged on a uniform that had been laid out for me, during the night. Miss Stewart and Lady Macdonald had consulted a few times about my needs. Then, last week, Lady Macdonald had her seamstress measure me for it and make it up, special.

It must've arrived when I'd gone out the day before.

I pinned up my braid. As I folded M'Lady's silk robe I looked at my fingernails. No blood.

Then I pulled my shoelaces tight. I needed to be able to walk on my own today.

I touched the thistle on the wall, though, for support, before I left my room. It wasn't Irish, but it had been carved by a Celt.

Mr. Macdonald and Pierce were awaiting me in the nursery.

"I'll fetch Clara's tray," Hortense said.

"Make sure there are four rashers of bacon, Hortense," said Mr. Macdonald.

"No bacon," I said.

They all stared at me.

"As Clara wants," said Mr. Macdonald. "Clara, sit in the rocker, Aggie tells me you're most comfortable there."

I was hardly going to be comfortable. I'd been chewing over one stone cold truth.

Hannah had let Jimmy hang.

After we'd all acknowledged that, I worked through how she must have justified it to herself.

"She did tell me at the trial that Jimmy would hang no matter what."

"Mike dying allowed her to feel she was the victim," Pierce said. "That the world owed her. That was a more comfortable place for her."

We fell into silence when Hortense arrived with my tray.

I let Mr. Macdonald set up the table, pour me tea with too much sugar.

"I'm sorry for your loss, Pierce," I said.

"Hannah talked of taking you with her to Grimsby." Pierce stroked his mustache. "Had she asked you?"

"Yes. At least—"

"Until she found another man?" Pierce said. "Ever the flirt."

"It's a long way from Hannah making big eyes at a lad, to taking such advantage of Jimmy," I said.

"She learned early—it wasn't a stretch for her Aylward grandparents," Pierce said. "From looking to their own advantage, to rage at being thwarted."

"Hannah's reasons were her own," I said. "Blood for blood. Not some politics. She was a Fenian only to feed her own grievance."

"There's a crossing where the two connect," said Mr. Macdonald. "People mistake their land for their lifeblood. The girl grabbed onto the Fenians' hatred of poor McGee, because it bolstered her own."

Another woman's grief came to mind. "Will Bridie have Jimmy's body for burial now?" I said.

"We can't have Whelan made into a martyr, Clara," Mr. Macdonald said. "We'd have Fenians staging protests in the same cemetery that holds D'Arcy's remains. No." The Prime Minister said. "I won't let those buggers know where we've buried the body."

"Clara, you do realize Jimmy was being pushed by Bridie, and pulled by Hannah, all along," Pierce said.

I slowly nodded. "Hannah said that Bridie's a Fenian. But you never knew for sure, Pierce?"

"Neither woman's name," said Mr. Macdonald, "was on our list."

XXXV

Little Miss Macdonald didn't die.

She didn't look any better as the days passed, only bigger. But she lived.

I called her Miss Macdonald around anyone in the house. For me, though, she would always be Mr. Macdonald's baboo.

He never treated her like anything other than his sweet baby girl. He always talked of her being 'better'. Sometimes at night he brought his work in where he could see her.

When I mentioned it, Miss Stewart said he's never slept much anyway; Miss Macdonald hasn't made things worse, she said, as the house had always been in an uproar.

Still, the Prime Minister noticed every little thing.

"Clara," Mr. Macdonald said to me, a few nights after Hannah's death, "I see that matters still don't sit well with you."

"No, Sir," I said.

We both knew I meant that, though he liked to play the common man, he was my Lord and master—and I his servant to do his bidding, until he decided otherwise.

"Clara, you need to wrap your mind around what's come to pass. It's not fair and it's not decent, but—well, needs must. I was thinking, though, you might want to set the true record down."

"I've been writing down everything that happened, since last September," I said. "Hasn't Pierce—?"

"—Of course, I'm sure Pierce has given your notes due attention, Clara," he said. "I'll give you this pledge now, though. Hand over your musings directly to me this time, and I'll ensure they receive a proper airing. When the time is ripe."

"You promise, Mr. Macdonald?" I asked.

301

"You have my word, Clara. Though Clara—you're to make only one copy."

I believed him—I didn't have the fight in me to do otherwise. Looking after a baby, always rocking, holding, taking her to Lady Macdonald for her feedings, watching her not become 'better'; it tired me in a way housework never did. After my shift and my breakfast each morning, I wanted only to sleep.

As the days passed, though, I often awakened from my slumber with a start. And an image of Mr. McGee, Jimmy, or Hannah. One of them would be there, lying on the ground. And I would be falling too, but never landing.

When that happened, I went to the library or the nursery, to write out this story. In the hopes that, when I finished, death would at last be done with me.

Pierce, with help from Eamonn's pub tales, spread the story that Hannah up and left for the States. San Francisco, of all places.

"California?" I said, as he drove away from the churchyard last Sunday.

"Had to be somewhere no one we know would venture," he said. "Any lad who knew her would look her up if he travelled through Grimsby. They were all lathered up at the pub that she disappeared without a sweet word in parting."

He spit tobacco and hawed the horses around onto the next street. "No, best they believe she's gone southwest for a new life after Mike's death. Eamonn and I are selling the Grimsby farm. To send Hannah the money to start over—that's our line."

We rode in silence for a spell. Then Pierce pulled up the buggy and nodded to a wooden door, cut into the stone wall where the yard met the jailhouse.

"The courtyard door's unlocked for us," Pierce said. "This is a measure of John's trust in you, Clara."

His words contained another message. I knew Pierce would never have called Mr. Macdonald 'John', like that, if he were going to keep working for him.

But I'd guessed already. From the moment he'd traded the cowboy hat for a tweed cap, and shaved off his mustache. I was startled every time I looked at his clean-shaven face, how much Pierce did look like Hannah.

The courtyard was so much bigger, when it wasn't full of gawkers. The ground was muddy, last year's grass just showing through. The steps of the scaffold staircase had been pulled against a wall. A few were still knocked together, steps to nowhere now. The rest of the scaffolding had been pulled apart, the planks stacked. There was no sun on that side of the yard; the wood looked stained by the damp.

I recalled how Jimmy had pushed aside snow as he climbed the steps.

Pierce closed the door after himself. Then he picked up a plank and held it out to me. "If you want to do this damn fooled thing, Clara," he said, "it's best done quickly."

I dug a shallow pit. Laid in the piece of Sow's skin with her blue knot brand. The sweetheart box Jimmy had made for Hannah. A copy of Mr. McGee's story about the Aylwards' violence, and the violent end he'd imposed on them in turn.

I filled in the mud.

Then I placed the plank on the ground and knelt on it, bunching up my cape open so it didn't catch dirt. Crossed myself, Father, Son, Holy Ghost. Tented my fingers and leaned my forehead against them.

But I couldn't call the angels and saints to me here. Just Mr. McGee's voice, telling me an Irish faery story.

"How many *Ave*s do you plan to say, Clara?" Pierce said. "It's past time."

I marked a circle with the edge of the wood, then an overlapping ring, and a third. Our everlasting knot. Stuck the wood in the centre. Pushed it hard into the ground. Like I was a Saxon hammering in a fence post, staking off safe territory, trying to keep the Irish beyond the pale.

"It's not the Black Rock, Clara," Pierce said. It won't stay fixed there."

"It will for me."

We were silent again all the way back to the Macdonalds'.

He steered down the lane, but he didn't take the wagon to the stables.

"So it's to be an Irish goodbye," I said.

He doffed his cap as I jumped down.

I ran down the lane and up the back steps. Down the hall to the front windows. The buggy was a trace line against the dusk. A ghost trail, like Mike's buggy the night of the murder. Then gone. Without so much as a by-your-leave.

He's off to the States. So M'Lady said. She shook her head, so I didn't ask more. I like to believe he'll be reporting in, even if it is to the Englishman.

I had a couple of visitors, just today.

One was accidental, the other a surprise only to myself.

M'Lady has been told Miss Macdonald may benefit from fresh air, though Hortense shakes her head at the thought. That's why early this morning, Monsieur Robitaille spied us in the garden from the Prime Minister's window.

"I had to pay my respects, Clara," Monsieur Robitaille said. "The boarding house I've been staying at is fine, but nobody looks after us the way you do. Or asks questions like yours."

I smiled at that.

"D'Arcy would be proud to see you here," he said. "I imagine you miss him still."

"Yes, Monsieur. Did you know, Monsieur Robitaille, that the Lacroixs are moving West? As soon as they are—able. They want to be near where their niece is being schooled."

"That poor man's been pilloried since the trial," he said.

I nodded. "That he has, indeed."

He looked at me, in a new way. Up and down, at my stiff nursemaid apron and cap, sprigged muslin dress, and spiffy buttoned boots. Like I was a person of some worth, not a girl off the boat whom he should be kind to.

"I can see John's looking out for you, Clara," Monsieur Robitaille said. "I just dropped off a copy of that book D'Arcy had such hopes for . . . .."

"Mr. McGee did make a copy of the *Apologia*?"

"He wanted me to run my eyes over his work, as usual. That didn't seem important . . . well, you know what his penmanship was."

So he didn't think it should be published either. I patted Miss Macdonald, and she gave me a burp.

"I received three letters, some time ago—from Woodmouse, Hedgehog and Bat," Monsieur Robitaille said. "They were inquiring about being compensated for the value of their trunks. I suggested they contact Desbarats for satisfaction. I don't suppose they ever will be satisfied."

"You call them that too," I said, a blush flashing over me from head to toe.

"Not as a rule, Clara. I wanted to cheer you, just for a moment. Oh, yes, I knew D'Arcy's nicknames," Monsieur Robitaille said. With a little bow, like he'd just performed a conjuring trick. Which indeed, he may as well have, for the reaction I'd given him was worthy of it. "D'Arcy had one for you too, did you know?" he said. "*Fáidbean*, he called you – he said that means 'wise woman'?"

"No, Monsieur," I said. "I never did know,"

It made me want to weep right there. Mr. McGee had thought enough of me to give me a pet name of my own.

"Well, I must be off." As Monsieur Robitaille said this, I realised how much more . . . English his English was now.

"Suzanne Lacroix's been teaching me a bit of French, Monsieur," I said. "Bytimes—we try and meet up at the market. 'Tisn't so different from Latin, it turns out." I smiled. *"À bientôt, Monsieur."*

"Au revoir, Mademoiselle."

That meant 'goodbye', not 'see you later'.

Later that night, I wondered exactly what Mr. Macdonald had told Monsieur Robitaille.

In truth, I find it as hard as the next one to be truly angry at the Prime Minister. But the scene I'd endured earlier this evening—

Mr. Macdonald asked me to wait by the front door, special, as he was expecting an important visitor in a few minutes' time.

"He's set to arrive at seven o'clock, and I expect him to be prompt." He said. "Be sure not to peer out the window, though, Clara. I want to create the right impression on this man."

Right on the hour, the knocker fell on the wood.

I opened the door, and my own da walked in, from under the rising moon.

"Clara." He held out his arms.

I grasped his wrists. Held them for but a moment.

"Look what the cat dragged in." I slapped my hand over my mouth.

"Was that you talking, Clara, or the old lady?"

He remembered. That's what Gram had said when he'd arrived at her sickbed. She wasn't out of her mind with pain yet, but she'd stopped couching her thoughts in niceties some time before.

"I'm sorry—I don't know, quite, sir. 'Tis—you've given me a shock, all right."

"Call me Da, Clara."

"Da."

He'd lost almost all his hair. His sideburns were streaked with grey, though the few hairs on top were still black as crow's feathers. They made his exposed head and face look all the redder underneath. Saxon skin, Gram had called it.

He didn't look like a man you'd want to cross, my da, for all his baby face. His neck was thick and stubby, his shoulders those of a labourer rather than a teacher.

He thinned out the farther down you looked, with hips no wider across than his solid shoulders. Gram said he was held in place by all his pride.

"Mrs. Swift and the boys are travelling straight to Fort Garry," he said. "I've been hired there as Superintendent of Schools—there's just the one now, but the job will expand with settlement of the Territory."

"You'll need woollens, then," I said. "And snowshoes."

"Yes, we'll all need to be well-equipped. I understand the winters are fierce."

I nodded. "You want me to help you outfit the boys . . .?"

"And yourself, if you've need of new winter things. A new coat, with fur lining? With you already used to the Canadian winters, you'll be able to teach us all a thing or two."

"You want me—with you?"

"Sir John A. Macdonald himself wrote to me," my father said. "It's funny, I'd almost given up the idea . . .. You see, I'd applied for a government position here, some time ago. After that priest wrote that you were taken on by McGee—well, it seemed a chance for all of us, didn't it? I was about to write to your employer, Clara, and mention that my family and I could use a good word. Last spring, in fact. But with McGee's death, and then you being in the Dublin newspaper accounts of the trial . . .. Well, I held off on that idea."

I was in the papers, in Ireland? And my da believed whatever was written about me.

"Then just recently, it seems, the Prime Minister's aide saw my application. And it turned out in my favour that I'm your father. A first-class passage all the way. I must say, it was fine of him to offer me the opportunity. Good fortune all round, right?"

Of course. Da had unbuttoned his overcoat. He was all spit-and-polished for the occasion, in a boiled-wool suit with a green silk vest. And chuffed to meet this country's Prime Minister.

"His study's this way." I felt the weight of my past and future, walking beside me. "I've a baby to look after here," I said. The look on his face . . . "Miss Macdonald herself."

"Ah," he said. "One housemaid's as good as the next, Clara."

"I'd like to hear that from Mr. Macdonald, Da."

But Mr. Macdonald had arranged this—

"Don't question your betters, Clara," he said. "I must say I expected a better reception."

"I'm fifteen past, sir. And two years shifting for myself, no matter what country you and your family have chosen to live in."

I sped up, so I could walk into the study ahead of my da.

Mr. Macdonald was perched on the front corner of his desk. He strode over and shook my father's hand.

"So pleased you've come, Mr. Swift," Mr. Macdonald said. "Call me John."

"Godwin Swift, Sir—though my friends call me Gwinnie."

This last was said tentatively, like he didn't know whether the Prime Minister of Canada would take him up on the familiarity. I didn't know anything about this 'Gwinnie' bit. But then, why would I?

"Your Ma married a Proddie, with a girlie name to boot." Och, that's what Gram had meant.

"A grand reunion," the Prime Minister said. As if saying that would make it so.

"It's most generous of you, John," Da said, "to look out for my family." Da took in Mr. Macdonald's genial way, his sharp eyes.

"Imagine, Clara," he said, "from home to here in three weeks, by steamer."

I couldn't, as my journey had taken sixteen, by sail.

"You've settled matters between you?" Mr. Macdonald said to Da. "Clara?"

"Mr. Macdonald, I think—" I said.

"Sure, we'll be grand, Sir," Da told Mr. Macdonald.

Mr. Macdonald could tell clear enough that none of this sat well by me. And yet. Did Mr. Macdonald look on this reunion as my—reward?

"You can be sure, Sir, that I know where my loyalty should lie," I said to Mr. Macdonald.

"Of course, Clara," Mr. Macdonald said. "You'll know what D'Arcy would do." He smiled, like he'd won the point.

And there it was.

Ten steps ahead of me, Mr. Macdonald was kindly leading me toward the explanation for all this.

Mr. McGee would have been so happy that the rebel threat to his new country had been destroyed.

People and money had turned from them, only because they wore the blame for the assassination.

That was the clearest answer I'd ever have.

That I let the truth be, and accept all my own losses. The McGee family left in ruins, Bridie a pariah, Jimmy a villain in the eyes of posterity, and Pierce and the Trotters gone. While Hannah's uncle, Eamonn Docherty, was taking home a tidy profit.

And for this, the Prime Minister had gifted me a family.

"Don't lose this chance by dwelling on your old Gram's judgements, Clara." A wise man's advice echoed. Leave Gram's words, Ireland's feuds, leave it all in the dust.

I felt light-headed as I returned the Prime Minister's smile. And then a laugh bubbled up, from a deep, hidden spring within me.

It rolled through me, and I didn't try to stay the tide, and when it burst into the air my voice sounded deep and loud and eerie, and I didn't care at all.

A measuring glance passed between Da and the Prime Minister.

"And what's made the cat laugh, Clara?" Da draped his arm across my shoulders and squeezed.

I didn't shrug him off, and I didn't let him quell my spirit. They stood and watched, Mr. Macdonald and Da, as my fit of nerves ran its course.

When I could talk again, I shrugged slightly and Da relaxed his hold—but kept his arm there.

"I learned how to laugh from Mr. McGee," I said. "He always said the Lord's given us humour in order to accept life's harshest jokes—and we should make best use of the Lord's gifts."

"What do you say to this title: 'Celtic Ballads and Funeral Songs?'
You know I am an old keener, and half my lays are lamentations.
It could not well be otherwise in this age with an Irish bard,
if I am worthy to be called a Bard of Éireann."

—*Thomas D'Arcy McGee, anticipating a new volume of poetry,*
in a letter penned on Monday, April 6th, 1868

Ottawa, Canada
Wednesday April 7th, 1869
Just before two o'clock in the morning

The baboo finally sniffles herself to sleep, after mewling half the night once more.

I rest my head atop the pages I've set ready to give over to Mr. Macdonald come morning, and rub my lips with the hardened bump on my pen finger. It feels better to think about Mr. McGee tonight, than to think about—what's ahead for me.

Dare I risk disturbing the baboo for a few more words? I've lain the last year down. Besides which, I'd need to light two fresh candles to form my thoughts properly on the page.

The light is lovely when it's low like this. I peer into the honey glow of wax created by a colony of busy bees, and ponder an old Irish story from the Otherworld. The one that'd come to me at the jail yard, in the place of a proper prayer.

Mr. McGee had first told me the tale fifteen months ago.

We were riding in a hack again. This time, from the Ottawa station to Trotter's Boarding House.

"The old folk say there are a thousand Fair People all around us, each time we cross a threshold, Clara," Mr. McGee said.

I knew Mr. McGee was trying to distract me from my nerves. But I was only half taking in what he said, for the hack had turned down Sparks Street, and pulled over.

I jumped down, with a boost from the driver.

Then we both helped Mr. McGee balance his cane on a wooden walkway.

"They're a funny bunch, those from the land of the Shee—why, I'll dare to call them by name, as we've both just travelled, safe and sound, to our new country's new capital city— Faeries," he said.

He raised a hand, to forestall my protest at his daring to name the Good People.

"They may be full of spite, yet take a liking to you," Mr. McGee said. "They may be kind, then laugh as they set you in the middle of calamity. Yet we frail humans pass through their peculiar magic each time we walk through a doorway, Clara."

He and I stepped through fresh snow, careful the cane didn't catch between the slats underneath, and headed to a door. It had been placed, strangely enough, where two buildings rubbed up against one another.

As we approached, a curtain was pulled aside, in a window of the building on our left. Above a stencilled sign that read 'Trotter's Bar', a woman waved.

Behind us, the driver grunted as he hoisted my little trunk onto his shoulder.

Mr. McGee mounted the stoop.

"When you open a door, Clara, you must never fear what's on the other side," Mr. McGee said, pulling a key from an envelope. "For once you've managed to slip past the faeries, what can a mere mortal do to you?"

The tower bell rings out two o'clock, as I set new candles in place of old.

AUTHOR'S AFTERWORD

"It was a time when the real and the imaginary shared the same space in the minds of men."

—James Behan & Leo Behan,
The Secret Gospel of Ireland

This book began when I awakened from a bad dream.

It was a night in September, 2012, a month after my mother's death, and I was left with the image of a girl and a candle, and one sentence:

"I was on the other side of the door when Mr. D'Arcy was shot."

I worship at the altar of Jane Austen, but this girl wasn't speaking of Fitzwilliam Darcy, hero of *Pride and Prejudice*. She was speaking, I knew—without knowing how I knew—of Thomas D'Arcy McGee. The saga of McGee's shooting, which my father had spun for me when I myself was but a girl, standing on the Sparks St. Mall in Ottawa, came rushing back . . . as perilous and fantastical as when I had first heard the saga.

I scribbled down this flash of story, in an urgent, young character's voice, and I had the nut of a scene. Then I told my husband that I was compelled to write this girl's tale. This haunting creature of my night terrors, this sending, was pushing me to pick up tools, as needs must.

In his wonderful, quick-to-the-bottom-line fashion, my husband said that was great, I had his full support—but how was I going to make this figment into a book?

So I dug out a scrap of paper I'd torn from a *New York Times Magazine* a few years earlier, and enrolled in an online fiction-writing course at Stanford University. Novelist Caroline Leavitt and premise guru Jeff Lyons kindly served as references,

313

when, thirty-eight years after my first piece of journalism had been published, I was accepted by Stanford's Online Writing Certificate (OWC) program.

I cannot speak too highly of the program. The generosity and guidance of my instructors and forty-four fellow cohort members—and their workshopping of tens of thousands of words—led me to a draft of this novel. Novelist and editor Angela Pneuman did a phenomenal job with the first edit-and-a-third of that manuscript. In October, 2016, as one of six graduates given a platform at San Francisco's LitQuake festival, I read *Celtic Knot's* hanging scene. (I have written about this transformative educational experience on the novel's website, www.annshortell.com).

After the reading, I Ubered to a Kinko/FedEx and couriered my opening five thousand words to Crime Writers of Canada's manuscript competition —meeting their midnight, October 15th P.S.T. deadline with minutes to spare. I flew home confident that I had a year and a half in which to edit and publish the book, before the April 7th, 2018 sesquicentennial of McGee's assassination.

Alas, my revision plans were themselves revised. Seven weeks later, I was hit by a rebounding door, and sustained a severe concussion with whiplash. Like poor McGee, I didn't make it across the threshold to my home.

Thus a year ago, almost to this January day, I was lying in the dark when my husband told me I'd been chosen for the 2017 'Unhanged Arthur' competition longlist. Crime Writers of Canada had given me three days to submit my complete manuscript. I pressed Send. On being named a finalist last April, I knew I must let this book see the light. Buoyed by a mystery author's salient edit notes, I donned special 'gamer' glasses, and for these many months have been training myself to look at screens again. I have thus been rejuvenated by the story of Clara Swift. She has shown me how to emerge from the shadow of a trauma, and deal with what life metes out.

I could not have done this without my Canadian editors. These include two close friends; author Angela Ferrante, my *donna saggia*, whose edit notes always insist on logic and clarity; and novelist Bryna Wasserman, invariably my most trenchant editor. I also had the pleasure of working with Friesen Press's Hayley Evans, whose edit was meticulous and insightful. Thanks also to Friesen's production team, for guiding the book to publication, and Oriana Varas, for advice and assistance placing the book in readers' hands. I am blessed to have my very own marketing guru, my friend Brenda South. Cam Craig, a talented graphic artist, designed the cover, and supervised Aindrea Skelly's evocative knot design and sketch of Ottawa. His expertise was crucial to many aspects of this book's production. Paige Quigley and her colleagues in Toronto have also provided design, graphics and printing assistance.

The detail of the portrait of Mary Lapsley Guest (née Caughey), by John Butler Yeats, is used with the permission of the National Gallery of Ireland. The painting has also gifted me with a story of its own, which I've published on the *Celtic Knot* website.

I have mixed fact and mythos and a girl's view of the world in a pot, and come up with my own distillation of truth and legend. For me, this is the essence of any historical fiction. You'll find a bit of the real Jimmy Whelan in my character Jimmy's words at his trial and in his last moments—though one of the scenes where I most deliberately moved away from factual detail was in describing Jimmy's hanging. Clara Swift needed to be closer to this brutal act, to witness it fully.

And, of course, as Clara didn't actually exist, she didn't open that door.

Aside from that, many of the events happened, perhaps not exactly when, or where, or how they are written.

That said, I must emphasize that, as a former journalist and non-fiction author, I have huge admiration for the level of research and scholarship that historians bring to their work. For McGee, the foremost historian is Professor David Wilson of the University of Toronto. Professor Wilson has written an award-winning two-volume history of McGee, and many other works about Irish-North American history. His scholarship has been a signpost for me (and provided, incidentally, the source material for the quotations which bookend the story.) Prof. Wilson was kind enough to exchange information with me regarding a manuscript, authored by McGee, which was indeed missing at the time of his death—and has never been found.

There are documents, articles, plays, books, even a musical now in the works, offering details about McGee and his assassination. There is even a trial transcript, originally published in the *Ottawa Times* and printed in book form in 1868 by Monsieur G. E. Desbarats, printer and landlord of the murder site.

McGee's voice in this book is an author's conceit, but McGee's own voice lives on in his writing. He was the author of a dozen books, including works of fiction, history, and politics; a prolific poet, journalist and essayist; and a legendary elocutionist. (Dare I again reference the ubiquitous website?)

Richard Gwyn, a dean among political journalists, has written his own highly-valued two-volume biography on John A. Macdonald. In it, Gwyn quoted

E. B. Biggar's 1891 description: ". . . there was something in his movement which suggested a bird alighting . . .", Biggar wrote. "His quick and all-comprehending glance, and that peculiar jerking of the head, bore out the comparison . . .". This descriptor so neatly fit my own lifelong image of our first Prime Minister, that I adapted the idea to limn my character, Mr. Macdonald.

Our first Prime Minister is both a focus for historians, and a continuing source of public and political debate. The perspectives reflected in this book are those of the mid-nineteenth century, through the lens of a young woman still learning about the new world to which she has immigrated.

For the book's Gaelic flavour, I consulted with art conservator and Irish language educator Danny Doyle, author of *Míle Míle i gCéin: The Irish Language in Canada*. He suggested how I might adopt and adapt the mid-nineteenth-century Irish-Canadian immigrant's Gaelic language and, in certain key instances, viewpoint; I utilized his expertise as best I could. (It is by happy accident that he bears the same surname as my character, Pierce Doyle.) *Merci bien* to Richard Marceau and Amanda Frohman for perusing my French (as with the advice of Mr. Doyle, any errors in language or in historical interpretation rest entirely with this author.)

My cadre of beta-readers includes Diane Abbey Livingston, Jack Livingston, Bill MacQuarrie, Marcia MacQuarrie, Susan Taerk, and Theresa Tedesco.

Other friends who cheered me on at points during this fictional journey include David Aisenstat, Peter Avis, Deirdre Bowen, Linda Law, Smadar Peretz, Arlene Perly Rae, Bob Rae, Richard Siklos, Howard Shrier, Cathy Stevulak, all the wonderful Walking Women, and Ellen and Dwayne Wright, as well as my Time Queens and fellow travellers, Jane Kingsland and Kathy Roeder. To Suzanne Dennis, a bouquet, for casting your artist's eye upon the landscape when I could not see it.

My family played a significant role in the book. Thank you to my sisters Susan Shortell and Carol Shortell, and my niece Emily Maniquet, for key research. My grandson, Henry Solway, demonstrated the workings of buggies through his mind's eye, in a manner that made me finally see them.

All of my family listened and asked and suggested and helped, and understood the demands on my time, none more than my husband Herb Solway. He is my heart.

In closing, there are three people I wish to remember. My late parents, Iris and Vincent Shortell, gave me their narratives, and they are part of this one, on every level: from word choice, to story choice, to the milieu in which Clara Swift moves. My lovely sister-in-law, Carol Solway, of blessed memory, smiled in her wry way, and told me, only a few weeks ago, how happy she was that the novel would launch this spring—and that, as ever, her timing was lousy.

—Ann Shortell, Toronto, January 2018

ANN SHORTELL was born in Kingston, Ontario, and raised on legends of John A. Macdonald, and of her Celtic ancestors. In a previous century she was a business journalist and author — and won an award or two. She wrote *Celtic Knot* in homage to the Irish storytelling tradition D'Arcy McGee embodied. She thanks Crime Writers of Canada for selecting *Celtic Knot*, her debut novel, as a 2017 finalist for the Unhanged Arthur Ellis Award for Best Unpublished Crime Manuscript. She lives in Toronto with her husband.

COVER PAINTING
John Butler Yeats (1839-1922)
Portrait of Mary Lapsley Guest (née Caughey) (1901-1964), 1916 (Detail)
Photo © National Gallery of Ireland

D'ARCY McGEE PHOTO
William Notman (1826-1891)
McCord Museum I-23790.2

AUTHOR PHOTO
Oliver Salathiel

COVER DESIGN
Cameron Craig